HEARTS AND MINDS

Also by Mark Bles

Non-fiction
THE KIDNAP BUSINESS
CHILD AT WAR: The True Story of Hortense Daman

Fiction
THE JOSHUA INHERITANCE

HEARTS AND MINDS

Mark Bles

'The answer lies not in pouring troops into the jungle, but in the hearts and minds of the people.'
General Sir Gerald Templer, Malaya, 1952

'Weapons are an important factor in war, but not the decisive factor. It is people, not things, that are decisive.'
Mao Tse-tung, *On Protracted War*, 1938

Hodder & Stoughton
LONDON SYDNEY AUCKLAND

First published in 1994
by Hodder and Stoughton
a division of Hodder Headline PLC

10 9 8 7 6 5 4 3 2 1

British Library Cataloguing in Publication Data

Bles, Mark
  Hearts and Minds
  I. Title
  823.914 [F]

ISBN 0 450 61008 X

Typeset by
Letterpart Limited, Reigate, Surrey

Printed and bound in Great Britain by
Mackays of Chatham PLC, Chatham, Kent

Hodder & Stoughton Ltd
A division of Hodder Headline PLC
338 Euston Road
London NW1 3BH

In Memoriam
Joy Wood
Sunday 10 January 1993

Contents

Author's Note

Hearts and Minds is a novel, set in the years of the Malayan Emergency, spanning 1945–55.

The principal characters are fictional and none is intended to portray a real person. Some characters come from my previous novel *The Joshua Inheritance* set in Palestine during the first of the British Army's post-Second World War campaigns, and reflect the historical fact that many people did move from Palestine to Malaya at the end of the 1940s, rather than return to England. Indeed, I have introduced numerous real-life historical figures, as well as places, institutions and crucial events – such as the assassination of Sir Henry Gurney – without which no picture of this period in Malaya would be complete.

I chose 'Hearts and Minds' as the title because General Templer made the phrase famous when he was High Commissioner in Malaya. It encapsulates the British approach to counter-insurgency (sadly ignored by the Americans later in the Vietnam war), and it also echoes the military and emotional problems faced by Edward Fairfax as he tries to understand the Chinese enemy in the jungle.

1 September 1993

HEARTS AND MINDS

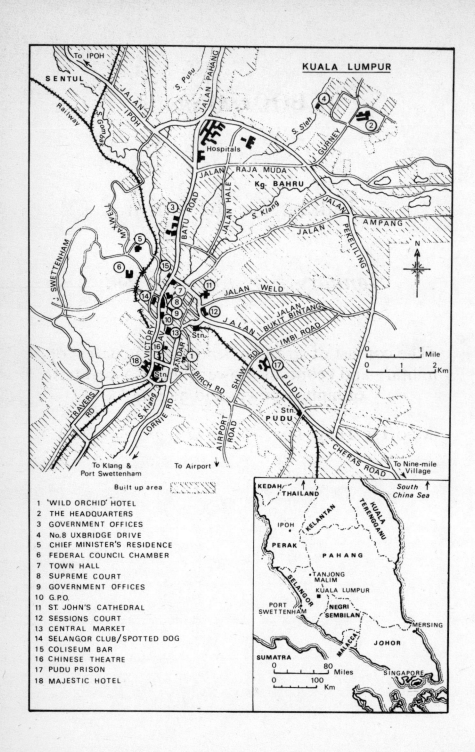

KUALA LUMPUR

1 'WILD ORCHID' HOTEL
2 THE HEADQUARTERS
3 GOVERNMENT OFFICES
4 No.8 UXBRIDGE DRIVE
5 CHIEF MINISTER'S RESIDENCE
6 FEDERAL COUNCIL CHAMBER
7 TOWN HALL
8 SUPREME COURT
9 GOVERNMENT OFFICES
10 G.P.O.
11 ST. JOHN'S CATHEDRAL
12 SESSIONS COURT
13 CENTRAL MARKET
14 SELANGOR CLUB/SPOTTED DOG
15 COLISEUM BAR
16 CHINESE THEATRE
17 PUDU PRISON
18 MAJESTIC HOTEL

BOOK ONE

Lull before the Storm

January 1945 to June 1948

'The contest of strength is not only a contest of military and economic power, but also a contest of human power and morale.'

Mao Tse Tung, *On Protracted War*, May 1938.

Chapter 1

'RED ON! GREEN ON!'

A big four-engined Liberator, painted black and showing no lights, flew low over the dark hills on course to a point which only the navigator could identify. Huddled behind the pilot and co-pilot in his flying jacket, poring over his charts, his target after six hours' flying time was nothing more than a spot in the most inaccessible tropical jungle where the three ancient Malay states of Pahang, Selangor and Negri Sembilan all meet.

The moon hung low over the ragged horizon on their right and cast long, weary, red shadows across the endless canopy of tree tops which spread under the bomber in all directions, like a sea of dark storm clouds lying over the undulating ground beneath.

The pilot rubbed his eyes and stared ahead, mesmerised by the continuous jungle rolling below them, and for a moment he wondered what went on beneath the canopy: a hellish, black nightmare of trees and tangled lianas, of snakes sliding through the rotting leaves on the soft dank floor of the jungle, dry scaly scorpions scuttling by, wild pigs rootling in the dark for food or salt licks, exotic birds sleeping high on branches out of reach of predators, and the endless cacophony of insects. He shuddered as he checked all round the sky for enemy aircraft. The last thing he wanted was to crash in the jungle.

'Fifteen minutes out, Sir,' said the navigator through the inter-com, his face glowing in the tiny red night light poised over his map.

'Raised anything on the S-phone?' asked the pilot. He hoped they could pick up the signal at 3,000 feet. He dared not fly too high just in case there was a Japanese night patrol out.

The navigator did not reply at once, willing the needle on the

3

instrument to indicate that the receiving party was in place.

Minutes passed.

The needle twitched. 'Yes, Sir!'

'Nine minutes out, Sir,' said the co-pilot. The relief was tangible. After 1,500 miles they had pin-pointed a tiny group of men in one of the remotest places on earth.

The pilot ordered, 'Action stations!'

In the belly of the converted bomber, the airloadmaster and dispatch crew sweated to prepare the Type-H containers to be parachuted to the reception party on the ground. Eight heavy, six-foot-long cylinders lay on rollers, like bombs, and the men fussed round, making last-minute checks that the casing was correctly fastened, the straps tight, and the static lines hooked up.

'These are bloody heavy tonight,' shouted one dispatcher over the roar of noise as he and another man rolled the big container towards the bomb-bay doors and fixed it in place with chocks.

The airloadmaster ignored him. It was none of his business what the resistance did on the ground. They were all brave men, but lunatics as far as he was concerned, and he was looking forward to a good breakfast when they got back to Ceylon. He opened the doors and the warm blast of slipstream air whipped round them, making conversation impossible. They worked on with handsigns and listened intently in their headphones. The pilot had picked up the men on the ground.

'Hallo seven-four, hallo seven-four, this is Bravo-two-one-delta, are you receiving me?'

Faintly they heard the reply, 'Roger, receiving you fives.'

The pilots strained their eyes ahead.

'Ten left, Sir, and two minutes,' intoned the navigator.

The pilot adjusted the plane and began to lose height for the run-in.

Suddenly the co-pilot jabbed with his gloved finger. 'There! Dead ahead!' He had spotted the dim triangle of lights which marked their target drop zone about two miles away.

The pilot nodded, immensely relieved. Only he of all the crew had been told how vitally important it was to make the drop that night, and if humanly possible to prevent the cargo of containers falling into Japanese hands. He was not a religious man but he thanked God for the weather – cloudy enough to hide in during their long flight but clear enough to see the torches of the reception party on the final approach. He dropped the big Liberator to 350 feet, skimming over the jungle trees, and spoke briefly into the intercom.

In the back, the airloadmaster acknowledged the orders crackling in his headphones and gestured at the dispatch crew. Hands on chocks, they tensed ready to shove, fascinated by the trees rushing past outside, so near they could see the chaos of branches, the occasional tree thrusting above the smooth undulating grey-green surface like a breaker from the sea.

'Red on!' said the pilot, throwing the switch.

In the rush of the slipstream, the airloadmaster flung his hand out to point at the glowing bulb. The dispatchers tensed and gripped the big containers.

Abruptly the jungle stopped as they raced over an open clearing of swamp and padi fields towards the three lights on the ground, where the moonlight glinted on the water between the mud banks and soft tufts of rice.

Seconds to go. The pilot concentrated, hand poised over the switch. Watch the lights below. Over the first. Over the second, lined up with the third, at right angles shining from the darkness on the left.

'Green on!' His fingers flicked the switch.

Behind him, in the back of the aircraft, the green bulb flared and the dispatchers heaved the first long cylinder into the night, swiftly following with the three behind.

Leaning out into the warm slipstream, the airloadmaster counted the four white chutes floating rapidly away in the darkness. 'All away, all opened,' he reported over the intercom.

'Any sign of enemy aircraft?' asked the pilot tersely. He turned towards his navigator whose attention was fixed over the dull glow of the small round radar screen.

'Nothing, Sir.'

Not yet.

'Going round again,' said the pilot. Eight containers meant two run-ins, as the length of the drop zone was 850 yards, long enough for only four containers each time. He wanted to get on with it, get away.

The Liberator strained round in a tight circle, hugging the contours inside a wide bowl of jungle-covered mountain ridges. Long, tense minutes later the pilot held her straight on the second run-in.

Again, the pilot held the Liberator on course for the three tiny lights on the silver-glinting padi fields ahead. Again, he throttled back the four Pratt and Witney engines to 115 knots, to reduce the distance the containers would be thrown forward before the parachutes opened.

'Red on!'

Watching the lights on the ground, the pilot fancied he could see the pale faces looking up at him as the Liberator roared over the reception party.

Over the first light. Dead on line. Over the second.

'Green on!'

A moment later it seemed, his airloadmaster's voice crackled in his headphones, 'Containers all gone, Sir, right as rain.'

The ground-to-air radio crackled for the last time, 'Thanks Bravo-two-four-delta, all stores landed safely. Good luck on the way back!'

'Let's go home,' said the pilot smiling with relief. There was a long dangerous flight ahead, looping north around Japanese ack-ack batteries in Kuala Lumpur, out to sea over the deserted mangrove swamps on the coast of northern Selangor, over the Andaman Sea and Indian Ocean to Ceylon. If they were going to be shot down, the pilot told himself, he would rather it was into the water. He hated the jungle.

In the jungle clearing there was frenetic activity. As soon as the last container splashed down into the rice fields, a crowd of Chinese in sweat-stained uniforms ran out from the shadows of the jungle to clear away every sign of the drop.

They flitted over the padi fields like thin shadows of the night, their bodies under their uniforms gaunt from years of hiding from the Japanese, and their faces pale from seeing no sunlight under the jungle canopy. They splashed through the rice padi, slinging their rifles across their shoulders, and sweated in the warm night air as they hurried to dismantle the heavy metal containers. Two steel rods down each side were loosened and the containers fell apart into five round drums. They worked in silence, confident in the orders they had received from the white officer before the drop. He was standing under the trees at the side of the wide clearing, a stocky powerful man quite different to the slight shape of the Chinese commander beside him.

'Bloody drums are heavy,' the big man said bluntly. Two Chinese were struggling in the muddy rice water to roll a drum round so they could slide wood poles they had cut from the jungle through webbing straps fitted to the side of the drum.

'They can manage,' said the Chinese commander. Like all the other Chinese soldiers, he wore a pale khaki uniform shirt and trousers and his leggings were fixed with puttees, Japanese style, down to his soft plimsole shoes. Ho Peng was impressed. The drop had worked out exactly as this vulgar British officer had promised; and the sight and sound of the great four-engined bomber roaring low overhead had been utterly thrilling, particularly when he thought of what was in the containers.

All eight containers had landed in the open. No time would be wasted searching in the jungle. The eighty men in the carrying party were busy in the padi fields bringing in the containers, two men to every drum, and more men waited silently out of sight on the edge of the clearing manning Bren guns in case of attack. Over years of clandestine activity, Ho Peng had learned never to take chances, but he thought it unlikely that the Japanese would interrupt them. There was no way they could reach such a remote place except by days of hard sweating slog through the trees, and they would not undertake such an expedition unless they had specific information. Betrayal was always a problem, but in this case only he and the British officer had known about the drop.

Trying to keep the excitement out of his voice, he mustered his best English and asked the big man beside him, 'Captain, how do we know which drums hold weapons and which have the bags?'

The British captain laughed unpleasantly and said, 'You're a suspicious bastard. You don't believe it, even now. You won't be satisfied till you've seen it with your own eyes.'

'Maybe the British Headquarters have not sent what we demanded?' snapped Ho Peng. He resented the other's patronising tone which had so often precipitated arguments during the months they had spent together in the jungle. 'It would not be the first time.'

' 'Course they've sent it,' said the captain crossly.

'I hope so. It is vital for our cause.' If the British had sent what he wanted, these differences no longer mattered and the action he had dreamed of for years was possible.

'Whose bloody cause?' asked the captain. 'That's the question, ain't it?'

'The fight against the Japanese,' Ho Peng hissed.

'Or for you and your mates?'

'No!' said Ho Peng furiously.

Behind him, in deep shadow under the fringe of the jungle, one other Chinese was watching the two men arguing and thinking how similar they were.

The captain grunted at Ho Peng and said, 'Well, you got everything you asked for. Eight canisters dropped, five drums each. Ten are marked "Bravo-seven", full of weapons.'

'What's the marking on the others?' insisted Ho Peng.

'They're the ones you want, aren't they?' the captain sneered. 'They're marked "Alpha-four-nine".'

At once Ho Peng turned and shouted at the line of porters as in pairs they stepped slowly and carefully over the uneven banks of the padi fields towards the jungle, the drums swung heavily from poles over their shoulders. Two men detached themselves and dropped their drum at the feet of the two officers.

Ho Peng dismissed them.

'Wouldn't do to let the others see, eh?' taunted the captain from the darkness behind him.

Ho Peng ignored the remark. The British officer was jealous. He bent down and peered in the gloom at the letters stencilled on the side of the drum. In halting English, he read, 'Alpha-four-nine'. With mounting excitement he demanded, 'How does this drum open?'

The captain stepped forward, knelt down on the wet earth, twisted a set of latches and pulled a knotted string on top of the drum. The lid came away. He put it down on the ground. He reached into the drum, shovelled away some cardboard packing and roughly pulled up the neck of a canvas sack inside. He needed both hands to lift it. He produced a slender pencil torch from his pocket and shone it at a small round object tied to the canvas.

'A lead seal,' he said. 'From the Royal Mint in Australia.'

He twisted the seal on the canvas sack to read the words stamped on it, the Chinese ducked down beside him and a knife flashed in his hand. The captain instinctively flung himself sideways and rolled away on the ground.

Ho Peng laughed as he stabbed his knife into the canvas sack in the drum. The sack burst and a shower of small gold coins scattered over the top of the drum. Some fell on to the ground where they lay gleaming in the moonlight.

'Impatient sod,' cursed the captain, clambering to his knees. But he stared fascinated at the coins.

Ho Peng ignored him, mesmerised. On his knees before the

drum, he pushed his hands into the sack of gold, feeling the smooth oiliness of new minted metal. The coins ran over his hands like drops of heavy water.

'Christ! Don't lose the frigging things!' said the captain. His aggressive tone had vanished. He reached out and picked up one coin, shone his torch on it, and read, 'King George V, 1929'. Awed by the sheer scale, he calculated out loud, 'Four bags of gold sovereigns in each drum and there are thirty drums. Jesus!' He dropped the coin back into the sack. 'That makes 120,000 gold sovereigns.'

The Chinese hiding in the darkness behind them silently wondered which of the two men kneeling before the drum of gold sovereigns, the communist or the British officer, would prove the stronger in the end, and vowed to see that the gold was used for its true purpose.

Ho Peng sat back on his haunches, his black slanting eyes glittering. In Chinese, he said emphatically, 'I have waited years for this. At last we have the financial backing to win the war.'

The big man beside him looked up sharply and asked, 'But who is your enemy?'

Ho Peng did not reply.

Chapter 2

'THE LAND OF GOLD'

'A heroic sacrifice is demanded of the proletariat!' shouted the Chinese speaker from the podium. A pale, slight figure in his plain grey Mao Tse-tung tunic, he looked insignificant under the enormous red banner which proclaimed in huge yellow letters, 'The Calcutta Communist Asian Youth Congress!'

He wiped the sweat from his forehead, and looked around the mass of faces staring up at him from the body of the hall: the smooth-skinned Chinese with their black hair, the darker Indians with their intellectual features, and a scattering of bearded and turbaned Sikhs. He picked out as well the sweating white faces of Europeans who had come from so far to represent their members in Calcutta, Trades Unionists and Party members from Russia and Australia, the sponsors of the Congress, from France, Italy and Britain.

He banged his fist on the wooden lectern and raised his voice so that it boomed statically from the loudspeakers at the sides of the stage.

'Working men and women!' he screamed, his magnified voice filling the hall. 'On this earth there is only one banner which is worth fighting and dying for. It is the banner of the Communist International!'

Cheering greeted these final words and the speaker realised that his long journey from China had been worthwhile. He had not wanted to leave the Chinese People's Army where it had been fighting Chiang Kai-shek's Kuomintang forces in northern Shensi, but Mao Tse-tung had told him his duty to the Party lay in going to Calcutta.

The mass of delegates spontaneously began to sing the anthem of the Communist International, the Red Flag. Linking arms and swaying to and fro, the jumble of languages from different continents was lost in the stiffing tune.

'Comrade, Ho Peng! There's nothing to stop us!' shouted a slim young Chinese leaning towards his older companion in the middle of the hall. His eyes shone with enthusiasm and even Ho Peng, carried away by the moment, sang as loudly as the rest.

But when they left the hall, Ho Peng did not allow his enthusiasm to overide his caution. He was a small wiry man of thirty-six with thin black hair and a pock-marked face, the indelible stigma of a smallpox epidemic which had scourged Shanghai where he had been born. Years of clandestine work in the Communist Movement had taught him never to relax. He nodded at a large black Humber police car parked at the side of the square, almost hidden behind crowds of Indians. 'Uniformed police. But where are the Special Branch men in plain clothes?'

'They won't be after us,' said Lao Tang, still buoyed up by the excitement of the speeches. 'They'll be looking for the red-hairs. The Russians, the Australians and British.'

Ho Peng gave him a sharp glance. 'Maybe, but don't ever allow yourself to be snared by the problems of others. It is still only days since Mahatma Gandhi was murdered, and the Indian police are still on the alert.'

Chastened, Lao Tang followed Ho Peng through the milling crowds as they plunged into the narrow alleys of Calcutta, where the dust danced in the hot sunlight between tattered jumbled houses. Dark-skinned Indians flopped past loose-limbed and barefoot, their shirt-tails hanging out, or sat on flattened haunches outside their shops and houses. The reek of hot curries and dry, sharp, spices, the stench of rubbish and the din of voices assailed Lao Tang's senses but Ho Peng's black eyes never stopped moving, left to right, sweeping the swarthy faces and liquid brown eyes for the element which was out of place, which would indicate danger.

After an hour Ho Peng decided that the Calcutta police were concentrating on the other more prominent communists at the Congress. They would take little notice of two insignificant Chinese from Malaya.

They walked into Chinatown. Here, instead of curries, the air was thick with the smell of frying; noodles, beans and bamboo shoots. Hands reached from the darkness inside open-fronted shophouses to pluck down scraggy pieces of chicken which hung at beams in windows or under the eaves. The soft indolent pace of the Indians was replaced by a brisk stir of activity. Chinese faces filled the streets. Barefoot men in baggy black trousers gathered at the knees pushed barrows, bicycles, and trishaws, or carried stuffed bundles on poles across their shoulders, and wrinkled old women genially watched groups of round-faced, black-haired children playing in the dust. Lao Tang relaxed. Here he felt at home.

The dingy wooden hotel where they were staying leaned on its neighbours as if exhausted by the weight of its own neon sign and the sweltering sweet heat of the Ganges delta. Inside the hallway, gloomy with dark wood, a thin Chinese in a string vest greeted them and they passed through to the ground floor café. Ho Peng sat down at a table at the rear with his back to the kitchens, where he could see the entrance and be nearest the exit through the back door. They ordered tea and fish with rice.

'Our movement truly spans the globe,' said Lao Tang. He had never been outside Malaya before, and was amazed by the power of an ideology which could bring together people from so many places and then bind them with such fervour in the service of the ordinary people.

'They were all most encouraging,' remarked Ho Peng.

Lao Tang detected a note of sarcasm and fell silent, afraid he had said something wrong.

The tea came and Ho Peng held the delicate teacup with both hands, enjoying the feel of warmth through the thin china. He sipped the hot green drink and stared at Lao Tang disconcertingly. In a low voice he added, 'We met the Russians and they were encouraging. We met the speaker from Mao Tse-tung's People's Army and he was encouraging too. These men represent the great Communist Movements. They are our models in the vanguard of the fight against Imperialism. But what substance did they offer?'

'What d'you mean?'

'The time for words is over. The struggle will begin and for that we need substance, support. Weapons and money.'

Enthusiastically, Lao Tang replied, 'But there are two million Chinese in Malaya. Nearly half the population! There can be no doubt of our success!'

'They will follow us, I'm sure,' agreed Ho Peng. 'But we can't succeed against the British Empire without arms and finance.'

'The proletariat will rise up,' Lao Tang insisted. 'Just as they have in Indo-China against the French, and in Greece against the British. The Malays are a lazy people and dominated by Islam, but there are more than two million of them. When they see how we are defeating the British who have stolen their country, they will join us. The Indians in Malaya will join us too, the Sikhs and the Tamils. It will be impossible for a few thousand bourgeois British bureaucrats to resist us. Look what happened in Palestine.'

Ho Peng sipped his tea. This was indeed the vision. The British Empire was fatally weak, bankrupt after the Second World War when the British had been so ignominiously defeated in Malaya by the Japanese in February 1942. Yet somehow, in August 1945, they had muscled back in and carried on, pretending nothing had changed. This time, they must leave for good.

An old Chinese woman appeared from the kitchen. She was fat and her skin was spotted with brown maculations and incredibly wrinkled. She put their food down on the table. Ho Peng was hungry and started eating at once, shovelling the rice straight from the bowl into his mouth with the chopsticks, as though someone might grab it from him.

When he had finished, he put the empty bowl back on the table, leaned forward and spoke fiercely, 'Of course we live on our ideals and success will be ours, Lao Tang, but until then we will grow lean, for there are going to be hard times ahead. That speaker from Mao Tse-tung's People's Army called them sacrifices. He was right. Men, women and children will be butchered for the benefit of the masses. It is the only way. Millions have died in the great fight in China. We know that because China is our homeland.' His hands tightened in fists on the table. 'But our losses will be nothing compared to the blows we shall strike at the British and their running dogs, the Malays, Indians, and even Chinese who support them. That is the message which I shall take back to Comrade General-Secretary Chin Peng in Malaya. We must delay our struggle no longer. The killing must begin!'

The following day, they left their lodging house in the Chinese quarter with a small suitcase each and walked to the docks. They found the big open quay where the SS *Nanyang* was tied up to battered rope fenders in harbour water covered with scum and rubbish. She was an ancient commercial steamer registered in Penang, Malaya, and was carrying cloth and a few passengers back to Port Swettenham in Malacca Province on the West coast of Malaya.

As he glanced up at the ship's name in chipped white letters on the battered black hull, Ho Peng's faced creased in a smile. 'Nanyang', translated literally from Chinese, meant the 'South Seas' and it was the clandestine name the Communist Party used when Ho Peng first came to Singapore in 1927. That was the year his family in Shanghai had been slaughtered by Chiang Kai-shek's forces. Ho Peng, still only a boy of sixteen, had fled to Malaya looking for work, like thousands of other mainland Chinese. He had found various jobs, as rubber tapper, tin-miner, in clothing factories and restaurants, everywhere preaching the benefits of communism and laying the foundations of his life's work. In 1931 he survived a disastrous police coup, when the Malay police arrested a senior agent of the Chinese Comintern carrying details of the organisation of the Malayan Communist Party, and he had survived the Japanese occupation, hiding in the jungle. Now it was fitting that he was returning to fight the British in the *Nanyang*.

The white bulk of the troopship *The Empire Orwell* glided south along the Suez Canal, towering incongruously over the harsh desert on each side.

Lieutenant Edward Fairfax was standing on the deck, leaning against the wooden rail which felt hot through his pale khaki tropical uniform. He switched his gaze from the shimmering blue ribbon of the canal ahead to the east. Beyond the arid sands of the Sinai Desert lay Palestine, where he had served his first two years in the army, caught between the Scylla and Charybdis of Jews and Arabs.

'Was Jerusalem ever as hot as this?' asked Diana, reading his thoughts. She stood close to him, her arm linked in his. A pleasant breeze set up by the ship's motion disturbed the unrelenting heat but she was wearing a wide-brimmed straw hat to shade her fair skin from the sun and, beneath it, her long blonde hair fell down her back over the thinnest cotton frock she had brought out with her.

Edward gave her arm a little squeeze and shrugged. He wanted to forget. The desert to him was synonymous with the past and personal loss. His father had died under tons of rubble when the King David Hotel in Jerusalem was blown up; and then he lost the American girl he thought he loved. He thought she had loved him too, but without a word she had disappeared from his life in the autumn of the previous year and he had given up trying to find her. His letters had gone unanswered and his friend in the Palestine police, Angus Maclean, had been unable to trace her.

When he returned to England, Edward found he had missed Diana Haike as much as she had missed him, and their long friendship as children grew into something promising much more. She was more vivacious and enthusiastic for his career in the army than he could remember. They saw a great deal of each other and, during his leave just before Christmas 1947, he had asked her to marry him. It seemed the most natural question in the world to both of them, and she had not hesitated.

In Palestine, Edward, had developed a strong interest in Intelligence. When he learned of a posting in Kuala Lumpur, the Parachute Regiment had been willing to release him and Diana's father, Colonel Septimus Haike, had smoothed his application through the War Office. Edward and Diana were both delighted, their decision to leave a war-torn Britain unanimous. The country was struggling in another cold winter, rationing was worse than it had been during the war, and industrial strikes were increasing. Diana hated the atmosphere of depression, the drab utility clothes and the cold. The attraction of a new life far away in the warmth and the colonial comfort of Malaya was for them both the answer to a prayer and offered a completely fresh start.

The slatted mahogany door to the passenger lounge opened behind them and a padre in a dog-collar stepped over the deep sill on to the deck. He introduced himself, 'Leonard Goodbury. I'm taking over as Chaplain in Kuala Lumpur.'

He was very dark and thin and would have worn a monk's habit had the war not intervened and put him in uniform.

'Malaya should be wonderful,' he said.

'We can't wait,' agreed Diana.

'Suvarnabhumi!' said Goodbury dramatically and then explained with an embarrassed half-smile, 'The Land of Gold, according to Indian writers at the time of Christ.'

'Better than Europe, or this,' said Edward waving a hand over the ship's rail at the desert.

' "Prepare ye the way of the Lord",' said the padre. ' "And make straight in the desert a highway".'

Edward smiled.

'Isaiah.'

'Really?'

'I don't suppose the old boy was thinking of a water highway but it fits the Suez Canal pretty well otherwise, don't you think? And today being Sunday, I shall be the voice crying in this wilderness.'

Edward looked a bit blank but Diana smiled and said, 'I promise we'll listen to every word.' Church Parade was an important part of army life and she was determined that Edward would rise to the top.

The padre departed on a brisk constitutional around the deck before the service, wondering if he would see more of Diana Fairfax in Malaya. Snatches of his sermon floated back to them on the warm breeze.

Edward wondered what the Arabs either side of the canal would think of a boat gliding between them filled with infidel Christians at worship. He remembered the posting officer in England telling him the Malays were also Muslims. He hoped he would find less bitterness in Malaya than in Palestine.

A month later, as *The Empire Orwell* cruised into the approaches to Singapore harbour, the officers and men crowded the rails in anticipation. The pale lines of uniforms on the upper decks were broken occasionally by coloured dresses where families stood together.

'It's very humid,' remarked Diana as they watched mile after mile of jungle hanging in tangled green confusion over the red laterite cliffs.

The big white liner passed a two-storey brick building patchily covered with sun-faded camouflage paint. The concrete gun emplacements facing the sea were empty, like eye sockets in a skull.

'Those are the guns which pointed the wrong way,' Edward explained how the British defences had proved so embarrassingly useless when in 1941 the Japanese invaded Singapore from the landward Malayan, side.

A comfortable-looking full colonel, standing the other side of Diana, overheard and said, 'My brother was in the Malay Police at the time and spent four years in Changi Jail. He says everyone felt terribly let down because the British Government hadn't done a damn thing to stop it happening. No-one believed the Japanese could move an army through the jungle.'

'I expect we've learned our lesson now,' said Edward. As he stared across the blue water at the sunlit jungle on the shoreline and imagined a place of green sunless gloom filled with dark biblical creatures which crawled and slithered on their bellies, he recalled learning a poem at school, by Kipling, 'Through the jungle very softly flits a shadow and a sigh; he is Fear, o' little Hunter, he is Fear.'

17

Chapter 3

A BOLSHEVIK WARRIOR

Ho Peng and Lao Tang reached Kuala Lumpur, the State capital of Selangor and the centre of the Federation of all the Malayan States, late in the afternoon after a bumpy ride in an old truck from Port Swettenham. At dusk, they crossed the bridge over the sluggish, filthy waters of the Sungei Klang into the busy streets of Chinatown. But Ho Peng, back on his home ground and surrounded by his own people, still did not relax. It was his vigilance which had kept him out of the hands of the Malayan Police for so long.

Unnoticed, they turned off Birch Road into Petaling Street in the middle of Chinatown, and walked under the tangle of red and white Chinese signs and neon lights advertising the shop houses all along the street. When they stopped outside a garishly decorated Chinese theatre, topped with gold dragons and hung with red Chinese flags advertising the fantasies inside, Ho Peng said, 'We'll meet tomorrow as planned?'

Lao Tang nodded. He had memorised his instructions. Ho Peng allowed no mistakes.

Without another word Ho Peng turned and slipped away. Lao Tang lost sight of him at once. Impressed, he walked off thinking the British would have to be very good to stop them when comrades like Ho Peng were leading the military wing of the party.

From the shadow of a shop selling Chinese medicines Ho Peng watched Lao Tang disappear into the evening crowds. After a moment he walked across the street to a rambling old-fashioned three-storey stucco building, with peeling ochre-painted pillars rising up the sides to a castellated façade fronting the flat roof. Flashing blue and red neon lights boldy announced, 'Ye Lan Hotel'

19

in Chinese characters and 'Wild Orchid Hotel' in English beside an advertisement for Tiger beer. A fat Eurasian woman with coils of black hair was standing in the doorway. She spotted Ho Peng as he emerged from the passers-by in the road.

'Back for long?' she smiled, showing a row of gold capped teeth. She bulged inside a rich silk cheongsam with a suggestive slit up the leg, and was so heavily made up with powder and mascara that her age was impossible to guess.

'One night, maybe,' said Ho Peng expressionlessly. He never told anyone if he would arrive, how long he would stay or when he would be back. Lu-Lu Suzie gathered gossip as easily as breathing air. He liked to hear what she found out about others, but kept his own plans to himself.

'Come in, come in,' said Lu-Lu. The gold teeth flashed again. She lifted aside a coloured bead curtain in the doorway, let him through and bustled corpulently after him on red high heels. The beads rattled as they dropped back into place, swinging like a dancer's skirts.

Inside, the smell of burning joss sticks thickened the warm air. Dark red paper lanterns hanging over the bar at the back of the room shed a lurid light on several young Chinese girls clustered round one of the little tables. They also wore silk cheongsams which hugged their slim bodies from shoulder to ankle with slits up the side. When Lu-Lu Suzie clapped her hands for beer, Ho Peng hungrily absorbed the alluring flashes of pale flesh.

Lu-Lu Suzie asked Ho Peng quietly, 'One or two?'

The journey had been long, the girls were deliciously willing and Ho Peng very conscious that there were difficult times ahead; but he asked, 'Is Liya here?'

Lu-Lu Suzie nodded. This one always wanted to see Liya. She said, 'Yes. She got back yesterday. I'll call her.' Liya lived in the Wild Orchid, buying supplies and helping out occasionally behind the bar, but in the Wild Orchid Lu-Lu Suzie could always make time for the foibles of a good customer and she knew Ho Peng would come back for her other girls.

'Send her up,' Ho Peng ordered bluntly. She nodded, and watched Ho Peng leave the bar for the stairs. He used a room at the back on the first floor, because it had its own bathroom. He always seemed to turn up filthy dirty. Privately, Lu-Lu Suzie was afraid of Ho Peng, but at least he spent money.

Upstairs, Ho Peng shut the old-fashioned hardwood door and

glanced suspiciously around the room to see if it was as he remembered it. The decoration was spare but overpowering, dominated by deep red patterned velours wallpaper. A big green armchair, a voluptuous soft curving model suggestively worn on the arms, stood on one side, a large round table with heavy legs and a marble top faced it on the other, and a double bed covered by a single sheet occupied the wall beneath the window. This big sash window overlooked the yard at the back of the building. Ho Peng padded across the bare boards, clambered over the bed and peered out at the roof of the shed outside. His escape route.

He drew the thick red velvet curtains and went to check the bathroom, also suggestively wallpapered in red velours. A huge white cast-iron bath stood like a whale in the centre of the room, exotically surmounted with glittering Victorian chrome taps imported from England. They were marked 'Royal Doulton'. Ho Peng was always amused to think how shocked that particular member of the British royal family would be to know what went on in this bathroom.

There was a knock on the door.

'Come in!'

A girl came in carrying a tray with four bottles of Tiger beer and a glass and shut the door behind her. She wore a sky-blue silk cheongsam on which richly embroidered fire-breathing gold dragons curled round her slender waist. Her long shiny black hair was tied up in a bun at her neck and her make-up was light. Her oval face was pale, her skin quite smooth and clear, and her dark slanting eyes watched Ho Peng warily.

'Shall I pour your beer?' she asked in a soft lilting voice.

'Yes, Liya.'

'Was your journey to Calcutta successful, Comrade?' she asked. He liked her to call him 'Comrade' when they were alone together and she guessed he would enjoy the flattery of being asked to talk about his important mission.

He took the glass of beer, sat down in the green armchair and began talking about Calcutta, and the Chinese communists at the Congress who had told them their campaign in Malaya must begin.

Liya, standing dutifully in front of him, thought how small and insignificant he looked in the big green armchair. It was strange how such an unimpressive man could be powerful enough for the Party to send him on such important missions.

The antennae of Ho Peng's mistrustfulness may have caught a

21

shadow of her thoughts in her face because he suddenly thrust his empty glass at her and shouted, 'Fill it up again!'

Shaken, she obediently slipped over to the table and poured another Tiger beer.

Ho Peng watched her slim fingers opening the bottle, thinking how deceptively weak and vulnerable she seemed to be. She was so soft, feminine and seductive, her small breasts swelling the front of her silk dress as she bent slightly to pour the beer, and her black hair brushing her cheek. He resented her advantages. He growled, 'Does Lu-Lu Suzie know what you do for me?'

She paused in her pouring and turned to face him, her eyes wide and candid. 'No, Comrade Ho Peng,' she said and continued filling the glass.

Abruptly he pulled himself from the padded green armchair and snapped, 'Did you do that job I asked you to before I went away to Calcutta?'

'Yes, I did, Comrade,' she said demurely and handed him the glass brimming with warm beer. She was no taller than Ho Peng.

'Show me!' Ho Peng screamed unexpectedly and smashed the glass from her hand, driving it against the wall where it shattered and beer splashed in a yellow arc over the red wallpaper.

Liya cowered back, expecting the next swinging blow to land on her shoulders, and quickly said, 'I have the answer! Here.' She reached into a secret pocket in her cheongsam, concealed in the pattern of the gold dragon roaring at her waist, and pulled out a folded slip of waterproof paper.

Ho Peng grabbed it, deliberately squashing her slender fingers as he did so. He turned away, moved to the double bed and sat down. First he inspected the packet, noting that the seal was still intact, then he broke the seal, opened it and began to read the columns of tiny Chinese characters.

At the end he read the name of the sender. Lao Yu. He swore. Why did that man always send him instructions to do things which he was going to do anyway? Unnecessary messages meant unnecessary risks. Ho Peng stared at the room carpet. General-Secretary Chin Peng might think Lao Yu was a great military strategist, but giving too many orders was dangerous stupidity in clandestine warfare.

Out of the corner of his eye, he caught sight of Liya edging towards the door. He said hoarsely, 'Open another bottle, Liya. And bring it over here.'

* * *

Lao Tang rose early, before dawn, and came down the rickety
wooden stairs to the kitchen of his mother's house. He supped tea,
and rice with milk. She seemed to guess what he was going to do and
that she might not see him again. When he left, almost without a
word being said, she watched him up the street for a moment before
bustling through the house again to beat her washing in a bowl in the
tiny yard at the back.

Men and women were already about in the calm shadows of early
morning, although the translucent dawn sky above the flat, grey
roof-tops promised a hot day to come. Near the edge of the Chinese
quarter, on a long straight avenue lined with palm trees, Lao Tang
waited by a bus stop. He had made this journey numerous times
before, but the decisions taken in Calcutta convinced him he was
doing these things for the last time.

The old bus arrived. Lao Tang boarded and saw Ho Peng sitting
at the back of the bus, near the emergency door, unconcerned and
apparently half-asleep. Lao Tang found a seat between an ugly
Chinese with short tufts of black hair and a large Indian dressed in a
flowing white overall who continuously stroked his black beard
which seemed to grow from every part of his fleshy face. Lao Tang
tried to ignore the continuous nudging of the man's fat arm and the
overpowering smell of chillies.

The driver swooped into every dusty bus stop, always braking
dangerously close to the deep flood channels which lined the sides of
the roads. Several bland-faced Chinese climbed aboard with grey
stains of tin slurry on their shirts, on their way to work in the tin
mines at Ampang. A slim Chinese girl in a cotton tunic shirt and
faded blue pantaloons struggled on with a raffia basket stuffed with
tins of tuna fish, hardware and clothes. Two barefoot Tamil
roadworkers dressed in dark skirts and thin white vests gangled
aboard behind two Indian women in long saris.

The bus quit the town for the open road as the sun began to warm
the air. It rose in a great orange circle above the bright green
patches of jungle between groups of wood houses on stilts beside the
road. Brown-skinned Malays, in sarongs and batik shirts, stood
beside the houses and watched the bus pass.

Ho Peng stared out of the grubby window. He hated these
indigenous Malays in the comfortable chaos of their villages, or
kampongs. They owned their wood shacks and worked their own
land, they cultivated plots of rice, sweet potatoes, sugar cane, maize

23

and tapioca or ubi kayu, which grew easily, like weeds, in the humid tropical warmth and good soil. They were a lazy lot, Muslims, stony ground for his communist gospel.

The bus lurched round a bend and swerved to avoid an old Austin saloon with a 'Taxi' sign on its roof weaving round a trishaw in the middle of the road. The turbaned Sikh driver hooted angrily and leaned out of the open window shaking his fist and cursing.

Out of town, between the Malay kampongs filled with doe-eyed brown children playing in the dust among the chickens, the low hills were covered by trees with mottled silver bark and waving glaucous leaves. Latex-giving rubber trees, the milky life-blood of Malaya's economy, marched away in straight lines up slopes, across streams and encircled kampongs, halted only by the jungle which encompassed everything, as the sea circled the land. Malaya's rubber plantations served forty per cent of the world's rubber market which made Ho Peng angry thinking how the Communist Party could use a fraction of those funds to save the country.

A mile past Langat, the District town, the Tamil workmen ambled off to work on a ditch at the side of the road, their puggarees loosely wrapped round their heads, protection against the sun and dust.

As the bus pulled away on a long straight, Lao Tang watched them till the figures grew small in the distance. Then the bus passed a sign announcing the Black Circle Rubber Estate where the road curved into hillier country. Ahead he could see the rolling hills covered with dark green jungle rising to a high broken ridge line of mountains in the distance.

The bus stopped again, where the brown waters of the Sungei Lui passed under the road. Here Ho Peng got off, and without a sign between them, Lao Tang followed. Behind them, the Chinese girl with the raffia basket struggled off the bus too. As soon as the bus had rumbled out of view round the next bend, Ho Peng led the way over a muddy ditch and uphill into a rubber plantation. Lao Tang padded silently along behind on the fallen leaves between lines of glaucous trees.

Liya watched them till they were out of sight. Then she hoisted her heavy raffia basket over her back, fixed the carrying cloth round her forehead, leaned forward to take the weight, and crossed the road. She enjoyed the sturdy plodding motion of her slim legs weighed down by the basket. She felt she was communicating with the earth with each step on the hard sun-baked path. This was her

24

life and her duty. She had work to do for the squatters in the village ahead.

Ho Peng and Lao Tang sweated as they walked steadily through the rubber. When they saw a group of tappers through the trees, dirty with latex encrusted clothes, they stopped and hid in a clump of scrub by a stream, and waited till they passed.

After an hour, Ho Peng breasted a slight rise and dropped into a natural dip in the ground on the other side where the rubber plantation was bordered by a thick wall of jungle. This was the far edge of the Black Circle estate. The dip concealed them from anyone following. Swiftly Ho Peng glanced at a little pile of stones in the low weeds at the base of a tree in the last row, to check they were undisturbed, took one last look all round, and suddenly slipped into the jungle behind a curtain of bamboo and the fleshy leaves of a Sweetheart plant hanging from the trees above.

Lao Tang ducked after him. As his eyes struggled to adjust to the gloom after the bright morning light outside, Ho Peng tapped him on the shoulder and set off into the shadows. He moved effortlessly, picking his way through the shrubs, lianas and palms with neat steps, his body poised, his head turning this way and that, noise-lessly alert, like a deer. After only thirty yards, he sat down, cross-legged, on the rotting leaves on the jungle floor, motionless and half-hidden behind young bamboo palms sprouting all round from the leaf mould. Lao Tang almost fell over him. They had worked together since the last months of the Japanese war but he still had not mastered Ho Peng's natural skill in the forest.

'Flow with the forest,' Ho Peng whispered hoarsely and then sat quite silent to absorb the jungle, the humid smell of decay, the insects flitting through the shafts of sunlight striking down from the canopy of leaves high above them, the sounds of frogs, crickets and screeching birds, and, faraway, the echoing howl of a monkey.

Suddenly Ho Peng gripped Loa Tang's arm in warning. For a moment Lao Tang heard nothing and thought Ho Peng was mistaken. Then he heard a twig snap. He stared in that direction, at a tangle of spreading green palm fronds. The fronds melted apart and three Chinese materialised in front of them. They wore pale khaki uniforms, two carried Sten guns and the third an American M-1 carbine, and their peaked khaki cloth caps were decorated with three red stars. These were soldiers of the Malayan People's Anti-British Army, the MPABA, the military wing of the Malayan Communist Party.

The leader of the group greeted Ho Peng deferentially and the two spoke for a moment in undertones. Then, he turned round and went back the way he had come. Ho Peng and Lao Tang followed and the other two brought up the rear.

They walked quickly through the jungle for two hours, always moving uphill. Lao Tang's leg muscles ached, the sweat ran off him drenching his clothes and he gasped the warm damp air into his lungs. Endlessly he stopped to unhook 'wait-a-while' thorns from his shirt and trousers, slipped on roots, and fought to ignore mosquitoes and leeches, while ahead of him Ho Peng slipped through the undergrowth like a shadow, ducking and weaving with practised ease.

Lao Tang nearly trod on the sentry at the edge of their camp. He was squatting down motionless and camouflaged behind thick leaves, a M-1 carbine cradled in one hand, the other on the long liana which disappeared into the bushes behind him and linked him to a cluster of big bamboo alarm bells in the camp fifty yards away.

The camp was too large to see from one side to the other. All the undergrowth had been cleaned away from the ground leaving just the huge tree trunks rising upwards for a hundred feet to the canopy of leaves which concealed the camp's existence from the air. Ho Peng stepped briskly away across the undulating leaf-covered jungle floor to a large hut made of wood poles, bamboos and roofs of attap palm leaves. This was the Camp Secretariat, where he lived.

Lao Tang, sweat streaming down his face and neck, walked across the camp to his own attap hut to rejoin his Armed Element. He felt safe. All around him were soldiers of the MPABA, all confident in the eventual success of the Malayan Communist Party. He ducked inside the hut to change into his uniform and clean his rifle.

A shrill whistle blast brought men from the shadows under the big trees on all sides. They gathered in the centre on the open 'parade ground' and formed up in squads. There were Armed Elements, a Propaganda Element, a Food Supply Element in charge of the kitchens, and a Self-Protection Corps which was Ho Peng's personal bodyguard element. Ho Peng, dressed in his khaki uniform, long puttees and plimsoles, stood at the front, outside his attap hut, and watched everything with a bad-tempered expression. Lao Tang, the squad leader of his Armed Element, marched forward to Ho Peng with the other squad leaders to state his Element present and correct.

As they returned to their places, Ho Peng waited for complete silence and, in spite of himself, felt a surge of real pleasure. Ranked before him were two hundred men wearing the new uniforms he had forced out of a Chinese clothing company in Kuala Lumpur, and they were all armed with a variety of weapons he had kept hidden after the war – Japanese rifles, British Sten guns and American M-1 carbines. For himself he preferred the M-1 which was light and fired a high-velocity .30'-round compared to the slower 9mm-round fired by the Sten sub-machine gun carried by squad leaders like Lao Tang. Now they were all ready, well practised after firing hundreds of rounds in training near the camp, safe in the knowledge that the British never came into the jungle.

This, Ho Peng told himself, was power. This was his command, the core of his forthcoming strike. 'You are the Malayan People's Anti-British Army!' he shouted in a surprisingly deep base voice. 'You are the striking sword-edge of a great struggle, the battle to rid the Malayan proletariat of the yoke of the red-haired British Imperialists, and you are the vanguard which will lead this country to the revolution of the masses!'

Excitement showed on every face.

Ho Peng lowered his voice dramatically but projected his words to every ear, 'After my important embassy to the Congress of Communist Asian Youth, I shall make a full report to our Comrade General-Secretary-Chin Peng. I have no doubt he will agree with my recommendation that the forces of the MPABA must be committed at once!'

He glared round, his hard gaze slowly sweeping from one side of the massed squads to the other, to be sure he had every last man's attention.

'You are the crest of the revolutionary waves sweeping out from our homeland in China. Together, we will liberate Malaya for the people!'

Wild cheering drowned these last words, and, when the noise faded, Ho Peng continued in a sombre tone, 'Today we honour a comrade of the Reserves who has proved himself worthy of the cause, who has absorbed our instruction, learned the basic skills of a jungle soldier, and worked hard to improve his knowledge as a true soldier of the revolution.' He paused theatrically and then shouted, 'Comrade Lao Tang! Step forward!'

Lao Tang marched forward and stood at attention in front of the whole parade. To his amazement, Ho Peng smiled at him, and then

27

continued to address the assembled soldiers, 'Lao Tang has worked hard, his progress has been assessed by the Executive Committee and he is to be accorded the most extremely glorious title of the Malayan Communist Party. He is appointed to the title of a Bolshevik Warrior!'

Ho Peng fixed Lao Tang with a hard stare, fanaticism burning into his soul, and in a voice which only Lao Tang could hear he said 'Comrade Lao Tang! You will join my Self-Protection Corp. Go now, and do your duty for the People and the Party.'

Lao Tang nodded, overwhelmed with pleasure, and left his place of honour in front of everyone at a run to join the bodyguards beside Ho Peng.

Ho Peng waited till there was complete silence again. Then he shouted, 'The Party is your life! Strive and fight for the Party! Fulfil your duty to the last!'

A roar of approval filled the clearing at these last words, rustling the myriad leaves of the canopy above. Ho Peng motioned for his bodyguard to begin singing the 'Red Flag'.

The noise carried a long way through the surrounding jungle, but, beyond the sentries staring silently out from their concealed positions on the edge of the MPABA camp, there was no-one else to hear them, and nothing reached the hot wind soughing listlessly over the canopy of dark trees above.

'Number eight, Uxbridge Drive,' Edward repeated in a loud voice, unsure whether the old Sikh taxi-driver had heard properly.

The square outside Kuala Lumpur's peculiarly vast, colonial Gothic-Muslim railway station was crowded with Malays, Indians and Chinese all come to meet the overnight train and to sell drinks, cigarettes, matches, socks and evil-smelling durian fruits to the new contingent of British soldiers up from Singapore. Edward and Diana had thankfully allowed themselves to be rescued by the bulky and grey-bearded Sikh who ushered them with old-world charm to his ropey old Austin saloon taxi in a way which could not be refused without fear of giving great offence.

'D'you think he knows where to go?' Diana whispered as the Austin jerked forward.

'Oh yes, please, Memsahib,' said the Sikh in a deep bass voice, turning almost fully in his seat to speak to them both in the back. Diana was surprised how white his teeth appeared against his dark skin and the grey whiskers of his beard. 'I have seen many, many

British officers to their quarters. I am Gandra Singh. Also, I am very well-known.'

He swerved to avoid a car and continued, 'Always, I am driving the British sahibs and their memsahibs. I can tell you very frankly that I have seen many, many years' service in the British Army. I was a Sergeant in the Punjab Infantry Regiment.'

Gandra Singh leaned out of his window to shake his fist at a Chinese wobbling dangerously close on a bicycle. 'They are very stupid, these Chinese,' he declared, shaking his head. 'And the Malays are very lazy.'

This account lasted, between interruptions when he had to concentrate on a junction or contend space on the road with a rubber lorry, as far as the married officers' quarters beside British Army Headquarters of Malaya District. Diana was exhausted, sticky and tired after a fitful night on the train, but she recovered at once seeing the spacious colonial villas laid out among neatly kept grass lawns and shady trees.

'The product of a century of Empire,' said Edward. 'But which one is ours?' He mopped his forehead with his handkerchief.

Gandra Singh drove along the curving avenues between the houses and they called out the roads, all reassuringly named after towns in the English home counties.

'Uxbridge Drive,' said Diana suddenly, pointing.

The road was a short cul-de-sac and Gandra Singh pulled up at the end, in front of a bungalow half-hidden behind a clump of Chinese fan palms and a mass of dracaenas with curving variegated leaves brilliantly green and white in the hot sun. Above, several tall acacias spread their delicate leaved shade over one side of the wide roof and a rampant bougainvillea covered in purple flowers hung along the verandah.

'Delightful!' exclaimed Diana.

'Thank God it's not a Nissen hut,' said Edward who had expected the worst.

'Indeed, this is Number Eight,' announced Gandra Singh proudly, reading a number on a white sign stuck into the grass. He racked up the brake handle and heaved himself out of his taxi to unload the suitcases.

Diana walked over the coarse grass to the bungalow. The grey-tiled roof sloped gently from a high ridge to eaves which spread protectively wide over a wooden verandah which ran all the way round the house. The windows had no glass, just mosquito netting stretched over the openings, and wood shutters covered with faded and peeling blue paint were folded back against the white-washed walls. The front door was ajar. Diana walked up a couple of wood steps on to the verandah and pushed through into a cool hall.

A sibilant voice greeted her from the darkness at the back of the hall and, as her eyes adjusted to the shade, she made out a slim brown Malay youth and an ancient bowed Chinese. The Malay was dressed in a brightly-coloured batik sarong, a white shirt and sandals. He said, 'I am Hassan, Memsahib, houseboy for you and the Sahib, and this gentleman is Lao Song, your cooking man.'

Savouring the novelty of being called 'Memsahib' Diana observed that Hassan had the most beautiful liquid brown eyes and flawless skin. She said, 'You are staying with us here?'

'Oh yes, Memsahib,' Hassan replied eagerly, 'We have living quarters the other side of the verandah, outside the kitchen under the acacia tree. We will do everything for you. This is our job. You will be our Sahibs now.'

Diana was delighted by the old-fashioned formality and turned her attention to the elderly Chinese. He was dressed in a black smock suit buttoned up the front to his thin neck and he gazed at her impassively, his expression lost in the dry wrinkles on his face. Wisps of grey hair on his head gave him the air of a monk. She decided to call him 'Mr Song', and said, 'We are tired after our long train journey and would very much like some tea?'

To her surprise, Lao Song did not move. Hassan, a shade embarrassed, turned to him and rattled off something in Malay. Lao Song fixed Diana for a moment with his ebony black eyes, bowed his head very slightly, then padded off down the corridor to the kitchen in his cotton rope-soled shoes. Hassan grinned quickly, showing perfect white teeth and explained, 'Song not speak any English.' He shrugged and slipped away, his hips swaying loosely under his silk sarong.

'Do they really belong here?' grinned Edward as he came into the hall behind her having paid off Gandra Singh.

Diana laughed. She said, 'Part of the furniture, it seems, but it's a bore Mr Song can't speak at least some English.'

Headquarters Malaya District was very British. Grass lawns spread in all directions under swaying palm trees, the roads between were lined with white-painted stones, and two red fire-buckets stood ready for use on the wood verandahs of every office building along

30

the roads, one filled with water, marked in white letters 'Water', and one with sand, marked 'Sand'.

A Tamil labourer ambling along the road with a shovel recalled seeing the same buckets painted with the same words in Japanese only three years before, though the buckets had always been British.

Edward passed him walking briskly to work for his first morning on duty. He could not help thinking how very black the Tamil Indian's skin was and to cover his stare, called out cheerily, 'Good morning!'

'Indeed, Sir, very good morning!' agreed the Tamil, puzzled by the need for so much energy among the British. In the distance two Tamil women were scything the grass, swinging sharp blades tied to short sticks round and round their heads in loose-limbed rhythm.

Edward marched on, feeling at once important and apprehensive. He returned the salute of several soldiers, saluted some senior officers in green aertex tropical shirt and trousers like himself and, keen to create a good impression on his new boss, he ran up the steps of the verandah marked 'Intelligence Office', pushed open the door and walked inside.

A captain was leaning over a desk in the middle of a large office absorbed in reading that morning's copy of the *Straits Times*. At the interruption he looked up, raised an eyebrow and frowned. He was tanned, fair-haired and wore a bushy moustache.

'Lieutenant Edward Fairfax, Sir.'

'Ah?'

Edward saluted and then went over to shake hands, whereupon the frown on the captain's face cleared and he became all bonhomie, like a man welcoming a new member to the Cricket Club.

'I'm Captain Denton,' he said. 'Harry Denton. You're the new chap?'

Denton was tall and broad-shouldered, with the manner of a keen sportsman. He sat back on his desk, folded his arms across his chest and said, 'Delighted to see you here, old chap. Arrived last night, eh? Everything all right? Can't say I'm sorry you've turned up, not at all. Been under a bit of pressure recently. Lots of talk of commies, you know.'

'Russians?'

Captain Denton laughed, 'No. Chinese. Not Mao Tse-tung's lot, of course. Local chappies y'know. We think it's all a lot of hot air,

31

really. Otherwise, there's not much to worry about, but you'd better meet the Old Man first.'

He led the way to a door at the other end of the office, knocked and went in. 'New chap, Fairfax, has arrived, sir,' he said, leaning round the door into the office beyond. He ushered Edward through and withdrew, thinking the new chap looked quite the sort of man he could get on with, fit-looking and bright too judging by his papers.

Edward quickly straightened his maroon beret and marched in. He came to attention and saluted smartly.

The colonel was a portly man, fair-skinned with a florid expression and he sweated profusely. Already, first thing in the morning, damp patches were spreading on his shirt under his arms and spotting the material stretched across his stomach while a ceiling fan uselessly churned the warm air at maximum speed. He grunted and looked Edward up and down for a moment, dabbing at beads of sweat on his forehead with a large handkerchief. 'So, you're Fairfax, eh?' he said eventually.

'Yes, Sir. Arrived yesterday, Sir.'

'Then, why didn't you report to me at once?'

'My wife and I were very busy, Sir, settling into our quarter,' said Edward, wishing he had at least rung in. The last thing he wanted was to set off on the wrong foot.

'Married, eh? Bloody fool.' The colonel smoothed thin strands of red hair over his balding head from one side to the other and looked for a piece of paper on his cluttered desk. He found it and read out, 'Fairfax. Lieutenant. Parachute Regiment. Commissioned May 1945 into the Sixth Airborne Division, short time in Germany, served in Palestine.' He broke off to look at the War Medal ribbon sewn above Edward's chest pocket. This single ribbon always embarrassed Edward as he had been too young to join up in time to qualify for the Defence Medal.

'Says here you speak good Arabic?'

'Yes, Sir,' said Edward warily, but the colonel made no further comment about Edward's language ability. He read on down the page summarising Edward's short career and suddenly said, 'You worked in Colonel Fergusson's special squads in Palestine?'

'Yes, Sir.'

'With Roy Farran?'

'No, Sir. With Major Erskine Meynell.'

The colonel grunted. 'Ridiculous! Those special squads caused nothing but embarrassment for the army in Palestine, and I want to make it quite clear that I'll entertain no such makeshift links with the police here. The police deal with civilian crime, though God knows the officers I've met in Malaya seem to spend most of their time bickering among each other instead. Some quibble to do with the poor devils who got locked up by the Japanese complaining at the ones who ran away into the jungle. However, that's their business. Our job is plain. I run an Army Intelligence department. The distinction between army and police is quite clear in my mind and all the better for it. Understand?'

'Yes, Sir,' replied Edward firmly, deciding the safest course was to agree with everything the colonel said. He hoped his new boss was not always so bad-tempered.

The colonel finished by saying, 'Standards are high here, Fairfax. I know what you Paras are like. Scruffy bloody lot. I don't want you to let me down. The good name of the Intelligence Office depends on you. Make damn sure your kit is in good order, your boots are polished and I'd remind you that saluting senior officers is a mark of respect. Don't forget it. Got that?'

'Yes, Sir,' said Edward, feeling as if he were back at his officer cadet training unit all over again.

'Right. Captain Denton will tell you what to do. Now get out. I've got a lot to do.' With that, the Colonel picked up a document marked 'Secret' and began to read, absently dabbing his face with his handkerchief.

Edward saluted and marched out. When he closed the door behind him, he stared in mock horror at Captain Denton who grinned widely: 'Quite a specimen, eh?'

Edward jerked his thumb over his shoulder and whispered, 'Is he always like that?'

'Worse at times. Especially when he has to brief the General.'

Edward said nothing for a moment, but he seemed to have an ally in Captain Denton and asked, 'Does he have a name?'

Captain Denton's grin broadened, 'Sorry, old chap, should have introduced you properly. He's Vincent Bleasley. Colonel Vincent Bleasley, of the Intelligence Corps. A pukka sahib, or so he likes to think, and very keen on good form.'

Chapter 4

NO MEN IN UNIFORM

Ho Peng emerged from the rain-soaked jungle on to the gleaming wet tarmac road by Bentong town and turned north. In the hot sun steam rose from the puddles and white mist hung over the jungle which rose steeply into the hills on both sides. As he walked, he caught reflections of the muddy rain-swelled Sungei Bentong through the trees on his left.

His blue shirt and workman's trousers dried quickly in the heat and he made good speed. The next few days would be momentous for Malaya, but whereas the prospect should have been something to look forward to, it was spoiled by one serious uncertainty. This made him unusually wary for his contact.

Just short of the river junction where the Sungei Penjuring joins the Sungei Bentong, a rubber tapper in filthy clothes stiffened with dried latex was sitting on the right side of the road, by a milestone marked '59 Miles to Kuala Lipis', a small town in the centre of Pahang State deep in Malaya's thickest jungles. From some way off he saw the wiry Chinese approaching and recognised his short black hair and pock-marked face. When Ho Peng drew level, the tapper asked his name and Ho Peng answered, seeing through his disguise at once, though British planters or District officers would have noticed nothing amiss in a tapper waiting for a lift beside the road. Ho Peng's searching eyes picked out several other 'tappers' sitting in the shade of some trees set back from the road and he guessed they were armed. He could not see their rifles but they were watching him very carefully.

The first tapper nodded and said, 'Follow me, Comrade.'

Both men checked up and down the road, but there was no traffic between the trees in either direction as far as they could see. The tapper led Ho Peng away from the road through a shady rubber plantation. As soon as they were out of sight, one of the other 'tappers' walked slowly over to take up position on the grassy bank by the milestone.

At the end of the rubber plantation, the tapper left Ho Peng just inside the jungle, and turned back. Ho Peng quickly adjusted to the natural gloom and saw another Chinese appear from deeper inside the forest. This man was armed with an American M-1 carbine. He gestured for Ho Peng to follow him. At first, there was no sign of a track and they ducked and weaved through thick undergrowth for a hundred yards or more with visibility no more than fifteen yards in any direction. Ho Peng recognised the trick. They wanted to conceal the main route they were to follow, just in case, so he was not surprised suddenly to find himself stepping on to a prepared track cut through the jungle. His guide checked to see Ho Peng was behind him and set off at a pace.

Ho Peng followed effortlessly, to the amazement of his guide who had conducted several less fit city members of the Party. After half a mile through the gloom, they stopped by the buttress roots of an enormous tree. Another armed guide, this time in MPABA uniform with red stars on his cap, emerged from the shadows and took Ho Peng on from there. The other man went back.

Every half mile, a new armed and uniformed soldier of the Malayan People's Army rose from the shadows to lead Ho Peng further into the jungle, while the previous man went back along the track. Finally, after more than three miles, two soldiers appeared. One stayed on sentry duty, the second took Ho Peng through the last four hundred yards of jungle into a large camp.

Ho Peng was impressed. All ground vegetation between the tall trunks had been removed, like in his own camp, but this one was enormous. Bright rays of sunlight filtered down through the green canopy of leaves on to large numbers of solidly-built wood and attap-roofed huts erected in a circle around a parade ground. A red flag hung limply in the hot windless air from a flag-pole in the centre. Behind on one side were kitchens, the latrines and a command post, to which vines trailed along the ground from all the sentry positions in the jungle outside the camp. On the other side were more huts built to accommodate five hundred MPABA soldiers and visitors.

Ho Peng was marvelling how the British had not found out about a place so big when a pleasant voice called, 'Comrade Ho Peng! How was your journey?' A Chinese of medium build, with pimply fair skin, emerged from the middle hut on the parade ground, which was the Secretariat. Ho Peng recognised Chin Peng, the leader of the Malayan Communist Party. He was dressed, like his soldiers in a simple pale khaki tunic uniform. They clasped hands.

'Comrade General-Secretary', Ho Peng replied. 'This is a famous occasion!'

'Not since the war have so many of us from Force 136 been together.'

'A good thing the British know nothing of this reunion', said Ho Peng.

Chin Peng smiled. 'Comrade Lao Yu, our People's Army Commander, and Comrade Siu Mah are here already.'

Ho Peng shook hands with Lao Yu, smiling politely, for good form was everything, and then greeted Siu Mah, a slight, wiry Chinese like himself.

'You know each other?' asked Lao Yu. 'Comrade Siu Mah is the Commanding Officer of the 11th Regiment in North Pahang.'

'Of course,' said Ho Peng. 'Comrade Siu Mah is my neighbour, north of my area. We see each other from time to time. We're fortunate that Comrade Chin Peng has chosen to have this important Central Executive Committee conference so close to our areas. We have had less far to walk than most of the other comrades.'

Chin Peng laughed pleasantly. 'We had to choose a place in the middle of Malaya, so all the comrades could reach us with the best equality of effort.' He had taken over as General-Secretary of the whole Malayan Communist Party during the chaos and supreme embarrassment after the previous Secretary Lai Tek had absconded with the Party's funds in March 1947 and, although he was only twenty-six, his leadership was undisputed. He ushered his visitors into the central Secretariat building, they sat on mats on the floor and tea was served in small cups.

'We should not behave like animals even though we are in the jungle,' said Lao Yu sanctimoniously, seeing a flicker of surprise on Ho Peng's face.

Ho Peng said nothing. For him, china cups and teapots were an effete nonsense in the jungle. The business of being in the jungle was to fight. There was no other reason.

Chin Peng was young but he had fought throughout the Japanese occupation, for which the British awarded him the Order of the

British Empire for his work in Force 136, though he had never collected it. He knew his senior commanders well, their strengths and weaknesses. He guessed Ho Peng's thoughts and said, 'We'll soon be drinking our tea in the sun, Comrade Ho Peng. We shall liberate areas and place them under our control, just as Comrade Mao Tse-tung tells us in his writings.'

'And what of the British?' asked Ho Peng.

'We shall declare war on them,' stated Chin Peng simply.

Ho Peng stared, hardly daring to believe what he had heard, and then exclaimed, 'Excellent!'

'It's what you recommended, isn't it?' Chin Peng asked, smiling.

'So you got my report on the Asian Youth Congress in Calcutta?'

'Of course!' said Chin Peng. 'Three days ago. Your courier, Liya, is most efficient, and really very attractive.' He paused, but Ho Peng was single-mindedly interested in war, not talking about women, so Chin Peng continued, 'Your report fits in with what I've heard from other sources. The Chinese and Russians feel this is the right time. They want to disrupt the Asian plans of our Imperialist enemies, especially the British and Americans, so they will support our effort.'

'The Comrade General-Secretary will explain his orders when everyone is present,' interrupted Lao Yu importantly, to Ho Peng's annoyance. He wanted to ask exactly what Chin Peng expected in support from Russia and China, how to arm the insurrection they planned, and more important still, how to finance it. However, the little group split up. Chin Peng apologised, promising, 'We'll talk before you go, Comrade Ho Peng, but now I must discuss tactics with Comrade Lao Yu.'

They left and Ho Peng walked round the compound with Siu Mah, only half listening to his chat. Ho Peng was worried about a question he thought Chin Peng wanted to ask him, and his inability to find the best answer left him feeling bad-tempered.

During that afternoon, numerous other important Party members appeared in the camp, guided along the three-mile-long track from the Bentong road. Ho Peng met men he had not seen for years, since the Japanese occupation: leaders like Ah Kuk from Malacca, nicknamed 'Shorty' because he was only four foot nine inches tall, Osman China, an intellectual who had passed his Cambridge University Entrance Examination at Singapore's Victoria School; and Hor Lung, a vigorous and capable fighter from the area around Segamat. By nightfall, nearly fifty of the Party's most important and aggressive leaders from all the Malay States were gathered.

Ho Peng enjoyed the reunion, the talk over old times while they sat round fires that night eating a feast of rice, vegetables and meat in pools of yellow electric lights hanging between the tree trunks and run off a generator. No-one worried about the noise, or the light, for there was an atmosphere of safety and confidence. Couriers, guards and participants had been careful not to let slip the slightest hint of this historic meeting to the Malay Police. Even if they had, there were over four hundred MPABA soldiers all round the camp, to guard the Party's most important men.

But Ho Peng never relaxed. Chin Peng's proposal to talk privately hung over him and he knew that, once they launched their campaign against the British and Malay authorities, all their lives would be at risk again as they had been under the Japanese.

He had to control his impatience for two more days in which they discussed routine Party business to take advantage of the rarity of having so many senior members present. At last, on the morning of the fourth day, Chin Peng gathered the Central Executive together in the Secretariat building and announced his plan of war.

He stood up in front of them all, a smiling young-looking man, and declared a campaign of terror and killing, 'There will be three phases to achieve our victory. In Phase One, you in the Malayan Peoples' Anti-British Army will attack the British Imperialists and their running dogs among the Malay, Indian and Chinese. You will kill petty government officials, miners, planters and sycophantic capitalist businessmen and destroy lines of communications, such as railways, telephones and bridges. You will terrorise them, shatter their faith in the Imperialist organs of government and break their spirit.'

Ho Peng looked grim but he smiled inside. This was what he wanted to hear.

Chin Peng went on, 'The British will have no answer to our assault in remote rural areas. Their police are divided among themselves and they will be unable to stop us. They will withdraw to the towns, just as Mao Tse-tung predicted would happen, and indeed has happened, in his successful fight through China.'

'Then, in Phase Two, we in the MPABA will emerge from the jungle and liberate areas of rural villages and small towns. We shall establish military bases in these "Liberated Areas", enlarging our forces with new recruits while we continue to attack outwards.'

'Finally, in Phase Three, our army columns will swarm out of the

Liberated Areas and seize the remaining towns and the cities, and the British will collapse.'

Cheers and clapping greeted this brief and concise declaration of intent, and Chin Peng, still genial, spent the next hours developing his plan, supported in tactical detail by his military commander Lao Yu. He emphasised, 'The Min Yuen, our "Masses Movement", will be crucial to our success. These men and women are not fighters in the jungle, like the MPABA, but waiters, clerks or officials and we have them placed everywhere, in offices, newspapers, companies, British clubs, bars,. hotels and kampongs. The Min Yuen are especially strong among miners, rubber tappers and squatters all over the country. They are ordinary people, but no less important than the soldiers in the MPABA. Their support is vital, for they will supply us with food and money and they will be a constant source of new recruits as our campaign progresses.'

The meeting went on all day, and that afternoon, while a group including Lao Yu stood chatting outside the Secretariat enjoying the dry heat of the sun on the leaves above, General-Secretary Chin Peng genially put his hand on Ho Peng's shoulder and steered him to one side. Ho Peng steeled himself for the awful question he could not answer. They walked into the middle of the compound where they could be seen but not overheard, and Chin Peng, smiling, softly asked, 'Are you ready for the fight, Comrade Ho Peng?' He scrutinised Ho Peng's pock-marked face and tried to read the hard expression there.

'I have enough weapons for the time being, Comrade Chin Peng, which the British were kind enough to give us in the war,' answered Ho Peng at once. 'I have Japanese weapons too, and my soldiers are trained. Yes, we're ready to go.'

'Good, good. You've picked your targets?'

Ho Peng described a few, and wondered if Chin Peng was playing with him, waiting for the right moment to ask the question he dreaded, but Chin Peng's face was plumply benign and he gave no sign of suspicion. So Ho Peng went on the attack. Speaking in a very low voice, he asked a question himself, 'Tell me, Comrade Chin Peng, there are 5,000 MPABA fighters in the jungle and you've told us they're all to be paid $30 Malay a month. How is this money to be raised?'

Chin Peng answered quickly, 'From the Min Yuen, of course.'

'But then we shall need millions of dollars a year for pay alone? And what about our war supplies, like ammunition, explosives and food, not to mention the expenses of the courier network?'

Chin Peng smiled and said, 'Have faith, Comrade Ho Peng. This war is for the People and the People will provide.' His face hardened, 'The People must realise, through force if necessary, that they must make sacrifices for the revolution to match our own sacrifices.'

Ho Peng nodded. This was the language of a theory he understood very well but he was a fighting man, and a practical man. He said, 'Today we've started a war-machine but it will seize up without money to oil its working parts.'

Chin Peng frowned, because he had worked it all out, and replied, 'There are more than a quarter of a million in the Min Yuen. They will raise your money and supply you with food in the jungle, but remember, Comrade Ho Peng, Mao Tse-tung says in his notes on the Three Stages of Protracted War, "Weapons are an important factor in war, but not the decisive factor! It is people, not things, that are decisive. The contest of strength is not only a contest of military and economic power, but also a contest of human power and morale." The People will support us and this is why we will win.'

Ho Peng had needed more than fine speeches to fight and survive during the Japanese occupation, but he kept such blasphemy to himself. Instead, to test Chin Peng's suspicions, he decided to ask one last question. Watching Chin Peng's open boyish face carefully, he remarked, 'I don't doubt our commitment, but surely Mao didn't mean that military and economic resources were neglected completely? Perhaps Mao himself will support us?'

Chin Peng had thought of it already and said emphatically, 'I don't think we need their support until we have Liberated Areas, in Phase Two. I'm in constant touch with the Red Army in China and we shall ask for assistance when we need it. Of course, we'll need heavy weapons and money to fight the British in open warfare in Phase Three, but I expect we shall capture much of what we need before then.' He added that he was expecting moral support from Russia in the United Nations, and then led the way back to join the others.

He asked Ho Peng no other question. He had wanted to speak personally to every one of his commanders before they left and Ho Peng's readiness to fight was expected and welcome. He controlled the important area near Kuala Lumpur. However, he was surprised to see a rare smile on Ho Peng's bleak face as they parted, and the unusual sight stuck in his mind for a long time afterwards.

Ho Peng was secretly delighted. Chin Peng had not asked about the gold sovereigns. This could only mean that, in the chaos at the end of the war, with communications so disrupted in the jungle, Chin Peng had never found out about the para-drop of canisters. Nor, it seemed, had the British informed him. The thought that really amused him was that, once Chin Peng's campaign of terror started against the British, they never would.

Later that evening, in the inky darkness of night under the canopy, Ho Peng was walking back to his hut to sleep when he heard the low voices of two people ahead in the shadows. Always curious for information, he slowed down, to pick up what he could before they noticed him. He was unwilling to sneak up on them and risk being caught. Too many of the men at the meeting had developed a sixth sense over years on the run in the jungle. Padding silently towards them over the soft earth, Ho Peng listened intently.

'Where will you go next?'

'To Seremban, then back towards Kuala Lumpur.'

'For the meeting in Kajang?'

'Yes.'

Ho Peng was almost upon them, moving like a wraith, and recognised them both in the faint yellow light cast from the electric bulbs hanging from the trees near the Secretariat.

General-Secretary Chin Peng and Comrade Lao Yu.

The following Sunday, Edward and Diana went to the Selangor Club, affectionately known as the 'Spotted Dog', to watch a cricket match between the Headquarters and the Police. The army won the toss, batted first and, just before lunch Captain Denton was at the crease and scoring freely.

Sitting on deckchairs, Edward watched the white figures on the field intently, while Diana preferred to check out the spectators who were a mixture of the most senior British officials in Malaya.

'Who's that?' she asked, pointing at a man in uniform in a group standing in the shade of some palm trees by the pavilion. 'He's got a sort of blob of silver on his shoulder and a black string round his arm.'

'For God's sake!' Edward whispered urgently, pushing her bare arm down. Like many of the men, he wore a civilian shirt and tie and neatly pressed cotton duck trousers but he did not want to draw attention to himself. 'That blob of silver says he's Malaya's Police

Commissioner. Top copper in the country. Chap called Langworthy. H.B. Langworthy.'

'Really?' said Diana. She shaded her eyes for a better look, holding her wide-brimmed white cotton hat with one slim hand. Her red and white cotton dress was stretched tight under her breasts as she twisted round in her deck chair, her long honey-coloured legs trailing behind her and she looked very blonde indeed with her hair loose and long. 'D'you know him?'

Edward nodded, trying to concentrate on the batsman again. He had seen most of the senior officers and policemen in the first few weeks, during Intelligence briefings for senior staff officers, but he could hardly claim to 'know' them and he felt somewhat on edge with so much 'brass' about. 'They're rather out of my league,' he said drily.

'Nonsense, darling. It's always useful to meet the top chaps,' said Diana smiling at him brightly. Her long fingers idly caressed his wrist. 'This is a social occasion, isn't it? And my background is quite as good as theirs.' She spotted a comfortably large woman in her forties wearing a voluminous printed cotton dress and said, 'Davina Bleasley's with them. I met her at a Guild of Saint Helena meeting in the Garrison Church last week. You've not met her, have you?'

'And this isn't the time,' said Edward decisively, shading his eyes to watch the game. 'Her awful husband is over there and I don't want him ruining my Sunday as well as the rest of the week.' Colonel Bleasley had not relented, except for grudging praise when Edward produced some well written material for the monthly Intelligence report.

Diana was not surprised and said, 'Well, Davina Bleasley is quite nice, and the padre's over there too, so I'm going over. Maybe they'll introduce me to that awfully important policeman.' She smiled wickedly, enjoying the feeling of being at the centre of Malaya's colonial life.

Edward watched her for a moment as she walked elegantly across the grass to the pavilion, and then turned back to the cricket. Ten minutes later, when the players came in for lunch, Edward went to the marquee to find a drink for himself and Diana.

A cold buffet luncheon was being served, and the open-sided marquee was full of talk and jostling people – the women in cool dresses and the men in lightweight suits and pale sandy tropical uniforms. Edward moved to a long table covered with a white tablecloth which had been set up as a bar and ordered a Pimms for

43

Diana and a whisky s'tengah for himself.

'Half water, half whisky, sir?' asked the barman in his starched white tunic as he poured the s'tengah and handed the drinks to Edward.

As Edward turned away with the two glasses, he knocked into a woman and spilled the Pimms across her arm.

'I'm terribly sorry,' said Edward appalled.

'Apart from the fruit salad, Pimms is not as sticky as some,' said the woman shrugging her bare shoulders. She was attractive, a guessing age somewhere in her thirties, with a slim boyish figure, short fair hair, deep blue eyes and a wide sensuous mouth tilted up at the corners, her lips pale pink with lipstick. She observed Edward critically and held her arm out to avoid the drips going on her pale blue dress.

Edward suddenly realised she wanted him to wipe her arm. Apologising again, he quickly put the glasses back on the table so he could fish out his handkerchief and began to dab at the drink on her arm.

'You're being rather pathetic with that,' she said trying to see his face as he bent over her arm. She liked the feel of his hands on her arm but she said, 'I'm not made of Dresden china.'

'You're American?' said Edward ignoring the remark but holding her arm more firmly.

She nodded and said, 'I'm Marsha. And you?'

'Edward Fairfax,' he said. Something defensive made him add, 'That's my wife, over there, with Colonel and Mrs Bleasley.'

'What a pity.'

'What d'you mean?' asked Edward looking up from her arm.

'What d'you think, Edward?' Marsha replied. She gave him a sudden brilliant smile and Edward was suddenly conscious of how close he was to her.

'Can I have my arm back now?' she asked softly.

Edward let go her arm rather quickly, apologising a third time, 'I'm frightfully sorry about all this. Can I get you a drink?'

Before she could answer, raised voices behind them made them both look round. In the centre of the marquee H. B. Langworthy, the Commissioner of Police was being harangued by a thin, fair-haired man in a crumpled tropical suit whose face was flushed. The thin strands of his fair hair stuck to the perspiration on his forehead, and he was shouting: 'The bloody bandits are armed and ready to go. Thousands of them.'

'What nonsense!' retorted Langworthy sharply. He drew himself up inside his uniform, the image of dependable authority, shook his head and stated firmly, 'I'll say it once more. There are no men in uniform lurking in the jungle. It's sheer panic-mongering to talk like that.'

'You don't have a bloody clue!' shouted the fair-haired planter. Gradually conversation died away and when the planter took another gulp from his whisky, the sound of ice chinking in his glass echoed round the marquee in the embarrassed silence. Langworthy stood his ground on the hessian matting, obstinately refusing to budge, but he searched the sea of pink and tanned faces for support, wishing someone would come to his rescue as soon as possible.

Marsha leaned close to Edward and whispered breathily in his ear, 'The drunk is Mark Bowman. Nice guy normally. He's a neighbour. He runs the estate next to ours but it's remote, so he and Jim Beam have made good friends recently.'

Bowman, swaying slightly, went on the attack again, prodding his finger at Langworthy's chest. 'You wouldn't be so bloody complacent if you lived on the edge of the jungle like me.'

Langworthy swelled a little more but said nothing. He noticed with relief some movement on the other side of the tent which looked like help and recognised the secretary of the cricket club in his striped blazer. Abruptly, his attention was gripped by another man who moved unconcernedly into the centre of attention to join the embarrassing little scene.

He was a big man in his forties run to fat, in a badly creased suit with his tie awry under the collar of his white shirt, the effort of a man unused to wearing a tie at all. He brushed one large, workman-like hand over his balding head and said, 'I'd like to apologise on behalf of Mark Bowman, Commissioner Langworthy, for his delivery so to speak, but there's no doubt as to the truth of his message.' The slow Irish brogue clearly reached every corner of the tent. 'My tappers were attacked and threatened yesterday and not a thing has been done about it.'

'Damned right, Sean,' interjected Bowman hotly and drained his glass.

'Nonsense,' repeated Langworthy feeling stronger now. The secretary was almost through the crowd, his face grim.

Sean Tallard shook his large head and said 'Of course, I won't be knowing what you know, Commissioner Langworthy, you being in the police, and the senior man at that, but, as true as I stand here, there are armed men in the jungle, and there's going to be a real barney. Mr Mark Bowman is certainly drunk, but what he says is right all the same, and I can see that we planters are going to have the thick end of it.'

Langworthy stared at him balefully, his jaw set. The club secretary emerged from the crowd into the open space around the three near the bar table. He announced briskly, 'Come along now, chaps. That's enough of that,' and he made to lead both Bowman and Tallard out by the arm. Bowman offered no resistance but Sean Tallard stepped aside to avoid the secretary's hand with surprising agility for someone so well built and said in a level voice, 'I make no apology, Mr Secretary, for telling the truth, but I'll find my own way out, if you don't mind.'

'Thank you, Mr Tallard,' said the secretary, mollified but still angry the club's day had been marred. 'I think that would be best.'

Tallard looked Langworthy straight in the eye and added, 'I'll take Bowman too. We're neighbours and he's going to need help.'

The secretary nodded, unsure whether Tallard meant Bowman needed help to reach his car or help to defend himself from bandits, but he let go of Mark Bowman and the Irishman led him out.

Conversation resumed in a babble of excited talk and, as Tallard and Bowman passed Edward by the bar, Tallard jerked his head at Marsha.

'I have to go,' she said.

Edward stared after the two planters and then back at Marsha who added, 'He's my husband'. She shrugged her bare shoulders. 'We live about twenty-seven miles down the road beyond Langat, on a place called the Black Circle Rubber Estate and I can tell you it's an awfully long walk home.' She pulled a face and pouted, 'I just knew something like this would happen. It's the first time I've been into town for weeks, and God knows when I'll be back.' Then her expression changed, she smiled warmly at Edward, put her long fingers gently on his arm, saying, 'Still, don't you forget me now, honey?' Then she turned on her heel and walked off to gather her things from her deckchair, knowing very well that Edward would be watching.

'Bloody bad show,' stated a man behind Edward, making him jump, guilty with thoughts about Marsha.

'Typical bloody planter,' agreed a major in uniform. 'Sean Tallard should know better. God knows, he's been here long enough.'

The cricket match ended in a draw, but the argument had left a sour taste and after the close of play everyone left as soon as they could. Edward had arranged for Gandra Singh to take him and Diana back to their villa and it was dark as they drove home.

Diana cuddled up to Edward on the back seat and asked airily, 'Who was that woman you were talking to?'

Edward was expecting this and replied straightforwardly, 'That chap Tallard's wife, actually. I bumped into her at the bar. Literally.'

Diana snorted and wrinkled her nose, 'You were pawing her. I saw you quite distinctly.'

'I was,' Edward admitted, enjoying her attention. 'I spilled your first Pimms all over her, if you must know, and I was wiping it off her arm.'

Diana made another deprecatory noise but wriggled closer to Edward. He slipped his arm around her and thought of the way Marsha Tallard had looked at him.

Gandra Singh began to hum a Sikh love song in a deep bass rumble.

Edward stroked Diana's bare arm with his fingers. She pulled his arm around her and cuddled in closer, enjoying the familiar smell of him and the pressure of his open hand through the cotton on her thigh.

Still humming, Gandra Singh dropped them at the house and waved Edward away when he tried to pay.

'Please, Sahib, you are always able to pay me the next time,' he said seriously and shooed him away with both large hands. He got straight back into the taxi, ground into reverse gear, and, sticking his head and beard right out of the window, he added cryptically, 'Also, please, it is now dark and you are not wasting this occasion.'

The old Austin reversed up the cul-de-sac belching smoke. Edward shook his head and followed Diana inside the house.

'Time for another tipple before supper?' he asked.

'I've had enough,' she said, her voice husky. She reached up on tiptoe and kissed him lightly on the lips. 'And besides, I'm not hungry any more.'

From the kitchen, Hassan heard Diana's high heels clipping across the hardwood floor to the master-bedroom and the sound of Edward's suede shoes following. He glanced at Lao Song. The Chinese cook was in his black working smock standing impassively at the kitchen table holding an enormous steel knife poised above some fresh bamboo shoots. Hassan put one brown finger to his lips and slipped out on to the verandah, breathing in the dusky scent of the Moon flowers, on to the grass of the soft Serangoon lawn which brushed coolly between his toes, and walked swiftly round the house to a clump of Clerodendron bushes outside the bedroom windows. The garden was his responsibility and he had planted them specially. All Malays knew these bright red pagoda flowers had magic properties and he nodded happily when he saw the bedroom windows were dark. Moments later he heard the rhythmic sound of springs and the occasional little cry which made him feel all liquid inside.

Being of a sensitive nature he did not wait any longer but returned to the kitchen where Lao Song appeared not to have moved. When he saw Hassan spread his smooth arms and his white teeth appeared in a brown smile, Lao Song's black eyes hardly flickered. He put his knife down on the chopping board and shuffled out to his room beyond the kitchen, slightly bent, like an old tortoise with a wrinkled neck off to hibernate. Hassan felt sorry for him. He had been absorbed in his habitually detailed way preparing dinner for the past two hours. He called after him, 'Song, please not to worry! The Tuans have very good food tonight.'

Later, Edward raided Lao Song's larder for orange juice and fresh fruit which he brought back to the bedroom. Moonlight through the open window cast shadows across the rays of light on the white mosquito net hanging over the big double bed. He slipped under the net and they lay together naked in the hot rumpled sheets, propped up on pillows eating sweet mangoes and yellow starfruit.

Diana felt deliciously relaxed. She gazed at the vault of white netting above them and murmured, 'It's very private in here, as though the rest of the world doesn't exist.'

'Our secret place,' agreed Edward, catching a dribble of mango juice running down his cheek.

She thought for a moment about the afternoon, and asked, 'I'm not harping on, but do you really think there are bandits in the jungle, out there.' She listened to the cacophony of cicadas and night frogs in the garden outside.

Edward frowned, 'There have been a few reports in the office, but I wouldn't have thought it was as bad as those two made out.' However, he resolved to make enquiries. He was beginning to realise there was so much of the East he did not understand and he wondered just what did go on in the secret, rotting darkness of the jungle.

'I hope not,' said Diana fervently and shivered. It did not seem possible that such an agreeable way of life in Malaya could be upset, then suddenly she remembered something. She leaned over him, squashing her soft breasts on the hard muscles of his chest, and said excitedly, 'I've decided to buy a car!'

Edward laughed, 'What with? I can't afford it.'

But she was serious. 'I can,' she said, provocatively scratching the skin on his chest with her long nails. 'I'm fed up going round in that taxi. It smells of old socks.'

Edward laughed, 'Gandra Singh is a great character.'

A little frown appeared on her forehead as she said, 'It's hopeless when I want to go to meetings and arrange "do-s" in the Headquarters. It's miles and I'm absolutely not walking in the heat.'

'True,' agreed Edward. Walking ten yards made everyone sweat. Furthermore, Diana could afford a car.

'We could go for drives at weekends,' she said. The idea of exploring the countryside really appealed to her.

'Okay, why not?' He stroked the smooth skin of her back all the way down to the rise of her bottom and she responded, slowly squirming up his body to kiss him full on the lips.

When Hassan heard the faint, sibilant sound of springs, slower this time, and gentler, he could control himself no longer. He slipped out of the house and across the moonlit garden to the red pagoda flower bushes, his body tingling with expectation.

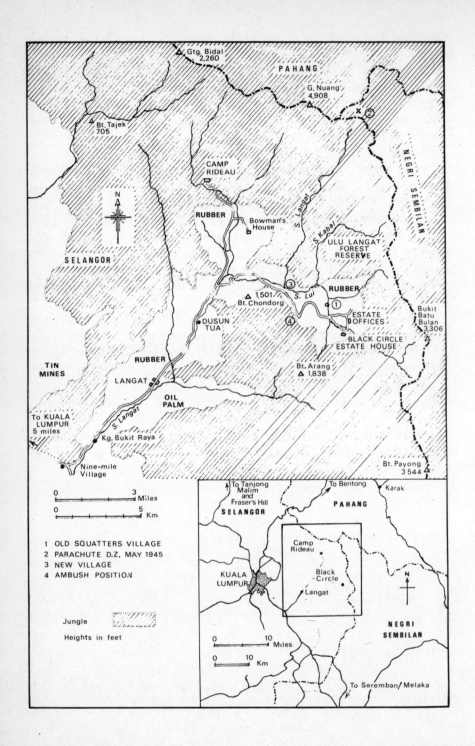

Gtg. Bidal
2,260

PAHANG

G. Nuang
4,908

× ②

NEGRI SEMBILAN

Bt. Tajek
705

CAMP
RIDEAU

RUBBER

Bowman's
House

S. Langat

S. Kabal

ULU LANGAT
FOREST
RESERVE

SELANGOR

③

S. Lui

RUBBER

①

1,501
Bt. Chondorg

④

ESTATE
OFFICES

Bukit
Batu
Bulan
3,306

DUSUN
TUA

BLACK CIRCLE
ESTATE HOUSE

RUBBER

Bt. Arang
1,838

TIN
MINES

LANGAT

OIL
PALM

S. Langat

To KUALA
LUMPUR
5 miles

Kg. Bukit Raya

Bt. Payong
3 544

Nine-mile
Village

N

0 _____ 3 Miles

0 _____ 5 Km.

1 OLD SQUATTERS VILLAGE
2 PARACHUTE D.Z. MAY 1945
3 NEW VILLAGE
4 AMBUSH POSITION

Jungle

Heights in feet

To Tanjong
Malim
and
Fraser's Hill

To Bentong

Karak

SELANGOR

PAHANG

Camp
Rideau

KUALA
LUMPUR

Black
Circle

N

Langat

NEGRI
SEMBILAN

0 _____ 10 Miles

0 _____ 10 Km.

To Seremban/Melaka

BOOK TWO

Revolution!

June 1948 to January 1949

'The art of the jungle is to enjoy it.'

Chapter 5

A STATE OF EMERGENCY

On Wednesday 16 June, at nearly nine in the morning, Mark
Bowman yanked the wheel of his old jeep round the last corner of a
red laterite track on to the short straight which ran to the offices of
the Empire Ringgit Rubber Plantations. He was whistling, 'A
Surrey with a fringe on top!', from the recent popular musical
Oklahoma! Rain during the night had settled the dust and freshened
the air and as always, he felt an intense personal satisfaction when
he saw the solid wood buildings with their red-ochre corrugated iron
roofs. He had built them himself before the war, when he took over
the lease of the rubber estate for his London-based rubber company.

His day had started as usual at a quarter to six, with the 'check
call' of his workforce in the dark before dawn. He and his foreman,
or krani, a meticulous Ceylonese called Sundralingam, had divided
his tappers between smoke-house duties in the estate's rubber
processing buildings and the rubber trees in the plantations which
needed attention most. The tappers usually managed to take latex
from 144 trees per day, finishing by about two o'clock, and, as
always, he had driven out to watch them at work. After two hours,
he was looking forward to a good breakfast of ham and eggs.

He stopped in front of the offices under a large chestnut tree,
eased his long shape from behind the wheel and stamped up the
steps into the airy building, shouting, 'Sundralingam! You there?'

'Yes, Sahib,' replied the krani, completing the morning ritual
they had established over the years. 'I am going through the books
and all is well.' Like Bowman, Sundralingam was thin, but he came
from Ceylon and his skin was as utterly dark as Bowman's was pale.

His black arms emerged from his short-sleeved white shirt like tubes, without touching the sides. He removed the shiny gold-rimmed spectacles from his nose and massaged his pinched nostrils with the long fingers of his other hand, waiting patiently, content in the order of things.

Bowman looked in the door, glanced approvingly at the spread of ledgers and invoices on his desk, and went across the hall to his own office shouting over his shoulder, 'Just a few papers to look at here, then I'll have a bite to eat.'

Sundralingam smiled to himself. 'Very good, Sahib. As you like. Rani has your breakfast ready when you want.' This too was their routine. His wife, Rani Sundralingam, cooked and cleaned for Bowman. She always watched out for his jeep when he came back from his routine rounds of the estate in the morning. Soon she would walk over from the house to remind him to eat, just to stop him staying at his desk all morning. Sundralingam admired such dedication even though he knew Bowman worked hard largely because he lived alone.

Rani, dressed in a purple sari, light and cool in the humid air, walked down the steps from the house and started across the yard towards the offices. As she approached the big chestnut, she stopped, and slowly, unconsciously, her hands clutched her sari tightly round her. Something was awfully wrong. Out in the bright sun where the red laterite road cut through green lallang leading to the rubber, six Chinese were walking briskly down the hill towards her. She stared at the red stars on their peaked caps, their pale uniforms stained with dark sweat patches, and their guns, and felt the power drain from her legs. Her throat went dry and she could not speak or move.

Disdainfully, the Chinese passed by her without a glance, their soft plimsoles scuffing in the dust. When they reached the offices four stayed outside while two marched straight up the steps and inside.

Sundralingam looked up from his desk. A short stocky Chinese with a terribly pitted face was staring at him from the door, his carbine pointing at his chest. The pen fell from Sundralingam's fingers and he opened his mouth.

Ho Peng shook his head in warning. Sundralingam shut his mouth, feeling guilty for not shouting a warning to Bowman but empty with fear. Another Chinese appeared behind him and both suddenly disappeared from view across the reception hall towards

54

Bowman's office. Sundralingam heard the Chinese give the usual morning salutation, 'Tabek, Tuan!'

Bowman's voice replied, 'What the devil?' and three quick shots shattered the absurd normality of the proceedings. Suddenly the two Chinese were back facing him again.

'What have you done?' whispered Sundralingam, the whites of his eyes enormous behind his glasses.

'Now, running dog, listen!' said Ho Peng, ignoring the dark-skinned Tamil's panic. 'The Malayan People's Anti-British Army rules this area. We need dues from the people to carry on the fight for true revolution. You will levy fifty cents a week from every man.'

In spite of his terror, Sundralingam exclaimed, 'That's impossible! They can't live if I do that.'

'You must! For the revolution.'

'But don't you see, they won't obey me?' His thin hands waved over the columns of figures in the account books spread on his desk. 'The tappers are mostly new arrivals from mainland China and they won't stay if I do that.'

Ho Peng paused, his eyes narrowed slightly and he shouted over his shoulder. At once, two Chinese ran up the steps into the office, seized Sundralingam from behind his desk, scattering his books on the floor in the struggle, and manhandled him outside. As he was pulled through the hall, he caught sight of Bowman sprawled head first across the threadbare carpet on his office floor. His fair hair was matted with blood which oozed thickly from the back of his shattered skull into the worn pile of the carpet.

The shock blurred Sundralingam's vision and he never saw his wife Rani standing forty yards away, rooted to the spot with terror. He only became aware of what was happening to him when he felt his arms being tied to the big chestnut tree in the centre of the sandy yard.

Ho Peng was talking to him quite calmly, legs apart, arms akimbo, 'You and all running dogs will learn that the revolution must be obeyed. The people depend on it.'

Lao Tang stood back from the tree feeling very powerful with a Sten sub-machine gun. He pitied Sundralingam, but Ho Peng was right. The Krani deserved no mercy for his rejection and exploitation of the ordinary tappers, poor Chinese fleeing their home in China and Tamils from Madras, but Lao Tang did not expect what happened next.

Ho Peng handed his carbine to Lao Tang, walked casually towards the tree where Sundralingam was tied and told him, almost conversationally, 'The revolution must be financed. The revolution is for the people and fifty cents is a miserable sacrifice for each man to make for the freedom of the whole people. If you won't collect money for the revolution, you must be an example to someone who will.' His hand slipped behind his back and reappeared quickly with a long parang, drawn from a leather sheath belted to the small of his back.

When Sundralingam caught sight of the blade he began to scream, 'Please, I will collect, I will collect! Whatever you want.' The circle of Chinese round him were expressionless. Rani stood rigid with fright, unconsciously screwing her sari into knots with her hands clenched over her breasts. Out of sight, estate workers watched from behind the shutters of the smoke-house.

The blade glinted as it fell in a steep arc and smacked through Sundralingam's thin wrist like a butcher's knife cutting pork chops. The severed hand dropped into the dust on one side of the tree. Sundralingam screamed, almost choking himself with desperation. His back arched and his thin body flayed about on the ropes holding him mercilessly to the tree. Without pause, Ho Peng stepped neatly round the trunk and the parang flashed again. Sundralingam jerked again as if electrocuted, his eyes standing out in disbelief at the dark red blood pumping from his stumped wrists.

Calmly Ho Peng wiped the parang on a tuft of lallang grass, sheathed it and took his carbine back from Lao Tang. Then, coolly ignoring Rani and Sundralingam's frothing cries behind him, he looked round at his soldiers and they padded out of the yard in silence.

Lao Tang followed, feeling strangely beaten. Ho Peng's implacable calm was as frightening as the foreman's horrible screams ringing in his ears. In seconds, he had learned just how savage the battlefield of his beliefs was going to be.

The six Chinese walked up the red track in the sun and disappeared one after the other over the brow of the hill. No-one moved in the yard. Rani and the other workers were transfixed with shock. Sundralingam's frantic screams faded to low moans and he hung twitching in his ropes. Blood was spattered over the tree trunk, it dripped steadily from his raw stumps and soaked into the dust. Greedy flies hovered and ants found one of his hands.

* * *

'Fairfax! Where's that damn report?' shouted Colonel Bleasley as he shoved through into the Intelligence room. He glared at Captain Denton, dabbing at his forehead with a handkerchief.

'Just making a few final adjustments, Sir,' said Edward cautiously.

'Adjustments?' Bleasley breathed heavily. 'Are you changing the draft I have already approved?'

They were interrupted by a knock on the door. The Chief Clerk appeared, took in the scene at once, and said, 'Good morning, Colonel!' Exuding an air of brisk efficiency which got him unchallenged into places where even quite senior officers dared not trespass, he strode across the room with a piece of paper in his hand to Captain Denton's desk, because that was the correct chain of command. It was Captain Denton's job to inform the Colonel.

'What's that?' grumbled Colonel Bleasley eyeing the flimsy paper. He could bully the officers but not his Chief Clerk.

'Signal, Sir!' declared the Chief Clerk with bright enthusiasm. He passed the sheet to Captain Denton as if he were producing a cheque for the winner of the Littlewood's Football Pools and marched out.

'Another Sitrep on these attacks, Sir,' said Captain Denton frowning. He pointed to a line on the sheet. 'Damn swine have murdered another planter. Chap called Arthur Walker, at the Elphil Estate in the jungle beyond Sungei Siput, north of Ipoh.' He looked up at Colonel Bleasley. 'That's the problem writing this report, Colonel. We keep getting more information. From all round the country! The whole thing must have been co-ordinated.'

'Bloody nonsense,' said Bleasley. 'Sheer coincidence. They're just a bunch of thieves, after his estate's pay-packet more than likely.'

Captain Denton shook his head slowly, reading from the signal, 'No, Sir. Apparently Walker had $2,000 just lying in the open safe in his office and they never touched it.'

Colonel Bleasley grunted, 'Does it say how many Chinese shot him?'

'Three, sir.'

'Well, there you are,' said Bleasley triumphantly. 'Three miserable Chinese criminals don't make a whole army hiding out in the jungle, do they?' He looked from Edward to Captain Denton, defying them to answer, and said, 'Get that brief ready at once. The place has been turned inside out since we heard Mark Bowman was murdered this morning.' He pulled at his shirt where it was sticking to his skin. 'The general wants to hear my assessment first, and then we're both going to Government House to brief Sir Edward Gent. The High Commissioner you know,' he added unnecessarily, looking at Edward. 'Where's that consolidated list of recent attacks, Fairfax?'

Edward gave him one of the annexes to the brief they were preparing and Colonel Bleasley walked back into his office and shut the door.

'I hope these murders stop,' said Edward glumly going over to the big map of Malaya which covered the whole of one wall. 'Or Bleasley won't give us a moment's peace.'

Captain Denton's handsome face cleared in a broad smile for a moment and then he frowned, thinking of the paperwork they had to finish. He hated writing reports. 'Do you really think there are thousands of armed Chinese lurking in the jungle?'

Edward shook his head. 'I don't know. Haven't been here long enough to judge. We ought to speak to the police. They should know.'

'Can't do that. Bleasley would have a fit. He says the police are all civvies.'

Edward snorted, 'But it's their job to keep their ears to the ground. They ought to know what's happening, at copper level, even if Langworthy doesn't think there's a problem. The fact is there've been a lot of murders, they've slashed rubber trees and sabotaged tin mines all over the place, and that can't be ignored.' He pointed at the big map of Malaya covering one wall of the office. 'At Bowman's estate by Ulu Langat, again near Sungei Siput by Ipoh, more in Perak, in Pahang, and in Johore in the south.'

'So how do we write this report, tying in all that with what Colonel Bleasley thinks?' asked Captain Denton worriedly.

'There'll be an uproar,' said Edward thinking aloud. The situation reminded him of the start of the terrorism in Palestine, when a similar spate of attacks all round the country had shocked the military and police establishments and proved to be the forerunner to a well co-ordinated campaign of terrorism. In the end the Jews had succeeded in tiring out the British who washed their hands of the Mandate and left. Would the same happen in Malaya, obliging the British to leave Malaya for the second time in ten years? He found the idea of being involved in another campaign rather exciting, but he said, 'We may not know exactly what the scale of

Chinese subversion will be, but there's no doubt the communists are out there and the number of attacks seems to be going up. Colonel Bleasley doesn't see it, but he won't thank you and me if we produce a report pooh-poohing the whole affair and then finds himself shot down in flames by General Boucher.'

'Good thinking, Fairfax, old man,' said Captain Denton, picking up the theme with a mixture of enthusiasm and relief. 'Just what I'd have said myself.'

Edward suppressed a smile and said, 'Why don't we give him a masterpiece of the middle road? Summarise all that's gone on, saying there's clearly evidence of armed aggression by the Malayan Communist Party, but without giving any guesses about numbers? Let the facts speak for themselves.'

'Excellent,' said Captain Denton. Edward Fairfax seemed heaven-sent. 'Is there much to do?'

Edward studied the paper spread around him on the desk with the satisfactory thought that he, the most junior officer on the Intelligence Staff was in effect producing the conclusion which would be heard by some very senior officers, including the High Commissioner himself. He said, 'We've only the conclusion left.'

'Which is?'

'Life as we know it in Malaya is over.'

'I say!' said Captain Denton genuinely shocked. 'That's a bit steep, don't you think? Bleasley won't like going out on a limb on that at all.'

Edward shrugged. He liked Harry Denton but here was a chance to influence the Staff so that the necessary steps were taken early enough to do some good. He said, 'The facts indicate we have a war on our hands. Judging by the number of attacks, there probably are thousands of bandits lurking about in the jungle. That poor man Mark Bowman was right, in spite of what Langworthy said, and he paid the full price. I think it's very probable they're coming out to do battle. Fired up by the Russians, I suppose, or the Chinese. The authorities will have to take exceptional measures to stop them. Road blocks, curfews, arrests, searches. All the things we saw in Palestine. Maybe worse. And all this is bound to change things in Malaya.' He glanced at Harry Denton who looked slightly bemused. Denton was a straightforward and brave officer, but he hated politics. Edward said, 'Of course, if you'd like me to say something else—?'

'No, no,' said Denton quickly. 'You crack on. Sounds like a firm batting wicket to me.'

They sat down and Edward wrote hard for an hour while Captain Denton collated the bald facts of the murders and attacks that morning. Captain Denton presented the final handwritten draft to Bleasley and left him to read it. Half an hour later, the door of Colonel Bleasley's office flew open again. Bleasley strode out and said, 'I think the whole situation is damned serious and I'm sick of saying so.' He looked quickly from Captain Denton to Edward, daring them to mention that it was the first time he had expressed such a view, but Edward's list had shown him just how many incidents there had been. 'The police are a bloody shambles to let things slip like this. I shall tell General Boucher, and I've no doubt he'll agree with me, that the situation can be wrapped up in a few weeks hard work by the army. Soon winkle the devils out, eh?'

Edward said nothing. He had poked his head into the small clump of jungle beyond the ditch near his house and the claustrophobic green gloom gave him no confidence the affair would be over so fast. He wondered if Colonel Bleasley had ever been in the jungle.

Wheezing slightly Bleasley stood for a moment under a ceiling fan to let the draught cool the top of his head. He enjoyed the warm climate, the food and drink but they all militated against a metabolism like his and he resented people with slim ectomorphic bodies. 'You, Captain Denton,' he growled aggressively. 'And young Fairfax here, will have this report in top copy on my desk as soon as possible. Get the Chief Clerk to type it up.' He glared fiercely at them both, and disappeared back into his office.

The typist produced the brief by one o'clock and Bleasley took it with him to lunch.

'Gone for his usual s'tengah and three courses in the Officers' Mess,' said Harry Denton, leaning back in his chair and thankful to see the back of Bleasley. He hated tension between people. 'I know he sleeps it off for a couple of hours after lunch but a chap his shape shouldn't eat so much in this climate.'

Edward shook his head. 'The thought of having to brief the General at two o'clock will spoil his appetite today.'

Harry Denton burst out laughing. 'Right ho! Then you and I will vacate the premises. I suggest we slip away to the Coliseum Bar in town, where all the planters go. Coming?'

Edward was pleased to be asked.

'Call me Harry if you like,' said Captain Denton. His years at school and in a cavalry regiment during the war placed him firmly in the English officer class. He felt safe with the well-understood rules of British social conduct, especially in sport, which was his main interest in life, and with the women in that circle who loved his muscular charm, but he was not a great brain and honest enough to admit it. Since Edward's arrival he had admired the young Parachute Regiment officer's grasp of the job and, now the security situation seemed to be deteriorating so rapidly, he was grateful to have Edward's help. Denton was a man of action. He groaned inwardly when Colonel Bleasley resorted to paper every time he was put under pressure from above. Edward Fairfax was likely to become indispensable.

They drove into town down the Batu Road in Denton's black Morris Cowley, passed the Government offices and the 'Spotted Dog' Sporting Club opposite across the cricket ground, turned left and parked in a dusty avenue lined with Royal Palms.

They followed the covered walkway on the pavement into the Coliseum Bar which they found very full. The bar was lined with mahogany panelling which gave it a gloomy club-like atmosphere but that day there was an air of excitement and frustrated anger. Everyone was talking about the murders.

Denton waved a greeting at Mr Wong, the owner, who was taking an order from a nearby table for another big steak, the bar's speciality, and he called back, 'Good day, Captain Denton. Nice to see you again.'

'Amazing man, Mr Wong,' said Harry Denton. 'Always knows your name, no matter how seldom you come in.' He turned to the Chinese barman and ordered, 'Two Tiger beers, Willie. Lot of customers today?'

'What d'you expect, Captain Denton?' the bartender said, pouring the beers. He was thin, about thirty, with an expression of world-weariness on his face as if he had known all along that the bandits were going to attack that day. 'They're all talking about what's happened on the estates.'

'Is this the place to find out?' Edward asked, enjoying the taste of the cooled beer.

'Who knows?' retorted the bartender safely. His smooth Asian features broke into a wide grin displaying several gold teeth.

'Trust you to go drinking at a time like this,' said a familiar voice in a gentle Scots burr. 'And lowering the tone of the haunts I enjoy.'

Edward turned to see Angus Maclean, the Scottish Chief

61

Inspector of Police he had known in Palestine. Delighted, he pumped his hand in greeting. 'In civvies as usual?' Edward laughed, seeing Angus was wearing a comfortable lightweight suit.

'In the CID, as before. When Palestine folded up, I moved out here at the start of '48,' said Angus grinning with pleasure. Finding Edward in Malaya was a real tonic, especially that particular morning. Edward introduced him to Harry Denton, explaining that he and Angus had worked together in Jerusalem.

'Chasing the Irgun, eh? Damn good,' said Denton, impressed. He liked the look of the slim dark-haired Scot. 'Rotten show, though, us getting kicked out of Palestine.'

'Aye, that's what it amounted to,' admitted Angus.

Denton nodded, 'I hope to God we can do better here!' He found it rather disturbing to think that, not far beyond the town limits, where the jungle lapped around the kampongs like sea unless actively checked by rubber cultivations or tin mines, there were Chinese soldiers waiting to strike again.

'We'll be fine,' said Edward, enormously cheered to find Angus Maclean. 'I feel better already.'

'Well I bloody don't,' said a voice behind them blurred with drink. The three looked round to see a large policeman in uniform, a crumpled beige shirt and voluminous shorts, long socks and black shoes. Edward noticed he was a lieutenant and, judging by his age in the mid-forties, guessed he had come up through the ranks.

The policeman reached unsteadily between them to slide his glass across the counter for another beer and said to Angus, 'You bloody Palestine police 'ave only been here a couple of minutes, 'aven't you? What the hell can you do?'

Smoothly Angus Maclean said, 'I'm sure we'll all do the best we can.'

This inflamed the policeman who said in a loud voice, 'Sounds just like the sort of bloody silly remark we used to hear in '41 before the fall of Singapore.'

A couple of planters at tables near the bar looked up. One said, 'That's right. We've been warning the High Commissioner for months.'

While the Chinese bartender filled his glass, Angus observed the policeman's flushed, tired face and hoped he would go away.

'Thanks, Willie,' said the policeman, shouting unnecessarily. With careful deliberation, he wrapped his large fist round the glass, lifted it delicately to his lips and drank deeply. Edward raised his eyes at Angus, but the man was planted to the spot and, like all drunks, single-minded. He wiped the froth from his mouth and returned to the attack, 'You newcomers haven't a bloody clue. Think you can just turn up from any old place and tell us what to do. Well, today proves you can't. The whole situation's out of control. It's up to the army.'

Edward sipped his Tiger beer. There was strong feeling in the crowded room. Everyone was watching the scene at the bar. They were angry, sympathising with the policeman. They desperately wanted the authorities to show a sign they would support and help them.

'It's a disaster for the economy,' said one planter. 'We'll have to close down if these murders go on.'

'It's a bloody disgrace. We all told Sir Edward Gent this would happen and nothing's been done.'

'They won't bloody give us rifles,' expostulated a tin-miner, 'so that we can fight the devils ourselves.'

'We can't do it alone. The army must guard us,' said another and they started arguing among themselves again.

'The army can't protect everyone,' said Captain Denton reasonably.

'We've all got to pull together,' agreed Angus in a placatory tone.

To Edward's surprise, the policeman shouted, 'What the hell do you know about pulling together?' He stared round at the three of them, his voice rising in outrage, 'Where the hell were you when we were left in the lurch in the war?'

Conversation died away again and several planters nodded.

Captain Denton bridled. He had joined up to fight Germans at eighteen years old and fought in Africa and Italy during the war. Bluntly, he said so.

'You weren't here though, were you?' the policeman stated with unanswerable logic, prodding his finger at Denton's chest. 'Where you were needed, eh? When the Japs came. Not like us.'

Denton stood up, high spots of colour appearing on his tanned cheeks above his bushy fair-haired moustache. He knew he was not clever, but he had never been accused of cowardice. 'I say, old chap, that's out of order.'

Edward said rather desperately, 'I think we should go.' He did not think fighting in the Coliseum Bar would go down well with Colonel Bleasley in his present mood. Not a good start to his posting

63

in Malaya. He reached into his pocket for the $3.20 to pay for the two beers.

'That's right,' sneered the policeman, breathing hops over them all. 'Bloody walk out when the going gets tough.'

'By God,' shouted Captain Denton and he began to swing his fist in a long haymaker.

Angus Maclean was quicker. He slipped between the two, shoved the big policeman off balance and grabbed Denton's arm.

'Calm down!' he bellowed. He pushed Denton back to the bar and whipped back to the big policeman who was rocking unsteadily forward to the attack. He jabbed him hard in the solar plexus, winding him badly, shoved him backwards with one hand on his chest and tripped him into an empty chair before he could think. The big man sat gasping for breath while Angus fished his warrant card from inside his jacket pocket. He leaned over the wheezing man flashing it close to his face, and spoke in a low hard tone, 'Pay up, Lieutenant, and leave, before you disgrace your uniform any more and force me to report you to the Police Circle. And remember, if we don't pull together, like I say, we shall all have to leave Malaya again. To the communists.'

The big man nodded vacantly, his temper fading as quickly as it had come. Suddenly, his body ached for sleep. A couple of planters came to his rescue. The brief scuffle had cleared the air. The country was at great risk and emotions were running at a pitch but everyone knew that fighting among themselves was not the answer.

Angus rejoined Harry Denton and Edward at the bar apologising, 'I'm sorry about that. It's the damn war again. When the Japs attacked, the British Government told everyone to stay where they were and everything would be fine. It wasn't, as you know. All the policemen and white managers were rounded up by the Japs and they had a bad time in Changi Jail or on the Burma railway. Many died and the survivors were only released three years ago, so memories are fresh and they don't have much faith in the Government.'

'What's that got to do with the situation now?' asked Captain Denton puzzled.

'There's a bitter split in the Malay Police between those who stayed and suffered, and those who got away,' answered Angus Maclean. 'And that's no way to fight the communists.' He smoothed his dark hair with a hand and pulled a face. 'Plus, that lieutenant was right in a way. I'm a new boy, like a lot of others who came here from Palestine, and neither of the two bickering groups of old Malay hands thinks we can be any use at all. So the Malay Police is split three ways.' He shrugged and added in an undertone. 'Trouble really starts at the top. The police need a lot of changes. I suppose in typical British Dunkirk style the crisis of these murders will get things going. God help us if it doesn't.'

Edward recollected Langworthy's remarks at the cricket match and asked, 'So you need a new chief?'

Angus said nothing, expressively.

Denton frowned, 'Seems everyone does. I don't think the High Commissioner Sir Edward Gent wants to accept the real extent of the bandit problems either.'

Edward was impressed with Denton's perspicacity.

'At that level, the discussion is too rarefied for me,' said Angus smiling. 'I'll stick to what I know. I've got to go out to interview a planter this afternoon. Chap called Tallard, out at the Black Circle rubber plantation.'

'Is that Sean Tallard? Big man, rather aggressive?' asked Edward.

'Aye. D'you know him?'

'Bowman ran the estate next door to Tallard,' said Edward and told Angus about Bowman's argument with Langworthy at the cricket match.

'Scant consolation to be proved right with half your brains lying over your office floor,' said Angus, his dark face bleak like the moors.

Edward wanted to be in on the action at once, and, the way Marsha Tallard had looked at him on her way out, he felt half-introduced to the Tallards already. 'Can I come with you?' he asked. 'Maybe give us a chance to catch up on news. I might even find a few real facts on the ground to please Colonel Bleasley.'

Denton agreed readily, 'Fine by me. We've finished the report and Bleasley will need a drink after briefing General Boucher before he visits Gent in King's House. He'll be in the bar till Happy Hour. You go off and see what you can pick up. I'm off to the nets, for a bit of practice. The Chief Clerk will deal with anything really important.'

Even with the windows right down, they sweltered in Angus Maclean's green Morris Oxford saloon, weaving slowly among the other traffic, logging trucks and bicycles crowding Jalan Pudu on the way out of town. They picked up speed past Pudu Prison and took the road to Kajang grateful for a warm breeze through the car. They passed kampongs, bananas trees drooping in the heat, and tin mine dredges working by slag-heaps like prehistoric metal dinosaurs.

'You really think we've got a problem here?'

'There's no doubt the Malayan Communist Party is on the offensive.'

'How can you be certain?' asked Edward.

Angus said, 'I was only telling a half-truth when I said I was in the CID. Actually, I'm in the Special Branch. Knowing what goes on among the communists is my business.'

'Why doesn't anyone believe you?'

'The Malay Police is badly set up at present,' Angus complained. 'Special Branch is part of the CID and that's far from ideal. A CID officer's aim in life is to catch and convict criminals, so the information he uses always becomes public at the trial. In Special Branch, we keep our information secret. We want to stop the other side finding out what we know. We want to infiltrate the enemy, and kill, trap or turn them without compromising our sources of information. Our enemy is political as well as being criminal. My boss is a fine CID officer but he doesn't really have a clue about what I'm trying to do. The sooner we get away from the CID the better.'

At Nine Mile Village, Angus turned left towards Langat and swerved to avoid a Chinese on a bicycle.

'How many bandits are there?'

'Five thousand or more in the jungle. A lot were on the run from the Japanese, but all the time they're dragging more from the towns into the jungle and training them.'

Edward whistled. 'That's more than we can put in the field against them!' He had been listing the security forces available in Malaya for Bleasley's briefing and found that although there were over 10,000 police and eleven battalions of soldiers in the country, the actual number of men who could go out on patrol was around 5,000. 'The battalions are up to strength but only four hundred out of the nine hundred men are in the fighting platoons.'

'What are the rest up to?' Angus demanded.

'Guarding things, painting things and driving things about,' Edward smiled.

'Then we're in the shit,' said Angus cheerily. 'A very experienced officer, Colonel John Dalley, estimates there are an additional 250,000 Min Yuen supporters in the squatter villages and towns.'

'Min Yuen?'

Angus said, 'In full it's Min Chung Yuen Thong which literally means the "popular mass movement", of communist sympathisers and activists. Mostly Chinese of course. They supply the MPABA fighters in the jungle with food, resources and most important of all, with intelligence on what we're doing.' A thought struck him. 'It wouldn't surprise me to find out that Willie the barman is a Min Yuen member. He'd certainly pick up some useful titbits in the Coliseum Bar.'

As they passed through the cluster of tatty buildings in Langat, Edward looked more carefully at the coolies wandering in the main street and said, 'That means one in ten Chinese is a communist. Does Sir Edward Gent know this?'

'He does, because Dalley told him,' said Angus. 'And he didn't like it. He has tried to play it down with the Government in London but now he'll have to declare a State of Emergency.'

'Why not declare war?' asked Edward bluntly. 'That's what it's going to be.'

Angus grinned cynically and answered, 'It is, but he can't. The British Government has told him that, if he declares war, then the insurance claims being put in for sabotage damage to mines and rubber estates won't be paid by Lloyds. There's no payout for an act of war, remember, and no payouts will jeopardise any re-building, destroy confidence in the Malayan economy and might even bankrupt the country.'

'Trust a Jock to know all that,' said Edward smiling, but the picture he was giving was intensely depressing.

'There's more,' said Angus matter-of-factly. 'As you've seen police morale is terrible, but we're also strapped for resources. Pay is bad, we need new armoured vehicles, the old ones need re-fitting, they need armouring, we need new carbines, lots of ammunition and training, and above all we need more men. All that means money. And that, my young friend, is the nub of the problem.'

'The politicians in London won't like that either,' said Edward. The *Straits Times* had carried a recent report that meat rationing in England was reduced again, to 6d worth of fresh meat and 6d of tinned meat a week, less than at any time during the Second World War, and another dock strike was threatened which made the use of troops likely. The British Empire was bankrupt.

'Aye, but the choice is simple,' said Angus. 'Finance and resources, or Malaya becomes a communist republic.'

Three miles after Dusun Tua village, they turned right on to a bumpy red laterite road signposted to the Black Circle Rubber Estate. As the road curved sharply over a stream running through a valley covered with lines of rubber trees, they passed a group of Tamils working on the side of the road, their black bodies covered with dust. Rubber trees lined the road on both sides and, beyond the plantations, the thick jungle rose steeply in serried green ranks to a high ridge of mountains in the hazy distance.

At the end of the road, where the jungle closed in on all sides, Angus stopped at the estate offices. A thin Chinese, the foreman, told him, 'Mister Tallard is up at the house'.

They drove up a short hill and pulled up in front of a rambling single-storey bungalow built off the ground on stout timbers. Slats hid the gap under the grey sun-bleached wooden walls and white shutters were tied back from the windows under a long low red corrugated iron roof which had been extended at one end over a garage. On one side a coarse lawn reached down the slope more than a hundred yards to the jungle and on the other, the house overlooked the estate offices, the rubber smoke house and the rubber plantations.

As they climbed out of the Morris, Edward lifted his sweaty shirt where it had stuck to his back on the hot seat.

Sean Tallard appeared at the front door and came down the steps. Without preamble, he stated rudely, 'You're hours late. Should've been here this morning.'

'I agree,' said Angus evenly. 'But we'd have been better off at Mark Bowman's place, had we known. Or did you get attacked too?'

Tallard shook his head, accepting the point. He had been lucky. 'Not this morning. The bastards usually visit me in the evenings.' They shook hands, Angus introduced Edward and Tallard led them inside, through a hall into an airy sitting-room.

There were two armchairs on each side of a fireplace, mute statement of the infrequency of guests to the remote estate, but the room was pleasantly decorated with local artefacts, Chinese paper lanterns, silver ornaments, dark hardwood carvings and richly-coloured printed Malay fabrics. Edward assumed that Marsha, not Sean, was responsible for these and wondered where she was.

Tallard stood legs apart in front of the fireplace and said bluntly, 'We've seen this coming for months.'

'Why d'you think they attacked Bowman, not you?' asked Angus.

Tallard gave him a sharp look and replied, 'I vary my routine, that's why. I go out at different times and I don't even tell my foreman, Hou Ming, where I'm going, or what route I'll take, how long I'll be or when I'll get back. Poor old Mark Bowman refused. Something to do with what you English call "bad show".'

'I'm a Scot,' said Angus.

'Ah well then,' said Tallard unabashed.

The conversation stopped at the sound of soft footfalls. Marsha Tallard came in wearing a light shirt and sarong, Malay-style, which seemed to make the contrast between her slim boyish figure and her husband's bulk all the more obvious. She was barefoot, her hair was tousled as if she had just got out of bed and Edward wondered if she was wearing anything at all under the sarong. Tallard introduced them.

'That's all right,' she said, shaking hands with Edward. 'We met at the Spotted Dog.' Edward could not help noticing the musky scent she was wearing. He guessed she had just put it on, in celebration perhaps of rare visitors.

Tallard grunted, remembering the argument with Langworthy but he said shortly, 'Marsha, would you step down to the kitchen and bring along some beers?'

'I don't know if there's any left,' she said blandly, without moving.

'There are some Tigers,' he insisted, his voice hardening. She looked at him crossly then walked out, her bare feet slipping dustily over the wood floor.

Tallard turned to Angus and said, 'You want to hear what happened to Bowman?'

'Yes, please.'

Tallard told them.

'How d'you find out all this?' Edward put in.

'My foreman, Ho Ming, went over to see his foreman's wife, Rani Sundralingam. She's terrified.'

'Can you trust this foreman of yours?' Edward asked, thinking of the Min Yuen supporters they had been talking about on the drive out.

'Yeah,' replied Tallard briefly. The English Parachute Regiment officer was only a lieutenant and he replied to Angus, 'I've known Hou Ming a long time. Since before the war.'

Angus asked various questions about the tapper workforce, the squatters' village where they lived and Tallard answered. Marsha came in with three beers, one each, and plumped herself down on one of the armchairs. She ignored Tallard who frowned at her to leave, crossed her legs and watched Edward drink his beer. He found her silent gaze and slight smile disconcerting. There were no glasses and he had to drink straight from the bottle. The beer was warm.

Tallard wiped his lips and suddenly said, 'Like to know who's in charge of the bandits in this area?'

'Go on,' said Angus, sipping his beer to hide his excitement. There was very little information about the communists in the area.

'Little short-arsed, pock-faced shit called Ho Peng,' said Tallard. 'He's been in the Communist Party for years. He hid out from the Nips in the jungle during the war, and he fought in Force 136 – the clandestine resistance group set up by British South-East Asia Command in Colombo.'

'How d'you know all this?' asked Angus intrigued.

'I was in Force 136 myself. I fought with him in the jungle.' He knew the police or the army would work it out sooner or later so there was no point in keeping quiet. Besides, he might be able to turn the situation to his advantage.

Edward looked at the Irishman in a new light. Instead of an overweight planter run to seed, drinking too much beer on a remote estate, he saw a man who knew the jungle intimately, who had lived in it for years, fighting the Japanese on their own chosen ground and finally beating them. He was reminded forcibly of his own ignorance of the jungle and a little knot of excitement tightened in his stomach.

Sean Tallard gulped the remainder of his bottle and gestured at where the mountains rose behind his plantation to the high mountains, saying, 'If you need any advice on the jungle in this area, I'd be happy to help out.'

When he saw them out, he pointed at the old green Morris and asked, 'That armoured?'

'No,' replied Angus shortly.

'Then find something that is, if you want to drive out here again in uniform and stay alive.' He glanced at Edward's tropical shirt, shorts and long stockings. 'There are some real fine ambush sites. I should know. I've used a few of them myself.' He roared with laughter again and stamped inside, leaving them to see themselves off.

On the way back Edward noticed they were both trying to peer into the jungle which bordered the road. With a hollow laugh he said, 'One imagines bloody bandits behind every bush.'

'Yes,' said Angus. They did not speak till they had regained the rambling Malay villages alongside the road nearer Kuala Lumpur.

Angus had been thinking about Tallard and said, 'I'll check Sean

Tallard's involvement with Force 136. Could be useful to us.' He negotiated a Malay pushing a handcart slowly along the side of the road and added, 'Planters like Tallard are brave men out there on the edge of the jungle, though he doesn't have to come into town for entertainment with a wife like that, eh?'

Edward grinned, 'Gave you quite a surprise, didn't she?'

'She's a skinny lass, but there's something highly attractive about her, don't you think?'

'I wouldn't know,' said Edward with mock severity. 'I'm a married man now.'

Angus looked at him in astonishment. 'You're not! When did this happen, and why wasn't I told?' Edward smiled, told him about Diana and their new quarter at Uxbridge Drive. He added, 'You're not very good at keeping in touch, so I had no idea where to contact you.'

'I could say the same about you,' Angus Maclean said and fell silent for a while. He was thinking of Palestine, where he had met Diana Haike. He himself had lost the girl he might have married there, killed, like Edward's father, in the King David Hotel bombing. He tried to suppress the memory and asked Edward, 'What happened to that other girl of yours, Carole Romm?'

'She vanished,' said Edward shortly. He had put her out of his mind. The affair was over. She had left him and he did not want to be reminded of how vulnerable he had been for her, especially so soon after marrying Diana.

Angus dropped Edward at the office and, when he walked home across the grass, Edward found a blue Plymouth saloon with white-wall tyres parked at the end of the cul-de-sac. He ran up the verandah steps into the house and called out, 'Diana, have we got guests? Better tell Hassan to sort out Mr Song for some extra dinner.' Lao Song had still not said a word of English, which was irritating, but his cooking was excellent.

'No, darling,' she said, coming through from the sitting-room from the garden verandah.

'Then whose car is that?' he asked, but she simply smiled at him. Incredulous, he asked, 'It's ours?'

She nodded, her blonde hair loose round her shoulders, took him by the arm, and said, 'Let's go for a drive.'

The Plymouth was beautiful, sky blue with a long bonnet flanked by voluptuous curving mudguards, big chromed headlights, the white-wall tyres and sweeping chromed bumpers. They circled it, touching it with the tips of their fingers to feel the smooth wax of the polish, and finally got into it. 'You drive,' said Diana, enjoying the amazement on Edward's face.

'The smell is superb!' he said, rubbing the palms of his hands over the luxurious tan hide.

'I love the smell of new leather,' said Diana breathing in deeply.

'How did you get it so quickly?'

'Oh, I went in to look for something, like we agreed, and there was this wonderful shiny thing sitting in the showroom. The Malay salesman said someone else had ordered it and changed their minds. He said there was nothing he could do about that, as the man was rather important apparently. A Datuk, he said.'

'That's a Malay titled rank, sort of like a Lord,' said Edward.

Diana looked pleased. 'I just fell in love with it,' she said.

'I'm not surprised,' said Edward. He put his hands on the leather steering wheel, grinned widely and said, 'Let's go!'

The engine made a rich and powerful burbling sound, Edward selected first gear on the column change and let out the clutch. They cruised through the quarters and Edward was amazed how smooth it was to drive. He was reminded of his bumpy ride with Angus that afternoon and said, 'Oh, by the way, I saw Angus Maclean today. He's out here too now.'

'Really?' said Diana vaguely. She remembered Angus well from Jerusalem, but there was something else on her mind. 'I know the car cost a bit more than I wanted to pay,' she said, 'but it's a sort of celebration too.'

'For what?' asked Edward as he negotiated a crossroads and listened to the expensive wet smacking noise of the white-wall tyres on the warm tarmac. He felt very important in such a splendid motorcar.

Diana hesitated and Edward glanced at her a couple of times as he accelerated along a straight avenue. She was blushing and he was about to ask her again, when she burst out, 'I'm going to have a baby.'

'What?' Edward cried turning to look at her. He nearly drove into a Tamil gardener, who was going home, slowly shoving his wheelbarrow along the side of the avenue. Edward swung back on to the road, saying all at once, 'Is this true? Wonderful news! When? I mean when is it due?'

'In December, according to Doctor Hazlitt.'

'Will it be a boy?'

'Who knows?' Diana laughed and flung her arms round his neck.

Chapter 6

FERRET FORCE

'D'you have to go off to work quite so early every day?' asked Diana sleepily from the bed. She was watching Edward, through the white gauze of the mosquito net putting on his shirt and trousers.

'Just going to listen to the news first,' he said avoiding the question and switched on his Bakelite radio set for the BBC World Service.

Diana was half covered with the sheet, half naked and alluringly blurred behind the soft white net. She looked at the sunshine streaming through the windows and unselfconsciously stretched her limbs, feeling gloriously warm and lazy.

Edward watched her, so tempted, with his fingers poised over the shirt button he had just done up.

The familiar brisk introductory music broke the spell. 'This is the seven o'clock news from the BBC World Service,' said the news reader in clipped tones. 'Yesterday afternoon, Sir Edward Gent, the High Commissioner for Malaya, was killed in an air crash over London. The Royal Air Force Transport Command York aircraft in which he was travelling collided with a Scandinavian Air Line Cloudmaster as both planes circled in bad weather waiting to land at RAF Northolt. All passengers and crew in both planes died.'

Edward stared at the radio and Diana sat up abruptly, clutching the sheet over her breasts. She whispered, 'How awful! Did you know about this?'

'Only that he was going back to England,' said Edward, shushing her. He concentrated on the announcer's voice rising and falling in classic BBC cadence, speaking, to Edward's mind, as if the whole world outside the acoustic isolation of the broadcasting studios in

73

the Aldwych was filled with semi-literate children, but his message left no room for doubt. 'Sir Edward was on his way back from Kuala Lumpur to London to discuss the serious breakdown in law and order in Malaya with the Prime Minister, Mr Attlee, and the Colonial Secretary, Mr Arthur Creech Jones. His loss will now present the Government with the serious problem of replacing him at a time when leadership in Malaya is most required, only two weeks after Sir Edward had been obliged to declare a State of Emergency.'

Edward switched off and turned to Diana. He said, 'This will cause real trouble.'

'How d'you mean?'

'No-one at the helm,' said Edward. Since the first planters were murdered two weeks before, there had been a non-stop series of attacks. The previous day, another bus had been burned out near Ayer Kuning, more rubber trees slashed on numerous estates, and a timber contractor's foreman had been found dead by a logging track in the high jungle beyond Ampang, not far from Sean Tallard's place. He had been tied to a tree, hacked to bits with parangs and left hanging with Communist pamphlets scattered round his bloody corpse. Edward felt sure Ho Peng was responsible. He said, 'As things are, we could contain the insurrection but not without leadership. The communist terrorists, as Angus calls them, are keeping up the pressure and won't give us the chance.'

'General Boucher seemed confident enough,' said Diana dubiously. 'Don't you remember at the cocktail party last week? He said he'd round them all up in a matter of weeks.'

Edward said, 'I hope General Boucher is right, but that's not what I'm hearing from Angus.' Without telling Colonel Bleasley, Edward was keeping in close touch with Angus. He walked towards the door shaking his head.

She said, 'Bye, darling,' flipping her hand weakly at him. She suddenly felt drained. She enjoyed being able to discuss what was going on with Edward but the delicious warmth of the morning was soured and now she felt slightly sick. Or, she thought putting her hand on her stomach, maybe it was her pregnancy.

'Bye,' said Edward, and then as he was about to pull the door shut behind him, he added casually, 'Oh, I meant to tell you, I've finally persuaded Bleasley to let me do some jungle training. I have volunteered for a thing called Ferret Force.'

Diana laughed and asked, 'How d'you get Bleasley to agree to that?'

'Easy. General Boucher supports the idea, to winkle out lots of communist camps in the jungle, and as soon as Bleasley realised that, he took very little persuading. I talked about intelligence gathering on the ground and he thinks it'll reflect well on the office and prove the army can beat the bandits without the police.' He checked his watch and exclaimed, 'I must go!' Quickly he blew her a kiss and disappeared.

Diana listened as his footsteps crossed the hall and the front door slammed. She thought for a moment about Edward joining Ferret Force and frowned. Bleasley was as ambitious for himself as she was for Edward, but Edward's description of the Ferret Force seemed glib, rehearsed even, as if he were deliberately concealing something from her. She wondered if it was really such a good idea. The army, she had heard her father, Colonel Septimus Haike, often say, was never keen on special units cobbled together in an emergency.

She shrugged off the sheet, slipped out of bed and took a leisurely bath. Hassan served her breakfast on the verandah in the sun, but the nagging shadow of the morning's news would not fade from her mind.

The Ferret Force volunteers started training at once, galvanised by the growing list of murders and attacks. They were divided into groups of twenty-five and, early one morning after muster parade, Edward found himself sitting in a truck on the way out of town. Soon they turned off the tarmac road on to red laterite which cut through thick jungle beyond Ampang, near the spot where the timber foreman had been murdered. After half an hour's jolting ride the truck pulled off the track into a small clearing and stopped. Edward and the others jumped out with their backpacks and the truck left them, rattling and bouncing on the pot-holed road out of sight behind the trees.

Edward watched it disappear with misgivings. He looked up at the blue sky and the tall green banks of tropical forest high above them on all sides, hanging over the road and the small clearing. As the last faint noise of the truck's engine faded an eerie silence settled on the place, hot and oppressive.

'Bloody queer,' said one of the soldiers. 'Where's this bloke that's supposed to meet us?' His voice sounded loud and flat in the silence and no-one replied.

Edward gripped his carbine and wondered what was going to happen next. They had been issued with jungle green shirts and trousers, green canvas boots with rubber soles, and everyone was armed with American-carbines. Round their waists they wore a belt with two ammunition pouches, two water bottles and a bayonet. Their army small-packs were heavy with a week's rations, but no-one had explained what they were going to do. It was hot in the clearing, with no shade, and he was grateful for his green floppy hat. Just standing in the sun made them sweat.

At a noise from the trees Edward whipped round. Two people emerged from the shadows of the jungle, one a short, stocky native, brown-skinned and almost completely naked, and the other a large European dressed like them in jungle greens.

'Tallard!' exclaimed Edward in surprise.

Tallard nodded in greeting and said, 'Lieutenant Fairfax, isn't it? To be sure, I never expected a man in a cushy job in Headquarters to volunteer.' Privately he wondered if there was another reason for Edward being there.

'You were wrong,' Edward replied, nettled by Tallard's tone and conscious that the other men in the group were watching with amusement. Edward was the only officer among a variety of other ranks in the group which included some civilians who had lived in Malaya for a year or more. In desperation, the army had accepted anyone with jungle experience or enthusiasm.

'We'll see,' said Tallard bluntly. 'Success in the jungle has nothing to do with rank.' He turned away from Edward and introduced the man with him to the whole group.

'This is Untam,' he said. 'He's a tracker from Sarawak.'

Untam grinned under a thatch of straight black hair, showing a bulging set of stubby teeth stained with chewing betel, and, close to, Edward saw his brown face and arms were covered in dark blue tattoos. He wore nothing but a loose cloth round his hips, a long parang hung on a rope round his chest beside a small bag and he carried a carbine. Edward guessed he was about thirty years old, but he was completely hairless and his skin agelessly smooth.

'Untam's job is to find the communists,' explained Tallard with crystal-clear economy. 'Your job is to follow Untam. My job is to teach you how to follow Untam. The trick is doing it all silently, so the communists don't know it till we hit them. Understood?'

Edward thought it all sounded too easy but Tallard gave him no time for second thoughts. He hitched up his green cotton trousers under his stomach, adjusted his belt of equipment, looked disdainfully around the motley group of people he had been given to train and said, 'So, gentlemen, we'll start as we intend to go on. String yourselves out in a single line and don't get left behind.'

Without another word, he gestured at Untam who padded barefoot through the buffalo grass on the edge of the clearing into the shadows under the trees. Tallard followed and Edward stepped forward first in line behind them into the green gloom under the canopy high above. He wanted to be next to Tallard, to learn as much as possible. Also, even on open ground the men at the back of a long line had to run to keep up, however slowly the leaders walked.

Within minutes he was soaked with sweat, the straps of his small-pack bit into his shoulders, he was plagued by mosquitoes and vegetation grabbed and tugged at his clothes as he blundered after Tallard through bamboos, vines and thorny palms. One long swaying tendril hooked him fast.

Tallard turned to unhook him, saying, 'That's a palm called Jenkensius Jenkensianus, or more colloquially "wait-a-while".' He let go the long tendril which sprang away like a fishing-line, and grinned at the expression of frustrated disgust on Edward's face. 'Don't struggle in the jungle,' he said. 'Learn to be in harmony with the forest, with the plants and creatures. It's a bit like swimming. You can't fight it, or you'll drown of exhaustion. You must slide through it, like a fish.'

They set off again, not fast, but relentlessly steady, and Edward found everything combined to sap his strength: the heat, the smell of rotting leaves, the sombre light under the canopy of leaves high above them and the clinging undergrowth which meant he could only just see Untam in the lead a few yards beyond Tallard, slipping confusingly in and out of sight through the green shadows. Even the weight of his pack, which he would hardly have noticed in England, racked his shoulders and back. His green canvas jungle boots were laced too tight and the rubber soles slipped on the decaying leaf-mould on the jungle floor.

They walked for an hour without stopping, Untam sliding effortlessly ahead and Tallard following him with infuriating ease in spite of his bulk. Edward slithered up and down steep slopes and waded several streams until finally they climbed a slight rise and Tallard stopped. He passed the word back down the line for everyone to gather round him and one by one they emerged noisily along the track, cursing, breaking branches and slumped to the ground exhausted. Several men lit cigarettes. Everyone took water bottles from their soaked canvas pouches and gulped down the warm water.

'This is the "ulu". The jungle. Home.' Tallard gestured at the leaves hanging claustrophobically all around them. 'We stay here till I'm happy you can live and work and fight in the jungle.'

There was a chorus of exclamation. Edward looked round and his own surprise was reflected in the tired, sweaty faces of the others.

'You've got a lot to learn,' said Tallard practically. 'The Chinese have been in the ulu all year, for years some of them. They're led by men who resisted the Japanese in the war. You've got to catch up. Untam and I will teach you all we can. It'll be hard work, but remember, the art of the jungle is to enjoy it.' To the sound of incredulous snorts, he insisted in his tough Belfast accent, 'You'll love it! There's everything you need in the jungle. It's warm, there's refreshing rain, trees and palms for shelter and food, streams for water and fish, bugs and plants for medicines, and animals you can trap, like pig and deer.' He drew breath and said with surprising intensity, 'And there's beauty. There are eight hundred species of butterflies and two hundred of dragonflies. There are parrots, flying foxes, wild orchids, flowering bromeliads, ferns, ivies, and red-arsed monkeys for them as like that sort of thing.'

There was a tired laugh but Tallard's description raised as many worries as it laid to rest. Edward asked, 'What about the snakes?'

Tallard gave him a sharp look. He disliked negative thinking, and said, 'There are creepy crawlies, certainly, like snakes, scorpions, spiders, centipedes and millipedes, and a host of other wee bugs, but they all hate you as much as you hate them. They'll leave you alone as long as you don't muck them about, by treading on them, for example.' Another nervous laugh.

'And leeches?' asked Edward. He had heard people talking about them in the Mess.

Tallard said, 'Surely, leeches love officers, Mr Fairfax. They're no respecters of rank. You'll see the little bastards waving about on the ground and you won't know they've hopped on as you brush past.' An idea occurred to him. 'Just check your legs now.' There was a sudden panic of activity as everyone peered at their sopping trousers. Edward scraped his hands over his damp buttocks and thighs and ran his fingers down to the tops of his boot leggings. He felt a soft cord-like object under his trousers and his heart missed a beat. He leaped to his feet, yanked his trousers out of his leggings and stared horrified. Just where the leggings ended a grey leech hung from the pale flesh of his leg, three inches long, its mouth parts embedded in his skin, the other end waving slightly in the air.

Disgusted, Edward was about to sweep it off in fright, but Tallard stopped him. Laughing, he gathered the others round.

'Don't just stand there!' said Edward fascinated at the small primeval thing sucking his blood. 'Get the frigging thing off!'

'Yeah, yeah!' said Tallard still grinning. 'But if you knock it off, you leave the sucker in your skin, where it'll fester and rot.' He took someone's cigarette, held it close to the leech and it dropped off. Edward stamped on it.

'Cigarettes, mosquito repellent or a pinch of salt all do the trick.'

Chastened by this first bodily contact with jungle life, everyone sat down and Tallard finished his initial briefing, 'To beat the commies, you've got to be better than them in the jungle. This three-day jungle course the British Army is running now is a lot of bollocks. You can't learn about anything in a few days! You need much longer. You've got to learn to absorb the ulu. You've got to live and breathe the atmosphere, use your eyes, your nose, your ears. You've got to see and observe, listen and smell.' He put his fingers to his temples, like a bulky Mephisto about to perform a miracle of concentration and his voice deepened with emphasis, 'You've really got to feel what's happening all round you'.

After a moment to let his words sink in, he hissed in a low dramatic voice, 'We'll start with the senses. You don't talk in the jungle. You whisper. Because sounds carry for hundreds of yards, especially along streams.'

It struck Edward that Tallard had been whispering all the time while the rest of them had been making a terrible noise fussing over the leech.

'And you all smell lovely,' he whispered grinning widely. 'Of Pears or Lux, and that carries too. Don't go thinking that just because you can't see through the jungle, no-one knows you're there. The way you lot are now, talking and smelling like a barbers' shop, you stand out like a turd on a billiard table and your communist will find you a hundred yards away. Then he kills you. So, in this training, we'll have periods of what I call hard routine, when we don't cook, we don't smoke or make any noise. In the mean time we've a lot to learn first.'

Edward thought he had worked hard training with the Parachute Regiment in England and in the open desert of Palestine, but Tallard worked them harder. He knew they had to catch up the communist bandits and he pushed them. Soon Edward was bending and turning around the thicker undergrowth and avoiding the spiky palms rather than trying to shove his way through, his feet sure on the steepest ground. He learned how to make a place to sleep, a basha, with poles to support his poncho waterproof, or just lie on a patch of dryer jungle floor after clearing the leafy layer so the insects would not bother him during the night. Most nights he slept undisturbed but occasionally he awoke with a swollen eye from a mosquito bite, and once he was revolted to find a leech hanging from his lip. It took all his self-control not to knock it off at once and wait till he could drop salt on it from a little packet in his rations.

They learned how to patrol, moving silently through the jungle on a compass bearing, counting their paces and checking the time to keep track of their location. They split into groups and one tracked the other, as if they were trying to find the communists, with Untam reading every sign of their track, every broken twig, turned leaf or soft indent on the ground. They learned to observe through the drooping leaves, palms and ferns for 'enemy', and practised ambushes and counter-ambushes, one group against another, till they were shattered.

Several times they walked back to the road, finding the route more familiar each time, to fetch heavy loads of more food and boxes of ammunition.

To Edward's surprise the days passed quickly. After a quick breakfast of a tin of beans, a few biscuits and a big mug of tea, they worked hard all day with nothing except more biscuits and tea for lunch. He particularly enjoyed the shooting practices which Tallard set up along the bottom of streams or in a safe leafy re-entrant between two fingers of high ground, firing at impromptu targets made of pieces of wood and the hessian sandbags in which they had brought their rations. By the time they stopped for supper at five o'clock, he was ravenous for a mess-tin of hot stew, biscuits, soup and anything else left in his day's ration which he could throw in. Tallard still teased him about being the only officer in the group, but he began to respect Edward's dedication and they often ate together. He gave him some curry powder for his evening tin-full of stew.

'Always bring curry powder. The goddam rations taste like cardboard otherwise,' he said. 'Whoever designed these never had to eat them himself.'

Edward found he was always wet, soaking with sweat when the

sun shone above the canopy, or drenched when it rained. He was often hungry and tired, especially when they lay awake in ambush positions all night, but he felt himself shrinking, hardening and beginning to become at one with the jungle around him.

After three weeks, they came out of the jungle for a break. A truck was there to meet them at the clearing and they drove back to the Headquarters. There was much laughter and talk on the way back, in contrast to the quiet oppressive self-conscious ride out. Their knowledge was still raw compared to Tallard and Untam, but they were no longer afraid of the jungle.

Edward went straight back to the house, feeling like a real warrior, fit and hard from the wars, to see his wife.

'Darling! I'm back,' he shouted, and dumped his pack and belt webbing on the verandah, still sodden and covered in ferns and bits of the forest. 'How are you? And how's the baby?'

Diana ran into the hall to greet him, thrilled to have him back, and stopped abruptly as if hit. 'My God! You stink!' She wrinkled up her nose and stepped back in horror. 'Don't you dare come near me, Edward Fairfax, till you've had a real clean-up!'

The following morning, as they ate breakfast on the verandah, Edward said, 'Sean Tallard has asked us to lunch. Like to go?'

'Didn't he cause that row with Langworthy at the cricket match?' Diana asked. She pictured a large rude man.

Edward shook his head. 'Not really. That was poor Mark Bowman, and Sean Tallard took him home.' He realised what was at the back of Diana's question and added, 'Anyway, Tallard is in favour now because he's volunteered for Ferret Force.'

'Then let's take the car for a drive,' said Diana cheerfully. Time had passed slowly on her own during the three weeks Edward had been away, made worse by morning sickness, and the idea of a day out appealed.

Edward drove the glistening Plymouth, which Hassan had taken upon himself to polish daily, and relished again the smooth column gear change, the powerful engine and the delicious smell of the comfortable leather seats. A downpour had cleared the heavy thunderous warmth of the mid-morning and the sun shone. Steam rose from puddles by the side of the road and the lallang grass sparkled clean and green.

Tallard's warning remarks about being ambushed on the remote road to the Black Circle estate jarred his well-being, but he pressed on. They were in civilian clothes and there was nothing remotely

81

military about the blue Plymouth. He accelerated down the long straight towards the hills covered with rubber trees ahead.

In the jungle at the edge of the rubber, Ho Peng could hear the throb of the big engine passing far away and he wondered if another policeman was going to see Tallard. Or, perhaps it was an army vehicle, now that bastard Tallard was working for the British again. He spat on the ground and peered out through the leaves into the lines of silver rubber trees for any sign of tappers who might compromise their exit place from the jungle.

No tappers about. Ho Peng stepped out of the shadows into the sunlight on the edge of the rubber plantation and watched his men follow.

Lao Tang stumbled as he stepped over a branch and Ho Peng hissed at him, 'Be careful!' He was strict about disturbing foliage which might leave signs which could be followed up later. The Japanese had used trackers to find them during the war, and his informants had told him the British were employing head-hunters from Sarawak. He wondered if they had put one to work with Tallard. He spat again, angrily. He wished he could kill Tallard.

The blue Plymouth cruised round a sharp corner and passed the sign announcing the Black Circle Rubber Estate. Ten minutes later they stopped in front of Tallard's house.

Marsha met them on the steps, sleek as a bird in a native sarong and brocade slippers. She greeted them warmly, and kissed Edward on both cheeks as if they had known each other a long time. He supposed that if one lived in such a remote spot, then anyone who took the trouble to visit twice in a month should be considered special. On the way up the steps, Diana frowned at him behind Marsha's back and Edward shrugged.

In the sitting-room, Marsha drawled, 'Sean will be back soon,' her eyes on Edward. 'He's in the office with Hou Ming, the foreman, catching up on paperwork after being away in the jungle. The boys have all the fun don't they, Diana?'

'I'm sure I shouldn't like the jungle,' said Diana firmly, looking around the room. She appeared not to see the way Marsha looked at Edward and picked up a black ebony elephant, stroking its polished flanks. 'Where did you find so many beautiful things?'

'Nothing much else to do here, honey, except collect,' said Marsha pulling a face, but she loved her collection. Soon she was deep in conversation with Diana, telling her where to buy various local products, and revealed a deep interest in each carving or design which entirely displaced the habitual sensuality of her gestures and manner.

Sean Tallard came stamping up the steps into the house, took one look at Diana and Marsha and said, 'You're watching money being spent there, Edward, as quick as if you poured it down the drain.' His broad face cleared in a sudden grin. 'Why don't we leave them to it and I'll show you round the place a bit before lunch. We'll go in the "Monster".'

He smiled at the puzzled look on Edward's face and took him to a shed at the side of the house. Inside was a truck which had been stripped down and re-built using a hotch-potch of steel plates welded together to form a homemade tank, complete with hinged armoured windows with narrow slits to protect the driver and passenger.

'That's real armour plate,' said Tallard patting the metal with obvious self-satisfaction.

'Impressive,' admitted Edward. 'Where did you find the steel?'

'Courtesy of the Japs,' said Tallard. 'From tanks and armoured cars they abandoned in the jungle, when they tried to winkle us out. They're overgrown now, but I know where they are.'

Edward wondered if there was anything Tallard did not know about the area.

The big man slapped the steel as he went round to the driver's side, saying, 'I armoured the engine compartment and I've even built in anti-mine plates under the cab. I remember seeing a British Army truck blown to shit on a mine back in Ireland, so I welded in some plates at an angle to deflect the blast under the cab and I filled the wheels with water, to absorb the energy of the explosion.'

Edward too had witnessed the effects of a mine on a truck, in Palestine, so he asked instead, 'You see much trouble in Ireland?'

Tallard did not answer for a moment. They climbed into the cab, slammed the heavy steel doors and he said finally, 'No.' He regretted mentioning his home at all. This was no time to bring up talk about the British in Ireland. He needed their support too much and did not want to upset his position in Ferret Force. He started up the engine, drove out of the garage and down the hill.

'You been here long?' asked Edward.

Tallard shouted back over the engine noise, 'Five years before the Nips.'

'What happened when they arrived?'

Tallard gestured at the lawn and said simply, 'I went down the garden and into the jungle.' His eyes glazed over at the memory. 'And learned the hard way.'

Recalling his first impressions of the jungle, Edward was fascinated. 'What happened to the estate?' he asked. It was hard to grasp how devastating it must have been to have suddenly found that the enemy controlled the entire country, leaving no alternative but prison. Or the jungle.

'My foreman, Hou Ming, looked after everything, including me. He got food to me, and clothes, smuggling it all past the Nip soldiers on guard duty. He's a miserable thin bastard in many ways, but he risked his neck and saved my bacon.'

'Sounds as if he's had good practice to join the Min Yuen,' said Edward and Tallard gave him a sideways look but made no reply.

They rumbled through the rubber plantations while Tallard explained how the tappers made a thin cut in the bark each morning with specially hooked knives, to let the sticky white latex ooze out into cups tied to the trunk. 'They go out at six o'clock each morning, about an hour before dawn, to empty the little cups tied to the trunks. That's when these bloody commies like Ho Peng get at them. There's very little I can do to protect them when they're way out on the edge of the plantations, miles from the centre of the estate.'

'Where do they live?' asked Edward.

'In a kampong, or village, not far from the estate offices,' said Tallard.

'Can we have a look?'

Tallard reluctantly turned the heavy armoured truck on the bumpy laterite track towards the house again. 'Just time on the way back to lunch.'

They drove past a thin belt of jungle along a watery padi field of rice and stopped the armoured truck in the middle of the tappers' kampong. Edward saw at once why Tallard had been unwilling. The village was a squalid mess, an open collection of ramshackle huts made of wood, pieces of corrugated iron, canvas and palm-leaf roofs. Naked black-haired Chinese children were running about, chickens and a pig rootled among a clump of bamboo near the padi fields.

'They're like this, all over Malaya,' said Tallard defensively. 'They're squatters. They don't own the land and they don't care.'

An elderly man with mottled brown skin, wearing a dirty white vest and baggy black trousers observed the two white men climb down from the armoured car.

To Edward's surprise, Tallard greeted him in Chinese, 'The tappers not back yet, Ah Chi?'

Ah Chi shook his head 'No, Tuan. Not yet.' There was nothing lost in being polite, maybe much gained.

An old woman in a simple brown 'samfu' peasant tunic and trousers appeared at the dark doorway of the attap hut nearby. She watched Tallard talking to her husband. Her family had come to Malaya just before the Japanese, to get away from the fighting in China, and ended up at the Black Circle rubber estates. She hated the smell of latex, but her sons and daughters-in-law worked hard as tappers and they owed the white man nothing.

Tallard motioned Edward back into the armoured car, saying, 'Ah Chi and his wife, Ah Po, are part of quite a big family here. I wouldn't be at all surprised to find the whole lot are in the Min Yuen!'

'Don't you ever worry about that? I mean, how can you live here knowing perfectly well that bastard Ho Peng is out there somewhere in the jungle?' said Edward. 'The same man who murdered Bowman?'

'I know him, and his cronies, well enough,' said Tallard coolly.

'They might be watching us now,' said Edward. He could see some jungle beyond a line of rubber trees. 'Just waiting for the right moment.' His voice trailed off, unwilling to say what he thought, even though Tallard seemed terribly unconcerned.

'To kill me, you mean?' said Tallard bluntly but without malice.

He slowed down to pass a young Chinese woman in a rough samfu walking along the track weighed down by a large raffia basket on her back. The weight was taken on a wide cloth strap round her forehead and she did not alter her steady pace as the 'Monster' approached. She peered up under the brow of the strap and her dark eyes met Edward's looking down at her in a bold stare.

'Who's that?' he asked Tallard.

'Liya, I think,' said Tallard off-hand, keeping a careful eye on the ditch as he pulled over to give her room. 'She's just one of the squatters. I think they use her to fetch things they need from town. She's always on the road.'

Edward nodded vaguely but the girl's slim face and black eyes stayed with him. There was more than dull peasant servitude in the expression he had glimpsed. He guessed there were thousands of educated Chinese who had had to flee from the ravages of the war in China and some of them must have ended up as tappers, a vital industry but the lowest form of life in Malaya.

Lunch, a delicious curry, was a success. Diana and Marsha were getting on well, having found common interest in Malaya's arts and handicrafts, so Tallard took Edward to the verandah at the back of the house where they sat down to relax with a couple of beers. Beyond the lawn, green undulating hills rose to the high mountains on the State border.

Edward asked, 'How d'you learn Chinese?'

'Real painful,' grunted Tallard. 'You thinking of it?'

'Maybe,' said Edward. Angus, with whom he had learned Arabic in Palestine, had suggested it but the prospect was daunting.

'It's a long hard road,' said Tallard. 'Hou Ming got me some books and sent them into the jungle and I used the Chinese I was living with to practise on.'

'Including Ho Peng?'

'Aye,' said Tallard non-committally. 'Nothing much else to do while we hid from the Japs.' He waved his bottle at the high mountains on the horizon. 'All up there. Over the Bukit Nuang ridge line. I got quite good.'

Edward wanted to talk about Ho Peng. 'Does Ho Peng speak any English?'

Suspiciously, Tallard wondered again whether the young Parachute Regiment officer had volunteered for the Ferret Force or been ordered, but a shattering rattle of gunfire stopped the conversation. Bullets smashed into the grey shiplap walls of the house, splintering the wood.

Edward flung himself to the verandah decking with Tallard who growled, 'Bastards! They're early!'

'Early?' shouted Edward in amazement. 'You mean you knew they were going to attack you?'

'Two or three times a week,' Tallard shouted back. A burst hit the palm-leafed roof above them, rattling the attap like rain.

Flat on the verandah floor, Edward lost his temper and shouted, 'You frigging idiot! Why in God's name didn't you say so?'

Sean Tallard shrugged carelessly, 'There didn't seem any point. The Chinese have got terrible sight. They never hit anything anyway.'

Edward took a deep breath, overwhelmed by the Irishness of the explanation. There seemed no point arguing. He just said, 'You

86

know Diana's three months pregnant?' and had the scant satisfaction of seeing surprise on Tallard's face.

Then it struck him there was no point grovelling about on the floor. All that mattered now was fighting back. He got to his feet and ducked inside the house. Tallard rolled sideways and joined him, breathing hard.

There was a cabinet by the back door. Tallard yanked it open, pulled out two M-1 carbines and dumped a handful of loaded magazines in Edward's arms. In moments they were returning a decent weight of fire accurately into positions Tallard said they often used at the jungle's edge and soon the enemy fire died away.

'Now the front,' said Tallard and ran up the corridor. Edward started after him, still furious.

In the sitting-room, bullets were tearing through the mosquito netting over the open windows and ripping into the walls and ceiling. Squatting down out of danger, Edward saw for the first time other marks, where the holes of previous attacks had been patched and painted.

Tallard noticed his look and grunted, 'Frigging house has never been so well kept. I won't let the bastards get us down, so the repair man is up here every week. I built this place and it's my home. The bastard is only doing it 'cos he knows I'll hate it!'

'Where's Diana?' Edward demanded looking at Marsha. In the madness of the attack, he was hardly surprised to see Marsha lying on the floor behind a Bren gun. The barrel poked through a hole in the wall, near the floor and she was peering intently at a target in bushes behind a bank on the other side of the yard in front of the house. She squeezed the trigger and Edward was fascinated to see her slim boyish body tremble with the stuttering recoil, her short fair hair brushing her brown shoulders.

'Sandbags and more steel plates in the walls,' explained Tallard tersely, gesturing round the room. A thick waist-high protective wall disguised by panels, shelves of Marsha's ornaments and rattan screens ran all round the room.

Plainly Tallard had been preparing for months, but Edward shouted again to Marsha, 'Where's Diana?'

A burst of firing drowned her answer and Edward ducked involuntarily. Bullets slammed steadily into the side of the house and Marsha returned two short economical bursts at the grassy bank down the hill. Her slim hands gripped the wood stock as she held it professionally on target. Then she wriggled away from the Bren and said, 'Sean, take over from me. Diana's in the bathroom and she needs help.' Her blue eyes were serious, all the teasing gone.

Edward felt sick. He glared at Tallard as he settled his bulk behind the Bren. Why the hell had he not said something about being attacked? He asked Marsha, 'Is she bad?'

'I can still remember a bit of nursing first aid and I've fixed her up as best I could,' said Marsha. She scrambled to her feet and ran out, bent over to keep beneath the protecting wall. Edward followed her along the corridor to the back of the house. They passed two bedrooms, one obviously Sean Tallard's, with trousers and heavy shoes lying about on the floor, and one as obviously hers, pink and white and feminine. Beyond, in a bathroom, Edward could hear sobbing. He hesitated, afraid of what he would find, but Marsha seemed to guess. Her long fingers gently closed over his wrist and led him forward, still crouching, saying, 'She's all right, really Edward, but it's hit her bad. The shock's always the worst.'

Feeling empty, Edward let her pull him inside the bathroom. Diana was sitting on the floor in the corner opposite the lavatory, furthest from the outside wall, her legs sticking straight out, staring at the floor. She was clutching a blood-stained towel in her lap and another bloody towel lay on the floor near the bath. Edward had seen wounded people before but seeing his wife like that was like being stabbed repeatedly in the guts.

'What's happened?' he whispered.

'You okay, honey?' Marsha asked kneeling beside her.

Diana looked up, her face streaked with sweat. When she saw Edward, she burst into tears and buried her face in the towel. He ducked across the floor and wrapped his arms round her. She was damp with perspiration, her hair matted and she was shaking. She let him pull her on to his chest. He stroked her damp hair, questioning Marsha with his eyes again.

'She was going to have a baby, wasn't she?' said Marsha, deliberate with the past tense.

'She's losing it?' said Edward stupidly.

Marsha glanced at the reddened towel by the bath and Edward saw there were others half-hidden beneath Diana's skirts.

'As I said, it was the shock,' Marsha repeated. 'The first burst of firing nearly hit Diana in the face when we were standing together in the kitchen. She's lucky not to be dead.' She felt sorry for them, but at least Diana was alive and could try again. She bent to check the towels under Diana's legs.

Another burst of firing thumped into the house and they could hear the sharper sound of Tallard's Bren echoing through the passages. When the shooting lulled for a moment, Diana forced herself to look up, and cried out in little staccato bursts, 'It's gone, darling, Edward, I'm sorry, I can't help it.' She buried her face in his shirt and kept repeating over and over, 'I'm sorry. I'm sorry. I'm so sorry.' And each time Edward felt the stabbing again.

He could not believe it. Everything had been going so well for them both. This was the last thing he expected and he felt utterly helpless. Marsha searched his face, waiting for him to speak. When she realised he had no idea what to say, she told him in a low urgent voice, 'We need help, Edward! She's losing a lot of blood. She needs plasma. You stay here and I'll go see Sean.'

Half bending, she was gone. Edward listened to her soft footsteps until the sound was drowned by Diana's sobbing and the firing at the front of the house. He stared round the bathroom. The normality mocked him, Marsha's bottles of scent and powder standing innocently on the shelves and basin, her fluffy slippers neatly side by side under the enormous cast-iron bath and her bath robe hanging behind the door. Gunshot wounds, riots and murder he understood, but this was different. He felt a terrible personal resentment boiling up inside him.

There was another savage tirade of shooting which went on for several minutes. Diana flinched and tried to press herself into his body. She felt terribly tired, and supposed distantly it was the loss of blood though it did not seem to hurt. Worse than that, she hated herself for being unable to control her feelings, for letting Edward down, for being unable to hold her place as a woman and fight back as his wife, like Marsha. She felt betrayed by her body when she had been so certain about herself and wanted so much to give him the son he wanted.

The firing stopped and, during the next long minutes of silence, Edward worried that their attackers were creeping round the back of the house and might surprise the two of them lying unarmed in the bathroom. His carbine was by the door, on the floor where he had put it down, but he dared not leave Diana to get it. He jumped when Tallard suddenly appeared at the door.

'I think they've gone,' he announced. His eyes flicked over the dark, sodden towels scattered round the tiled floor. 'Marsha tells me she's losing a lot of blood?'

Edward nodded. Diana was desperately pale.

'I've got no estate medical centre, no plasma here, so we have to get her to hospital,' said Tallard, his face set and hard.

'How?'

'In the Monster.'

'What about the house?'

'Fuck the house,' said Tallard. 'That bastard Ho Peng wants me, not Marsha, not Diana, not you, nor the bloody house.'

Edward did not notice the bitter irony in Tallard's voice till much later. Tallard said urgently, 'You carry Diana to the shed. There's a door from the house. Marsha will join us when we're inside the Monster. We can't leave her here on her own and we need her to look after Diana. I'll drive and you'll ride shotgun on the way out. They won't like us leaving their shooting party.'

The withdrawal through the house to the Monster took seconds, as Tallard had directed. Edward slammed the passenger door and looked at the two women on the seats behind, arms tangled, towels, sweat-soaked hair and clothes, intimate in their feminine complicity and understanding. He gripped the cold hard carbine angrily, feeling utterly useless, as pointless as the carbine until required for an occasional brief ecstasy of destruction. The engine roared in the confined space of the shed. Tallard waited a few moments to make sure it was running smoothly, then eased forward, pushing open the shed doors he had unbolted before getting in, and they were in the open gathering speed.

An ear-splitting burst of firing exploded on the armoured steel plates. Both women cried out in terror, Tallard shouted, 'Jesus! Holy Mother of God!' and Edward lost his temper. He stuck the carbine through the slit in front of him and squeezed off a whole magazine into the bushes at the side of the track where he thought he had seen movement. When it was empty, he rammed in a new clip and used that too, swinging the carbine to rake the bushes as Tallard accelerated the heavy truck down the hill. Then they were through the ambush. Edward's clip emptied again and the beating noise of bullets on the armour stopped. The silence, except for the engine noise, was surprising.

'It worked, then,' announced Tallard jovially. 'The armour, I mean.'

'We didn't come out here to be your bloody guinea-pigs,' said Edward furiously. He released the front armoured windows and shoved them forward on to the bonnet. Warm air rushed in.

Tallard looked surprised, 'How was I supposed to know they would attack now?'

'You worked with that bastard Ho Peng in the war,' Edward reminded him. 'Must've learned something about him.' He made up his mind to ask Angus Maclean just what he had found out about Tallard and Ho Peng in Force 136 in the war.

'Maybe, but I'm not a frigging clairvoyant!' shouted Tallard, sweating as he pulled the heavy truck round the corners, his powerful arms stuck out either side of the steering wheel. 'You can't blame me for this. How was I supposed to know Diana was pregnant?'

'Stop arguing!' shouted Marsha from the back. 'For Christ's sake, what matters now is getting Diana to the hospital!'

Edward glared furiously at Sean Tallard, hating him, and wanting someone to blame. At the same time he hated himself for ignoring Tallard's warning the first time he came out to the 'Black Circle'. They should never have come. He fell silent, staring out through the window and the winding road ahead, with blame and guilt churning round inside his head making him feel physically sick.

The journey back to town was a nightmare. He was helpless. Oblivious of the road, the rubber plantations and the kampongs they passed, he bounced about on his seat in the front with nothing to contribute. Tallard said nothing, busy driving, and Marsha helped Diana lying across the seats behind them.

'Doesn't this thing go any faster?' Edward shouted over the noise of the engine.

'I'm going as fast as I can,' Sean Tallard snapped back. The engine was at its limit for the weight of the armour. The afternoon sun beat down on the steel cab and they sweated for another hour before reaching the outskirts of Kuala Lumpur.

At the 'T' junction in Nine Mile Village they ran into an army road block. Soldiers at a chicane of barbed wire pulled over the road were methodically checking everyone in a line of cars, taxis, bicycles and logging trucks.

Tallard braked to a halt and swore. 'This'll take ages!'

'We haven't got ages,' said Marsha quietly at the back.

Edward's self-pity and anger swelled at the injustice of the situation. He snapped, 'Drive on, for Christ's sake!'

'You must keep going,' Marsha insisted. Diana had not said a word throughout the journey, determined not to make a fuss, and her skin had become waxy white. 'She's lost too much blood, Sean. We can't wait.'

Edward twisted round, saw Diana's face drained of colour behind him and shouted at Tallard, 'Sean, for God's sake, go!'

Tallard was already in first gear, and pulled out to overtake. The big truck accelerated up the line.

At the control point a corporal ran out waving his arms. 'Oi!' he shouted angrily, 'You can't queue-barge like that.' He stood in the middle of the road and Tallard braked.

Edward leaned out of the window and shouted, 'Out of the way! We're on our way to the hospital!'

'What's this 'ere then?' asked a sergeant stepping ponderously into the middle of the road with a stick under his arm. He joined the corporal and screwed up his eyes against the sun to scrutinise the tank-like truck trying to bulldoze its way through his road block. Another planter throwing his weight about, it seemed.

'Jesus Christ, Edward!' said Tallard under his breath. 'Pull some bloody rank or something!'

'I'm Lieutenant Fairfax,' Edward began as politely as he could, showing his identity card, but the sergeant shook his head and said, 'You'll have to wait in turn, Sir, with all these others. Orders is orders and we've been told that whites must get the same treatment as all these 'ere wogs.' He gesticulated at a taxiful of Malays and Sikhs, and two Chinese on a trishaw.

'My wife is dying,' Edward said as calmly and forcibly as he could, looking down on the sergeant. 'We have to get to Kinrara at once!'

For a moment the sergeant tried to decide if the frantic young officer in civvies was swinging the lead. Then he climbed swiftly up on the running board, peered past Edward into the cab where he could see Diana's white face in the shadows and towels littered on the floor. He was a wartime soldier and the cab stank of cordite, sweat and blood. Without wasting another word to Edward, he jumped down and started bellowing instructions to the other soldiers to move the barbed wire caltrops at once. In moments, Tallard had negotiated the big armoured truck through the block and before they had reached the end of the street, a military policeman on a motorbike overtook them, waving them on, and riding ahead of them to wave traffic out of their way.

Kinrara Military Hospital, fortunately on the south side of Kuala Lumpur, was a solid white-painted building set in neat grounds with imposing colonial pillars at the front entrance.

Edward's immense relief at reaching the hospital was spoiled for when the truck stopped, he was again unable to be any real help to Diana. The military policeman parked his bike and was first inside, shouting for help. He reappeared at a run with several nurses. They took no notice of the strangely armoured truck. Such bizarre sights were now common. They brushed straight past Edward, with Marsha's help eased Diana from the cab, lifted her on to a trolley and whisked her away in a cloud of crisp white uniforms.

After a moment staring after them Edward wandered back to the Monster. He looked at the mess of towels in the back with the smell of blood in his nostrils. With automatic gestures, he unloaded his carbine and left it with the magazine on the seat. 'What about the car, the Plymouth,' he asked Tallard dully. There was no point being angry with Tallard any longer. His mind was searching for balance in the order of detail.

'We'll get it tomorrow,' grunted Sean Tallard. 'If it's been hit, we'll get it fixed. Don't worry.'

'There's nothing more we can do now,' said Marsha. Her sarong was filthy, her face tired and damp with sweat, but her eyes were soft after the tension of the past hours. She took Edward's hand, and said, 'She'll be fine now, really.'

Edward nodded. He wanted to be alone, but he could not persuade Sean and Marsha to leave him. They insisted on staying. It was too late to drive back to the estate and they decided to stop overnight in the Station Hotel in the centre of town. It crossed Tallard's mind to offer to join Edward, in his house in the quarters, to keep him company, but there was something distant about him which demanded privacy and he did not mention it.

They sat in an empty waiting-room on hard chairs, hardly speaking, all of them exhausted while a fan flicked slowly round under the high ceiling. A nurse came, once, with tea, but the shadows were lengthening nearly two hours later when a doctor came to find them. Edward was standing at the open window, gazing vacantly across the neatly kept lawns at the red sunset behind the big spreading Rain Tree and several pink flowering Bungors.

'Mr Fairfax?' said the doctor introducing himself. 'Lucky you got her here when you did. She'd haemorrhaged rather badly, but we've tidied her up now and she'll be fine.'

'Can I see her?'

'Better not. She's sleeping now,' said the doctor. 'We'll keep her

93

here for a few days and then she can go home, right as rain.'

'Just like that?' said Edward bitterly.

'Yes.' Matter-of-factly, the doctor added, 'It's not your fault, you know.'

'No, I suppose not,' said Edward, but he felt soiled, different. And resentful. Someone, he promised himself, would pay for this.

He telephoned Gandra Singh to drive him home. He thanked Marsha and Sean Tallard but he wanted nothing further to do with the armoured truck. When he got back to Uxbridge Drive Hassan gave him a large whisky s'tengah and he went and slumped into a rattan cahir on the verandah. The night air was heavy with the sweet scent of a stephanotis climbing up a pillar by the steps on to the lawn but he found it impossible to relax. The racket of cicadas and frogs suited his mood better. He desperately wanted to come to grips with the men who had killed Bowman and others, but he had simply not been prepared for them at the 'Black Circle'. He told himself it was absurd, but he blamed himself for being too late to fight in the Second World War. Then he reminded himself that he had seen plenty of violence in Palestine. What grated was that, just as he had the good fortune to see a serious new campaign erupting right under his feet, his professional commitment was spoiled by personal loss. He felt awful thinking of Diana, lying drained in the hospital. Blame and counter-blame, accusation and excuse dipped and flashed through his mind like the fireflies over the clump of jungle beyond the gulley at the back of the garden.

Hassan silently watched from the shadows inside the house, squatting with his back against the frame of the sitting-room door, his brown eyes huge with concern. He was terribly upset by Edward's curt description of what had happened and wanted to help. Whenever Edward emptied his glass, he slipped forward to refill it.

Edward's sense of injustice gradually focused on Ho Peng. Finally, as he swore to find and kill him, he fell asleep, slumped over in his rattan chair.

Chapter 7

A FATAL PAUSE

A month later, a thin Chinese in a shirt and black trousers stood in a telephone booth behind a bar, waiting impatiently. It was mid-morning, too early for customers, and the foyer was deserted. Suddenly the telephone shrilled.

'Hallo? Hallo?'

'I want to speak to Chang Cao Lin,' said a metallic voice in Chinese.

'He will be back in six minutes,' replied the Chinese. Recognising the name, he used a number at random and waited on edge for the expected reply.

'Then I'll call again tomorrow at ten.' The voice sounded faint, as though phoning long-distance.

Six plus ten made sixteen, the current code number. Correct. The Chinese smiled his relief and asked, 'Perhaps you would like to leave a message?'

'Thank you.' The words came more slowly and very clear, 'Please tell him that the stores which he has been waiting for will leave this evening on schedule on the night train, and he will be able to meet them as planned.'

The Chinese repeated the message and hung up. Quickly, he slipped through the foyer into the brassy sunlight and turned left through a bustle of people into Chinatown.

He made himself take a circuitous route through several alleys, to see if he was followed but after ten minutes he was bored. He had noticed no-one, so he doubled back into Petaling Street, turned right, and stepped down into a Chinese apothecary's shop. The small space inside was lined with bottles on shelves, some filled with

95

liquids, others with nameless parts of animals, vegetables and minerals, all with secret properties good for the Chinese body or soul. An emaciated Chinese of indeterminate age in a worn grey tunic waited behind a counter.

Liya, looking sleek in her silk dress and high heels, was standing behind a colourful bead curtain in the door of the Wild Orchid Hotel and saw the Chinese go into the apothecary's shop. After a few minutes, she saw him leave and walk swiftly into the crowds on the pavements. She stayed behind the bead curtain for another half an hour, watching life in Chinatown ebb and flow along the sunny street, the hawkers, people bowed under bundles of clothing, barrows of Chinese vegetables shoved energetically along by young men between the shafts, children playing in the dirt, bicycles wobbling through the crowds and the occasional truck creeping along as people parted to let it through. Finally, feeling safe, she slipped out between the beads into the bright sunlight, crossed the street and entered the apothecary's shop.

The same morning, Colonel Bleasley was standing with Edward and Captain Denton in the Intelligence room looking at a new wall-chart of the MPABA, laid out like a family tree, with names and ranks where known, starting with General-Secretary of the Central Executive Committee, Chin Peng, at the top and spreading down through State and District Committees, to Element leaders and finally to the rank and file communists at the bottom. Many names were missing. A few had small police identity photographs pinned against them.

'Long way to go before we know who they all are,' Edward observed. He and Captain Denton had made the chart together.

'Exactly,' stated Colonel Bleasley. 'This is more important than wasting our bloody time putting ambushes round Tallard's place.' He glanced aggressively at Edward.

'At least they've killed one MPABA member, Sir,' Edward replied. The ambushes had been his idea, to trap the communists when they came back to shoot up Tallard's house, and he was still furious that Bleasley had refused to allow him to take part with the local infantry battalion.

'Yes, but that was two weeks ago,' said Bleasley dismissively. 'Trail has obviously gone cold now. What d'you think, Denton?' He swivelled weightily on his heel, his hands stuffed into the pockets of his voluminous green shorts. His fat legs stuck out below like pink sausages pushed into long socks and shoes. He stared at Denton with his narrow piggy eyes. He liked keeping his subordinates on edge. It was good training.

'I'm sure the bandits will come back, Sir,' Edward butted in before Harry Denton could reply. 'We must keep the ambushes in!'

'Rubbish,' Colonel Bleasley retorted unpleasantly without looking round. 'You're obsessed, Fairfax, just because of your wife.'

'Diana all right now, Edward?' Captain Denton put in smoothly, seeing Edward about to lose his temper.

'Thank you, yes,' said Edward shortly. Diana had spent ten days in hospital. The doctors had pronounced her fit again, but she still seemed listless and lacking interest in life.

Harry Denton looked obliquely at Colonel Bleasley and remarked, 'Must've been quite a shock. Mrs Fairfax nearly died.'

Colonel Bleasley grunted, but the rebuke irked. 'No place for emotions on operations,' he blustered. 'That's exactly why I wouldn't let Edward go on the ambushes.' He mopped his sweating forehead with his handkerchief. 'Besides, why should we waste a lot of effort on Tallard's estate? God knows, plenty of other places are being attacked.'

Edward took a deep breath and said, 'Because Sean Tallard and Ho Peng were together in the war.'

'So what?' said Bleasley, staring at Ho Peng's name on the wall chart. He was marked as something to do with the Selangor State Committee. 'I'm damn certain that Tallard is using his time in Force 136 during the war as an excuse to get us to protect his estate, and you've fallen for it, Fairfax.'

'I feel certain there's something between them, Sir,' insisted Edward. With Angus Maclean's help he had searched wartime records but papers on Force 136 had been frustratingly scanty and revealed nothing of interest. 'Ho Peng wants Tallard personally, for some reason. Not just to attack his estate.' He remembered Tallard's words before they burst out through the communists around the house.

'Nonsense,' Bleasley replied. 'You've got to be balanced in Intelligence. No good concentrating on one small detail when there's so much to do here overall. No, you've wasted too much time with this Ferret Force, mucking about in the jungle while Captain Denton and I have been working our backsides off with the big picture.'

97

To keep the bloody General briefed and sweet, thought Edward, his heart sinking.

'Yes, indeed, Fairfax,' Colonel Bleasley continued, warming to his theme. 'Meticulous staff work is how we'll defeat these bandits and you won't learn that farting about in the bushes. From now on, you'll stay in the office, Fairfax. Understood?'

Before Edward could reply, they heard a jeep pull up in the road outside and Captain Denton said with relief, 'Ah, a visitor, Edward. Your friend, Chief Inspector Maclean.'

'Bugger!' said Colonel Bleasley. 'What's that bloody policeman doing here in HQ?'

They heard footsteps across the verandah boards.

'Bit of Int for us, perhaps. A scrap off the police table?' said Edward carelessly. He was furious at being told to finish with Ferret Force before it had been given a chance to show its worth.

Colonel Bleasley glared at him.

The door opened, Angus Maclean stuck his head into the room and said cheerily, 'May I come in? Not interrupting anything?'

'You're looking very pleased with yourself, Chief Inspector,' said Colonel Bleasley grumpily, waving him in.

'With good reason, Colonel,' replied Angus joining them at the wall-chart. He came straight to the point before Bleasley could say another word. 'We've killed Lao Yu.'

He pointed at the chart where, at the top, next to Chin Peng, a small photograph was pinned by the name, 'Lao Yu, MPABA Senior Military Commander'.

'Excellent,' said Edward enthusiastically. Good news had been in very short supply since the Emergency began.

Captain Denton grinned broadly and asked, 'How did it happen?'

Colonel Bleasley stared morosely at the small photograph.

Angus said, 'I was with a chap called Bill Stafford, a very good man indeed, a police superintendent in town, when a source turned up to see him while he was having a shave in a barbers' shop.' He smiled at the recollection. 'The source said that Lao Yu was going to be at a meeting in a hut on the edge of the jungle near Kajang, fifteen miles south of Kuala Lumpur. So up we went, just before dawn. Led by the source, we attacked the hut and killed all the Chinese in the subsequent shoot-out. One was Lao Yu.'

'Splendid,' declared Captain Denton. He enjoyed a straightforward operation, cut and dried.

'Well done, I'm sure,' said Colonel Bleasley condescendingly, thinking the body might well have been misidentified. 'But so what?'

Angus frowned and glanced at Edward, realising for the first time what Bleasley was really like. Speaking deliberately slowly, he explained, 'Lao Yu was Chin Peng's most important military commander, Colonel Bleasley. It's a major coup against the terrorists. Makes a change to be on top and we must keep up the pressure.'

'The army, anyway, is doing just that,' said Colonel Bleasley obstinately. 'If the Malayan Police hadn't allowed the security situation with these bloody communists to deteriorate in the first place, the army wouldn't have to be involved at all. As it is, the army is damned busy. Our chaps don't sit about having their hair cut in barbers' shops. They're out on patrols all the time.'

'Trampling about in the jungle?' asked Angus blithely, unable to resist the jibe. Being a newcomer to Malaya, from Palestine, Bleasley's remarks about the past made no impact. 'Or working on good information?'

'Of course,' Colonel Bleasley retorted. 'We have our successes too. Killed one at Sean Tallard's estate, for example, and that was all on army initiative. No thanks to the police.'

Edward stared, amazed at his gall, and opened his mouth to speak but Captain Denton silently shook his head behind Bleasley's back.

Angus glanced at Edward too and said, 'So I heard, Colonel Bleasley. Ho Peng's gang. Then you will appreciate that, after Lao Yu's death, Ho Peng is even more important than before.' He stabbed his finger at the name on the wall-chart and said, 'You can write in here that Ho Peng is top man in Selangor State round Kuala Lumpur.'

Colonel Bleasley looked cross and said with obvious insincerity, 'Well, it's very good of you to take the trouble to drop by and let us know all that, Chief Inspector. Now, do excuse me. Lot of paperwork to be done before lunch. Fresh troops coming up tomorrow from Singapore, you know, and we're damn busy working on a good brief for them. No time for haircuts, what!' He laughed and waddled off to his office, mopping his face, very pleased with the encounter.

Edward exhaled a long breath and said, 'I'll see you out, Angus.'

'Aye,' said Angus staring after Colonel Bleasley. 'No point staying here. Thought I might interest him in combining forces, supplying army patrols with Special Branch source intelligence, of the kind we used to nobble Lao Yu. The police aren't organised or numerous enough yet to act on the information we can supply and we can't sit about till they are. They haven't found a new High Commissioner to replace Sir Edward Gent yet, so we're sadly lacking in leadership. The brutal fact is that the communists are gaining the upper hand.'

'Trouble is the majority of soldiers aren't yet good enough in the jungle either.'

'They'll have to learn fast if we want to catch Ho Peng,' said Angus. 'Your Ferret Force boys can teach them, if they're allowed.'

'What have you heard about the Ferret Force?' Edward asked at once. Perhaps this explained Colonel Bleasley's attitude?

'Let's just say the British Army doesn't like irregulars,' Angus replied. 'You should remember that, from Palestine.'

Edward nodded glumly. 'But people like Tallard are the only ones who can teach us about the jungle, to catch the likes of Ho Peng.'

They stood on the verandah overlooking the unruffled grass lawns of the British Headquarters. Angus said contemplatively, 'I'd love to get my hands on Ho Peng. He knows so much. I'll bet he was involved in Lao Yu's death.'

'How?' Edward wanted Ho Peng too.

Angus frowned, 'After we'd shot Lao Yu, we found five women in the hut. Couriers, probably. Or bits of skirt to keep the fighting men happy.'

'Or both,' grinned Edward.

'We handcuffed them and put them in a hollow while we searched the hut. Then, just as we were about to leave, all hell broke loose from the edge of the jungle. About forty enemy, Bill Stafford reckoned, opened up on us, with Bren guns, Stens, the whole bloody issue! I nearly shit myself, I can tell you!'

Edward burst out laughing and said, 'What happened?'

'Bill Stafford bravely led a charge into the jungle, whereupon the attackers miraculously melted away. More than that, when we came back, we found that none of us had been hit but all the Chinese women in the hollow were killed.'

'You were bloody lucky.'

Angus turned to him, 'Luck? Don't you see? They weren't aiming at us at all. You know how hard it is for forty men to creep up silently in the jungle, yet we never heard a damn thing, nor was Lao Yu warned off when we attacked in the first place, so these guys must have been waiting for us. They knew we were going to be there, to attack Lao Yu and when we had done the dirty deed, they made sure there were no Chinese witnesses or survivors.'

Edward said slowly, 'Ho Peng?'

Angus nodded. He said, 'With Lao Yu out of the way, he becomes the most important man in three States, in Selangor, Pahang and Negri Sembilan.'

Angus got into his jeep and started it up. As he was about to leave, he added, 'And there were two reporters with us too, from *Time* Magazine. Bill Stafford wouldn't have let them come along as well unless he had known we were on for some success. The whole thing must have been a set-up.' He paused and said, 'By the way, Edward, how is Diana?'

Edward frowned, 'All right, I suppose. Trouble is, she's not the same any more. She keeps busy enough in the Headquarters in a determined sort of way, with people like Leonard Goodbury, the garrison padre, but she refuses to leave town.' She had used every excuse not to try another day out in the car. 'She acts as if there's a bloody communist under every bush.'

'She may well be right at that,' said Angus dourly.

As if he had not heard, Edward continued, 'And she loved the place when we first got here.'

'Aye, it must have been a shocking experience for her,' said Angus sympathetically, thinking of the girl, Liz Warren, whom he had lost in the King David Hotel. 'But I expect she'll recover soon enough.' He let out the clutch and Edward went back into the office.

Liya's hearing was so acutely tuned to the distinctive sounds of police and army vehicles that she easily heard the jeep approaching the Sessions Courts on the junction of Mountbatten Road and Jalan Pudu. She was on her way to take the bus out to the Black Circle estate dressed in her samfu working clothes with her raffia basket on her back. Behind her, Ho Peng walked briskly along in her wake.

She tensed as the jeep emerged through other traffic and then relaxed. Instead of a police patrol, which might stop at any moment to search people, the driver was alone. She recognised him as a Chief Inspector, and wondered at the great gulf which separated them, he a British colonial official in his jeep, she a Chinese immigrant from mainland China, a peasant on the road.

Up ahead, the engine hooted. A whiff of smoke drifted past the compartment window, obscuring the endless stream of green jungle outside for a moment and the colonel said, 'Damn sun only just up and blazing hot already. What a bloody climate, eh, Captain Haike?'

Roger Haike nodded damply. The colonel had done nothing but complain about the heat since leaving Singapore, which only made it worse. He had not slept a wink during the night in the stuffy compartment, in spite of leaving the window open.

A black-skinned Tamil Indian cha wallah opened the compartment door and said, 'Cha, Sahib?' He grinned at both British officers with a mouthful of white teeth. Somehow, despite the swaying train, he was carrying a tray piled precariously with small cups and a teapot.

Roger Haike waved him away. No amount of tea seemed to make any difference. His body seemed to be melting in sweat, softening his neat black moustache and running down his flanks and thighs where his tailored khaki trousers stuck uncomfortably to the seat, He found this intensely irritating. He liked to be properly turned out at all times and hoped the colonel had not noticed.

'Go away,' said the colonel to the Tamil, who disappeared.

'Bloody cha wallahs,' said the colonel. After some moments staring through the window, he added, 'I've been doing a co-ord job in HQ FARELF in Singapore, you know.' He sat legs apart, fanning his shiny face with yesterday's *Straits Times*. 'Now they're sending me to KL. Important job there. Need someone to galvanise things. As you know, bit of a fatal pause in command since poor old Gent was killed. No-one to replace him yet.'

'You been out here long, Sir?' asked Roger. The colonel had been through the same story several times since leaving Singapore Railway Station the night before but Roger Haike believed in treating senior officers exactly as they wanted to be treated.

'Came out several months ago. On the *Empire Orwell*. They need chaps like me with experience, you know, to get things going against these beggars in the jungle.' As he talked, he waved his newspaper at the dense blur of green trees passing the window.

Roger Haike looked at his watch. Not long to go before this awful journey was over. He decided he hated the heat and cursed ever listening to Edward, his brother-in-law. At their wedding Edward had said he was taking Diana to Malaya for an agreeable colonial lifestyle, but Roger had suspected at once that there was an underlying career opportunity. Like Edward, he took one look at the chaos in Europe, used his father's influence in the War Office and arranged his own transfer to an artillery unit near Kuala Lumpur.

Had he done the right thing? In Germany, the British Army was once again in the front line, only this time Russia was the enemy, and he knew that careers were being made and medals won in the frantic efforts to break the blockade of Berlin.

From the front of the train he heard a dull explosion, then a wisp of smoke from the engine floated past and the carriage lurched.

Fear washed through him and he gripped the seat. He stared at the colonel, still talking, who seemed oblivious. The carriage lurched again, as if checked by the engine's brakes, then rocked on. The wheels clicked comfortingly over another join in the rails. For an instant Roger imagined the noise was his imagination, but the colonel had stopped in mid-sentence, his mouth open in his round surprised face.

Suddenly their compartment began to tilt rapidly on to its side. Roger's head snapped round to look through the window. Detachedly, he observed that they were on a bend, the jungle about forty yards away, the thin band of blue sky framed in the top of the window above the tree tops had disappeared and the embankment was rushing up to the window.

The colonel stood up, his mouth open, lost his balance and fell towards the window which burst in silver shards as the carriage bounced on its side on the embankment. The colonel disappeared head-first through the window in a spray of exploding glass which turned blood red. Roger was flung forward on to the bulkhead of the compartment as the carriage leaped and bounced to a standstill, and lost consciousness.

In the thick undergrowth at the jungle edge Lao Tang's Bren gun grew hot as he fired burst after burst into the roofs and sides of the carriages lying on their sides, twisted and smashed in the ditch in front of him. Looking down the embankment to his right, he could see the fallen engine belching steam and smoke, its wheels slowly turning in the air, like a vast iron insect on his back. Thrilled with their success, his nostrils thick with the smell of cordite, he fired frantically until a voice screamed behind him, 'Fire at people! At the red-haired Imperialists! Not unless you see them!'

Ho Peng's fingers pinched hard into Lao Tang's shoulder, and Lao Tang checked his firing. He changed magazines on top of the Bren and watched the carriage in front of him. The doors flapped open and bemused figures in khaki clambered out and stood up on the side of the stricken carriage.

'Now!' shouted Ho Peng venomously. 'Fire!'

Lao Tang opened fire again and was sure he hit two. The rest dived out of sight. Elated he continued to fire short bursts into the top of the carriage, at places where he imagined the British could be hiding. Ho Peng ducked away up the line of his men firing at the train from their positions on the jungle's edge.

Roger Haike came to with the din of gunfire in his ears. He looked round. The compartment was wrecked, clothes, suitcases and bench seats scattered about covered in glass. One of the colonel's hand-made brown brogues was lying in the thick lallang grass which poked through the broken carriage window. Roger could see the bright stamp of the maker's name quite distinctly inside the heel, Lobb's of St James's, and, in a moment of clarity, he deduced the colonel had had them made specially before coming out to the Far East.

Several bullets smashed through the roof of the compartment and ripped into the floor behind him. Terrified, Roger crawled into the corner between an upturned bench-seat and the floor of the compartment. He heard shouting. The compartment door over his head was open and the carriage window above that had fallen out. Someone outside was shouting fire orders to fight off the bandits. He crouched into his corner and prayed the shooting would stop.

Ho Peng came back to Lao Tang and hovered behind him like a banshee, spitting out a stream of instructions. 'Aim before you fire!' he screamed. 'Squeeze the trigger, don't pull at it!' His arm jabbed out at a target, 'There! That man on the carriage. He's an officer trying to rally the British soldiers. Shoot him!'

Lao Tang wiped the sweat pouring down his face, adjusted the position of his Bren on the flying buttress roots of the big tree soaring above them and peered down the sights. He picked up the little figure on the carriage. He concentrated fiercely, determined not to fail with Ho Peng perched like a hawk behind him, tightened his grip on the machine-gun as Ho Peng had taught him, and squeezed the trigger with his forefinger. The figure toppled backwards out of sight, like a small puppet whose strings have been cut.

Roger Haike nearly died with fright as a body fell through the corridor window above him, bounced back and forth on the jamb of the compartment door above his head, like a ball-bearing in a pin-ball machine, and thudded face down on to the grass beside his feet, close to the colonel's shoe. For a moment Roger did not move. He watched the body with a glazed look until he became aware that the shooting outside had died away. The uniform was that of a captain like himself. He stirred and crawled over to inspect the still form. He pulled the man towards him and recoiled, retching. Great wounds punctured the man's shoulder, his neck was ripped open and half his head had been shot away. Brains hung out over the clean white edge of his skull, wetting the grass. Roger fell back gasping for air.

Above him a voice called down, 'You all right, Sir?' He looked up. A head and shoulders was silhouetted in the corridor window directly above him.

Shaken, Roger called out in a brave voice, 'Just a few bruises, thanks, but I'm afraid this poor chap has had it.'

'No matter,' shouted the head. 'We've driven the little bastards off, thanks to you.'

'Yes,' Roger shouted back automatically. Then he frowned. He thought for a moment, shrugged and stood up, straightened his uniform and clambered out to take charge.

Edward had hardly sat down for lunch on the verandah with Diana when he heard someone bellowing in the road outside.

Edward pulled a face of apology and walked briskly through the sitting-room to the hall.

'Don't be long,' Diana called after him.

The shouting grew furious and Edward yanked open the front door. In the road, he saw Sean Tallard sitting in a jeep, in jungle greens and floppy hat. Untam sat in the back with two others from the old Ferret Force group. Tallard shouted, 'Come on, Fairfax! I can't wait all bloody day.'

Edward said, 'What's going on?'

'The troop train from Singapore was ambushed this morning. A group of survivors marched out along the track to report what had happened. They've asked me to track the bastards from the ambush. If we find them, we'll radio out for more troops to attack them. Harry Denton said you'd come home for lunch, to see Diana.'

Edward nodded. He had been coming to the bungalow to keep her company every lunchtime since she was released from hospital.

'Well, then?' said Tallard exasperated. 'Untam's got your carbine. The other two dozen are waiting in trucks at the main gate. Go and get your gear!'

'Didn't Captain Denton tell you Colonel Bleasley has ordered me off the Ferret Force?'

'Fuck Bleasley,' Tallard swore exasperated. 'I know what he's said, but are you really going to let a useless git like him put you off? Shit, I'll wager a month's pay that Ho Peng was leading that ambush.'

'How d'you know?' asked Edward.

'Just things I heard in the de-brief. His trademarks, so to speak. Jesus, we did enough ambushes together in the war, Ho Peng and I, and it was all there, in HQ, not five minutes ago.'

'Who told you?'

'The man who led out the survivors,' shouted Tallard impatiently. 'An artillery captain. Man called Haike, I think.'

Edward groaned, 'Roger Haike?'

'Yes, that's him. What's the matter?' Tallard demanded. 'He seems to have done rather well.'

Edward grunted but it settled his mind. With sudden determination he shouted, 'Give me two minutes, Sean!' and ran back into the house.

Sean Tallard turned to Untam, grinning, and said, 'I thought he'd come for Ho Peng.'

'What's happening?' asked Diana appearing at the door of their bedroom. She watched Edward struggling into his jungle greens and stuffing things into his back-pack at the same time. She had an awful premonition of disaster. 'You're going off with Tallard again, aren't you?'

Edward nodded, wishing Diana had not been around. He shouted past her, 'Hassan! Fill my water bottles!'

'Yes, Tuan!' came Hassan's clear voice, muted from the kitchen.

'I thought you said Colonel Bleasley had taken you off the Ferret Force?' Diana asked. She backed out of the way to let Hassan through.

'Yes,' Edward admitted, grinning and rapidly buttoning his shirt. His hands flashed to loop the long tabs holding up his trousers at the side.

'For God' sake, darling, you'll get into terrible trouble,' said Diana. She had heard from Mrs Bleasley that Ferret Force was no longer in favour.

'Ho Peng ambushed the train,' said Edward. 'Doesn't that mean anything to you? And your brother was on board. On his way up from Singapore. This is a real chance to nail the swine.'

106

Diana shook her head hardly registering the news about Roger. She had tried to erase the memory of the CT from her mind.

'Well, it bloody well does to me!' He picked up his pack and belt kit and started for the door.

Very quietly, she pleaded, 'Please don't go.' She was terrified of losing him.

Edward kissed her rather fiercely in the doorway, to settle her fears, holding her face, and she let him, her hands loosely on his sides. Then he was gone.

They reached the ambush by midday, on a relief train, and the scene drove Diana from his mind. The engine was still steaming, like a manic wounded beast on its side at the head of a tangled line of carriages holed and ripped with gunfire. A swarm of medics and soldiers laboured and shouted instructions in the blazing sun to release the injured, helped by a variety of people, civilians and soldiers, men and women, their clothes torn and bloodied. Little groups of wounded sat dazed and bleeding in the shade of the upturned rolling stock.

Sean Tallard, solid in his army uniform, spoke briefly to a harassed platoon commander who pointed at the jungle. 'You know they robbed the Post Office van too?' he said. 'A party of them killed all the Post Office workers and robbed the van while the others shot up the train. They got away with quite a lot of money.'

'Did they just,' replied Tallard, with a tuneless whistle. 'Now isn't that terribly interesting?' So, Ho Peng needed money.

The platoon commander turned away, thinking Tallard was being sarcastic. How could anyone so overweight possibly cope in the jungle?

Tallard was already looking towards the ambush site. He nodded at Untam who led the thirty men directly into the trees. Edward was immediately struck with the peace in the green shadows under the canopy compared to the hot, noisy scene behind them on the wrecked train.

Untam wasted no time. He began casting back and forth behind the ambush positions for the bandits' withdrawal route. Edward, fourth in line behind Tallard and a Bren gunner, watched the slim brown tracker at work, darting back and forth as he dipped and peered at bent leaves, squashed fronds and depressions in the soft jungle earth which were hardly visible, building a picture of where each of the communists had hidden, pointing at the shiny piles of empty cases which had spewed from their weapons. Finally he decided where they had set off from, back into the jungle.

When Untam grinned with yellowed teeth, held up his roughened thumb and pointed into the trees, Edward felt a surge of adrenalin The chase was on.

'Take care!' warned Tallard as they set off. 'The little shits will be weighed down with their loot, but they might ambush us too. Don't make a fucking sound!'

The caution was hardly necessary. Edward and all the others were well aware that they were now on their own, with no support available except by radioing for another patrol; and the deeper they went into the jungle, the longer a relief would take to walk in to help them out. They were committed.

Soon, they were a mile from the railway track, Untam working steadily at the front of the line. He advanced a few paces at a time, then stopped to examine the ground sign, the footprints and faint straight edges in the soil, the grasses and ferns brushed forward by the bandits' feet which gave away their direction of travel, and then the top sign higher off the ground where arms or packs had snapped twigs or turned leaves to show their pale undersides.

Tallard hung behind him, Untam's cover man, adding his experience and diagnosis of the signs. Gradually they paced forward, sometimes swiftly, sometimes agonisingly slowly. Edward's enthusiasm for coming to grips with the enemy changed to frustration at the time it took, and he feared they could be caught out themselves. He moved forward in a permanent crouch, instantly ready to fight, peering into the foliage all round, and the sweat poured off him, soaking his jungle greens almost black, getting in his eyes and making his hands slippery on his carbine.

Ahead of them, Ho Peng called a halt after three hours continuous walking and Lao Tang slumped to the ground exhausted. Thankfully, he dropped his pack and the Bren gun and gulped from his metal water bottle. The humidity was intense and he was worried about dehydrating. Ho Peng emerged through the leaves, his pale khaki shirt and trousers dark with sweat, his cap with its three red stars still square on his head. He bent down and whispered harshly, 'They're following us!'

Lao Tang stared and whispered, 'How d'you know?' Suddenly he felt less victorious.

'I know it,' was all Ho Peng would say. He could feel it, in his stomach, in his skin. He hissed, 'We shall ambush them!' He was sure the British were using an Iban tracker from Sarawak, though he did not want to alarm his men by saying so, and he wanted to teach them a lesson, like he had taught the Japanese. Swiftly he explained the ambush to Lao Tang and moved on to the next man. Twenty minutes later he returned down the line of men and took the lead again. He gave the sign to move. Lao Tang struggled to his feet, lifted his pack to his sore shoulders, picked up the Bren and followed the man in front.

Ho Peng led them to the top of the next rise, then the front section broke track to the right, looping round in a wide circle over the ridge and back again, while the men at the rear carried on, walking careless of the signs they left to cover the spot where the first group broke track over the ridge.

Lao Tang, in the first group, followed Ho Peng round the loop and, when they stopped, he realised he was no more than ten yards from the track they had just made coming up the hill, looking down on it from rocks in thick jungle cover, perfectly placed to ambush the soldiers following them. Ho Peng appeared out of the gloom once more, and placed each of his men exactly where he wanted to maximise the killing on the track below. He put Lao Tang behind a palm bole, his Bren hidden from view by thick vine leaves and whispered with savage intensity, 'Do not open fire till you hear my carbine! I'll be on your right. Understood?'

Lao Tang nodded nervously. He had not prepared himself for a second fight in the same day and was badly frightened. The soldiers following him would be on full alert, not like the men in the train. He shrank behind the palm bole, gripped his Bren and waited, his mouth dry.

Ho Peng settled down concealed on his right under pale green ferns. Utter silence descended on the jungle, the silence of humans, while the birds and insects filled the canopy around them with noise.

Sweat ran down Lao Tang's face and neck, and in rivulets from his armpits across his chest, but he dared not move a muscle. He strained his ears for the approaching soldiers.

Edward slipped as he crossed a stream, and swore softly. He knew the high pitch of concentration was tiring him out. Ahead, Sean Tallard seemed indefatigable, peering at the track with Untam, and moving effortlessly, like an animal, poised for the scent of trouble.

Abruptly, Tallard stopped, frozen in place. As one man, the

line behind him stopped moving too. Edward watched Tallard whispering to Untam. His whole body position spelled alarm.

After a moment, Tallard came back, walking very softly indeed. He knelt down beside Edward and whispered, 'The bastards stopped here. For several minutes. Look!' He pointed by Edward's foot to an indentation in the soft leaves, a clear imprint of a Bren gun butt. It could only have been put there when its owner stopped and rested its weight on the ground.

Tallard looked round the green backdrop of leaves which concealed everything further than a few metres away. Somewhere not far away was Ho Peng, he was sure. But doing what? He thought of the money he had robbed from the Post Office van on the train.

'What are you thinking about?' asked Edward. He felt Tallard had lost momentum and, remote as they were in the jungle, far from help, that could be fatal.

Tallard swivelled to look at him and decided he needed Edward's support. He replied, 'I'm sure we're very close. Untam thinks they were here only half an hour ago. What worries me is the chance of ambush. Ho Peng's a bastard for that. We have to keep going, but Jesus, keep your eyes peeled!'

Lao Tang heard the secret human noises approaching along their track at the same time as Ho Peng. Tiny scraping sounds of rubber soled boots and leaves gently brushed aside by arms and guns. He tensed, gripped his Bren tighter and glanced across at Ho Peng whose pocked face, streaked with dirt and sweat, was intent, his black eyes narrow slits. Very slowly, Ho Peng raised his carbine and pointed it towards the track they had used to come up the hill.

Lao Tang jumped. A small brown man with jet-black hair had materialised through the curtain of leaves, hardly ten yards away, virtually naked and stepping lightly up the slope, quite soundless on bare feet, his eyes casting left and right. Lao Tang froze, in desperate self-control, masking his terror at the proximity of his enemy. His finger stiffened on the trigger. Behind the Sarawak tracker, a second man appeared, big and sweating profusely, but moving with surprising grace and almost as quietly as the first.

Only his eyes moving, Lao Tang risked a quick glance sideways at Ho Peng, expecting him to fire the first burst. Ho Peng, hardly visible behind the ferns, never moved.

Ho Peng was staring through the leaves at Tallard. He picked him up in the iron sights of his carbine. Then he exhaled a long silent breath and swore fiercely to himself. Somehow he had not expected

Tallard to be among the pursuing British soldiers. He cursed silently. And let him pass.

The next soldier, carrying a Bren, made more noise, and the fourth. He was fair-haired, and moved with care through the vines and lianas. Ho Peng fixed his face in his sights and started! This was the officer who had been to Tallard's place more than once. He studied the keen sweat-stained young face, recognising the signs of animal alarm and realised his enemy knew he was close.

Edward felt his skin shrinking. His sweat had gone cold and he shivered to feel the air on his neck. Creeping, bending and weaving he strained to minimise the sound of each footfall, yet each careless noise sounded like a thunderclap. Sean Tallard's last words kept churning round in his head, that Ho Peng would strike back. More telling still, he felt he could sense danger in the opaque green shadows around them.

Ho Peng watched him pass out of view, and still did not fire. With a jolt, Lao Tang realised the advantage of surprise was fading fast. The danger of being rolled up by a British counter-attack increased with each step the British took unmolested along the track through the ambush killing zone.

Ho Peng knew it too, but he lay quite still. And he watched every single one of the soldiers pass by him without moving. The men at the back were less alert, made more noise, and were plainly exhausted.

Glancing repeatedly at Ho Peng, Lao Tang tried to will him to open fire, even just to relieve the tension. When the last man passed and still nothing happened, Lao Tang let his head fall on his Bren and silently cursed him, desperate to know why Ho Peng had let the opportunity pass.

Ho Peng was so cautious he made them wait another hour before he got to his feet. Lao Tang's impatience burst in the relief of tension and he almost shouted, 'Why? Comrade, why!'

'Tallard!' snapped Ho Peng in a harsh whisper and they marched on. The look of savage frustration in his face silenced Lao Tang but the confusion in his mind about what had happened absorbed him for a full hour more before he realised that Ho Peng was now tracking the trackers. In line, they were slowly, painstakingly following the British soldiers.

Edward checked his watch. Five o'clock. More than four hours tracking and the feeling of danger had not passed. The heat of the day had not abated, even worsened. He had never sweated so much in his life, with fear, and with the relentless pressure of moving silently in thick jungle. His system was poisoned with the adrenalin burning round his body. From time to time, he glanced back down the line at the strained, filthy and haggard faces of the few others he could see behind him and he knew they were as drained as he was.

Even Tallard was showing the strain, every few minutes stopping to argue furiously in low tones with Untam who seemed reluctant to go on. No doubt Untam could feel the enemy close to as well.

They needed to, had to, stop. Edward was about to speak to Tallard when drops of rain began to tumble through the layers of leaves above him. Abruptly the sunlight faded, blotted out by dark clouds, the temperature suddenly dropped, the wind whipped the canopy top high above. Thunder burst over them and water streamed vertically into the jungle in a drenching downpour.

The beating, deafening rain eased the tension for British and Chinese alike, cooling the skin, almost freezing them by comparison with the intense humidity before, and making their concentration on silence quite pointless.

Five minutes after it started, Untam stopped cautiously on the edge of an enemy camp. The open space cleared between the big trees was all the more surprising for the unrelenting jungle they had been in all day. The tracker sank slowly to his knees, his brown skin glistening in the rain. Sean Tallard and Edward closed up behind him. They searched between the trees for signs of life. Nothing moved, but the sheets of rain and gloom made it impossible to be sure. Edward could just make out a cluster of atap and bamboo huts between the hardwoods in the middle of the camp. He wished the Commissioner of Police could have seen the place.

'The bastards have beaten us,' Tallard swore loudly. There was little point whispering in the dinning rain.

'Why?' asked Edward. He was damned if he would give up after so much effort. 'Can't we follow them across the camp? It's open enough.' He estimated the camp was more than a hundred yards across, though the rain obscured the jungle on the other side.

'No good,' said Untam shrugging his shoulders. He pulled a face to demonstrate complete lack of interest. He seemed unaffected by the rain falling on his naked body.

'What does that mean?' asked Edward, half to Tallard. Untam's English was not very good and Tallard had found he understood Chinese better.

Tallard said, 'He means the rain is washing away the tracks.'

112

Untam looked cross and shook his head.

'I think the commies have come here on purpose,' Tallard said, ignoring him. 'To split up and follow various different escape routes out of this camp which makes it impossible for us to follow them with only one tracker.' Water streaming off his hat, he lifted his powerful shoulders hopelessly. 'This is the end of the line.'

'No good,' repeated Untam, wagging his finger and scowling at Tallard.

Tallard lost his temper. He snapped, 'Shut your mouth, Untam!' and let fly a burst of Chinese. The Iban tracker shrugged and sat down among some ferns.

'What's the matter with him?' Edward asked.

Tallard swore and said, 'He doesn't like being close to the enemy.'

Edward noticed that Untam was listening and shaking his head, but Tallard was saying, 'This camp would house two hundred or more.'

'Then I'm with Untam,' stated Edward practically, peering nervously at the camp through the rain. 'This is like Goldilocks and the two hundred bears. We're only thirty, Sean. What d'you suggest we do if the frigging bears come back and find us sleeping in their house?'

Tallard laughed, 'Don't fuss yourself over that. The camp is unoccupied. No-one will bother us.'

'How d'you know?'

'Just you take it from me,' snapped Tallard.

Edward ignored his aggressiveness. They were all under pressure. He said, 'All right. We better tell the others what's going on.' He paused, then added, 'What is going on?'

Tallard grunted, 'We sleep here the night. On the ground.'

Safely hidden behind dripping palm leaves and confident that every sound he made was lost in the rain beating down, Ho Peng peered across the open camp at the British soldiers settling in for the night. He recognised typical British Army training as they dug shallow shell scrapes in case they were attacked, and positioned the Bren guns to guard their most vulnerable points.

'What are they doing here?' asked Lao Tang crouching close by him. The two had crept round the British position to see what they were doing. 'Our rear party didn't come to this camp.'

'I know,' said Ho Peng grimly. This was one of his camps, but he had ordered his men to step off their line of march one by one soon after the ambush position, and make their way separately to another rendezvous.

'Why are they here?'

'We shall see,' said Ho Peng.

'Will we attack them?'

'Not till we see what they're doing.'

Dusk deepened the gloom of the storm and they watched the British light a few solid fuel fires under their ponchos, half hidden by the scrub they were lying in, and they saw the odd flare of a cigarette being lit. Ho Peng seemed untroubled by the rain or cold but when Lao Tang caught the faint smell of cooking, he ached for something to eat himself and to rest. Finally Ho Peng withdrew into the jungle again as total darkness threatened to cut them off from the rest of their group.

Edward, cold and wet, spent a miserable night. After a check for leeches, he took the first two hours sentry duty with the Bren gunner beside him, both wrapped and shivering in ponchos in the pouring rain. He doubted anyone could attack them in such inky darkness but he had insisted on posting sentries just in case. Then, utterly tired out, he lay down to sleep under his poncho. However, unconvinced by Sean Tallard's optimism that they were in no danger, his mind refused to rest. When they all stood-to again at first light, which came as a cold grey mist hanging in the trees, he was still as exhausted as he had been the night before.

'At least the rain's stopped,' said Tallard trying to be cheerful.

'I can't shake off the feeling that we're being watched,' said Edward. Droplets of water fell from every leaf in the drenched jungle and would cover sounds as well as the rain had the night before.

'You too?' said Tallard nodding, impressed. 'I bet that bastard's out there. I hope he's as miserable as the rest of us.'

'What's the plan?' asked Edward. 'Look for the tracks?' He hated the idea of leaving, giving up, though he had to admit that after a night of continuous rain, the chances of finding anything to follow were slim. Tallard was categoric. He shook his head, 'No point. We'll search the camp, then turn back home.'

'Shouldn't we call in support?'

Tallard gave him a nasty look and snapped, 'Not necessary, unless we find anything.'

Reluctantly Edward agreed. After all, Tallard was the expert, but he insisted that they report their intentions on the radio.

They left ten men in all-round defence with everyone's rucksacks, sent another section round the camp leftwards and Tallard took Edward with the remaining ten to the right.

They moved carefully, in pairs, alert for ambush or booby traps, their footsteps padding silently on the sodden earth and leaves.

'Watch the trees,' warned Tallard, moving bulkily from the cover of one large tree to the next, covered by Untam. He pointed up, to an old look-out perch high in the branches of a big hardwood. After twenty minutes, it became clear the camp was deserted.

'Just as I thought,' said Tallard.

Edward let himself relax, slightly, though he still felt uneasy.

Tallard pointed with his carbine at a large atap hut in the centre of the camp. 'This is the command post. Ho Peng's basha.'

Edward observed the hut with more interest, trying to imagine his enemy there, sleeping on the low bamboo cot and planning the brutal attacks he had carried out continuously since the middle of June. It was very frustrating. They had come so close, but, in jungle like this, just being close was no good at all.

'He ain't far,' said Tallard, reading his thoughts. 'He'll have several places like this.'

Edward wondered what sort of man wanted to spend his days in the shadows of the jungle, on a bed of leaves in a primitive basha, on a tasteless diet of rice and vegetables, while Edward and Diana lived in their comfortable home in the sun, surrounded by garden and grass, with a houseboy, a cook and cool drinks. Such sacrifice and conviction was impressive. Unnerved, he wondered if all the bandits were the same.

A grunt of satisfaction from the other side of the hut broke into his thoughts and he walked round. Tallard was on his knees scraping away with a piece of wood in the damp black soil behind the atap wall.

'Look,' he said. 'Directly behind Ho Peng's goddam sleeping place, so he can keep an eye on it.'

'On what?'

Tallard ignored him, intent on digging the earth away with his fingers to reveal the top of a metal drum about a foot down. He said triumphantly, 'Type-H para drums!'

'How did you know where to look?'

'Tricks learned during the war,' said Tallard without looking up. 'Ho Peng always hid stuff from the Japs like this.' He had exposed the top of a box, where a white stencil was clearly marked on the

115

green paint. He read out, 'Bravo-seven'.

At that, he sat back on his haunches, called over two privates and ordered them to dig it out. 'Give them something to do,' he said to Edward and went off to smoke a cigarette.

Edward sat with his back to a big tree to watch the two soldiers at work. He was intrigued, but he still feared an attack and did not want to present the bandits with a nice target by bunching close to the two men digging.

Sweat pouring down their faces, the privates cleared the earth to reveal four drums side by side. One man stood up while the second bent down to lift the first drum. His hands reached round to the handles, he tugged upwards and suddenly there was a roar of sound and a flash of orange light. His body lifted, flipped backwards and crashed through the dried leaves of the atap wall of the hut. The other staggered in the blast, clutching his face, and fell full length on the ground where he lay screaming and writhing, blood pouring through his fingers.

Shocked, Edward rolled sideways to the ground and by the time he looked back, he saw Tallard running round the atap hut with Untam and two or three others. Edward leaped to his feet and joined them by the man who had fallen through the hut wall.

Tallard's large hand reached through the atap leaves to find the pulse in his neck where his head lolled sideways on to the dried leaves. After a moment he said, 'Not a flicker.'

Edward stared at the dead man on his back and the mess of blood and flesh in the centre of his chest where he had caught the full force of the booby trap under the drum.

'Leave him! He's dead,' shouted Tallard already stepping over to the second wounded man. 'Go fetch the medic!'

Edward turned to obey but the corporal medic was already running through the big tree trunks towards them. Together, they prepared a 'shell dressing', a large pad of gauze and cotton wool, and pressed it firmly over a huge gash in the man's face where his cheek was slashed to the bone. A flap of flesh hung down exposing his teeth from lips to eye.

'Poor sod,' said the medic, kneeling and taking over as Edward carefully held the tortured man's hands away from his face.

Tallard stood back grim-faced and remarked, 'Pieces of metal stacked on top of the bomb, to make shrapnel.'

Edward whipped round and stared, 'How d'you know?'

'That's how Ho Peng made them during the war.'

An appalling thought occurred to Edward, that Tallard had deliberately let the two privates take the risk of unearthing the drums. He said, 'You knew it was booby-trapped?'

'Don't be a fool!' Tallard retorted angrily and turned away before Edward could ask any more questions.

Dully, Edward supposed they were at the black edge of what people called civilisation, in the primeval jungle, at the working coal-face of death. He watched the medic at work, patching and binding the man's face. Inside, he seethed with the pointless loss of life and hurt, all for a few weapons.

The medic worked fast, dressing the man's face and left side where he had been lacerated with shrapnel and soon his screams faded to low moans. Ignoring Tallard, who was not really a regular officer at all, he spoke directly to Edward, and said, 'We'll have to carry him out, Sir. I've done my best but he can't see and he's in shock.'

Edward nodded. Aggressively, he added, 'And the dead man. We can't leave him here.' The medic glanced over to the body whose legs protruded from the atap basha behind.

Tallard was busy lifting the boxes of weapons out of the cache. He prised open the first and revealed a neatly stacked pile of Sten guns still in their factory grease-proof wrappings. Evenly, he said, 'It would be a terrible shame to leave these. Like these two were hurt for nothing.'

'What d'you suggest?' demanded Edward bluntly.

'Call in support,' suggested Tallard, knowing the other soldiers now looked to Edward for command. 'To help us carry out the wounded, and the weapons.'

Edward stared at him resentfully. If this was typical of what had to happen all over Malaya, it was going to be a long war. He wondered how many people outside the jungle knew it.

'All right,' he said eventually. 'I'll speak to the signaller.'

The relieving patrol found them in the enemy camp only two hours later with the good news that they were closer to the edge of the jungle than they thought. A lumber track cut into the jungle quite close and transport was waiting. Even so, the journey out was back-breaking. A vanguard laboriously cut a path through the twisting lianas and vines. Behind them, the soldiers took it in turns to carry the dead man, slung from a pole like an animal, because it was the only way to bring him out. The injured private followed, blinded with bandages. Drugged with

117

painkillers and hardly conscious, he staggered along between two men who guided his footsteps. Edward struggled along with his pack strapped on top of his own. The weapon drums were carried out by the relieving patrol and the dead man's kit was shared between the rest.

Only when Edward finally stepped out of the dark jungle on to a red laterite track and felt the blazing heat of the sun on his sweat-soaked shoulders did the unnerving feeling that he was being watched leave him.

He was delighted to see several trucks parked on the track with an ambulance which set off at once to the hospital with the dead man lying on one bunk, ignored, and the injured man on the other, tended by a nurse and two medics.

'The quick and the dead,' said Tallard without a flicker of emotion.

Before Edward could reply, he heard a familiar voice among the crowd by trucks, shouting, 'Fairfax! Where the hell have you been?'

'Your friend Colonel Bleasley,' Tallard said, grinning.

Between the soldiers making their way to the trucks, they saw Bleasley waving from a jeep. He was dressed in crisply-ironed and spotless jungle greens, and wore an especially wide-brimmed green jungle-hat. A driver sat stony-faced beside him, hands on the wheel.

'I'd better go and see him,' said Edward, knowing he was in trouble.

'I'll come too,' Sean Tallard said grimly. 'This was my patrol. If Bleasley's got any criticism, he'll have to make it to me.'

Bleasley eyed their filthy clothes, their sodden canvas pouches covered with bits of ferns and twigs, and the way they carried their carbines in the crook of their arms, with extreme distaste. When they got close to, he noticed neither of them had shaved.

Edward stood by the jeep and saluted, hoping to defuse the situation. Tallard did not salute. He did not care for the British Army parade ground.

Colonel Bleasley ignored him. He said, 'Splendid show!'

'What?' said Edward, thinking his tired mind was playing tricks.

'Finding these weapons. Jolly good show,' said Colonel Bleasley. His pale face was running with sweat. 'Every weapon found is one less to kill one of our chaps.'

Edward guessed at Bleasley's thinking and refused to play. He gestured at Sean Tallard and said, 'He found them. It was his patrol.'

'Well, what happened, Tallard?' Bleasley demanded with uncharacteristic enthusiasm. He was determined to make the most of coming all the way out to meet one of his officers straight out of the jungle. It gave him the excuse to be first back with the news.

Tallard told him, speaking in flat, unemotional tones which made it all sound very cut and dried. There was nothing of the heat, the sweat and fear of being ambushed, the torrential rain, the unnaturally deserted camp shrouded in rain mist, the sudden explosion of the booby-trapped cache and the final gruelling march out to the trucks following the two stricken soldiers, one ignominiously slung from a pole.

When Tallard had finished speaking, Bleasley said, 'Capital show. Pity about the two chaps. The medic just now said the wounded man will lose an eye, but capital about the weapons. One up to us, and nothing like going out with a bang, eh?' Edward had never heard Bleasley so cheerful.

Tallard did not like this fat, sweating, pink British officer, much less his tone. He folded his brawny arms over his sweat-drenched shirt and demanded, 'What d'you mean, "going out"?'

Bleasley looked up from the jeep in surprise and said, 'Haven't you heard? Of course not. Decision taken while you've been away. Ferret Force is disbanded. Finished.' He looked smug.

Edward was speechless with amazement. So that was why Bleasley had not bothered to make a fuss about his going on the patrol. He had scotched the whole idea. Tallard gazed malevolently at Colonel Bleasley and demanded in a loud voice, 'Then who the hell is going to go find these bandits?'

The soldiers loading gear on to the trucks cocked their ears. Everyone enjoyed a row between officers.

Colonel Bleasley said blandly, 'You chaps have done a jolly good job, but it's infantry work now. I gather some of you might be attached to various battalions to advise them on jungle work, in a thing they're going to call the "Civil Liaison Corps" but certainly not you, Fairfax.' He poked at Edward with his Malacca cane. 'I need you in the office.' He pretended not to notice Tallard's furious expression and waved his stick, like a Grand Duke addressing peasants. 'Still, look on the bright side, Tallard. Ad hoc units cobbled together like this never work in the long term.'

'It's the short term that I'm concerned with,' Tallard boomed back. 'While you're slotting everyone into neat little staff boxes, who's to stop the bandits shooting at planters like me?'

119

'Is that what really bothers you?' Colonel Bleasley asked, quick as a knife.

'I'll put it another way!' Tallard shouted at him, exasperated. 'If you don't go into the frigging jungle to look for the goddam communist bastards the shooting won't stop at all! Will it now?'

Bleasley leaned back in his seat and said smoothly, 'The army will do its job, and the police theirs, eh? That's the best way.' Bleasley did not blame Tallard. He was simply exhibiting his regrettable civilian prejudices and did not understand.

'Then we'll lose the war,' Tallard snapped and stamped off to find a jeep.

Colonel Bleasley was appalled. He said, 'That man is a defeatist, Fairfax. Best not let him go to Headquarters talking like that. I'll deal with the oral report and you can put something down on paper tomorrow. All right?' In fact, the arrangement suited him very well. The trip had turned out better than he hoped. He smiled briefly at Edward, then tapped his driver on the knee with his Malacca cane and ordered, 'Back to town, Driver. Chop, chop!'

Edward stood and watched the jeep accelerate away along the track, Colonel Bleasley's floppy jungle hat bobbing about as the vehicle bounced through pot-holes. He turned to find Tallard. He suddenly felt terribly in need of a drink.

The breeze, as they were driven back to town in another jeep, was glorious after the sweltering humidity of the jungle. A few moments later, Edward, who was sitting in the back, said to Tallard in the front, 'Bleasley doesn't think it's necessary for you to report to HQ this afternoon.'

To his surprise, instead of being angry, Tallard roared with laughter and said, 'Old bastard wants to do it himself, eh? Make it all sound like his idea in the first place, I don't doubt.'

Edward frowned, thinking the driver should not be hearing this, but Tallard twisted round in his seat and said, 'Well, he's welcome, Edward. He can say what he likes, but you and I know the patrol was not a success. Not a failure, mind, because we recovered some weapons, but not a success, and I'll tell you why? In war, in the end, you fight people, not things. And it won't matter how many weapons the army finds to boost its lists of statistics if they don't also think of a way to find the people who are using the weapons, and stop them supporting the communists.'

'You mean kill them?'

Again, Tallard surprised him by saying, 'Not necessarily. You can't kill everyone, and you can't kill ideas. Jesus, look at Eire and Palestine. The British Empire couldn't change the people's ideas there and got flung out. You have to change their minds, Edward. And we won't win here till they realise that.'

He twisted back and they continued in silence to the edge of Kuala Lumpur, when he announced in a loud voice, 'I'm just dying for a fuck. I think it must be all that sweating and hard work. What say we go find some tarts, Edward?'

Expressionless, the driver negotiated a junction up Cheras Road and waited with interest for Edward's answer.

Taken aback, Edward asked, 'At this time of day?'

'Best time. They'll be fresh as daisies,' Tallard grinned at Edward. 'Before they're worn out by all the drunken soldiers tonight.'

'Where then?'

'There are several places,' Tallard said airily. 'You can take your pick. Anywhere you like.'

Edward was certainly curious to see the red light district which he had heard talked about so often in the Mess. He reflected that since their carbines and equipment were being taken back in the truck, and since Colonel Bleasley intended to make an initial report, there was no rush to get back. He said, 'I'll come for a beer and take it from there.'

'And you can check out the ladies at the same time, right enough,' laughed Tallard.

They cruised down Birch Road and plunged among the hanging Chinese shop signs and crowded streets of Chinatown. Tallard ordered the driver to stop. They pulled up by an apothecary's shop.

'And don't wait!' he told the driver as they climbed out. Without a backward glance he led Edward across the street into the nearest place, called the Wild Orchid Hotel, pushed through the hanging bead curtain and marched straight to the bar at the end of the room.

'Dua bir Tiger!' he said to the plain young Malay girl behind the bar, and, when she lifted two bottles on to the bar, Tallard reached over, took them in his big hands, passed one to Edward and poured the other straight down his throat, groaning with delight.

Edward was parched and copied him without hesitation. He could never remember when a beer tasted so good. He set his bottle back on the bar, empty, and ordered two more, 'Tolong dua bir.'

To Tallard, he said, 'What are you going to do now, Sean?'

Tallard suspected Edward was asking about the demise of the

Ferret Force, so instead he declared, 'I'm going to take a room here, in this hotel, and then fuck the arse off one of those young ladies over there.' He pointed into the deep red shadows at the end of the bar where Edward noticed for the first time a group of Chinese and Malay girls sitting round a table. They were dressed in thin Chinese cheongsams and Malay sarongs, low-cut over their soft breasts and with long slits up the sides. They knew the two soldiers were looking at them and smiled with simulated coyness.

'You want one?' asked Tallard grinning at Edward. 'Sweat, blood and sex. I can't think of a better way of finishing a patrol.' His large hand closed round another bottle of Tiger beer.

'You're too kind,' said Edward sarcastically. Thinking of Diana he peered into the red gloom at the girls and observed, 'I don't think they'd look so attractive in the broad light of day.'

Tallard laughed, 'The lighting's part of the deal. You can't see the wrinkly bits on them, and they can't see the sweaty bits on you. It's quits both ways.'

'They'll certainly smell the sweaty bits on you tonight, after two days in the ulu,' said Edward.

'They'll have baths upstairs, to be sure,' said Tallard off-hand.

Two of the bar girls crossed the room and they appeared not to notice the reeking damp smell of the jungle. Edward slid out of the grasp of one, leaving Tallard to entertain them both while he used a phone behind the bar to call Gandra Singh at his usual café waiting place.

When he came back, Tallard had one arm round each girl and was saying, 'They're charming.' Roaring with laughter, he ordered more beer and hugged them tight. They seemed to enjoy his bulk, smiling encouragingly, and looked tiny beside him. The more suggestive he became, the more the girls liked it and the more Edward thought of making love to Diana. After their fourth beer, he wondered hazily what had happened to Gandra Singh.

Another girl came into the bar through an archway from the back of the hotel. She was wearing a blue silk cheongsam decorated with gold dragons curling round her hips and breasts and she had an excellent figure. Her black hair was drawn back from her face into a loose plait at her neck. She watched the soldiers at the bar for a moment and her pulse quickened. The fat one with the two girls was no good, but the other certainly looked interesting. In spite of his filthy jungle uniform, he was obviously an officer. And he had noticed her too.

Taking her time, she sauntered nearer the bar, chatting to a couple of girls on the way and watching him out of the corner of her eye, looking at her as she came. She stopped in front of him and smiled. Under the dirt, he was good-looking, fair, which she liked, as the Chinese all had black hair, and his face was lean with a hint of hardness in the set of his mouth and blue eyes. Standing, she was the same height as Edward sitting on his barstool. She put her hand softly on his knee and asked, 'What is your name?'

Edward blinked at the unexpected question but her slanting black eyes looked at him with such surprising candour he replied automatically, 'Edward, and yours?'

'Liya,' she said softly. She lifted her head very slightly at the girl behind the bar and said something rapidly in Malay. In the brighter light, Edward noticed she had flawless skin and was extremely pretty.

The bar girl slid another beer over the counter.

'This is for you,' said Liya, smiling. 'On the house.'

'Thank you,' said Edward, beginning to enjoy the game. He could not help thinking there was something familiar about her but she moved with such grace he put the idea out of his mind and asked, 'Are you in charge here.'

She laughed at the idea. There was much she wanted to do in her life, but she had never dreamed of managing a brothel and, still laughing, said so.

Embarrassed, Edward apologised.

She enjoyed his embarrassment, but she did not want to upset him. The game, as she wanted to play it, had a long way to run. She slipped her hand to his arm and reassured him. 'Lu-Lu Suzie would be very pleased to hear you say that,' she said, smiling.

'Who's she?'

'She runs this place. She is very large.' She tried to make herself look fat by holding her hands in front of her and sticking out her flat stomach, and then burst out laughing. 'Like this. But she is not here tonight.'

'You speak good English,' said Edward laughing too and beginning to relax.

'Getting on well, there?' shouted Tallard from the other end of the bar. 'And a right cracker if I may say so too!' They looked like a pair of schoolchildren eating forbidden sweets together.

Outside in the street, they heard a car hooting.

Tallard shouted again, 'Your taxi, Sir!' And then in a frightful stage whisper he added, 'Or have you changed your mind?'

Liya knew perfectly well what the big man was insinuating and smiled. Edward slid off his bar stool and said, 'I'm sorry, Liya. Sean's right. I have to go.'

Her smile faded and she watched him walk unsteadily to the bead curtain, feeling curiously let down.

Edward shoved through the beads telling himself it was absurd apologising to a girl in a brothel, however upset she might have seemed to see him go.

Outside, he was surprised to find it was already dark. All along the street, garish neon signs hanging over the shop houses cast a sickly light and Gandra Singh was standing by his taxi, one hairy arm through the open window hooting the horn. He took in Edward's filthy clothes and a glimpse of Liya's blue dress as she parted the beads to watch them from the doorway and shook his head. Expressively silent for a change, he showed Edward into the old Austin. Personally, he always liked to bathe before visiting places like the Wild Orchid, but although he had served for thirty years with the British Army he was for ever being amazed by the white man.

As the taxi moved slowly between the white shirts of the people crowding China town, Edward apologised for his clothes.

'I am expecting that you are being very busy, Sahib,' replied Gandra Singh tactfully.

'You'll see more and more of this,' said Edward shortly. 'For years maybe.' Whatever Bleasley thought.

'More of what, Sahib?' asked Gandra Singh, puzzled. There had always been hotels like that.

'Soldiers in uniform, from the jungle,' replied Edward but he was already thinking of Diana. The last hour in the brothel, the beer and Liya's suggestive innocence had fired him up to take her straight to bed. He said, 'Step on it, Gandra Singh.'

'Yes indeed, Sahib. I'm sure the Memsahib will want to see you very much.' After religion and work, Gandra Singh reflected, there were women. He wriggled his toes in his battered shoes and stroked his beard.

Edward walked into the house, threw his jungle hat on the hall table and frowned, hearing voices. He went through to the sitting-room and to his annoyance he found Diana drinking Martini with her brother, Roger Haike. She looked up and exclaimed, 'Edward! Darling!'

In her relief that he was back in one piece, she jumped up to give him a hug. Then she stopped theatrically, telling her brother, 'I long to give him a real hug, but look at the state he's in!' Although she had been terrified by the rumours she had heard while the patrol had been out, she wanted to let Roger know she was fiercely proud of what Edward had been doing and loved him for it.

'Righto!' said Roger taking her literally. He sprang out of his chair, marched over to Edward and shook his hand before she could move. When Diana finally kissed Edward, she felt second-class and his obvious irritation upset her even more.

She determined not to let the silly little incident get her down and said brightly, 'Edward, darling, isn't it grand to see Roger? He's just been released from the hospital. He was actually on that train when it was ambushed.'

Roger sat down again on his armchair and elegantly crossed his legs. He was a neat figure, in his pale khaki tropical uniform, laundered and clean, with his dark hair smoothed back from his forehead and his clipped black moustache. Apart from a few cuts on his face he seemed untouched. He peered for a moment at Edward's torn jungle greens before saying, 'I'm sure you'd like to hear my story, eh?'

Edward said nothing, so Roger added, as if the place was his own, 'Perhaps after you've changed, old man? Plenty of time. Diana's kindly offered me a bed for a few days. Till they've finished de-briefing me on the train thing.'

Edward's spirits sank. His plans for an evening alone with Diana, to enjoy Lao Song's excellent cooking, several whiskies and a night in the sack, were in shreds. He left them without a word. On the way to his room, he shouted down the kitchen corridor for Hassan to bring him a beer.

He stripped off and angrily flung his filthy things in the corner. Sharing Diana with Roger was the very last thing he had expected, or wanted. Resentfully, he felt very much a weary soldier home after a hard, frightening and bloody patrol, and he wanted his wife to himself. Hassan appeared silently with his beer, condensation jewelled on the glass, and slipped out as quickly again, puzzled and upset that the Tuan was angry when he had only just come home.

Edward stood under the shower and let the torrent of warm water wash away his irritation. Images of the previous twenty-four hours filtered through his mind but they always came back to the slender and beautiful Chinese girl in the bar, tantalising him with thoughts

125

of Diana out of reach in Roger's grasp.

He put on a white shirt and cotton duck trousers and reluctantly rejoined them for dinner. Taking instructions from Diana through Hassan as usual, Lao Song produced an excellent dinner but Roger dominated the conversation with every detail of his experience on the train. For the third time, he said, 'As soon as the carriage stopped moving, I clambered out and rallied the men together. Soldiers need that kind of leadership, you know.'

'How very brave!' said Diana vaguely, suppressing a yawn.

At the end of dinner, Hassan served coffee, wondering why the Tuans were so stilted and silent when they were all in the same family. They had all been in danger and all survived. Surely, he thought, there was reason to celebrate.

Edward said forcefully, 'You will be exhausted, Roger, after so much.'

'No, no, really,' Roger began but Edward had had enough. He moved round behind him, winking outrageously at Diana who smiled. Edward had recovered his sense of humour.

'I'd love to hear the story again, Roger,' Edward lied charmingly. 'But it's late now. What about tomorrow?'

'Really?' said Roger and allowed Edward to guide him politely but firmly to his guest room on the other side of the house.

In their bedroom moments later, Edward threw himself backwards on to his bed and said in mock horror, 'You said he could stay for three whole days?' Diana stood by her dressing-table, slipping her dress from her shoulders, tall, very beautiful and desirable and he felt his sex stirring.

Diana laughed as she walked into the bathroom and called back through the open door, 'I think he's so amazed at having survived, he can't stop talking about it.'

Edward sat up, kicked off his shoes and socks and took off his shirt.

In the bathroom, Diana flung her underclothes in a wicker basket and pulled on her flimsy silk night-dress. She brushed out her hair in the bathroom mirror, held it bunched in one hand as she quickly cleaned her teeth, and walked over to Edward on the bed saying, 'I'm exhausted. I don't know what I've done all day, but I feel tired out.' With that, she slipped past him on her knees as he was taking off his trousers, slid under the single sheet and curled up on her side to go to sleep.

Naked and aroused, Edward stared at her long shape hidden

under the white cotton in amazement.

Diana added, 'Put out the light darling, when you've finished in the bathroom.'

Edward's jaw set. With great deliberation, he slipped under the sheet after her and wriggled up to her back. He kissed her shoulder lightly, pushing the thin silk strap down her arm a little, and said, 'Don't I even get a kiss goodnight?'

Diana paused a moment, enjoying his attentions but feeling a helplessness inside her, which had refused to go away since she lost her baby and which always seemed to inhibit her now with Edward, however much she wanted it not to. She turned on her back, hoping he was too tired and even a little too drunk, but as she faced him she felt him hard on her thigh. She said hopefully. 'Aren't you tired, after that patrol?'

'No, darling,' he said, tracing kisses over her neck to her lips. She did not move, so he lifted her arm round his shoulders and she held him, trying to suppress the fright in her stomach.

He went to work on her with lustful determination. His hands explored her, feeling her thighs and breasts. He pulled apart the bows of her night-dress, moving her with him, stripping her, pinching and biting her nipples and finally mounting her. He moved on her slowly and relentlessly, in reaction to the extremes he had experienced in the jungle, fired by the drink in him, by the images of raw sex in the hotel in Chinatown, by the memory of the slim beauty of the Chinese girl, and by the voluptuous reality of Diana's pale flesh under his sweating body. He drove her relentlessly until she felt swamped by his endless domination and cried out for him to stop, at the same time desperate for his love and commitment, wanting to be enveloped and to be protected by him from the cloying jungles of Malaya beyond the diaphanous white net over their bed.

Later, Hassan reported to the impassive cook that the Tuans were happy again. He did not think he was prying to listen to the soft rhythm of the bed springs from the Dragon Flower bushes in the garden. More, he said, a case of being an acolyte in harmony with the forces of his life.

'So gentle,' he sighed wistfully, stroking his bare brown arms.

'Like a dream?' asked Lao Song cryptically, uncharacteristically, his eyes like pools of jet in his wrinkled yellow skin.

Chapter 8

IN THE HEAT OF THE AFTERNOON

Lao Tang heard a distant rumble, like thunder, beyond the clatter of insects and screeching birds. He looked up at the canopy but there was no indication of bad weather. Long darts of early morning sun cut through the shadows from the trees above and splashed brightly on the crinkled, curving leaves and palms.

He squatted on the ground, half hidden by ferns, eating a mess of vegetables and rice from a British Army mess tin. As he ate, he stared at a stream, mesmerised by the yellow water tumbling over rocks and tugging at palm leaves hanging in the surface. He longed to feel the heat of the sun on his neck. Mao Tse-tung's troops were in the open, marching through China on Peking, smashing the Kuomintang, and Lao Tang felt an extraordinary delight in thinking of the bond between the revolutionary armies in mainland China, and himself, a poor exile sitting on a log in the Malayan jungle.

He asked, 'Comrade Ho Peng? When are we planning to leave the jungle and seize the Liberated Areas?'

Ho Peng picked his teeth with a sliver of wood without answering. He stared bleakly at the stream. Lao Tang was too thoughtful, and too observant, but he was dedicated. So far. He threw the sliver of wood into the stream where he watched it carried off swiftly on the surface, and said, 'When the Central Committee orders us to do so.' The Party was supreme.

The jungle floor was broken and rocky, some way from the big camp which they had not used for three months since the British patrol found it after the train ambush. The majority of British soldiers and police were still not competent in the jungle but they had been finding big camps and had had some success surprising

129

large bodies of MPABA moving on tracks. In his command, Ho Peng had prevented this by ordering the MPABA regiments in the jungles around Kuala Lumpur – the 1st, 2nd, 5th and 6th Regiments – to split into smaller groups of companies and platoons of forty or so and to keep on the move which made it difficult for the British patrols to find them. He stood up and looked at his personal bodyguard, or Killer Squad as he preferred to call them now, dotted round among the rocks and ferns bordering the stream, eating their food. He always ate faster than everyone and wanted to go. 'Time to work again, Comrade Li Chi-Chen,' said Ho Peng looking at a young Chinese wearing steel-rimmed spectacles sitting by Lao Tang.

'Where to, Comrade Ho Peng?' asked Li Chi-Chen. The red star on his cap was clean, his pale khaki uniform was unblemished by rips and patches, and both marked him out as a recent arrival. He had been recruited after the train ambush three months before and been in the jungle only a month. He wanted to finish his food in peace.

'To caves, up this stream,' answered Ho Peng, lifting the rectangular pack they all carried on to his shoulders. 'We have another place to search.'

'Not more digging?' said Li Chi-Chen before he could help himself.

They heard the thunder again, closer this time, somewhere over the ridge, shaking the ground and rattling the leaves in the trees, but no-one paid any attention.

Ho Peng sneered, 'Tired of the jungle, Comrade?'

'No, Comrade,' Li Chi-Chen said without the conviction he knew he was expected to show. 'I want to fight but—'

'But what, Li Chi-Chen?' hissed Ho Peng, anger boiling inside him. These young recruits had none of the resilience he had needed to survive the Japanese.

Lao Tang edged away from Li Chi-Chen. He knew what was going to happen.

'But what?' screamed Ho Peng, his voice echoing through the trees. The noise did not matter. There were no British patrols in the area. Down near the squatters' village, Liya had told him of considerable troop movements on the roads in recent days but the British had still not learned how to move silently enough to catch him unawares.

Besides, he wanted all his men to hear and understand he tolerated no slackening of discipline. They would not survive in the jungle unless they followed certain cardinal rules, Party rules and soldiers' rules, implicitly.

He shouted, 'Li Chi-Chen, you are a Reserve soldier, but you are not working hard or making progress. You will not qualify for your Circular of Approval, like Comrade Lao Tang here. For example, have you learned our Comrade General-Secretary's Ten Points of good conduct for jungle operations?'

'Yes, Comrade,' said Li Chi-Chen quickly but his eyes behind his glasses refused to meet Ho Peng's furious look.

'Then what is Point Number Three?'

' "Return borrowed articles",' quoted Li Chi-Chen miserably. He had forgotten to return an oil bottle to Lao Tang. He had not meant to cause trouble. He had joined the MPABA from the Min Yuen and come into the jungle to kill the Malay Police whom he hated, but they had done nothing but search old wartime camps and hiding places and he did not understand.

Ho Peng hit him on the side of the head with the butt of his carbine, knocking him sideways to the ground and shouted, 'Well, why did you—'

Thunder drowned his words, bursting nearer still, just over the ridge above them, and they all distinctly heard the whining metal screams before the explosions.

'Artillery!' shouted Ho Peng.

Li Chi-Chen was on his hands and knees looking for his spectacles, blood dripping from the blow on his cheek, his fear of Ho Peng abruptly transcended at being blown apart by enemy shells.

'Run!' shouted a voice.

'Stand still!' Ho Peng bellowed.

In spite of themselves they obeyed, and stood terrified among the bushes and ferns by the rocks near the stream. Coolly Ho Peng waited, scowling round at everyone, daring them to disobey him. He wanted to listen to one more salvo before deciding what was happening and what they should do.

Lao Tang's body itched to run. He crouched down with his carbine, certain he was going to die. Li Chi-Chen was on his hands and knees desperately scrabbling among the rocks and ferns to find his glasses, knowing he must not leave without them. Lao Tang could not risk helping with Ho Peng standing over them and he wondered detachedly if Li Chi-Chen would find them before the shells hit him.

Another salvo screamed in and exploded, nearer, making the

ground tremble and the stream water ripple. Lao Tang imagined some ghastly jungle creature of apocalyptic proportions taking great crashing footsteps through the trees towards them.

'A creeping barrage, up the stream bed,' said Ho Peng half to himself.

'What do we do?' asked Lao Tang, aching to run, to hide, to do anything but wait.

'To the caves,' replied Ho Peng grimly and set off upstream. Lao Tang tucked in swiftly behind him, followed by all the others. Ho Peng ran. His short wiry shape seemed to flow like water through the dense undergrowth, ducking under thick branches, sliding around spiky palms and stepping lightly from rock to rock. Lao Tang was soon gasping to keep up. Behind him, the rest crashed along through the bushes, careless of the noise they made as the barrage marched relentlessly up the stream bed on their heels.

Another roar shook the forest. This time, they could all make out the individual shells in the salvo. The barrage was closing on them.

Ho Peng stopped to let them catch up and shouted back, 'The British don't really know where we are! Their soldiers aren't good enough to come into the jungle to find us so they're bombarding features off the map in the off-chance of catching us out.'

A thunderous roar exploded closer than ever and shrapnel cut through the foliage high above them.

'How much further, to the caves?' Lao Tang gasped, sweat pouring off him. He was beyond caring why the British were wasting shells, just that they seemed close to killing him.

Ho Peng ran on. The barrage was moving faster than he had estimated.

When Lao Tang heard the next salvo shrieking over the canopy towards him, he flung himself into the stream and cowered against the bank. The shells ripped his universe apart, shaking his body with each explosion, deafening him and blinding him with dirt whirling in the air. The blasts blew the jungle apart, ripped great holes in the canopy, and filled the air with a terrifying rush of shattered foliage and deadly splinters of trees.

Then the storm suddenly passed, churning up the valley ahead, like a manic giant, ripping out whole trees as it went.

Silence returned and Lao Tang raised his head. The undergrowth had been cleared all around for a hundred yards or more, tree stumps stood up from the ground shredded like chewed sticks, and the sun shone through holes in the canopy from a clear blue sky, warming his back just as he had wanted.

A roar of airplane engines above the canopy made him duck again instinctively and he heard the pointless rattle of machine-guns strafing the jungle several hundred yards away. More wasted British effort. The members of Ho Peng's Killer Squad dazed but alive, grinning and chattering with relief, were standing up and shaking broken foliage off their uniforms. He wondered if Li Chi-Chen had survived.

As Roger Haike watched the two Spitfires fly over he said, 'That'll do the trick. Wonderful machine, the old "Spit".'

Edward looked at him in disgust. They were standing outside the sandbagged sangars and barbed wire of a newly constructed army camp which stood in a wide clearing hacked out of the jungle on all sides. A sign, nailed on the wriggly tin main gate, read, 'CAMP RIDEAU' and underneath someone had scribbled, '6,590 miles from Bury St Edmunds'.

Roger Haike's artillerymen had laid a line of 25-pounders for firing on the open ground between the camp and the jungle. Piles of shining empty brass shell cases had built up behind each gun in the line, some still smoking, and sweat poured down the gunners' faces as they worked in the harsh sun. Roger Haike observed them critically, neatly dressed in his jungle greens, a clean green floppy hat shading his eyes and one booted foot elegantly poised on an ammunition box. He said in an authoritative tone, 'We'll soon sort out these bloody bandits now Sir Henry Gurney's the new High Commissioner. Took them long enough to get him, but with a bit of leadership from the top, and some artillery up the arse from the bottom, we'll soon show the Chinks who's boss. Drive the bloody bandits out of the jungle like pheasants on to the guns. That's the job.'

Edward snorted his disagreement, 'Rubbish! This "Operation Tasek" is a total waste of time. You can't surround a huge patch of jungle with a ring of soldiers, shell bits of it or get the Royal Air Force to bomb it, and then expect the enemy to come running out in terror!'

'Why not?' asked Roger in genuine surprise. He flicked his hand at a mosquito.

'Jungle sweeps don't work any better than urban ones. This operation is like "Operation Shark" in Palestine, when the Staff got 6 Airborne Division to surround the whole of Tel Aviv and search every house on the off-chance of finding something. Doing that in a city is almost as ludicrous as searching a whole area of jungle.'

'As I recall, you didn't even take part in the Tel Aviv search,' said Roger smugly. He shouted an order and the guns fired another deafening salvo. The empty brass cases shot out of the smoking breaches and were tossed on top of the piles behind each gun.

'True,' Edward admitted after a moment. 'I was doing something else, in Jerusalem.'

'Chasing the girls, I expect,' suggested Roger.

Edward snapped, 'I wasn't chasing girls. I was doing an undercover job.' For three weeks, he had hidden in a derelict building, with snow on the ground outside, waiting to catch a terrorist.

Roger grunted and said, 'I hope you don't behave like that here. Remember, you're married now.'

Edward took a deep breath and said, 'What I do anywhere, Roger, is none of your bloody business.'

'It certainly is if it's to do with my sister,' Roger replied pompously, 'Someone's got to look after her now she's pregnant again.'

'Meaning?'

'Well you didn't make a very good job of the first time. Never should have taken her out to see that Irish chap Tallard.'

'Typical of you to be wise after the event,' Edward said sarcastically. He supposed Diana had to tell her brother something of what happened, but she knew what he was like, how he loved to interfere, and Edward resented her confiding in him at all.

Roger, impervious to innuendo, said, 'I've warned her to take the greatest care this time.'

Edward took a deep breath. 'What exactly have you been saying to Diana, Roger, old chap?'

'No stretching up, no lifting, lots of rest and no intercourse. That's the ticket!' Roger stated, and signalled another salvo.

Edward stared at his brother-in-law in amazement as the guns fired more high explosive over the green trees and wondered if there was any truth in what he was saying. Diana had indeed become very cautious since finding she was pregnant again, resting and refusing to make love, which, in the light of her miscarriage he understood, even though it was frustrating. She saw the garrison doctor regularly, but the idea that she was taking advice from Roger was infuriating. He exploded, 'You've got a bloody neck!'

'Not at all! Can't risk losing another baby like that. She nearly died!'

Edward supposed Roger thought he was doing his sister, though certainly not his brother-in-law, a favour by meddling. He said, 'All done for the best possible motives, eh, Roger?'

'Glad you see it that way, old chap.'

'Just as well the army employs you firing shells into a target as big as the Malayan jungle,' Edward replied.

Roger Haike frowned. Edward's frivolous reaction was disappointing, though not unexpected. He disliked Edward's athletic spontaneity and could never understand what Diana saw in him. Speaking slowly and distinctly, as if he were addressing a small child, he said, 'I'm firing at the bandits, Edward. At Ho Peng, to be precise.'

Edward snapped, 'We don't even know Ho Peng is out there. Remember, Roger, I work in Intelligence now.'

'Of course he's out there,' retorted Roger crossly. He had little time for Intelligence officers.

'But no-one knows in which little part, do they?' said Edward, angry again. He did not expect Roger Haike, with his unthinking addiction to good form, to criticise what his superiors had ordained, but it was the very vagueness of 'Operation Tasek' which annoyed Edward. Of course Colonel Bleasley thought the operation an excellent idea, and had ordered him to visit Camp Rideau to discuss intelligence aspects of the operation with the infantry Company Commander. However the operation was so prophylactic there was nothing much to say. The infantry platoons were deployed in stop groups along the jungle edge waiting in ambush in the vague hope that the communist bandits would be driven out by Roger's guns or the bombing.

Before the operation Edward had talked to Angus at length and was convinced that the only way to catch Ho Peng was through specific information. He himself harboured a secret ambition to find and control a source, perhaps among the Min Yuen, or even one of the MPABA jungle bandits. To Roger however, he merely said, 'You've never even been into the jungle.'

'But I have,' replied Roger smugly brushing his neat black moustache with his finger. 'When my train was ambushed.'

'You didn't exactly break sweat under the canopy, as I recall. All you did was walk down the track for help, and that was three months ago.' Something about Roger's self-satisfied expression made him add, 'Anyhow, what's this about "my" train?'

Roger was delighted to explain, 'As you're my brother-in-law, you may like to know that I've been put up for a medal.'

Edward was flabbergasted. He hardly thought walking along the railway line to raise the alarm was worthy of an award, but if someone thought it was, then it was extraordinarily bad form that Roger should know about it, and worse still that he should have the gall to talk about it. He gasped, 'What on earth for?'

Diffidently Roger quoted, as if he had somehow been able to read his own citation, 'For rallying the soldiers and organising resistance to the attackers.'

Edward gaped stupidly. Roger, delighted with his reaction to the news, glanced at his watch and said, 'Excuse me, Fairfax. More important things to do than waffle with you. Got to keep the creeping barrage going, you know. Drive these bandits on to the stop groups.' He turned and walked over to his gunners.

Furious, and hot, Edward watched Roger shouting orders. The gunners moved like marionettes through their age-old sequence of fire drill. Roger, he guessed, had written his own flattering patrol report about the train ambush, thereby providing the glowing prose for his citation. He hoped Colonel Bleasley's self-congratulatory report of the follow-up Edward had done with Sean Tallard had not contributed.

Edward's irritation faded a little in the roar of the guns. There was something hugely satisfying about the smell of cordite, the sight and explosive power of a gun barrage.

His jeep was parked by the wriggly tin camp gates and Edward walked back wondering what to do next. There was nothing more to say to the Company Commander or to Roger Haike.

He climbed into the jeep and sat down, undecided. He wanted to see Sean Tallard to ask him if any of the Chinese he knew might be developed as a source, but a new regulation restricted him. The communist terrorists had ambushed so many roads that HQ had banned all the security forces from driving about on their own outside the towns without an armoured car escort. The infantry had provided his escort out to Camp Rideau but would not go back to Kuala Lumpur till the evening.

The guns fired another salvo.

Surely, the communists would hardly dare ambush the roads during 'Operation Tasek', when there were British soldiers deployed everywhere? He chewed over the risks of ambush against being caught without an escort. The Black Circle estate was frustratingly close, maybe half an hour, and much of it on good tarmac road.

The guns fired again and Edward made up his mind. Hang the consequences. Sean Tallard knew Ho Peng and his methods better than anyone. The opportunity to find a source was too good to miss. Colonel Bleasley would be especially pleased to have an army source. He enjoyed stealing a march on the police. Edward could always use his independence as an Intelligence liaison officer to excuse driving about on his own.

Roger Haike looked up when he heard Edward's jeep start up and frowned as he watched him drive across the clearing on the road back to town.

Edward pushed the jeep as fast as he could on the straights and gripped the wheel hard as he sped round the bends, trying to read the road ahead for ambush positions. He peered into the dark shadows of the jungle, at the ditches and clumps of lallang grass in the open padi fields, and he glanced up rows of rubber trees as he shot past the rubber plantations, trying to rationalise the same fearful tightening in his guts that he had felt when they tracked Ho Peng after the train ambush.

He passed a few tappers strolling back home after a day's work, but the road was deserted of traffic. He reached the Black Circle estate without incident and pulled up in front of the wood office building in the yard. He jumped out of the jeep and walked over the verandah into the offices. He found Sean Tallard's foreman, Hou Ming, at his desk, thin, austere and distant in white shirt and slacks.

'Mister Tallard is not here,' said Hou Ming looking up from the papers on his desk. His black eyes were very slanted and hooded in his thin face which made it impossible to tell what he was thinking.

'Where is he, Mr Hou Ming?' Edward asked.

The foreman remained seated. He said nothing to Edward, but called out something in Chinese and then made Edward wait, standing in front of his desk.

Hou Ming sat and stared at Edward shifting about with typical Western impatience, at his sweat-stained British Army shirt and shorts, at the green canvas belt and pistol, at his long cotton socks and brown shoes. He looked forward to the day when Malaya would no longer be occupied by foreign soldiers.

The delay niggled. Edward felt he was being made to wait on purpose. He assumed the foreman had been shouting at someone outside to find the answer to his question about Tallard, but nothing happened and the man's silence was unnerving, almost aggressive. For a few moments Edward resisted the temptation to repeat his question and give Hou Ming the satisfaction of telling him to wait. He was on the point of opening his mouth to ask again when they heard steps on the wood verandah outside.

A Chinese tapper in filthy grey clothes appeared in the doorway and a rapid conversation ensued in Chinese at the end of which both men laughed, looking at Edward.

'Well?' Edward snapped crossly, wishing he understood some Chinese.

Hou Ming switched to English and said simply, 'He's in town.'

'In the armoured truck?'

Hou Ming dipped his head.

'When's he due back?'

Hou Ming shook his head slowly and said, 'He never says when exactly nowadays, but not I think, tonight.'

He said something briefly in Chinese to the tapper and they both laughed again. Hou Ming's smooth face hardly creased but the tapper threw back his head and his laughter was suggestive in a way which transcended language.

'Thanks,' said Edward briefly, for nothing, and marched out. The quick chatter of Chinese and more laughter as he stepped off the verandah into the hot sun made up his mind. Somehow, he must learn some Chinese.

Hating Hou Ming's condescending attitude, he tried to reconcile his instinctive dislike of the man with Tallard telling him how brave and faithful he had been during the Japanese occupation. Or, maybe Hou Ming had been lying about Tallard being in town, and they had really been laughing at him? Edward decided to go up to the house and see for himself.

He drove up the hill, parked and ran up the steps. The front door was open, so he walked in and called out, 'Anyone around?'

'Edward?' Marsha Tallard's voice floated from somewhere at the back of the house. 'Just me. Come on in, honey.'

Edward walked briskly through the hall and found Marsha on the verandah at the back of the house. She was stretched out full length on a bamboo lounger, wearing a colourful silk sarong and reading a book. A long iced drink topped with slices of orange stood on a table. 'A Whisky Cooler', said Marsha following his eyes. 'Like one?'

Edward nodded, 'I'm gasping for a drink.'

She stood up, swinging her long legs off the lounger and the sarong slipped to reveal shadows of her thighs. She quickly tucked it back around her slender waist and, before he realised it, she stepped up to him and gave him a kiss of welcome. With one hand still lightly on his arm, she asked, 'You look as if you've had a rough day?'

'Frustrating,' Edward admitted, pulling a face.

She pointed at the revolver holster on his belt and smiled, 'You want to relax and put that thing down somewhere?'

'Good idea.'

'Or are you going to just rush in and out?' she asked, gently forcing his commitment.

'Certainly not,' Edward assured her. 'I've had enough of the army for today.'

'Hang 'em all, what?' Marsha mimicked the British accent. Her blue eyes studied Edward's face for his reaction, and she was delighted to see his smile broaden.

Barefoot, she walked ahead of him to the drawing-room to the drinks cabinet and he watched her firm boyish hips swaying under the sarong, pulling the thin material back and forth at her narrow waist.

'You go and sit down outside when you've got rid of that three-eight,' she said. 'I won't be a moment with these drinks. We don't see any company out here and it's a pleasure to mix drinks for someone else for a change.'

When she joined him a couple of minutes later he was lying on another lounger, beginning to relax.

'God, it's hot today,' he said.

'Humidity's terrible,' she agreed. 'Going to be a storm.' She handed him a tall iced glass. 'This Whisky Cooler will sort you out.'

Edward gulped the long soda drink. 'It's whisky and soda,' he said admiringly, 'but there's something else in it?'

'Orange bitters,' she said.

'And a real kick!'

'Yeah, plenty of Scotch. I thought you needed that,' she smiled and lay down on her lounger. 'I'm giving away all my secrets. I worked in a cocktail bar once, in New York. I could mix you some real fire-balls!'

He laughed, 'If they're as good as this, I'll hold to you that.'

'It'd be a pleasure, honey.' She emphasised her soft American drawl and looked at him over the top of her glass, her blue eyes sparkling in the most suggestive and theatrical way. He held her gaze, enjoying the game.

Swiftly she changed tack and asked, 'Can you tell me, Edward, what all the goddam noise is about? They've been firing shells over the jungle all day. What in hell's name is the British Army trying to do? Flatten all the trees in Malaya?'

Edward laughed out loud. He told her about 'Operation Tasek' and Roger's 25-pounders.

'You British are nuts!' said Marsha genuinely surprised. 'I thought the army would have learned all there was to know about jungle fighting after beating the Japanese in Burma in the last war?'

Edward snorted cynically, 'They did. Now we've forgotten it. Like we always do. We'll have to learn it all over again.'

'Or lose?'

Edward nodded, 'Correct.'

'Well, you tell them from me to cut the artillery in future,' said Marsha with feeling. 'Gives me a goddam headache.'

She shifted on to her side on her lounger, to show the full length of her body, one leg long, smooth and bare, the other drawn up to the knee, curving her hips, and she leaned forward on one elbow to drink her whisky cocktail, enjoying Edward's surreptitious glance inside her sarong. She wriggled her toes and said, 'So why did you come over here?'

'To see Sean,' said Edward quickly without thinking and then realised she had asked the question on purpose to catch him out.

When she said, 'You disappoint me,' pouting theatrically, he laughed and added, 'Of course, Marsha, I was delighted to find you here instead!'

'Well, sod him,' she said suddenly, slugging down most of her drink. 'The bastard has gone off for a couple of days leaving me here on my own.'

Edward hesitated to get involved, but the drink and heat of the afternoon made him careless and he asked, 'What's he doing?'

'What d'you think, honey?' she said and this time the look in her blue eyes spoke of pure sex. 'He gives me some shit about giving you guys advice for jungle training, but I know he's up to no good in town. Probably spending some of the money he got for finding all those submachine-guns with you.' She stood up in a huff and once again, Edward could not help seeing flashes of her thighs and breasts, but he asked in surprise, 'What money?'

She looked down at him wondering if he was being deliberately slow and said, 'The reward. You know, the authorities are giving reward money for guns, grenades and so on?'

'Yes,' said Edward feeling his amazement grow in anticipation of what she was going to say. 'But that's supposed to be for communists' weapons.'

'Well, they were, weren't they? In a manner of speaking,' she said cynically. 'I think he said the reward money was $50-Malay for a machine-gun and $1 for every bullet. There were twenty Sten guns and somewhere around 5,000 rounds and he was cross they only paid him $5,000 for the lot.' She shrugged, dismissing the subject, and walked back into the house. At the door, she looked over her shoulder and said, 'I fancy another drink. What say I mix you a real cocktail?'

'Yes, of course,' said Edward and leaped to his feet to follow her into the drawing-room. He could not believe Tallard was so mercenary as to insist on reward money.

'Yeah,' she said, when he caught up with her standing at the drinks table. 'He'd kill for cash. Then he drives into town for the tarts.'

'But what about you,' said Edward lamely.

'He seems to have a real short attention span.' She shrugged again and gave a little smile, looking vulnerable.

The 'Black Circle' was no place to leave a woman on her own, on the edge of the jungle, even if she was competent with guns. He said, 'I'm sorry.'

'Don't be.' She caught his sympathetic look and smiled again. She liked his expectation of honesty. It made him vulnerable, like her. She said, 'You just watch what I'm mixing you here.'

'What's it called?'

'Monkey Gland cocktail.'

'You serious?'

She laughed out loud at the expression on his face. 'Not real monkeys, you fool. Just plenty of gin, orange juice and absinthe. All on the rocks.'

'Fine by me,' he said. He admired her slim figure as she mixed the ice and alcohol into the shaker. If she was prepared to dismiss her husband's selfishness without a second's thought, then so was he.

She returned his smile as she rattled the shaker, smashing the ice inside. Then she strained the drink into two wine glasses, slipped a sliver of orange peel in each glass and came over to him in the middle of the room.

141

'Try this, honey,' she said. 'Blow your socks off.'

He sipped his drink, watching her sip hers. It was fiery and delicious. To his surprise, she continued to drink without stopping, signalling to him with her eyes to copy her, smiling at him as she tilted her head back. As he drank, he watched her pale throat pulsing as she swallowed.

She finished first, gasping and laughing, and grabbed his glass as he drained the last drop, putting both on the table.

'What d'you think, honey?' she asked, standing close to him and looking into his eyes for his reaction. Her cheeks were flushed with alcohol, her eyes sparkled, and he could smell the scent of her warm body.

'Dynamite,' he said, catching his breath from the searing alcohol. Her blue eyes suddenly became serious and he felt like a man with vertigo on the edge of a great precipice, irrevocably drawn yet knowing the fatal consequences. 'What was the secret ingredient this time?'

'Tell you later, honey,' she said huskily, without moving, her eyes on his. She stood imperceptibly closer, her arms loose at her sides, offering herself without a word, sure she would eventually win, but not sure if this was the right time or even the right day.

He put his hands on her arms, as if to steady himself after the cocktail, but his eyes were ice-blue with intent and he bent to kiss her, unsure of her but determined. She stood quite still for a moment, relishing his lips softly on hers, lifting her head to meet him. Then her breathing quickened with the first thrill of the kiss, feeling him pressing towards her, demanding and strong and she slipped her arms around his neck in total submission.

The movement released him, as the heat, the frustration, anger and alcohol had primed him. His hands pulled her hard towards him, enveloping her, exploring the warm curves of her back and the mounds of her bottom under her thin silk sarong and then, increasingly frantic, he began to pull the folds apart and slid his fingers on to her bare flesh. She matched his frenzy, holding his head as they kissed, mashing her lips to his, pulling him down to the floor, then tearing at his clothes, helping him undress as they rolled on the carpet between the two armchairs.

She was as desperate as he, as ready, and she arched at him as he thrust into her, rutting and grunting like animals, sweating and gasping in their lust, until, quickly, they were spent in a torrent of shouts and thrashing, sweating limbs and lay stilled.

'You're a lump,' she said after a moment, caressing his cheek.

He laughed down at her. Her face and chest were flushed and sweat ran between her breasts. He rolled off her body and bent forward to kiss a nipple. She let him tease her, one arm loose above her head, the other stroking his back with her fingertips and exciting him again with her abandon. Then she wriggled out away from him, saying throatily, 'We don't see each other too often, honey, so let's go somewhere more comfortable.'

An hour later, the light went, clouds blackened the sky and the day finally burst about their heads. An ominous rush of torrential tropical rain swept over the jungle and on to the house, beating over the corrugated iron roof and cascading in a solid wall past the window of her bedroom, blotting everything from view.

'You can't leave now,' Marsha whispered as Edward sat up on her bed wishing he had put up the jeep canopy.

She looked at his broad back and strong arms and listened to the rain. There was something very private about the way the downpour enveloped the house and her hands began to explore his body again. She said quietly, 'Your skin is so soft.'

Edward cast a quick glance at her bedside clock to make sure he had time in hand, and turned back to her, grinning, 'What the hell was in that cocktail?'

In the middle of the afternoon, Hou Ming noticed that the rain had stopped drumming on the corrugated tin roof. It died away as quickly as it started and the sun came out in a blue sky. The sodden jungle steamed. Round the yard, delightful patterns of mist rose lazily in the heat from the water-soaked lallang grass and from wide pools in the red laterite yard.

An hour later, when the earth was almost dried out, the colours fresh and bright everywhere, he heard a jeep start up and take the top road from the house which led behind a belt of rubber to the road off the estate. He guessed what had happened and made a mental note. He prided himself on knowing everything that went on in the area. No detail was too insignificant. Certainly not this.

Two Tamil roadworkers, their black skins and loincloths filthy with dirt from being caught out in the rain, squatted together on the bank of a stream washing the mud off their black bodies and rinsing their shirts. A jeep passed them on its way to Kuala Lumpur town.

'Manilingam,' said one thoughtfully. 'Haven't we seen the British officer in that jeep before?'

'I don't know,' replied Manilingam. He splashed the pale white opaque stream water over his glistening ebony skin. 'A lot of people pass us by while we work on the road.'

An hour later, they walked home. The sun dipped towards the tops of the palm trees and cast long shadows across the bare earth around the poor wood and attap huts where they lived with their families and children.

Later, they sat outside their wood huts replete with a vegetable curry, smoking contentedly. Scuffling noises in the rubber in the plantation on the other side of the metalled road, directly opposite their house, alarmed them and they sat quite still, thinking of snakes. Two Chinese tappers appeared out of the shadows under the trees. One was tall and slim, a young man, while the other was short, and, even in the fading light, they could see he was scarred by smallpox. The two stepped over the ditch beside the road with hardly a glance at the Tamils, and began walking briskly towards town.

The two Tamils said nothing till the Chinese had faded into the warm grey dusk, then one said, 'There are some things we see, and some things we do not see.'

'That is very true,' said Manilingam, shaking his head.

'We do not know who will win, between the white men and the Chinese. We must be very careful.' His long black fingers caressed his thin flanks thoughtfully.

BOOK THREE

The Killing Years

February 1949 to October 1951

'It is thus obvious that the war is protracted and consequently ruthless in nature.'

Mao Tse Tung, *On Protracted War*, May 1938
Yenan, China.

Chapter 9

RED FISH, GREEN SEA

The second jungle conference of the Malayan Communist Party Central Executive Committee in February 1949 was not in the same place as the June meeting of the previous year, for repetition spelled the risk of betrayal. The death of Lao Yu was still fresh in everyone's minds.

This time Ho Peng took Liya with him, in case he had to send messages back to Lao Tang who was left in command of his jungle group near the Black Circle squatters' village. Dressed as workers and pretending no connection with each other, they took a bus early in the morning from Kuala Lumpur north through Kuala Kubu Bahru, past Fraser's Hill rest station on the high mountain ridge which ran up from Gunong Nuang above the 'Black Circle', and down the steep curves and bends cut through the jungle the other side to Tranum in Pahang State. From Tranum, in the afternoon, they continued on foot for three miles south on the Bentong road, as far as the brown waters of the Sungei Delum, before striking off the narrow tarmac road into the dense jungle of Ulu Semangko.

The jungle camp was new, but the secret ring of communist guards hidden around it was the same. Liya was both frightened and impressed by the discipline and organisation – meeting a 'tapper' on the road, being led deep into the trees by a relay of soldiers who appeared out of the jungle shadows – and finally by the large camp hidden under the canopy, well guarded and surely impossible for the British to find.

She quickly settled in and made friends with the soldiers guarding the Secretariat, a long attap hut where the Politburo was meeting. They were flattered by her attentions, as women were rare in the

147

jungle, and impressed by Ho Peng's influence, so they let her sit in the shadows at the back. She could just see Chin Peng's round face at the other end of the hut over the silhouetted heads of the twenty Politburo members sitting on mats on the floor in front of her, and she listened very carefully indeed.

'It is not enough to fight. We must pursue the political programme at the same time. We must inform the people of the advantages they will have under Communism,' Chin Peng announced. 'Most important, we promise everyone in the country over eighteen years old will have the democratic right to vote.'

A spontaneous burst of applause greeted this announcement. There never had been free elections in Malaya and much more than half the two million Chinese in the country were immigrants from mainland China, squatters without land, rights or citizenship. Such a promise would transform their lives and give the Chinese a sizeable electorate among the five-and-a-half million total population.

Chin Peng smiled cherubically. 'At present, Malaya is ruled by a convenient arrangement between the despotic State Sultans and the British colonialists, who are less than one per cent of the population. We will give everyone the vote. We will hold democratic elections, and, with their votes to support us, we will create the People's Democratic Republic of Malaya!'

The applause was louder than before. At the back of the hut, Liya clapped as hard as the rest, carried away by the sheer equality being offered.

'Malaya will become a model People's State controlled by the united revolutions of all races!' said Chin Peng and described his manifesto: 'Workers will have equality with the state-controlled industries. Unlike the slave labour they now endure, in tin mines and rubber plantations, they shall be properly rewarded for their labour.'

Leaning forward, he thumped out the detail of his plan with his fist: 'Everyone will be entitled to national insurance. Children of all races, not just the Malays, will have free education. Farmers will have grants of free land, and be given free supplies, such as seeds, farm implements and pedigree pigs to establish good breeding stock. And everyone will be entitled to pensions starting at the age of fifty-five years.'

All day Liya listened fascinated. She had never heard promises like these in her life and wanted to talk to Ho Peng about it, but he was more than usually taciturn.

On the second day, she saw General-Secretary Chin Peng in close discussion with Ho Peng. The two presented a complete contrast, as between fighter and politician. Chin Peng was plump, almost overweight, a few pimples on his smooth face and comfortably dressed in a clean white shirt and shorts, while Ho Peng was short, hard and wiry, in dirty tappers' clothes, his pitted face cunning and alert. They even walked differently. Ho Peng stepped along aggressively, looking warily about him like a crow over a piece of carrion, while Chin Peng strolled easily, turning genially from time to time to watch Ho Peng when he spoke. Liya wished she could hear what they were saying but they were too far off and kept their voices low.

'We were all very upset by the murder of Comrade Lao Yu,' said Chin Peng experimentally.

'Lao Yu's death was a great tragedy for the Party,' said Ho Peng. He knew how much Chin Peng had relied on him.

'It was,' said Chin Peng reflectively, with genuine regret. 'Someday, I will find out who betrayed him.'

'We were betrayed at the time of our greatest struggle,' added Ho Peng sanctimoniously. He knew Chin Peng could not afford to upset the armed effort against the British with a witch-hunt to find out who had betrayed Lao Yu.

Recovering himself, Chin Peng said, 'After Lao Yu's loss, we need new strategic military direction. I have formed a new Central Military Committee, directly under my control, which will direct all operations in future. It will be like what the English call their GHQ, or General Headquarters. I want you to be a member.'

After Lao Yu, it was exactly what Ho Peng had hoped, placing him higher than ever in the Party's structure, but the shadows under the green canopy above masked the pleasure in his narrow eyes and he answered calmly, 'It will be a great privilege, Comrade General-Secretary. I will do my best for the Party.'

'And what is your first recommendation?' asked Chin Peng straightaway, watching Ho Peng carefully.

'We must attack, Comrade Chin Peng!' said Ho Peng. 'We've not established any Liberated Areas. We need new impetus.'

Chin Peng agreed. He had made his own assessment called 'Our Opinion of the Battle' and realised his campaign had not been going well. He said, 'The people need to understand that our military effort exactly reflects our political aspirations. Therefore, we shall change the name of the military wing of the Party from the Malayan People's Anti-British Army, which harps back to our old wartime

149

role, to the Malayan Races Liberation Army, which looks forward
to the future.'

'Let's hope this will encourage the Tamils and Malays to join us,'
said Ho Peng but privately he doubted it would make much
difference. So far, only three Malays and a few Tamils had joined in
his area, in Kuala Lumpur, and they were from mixed parentage
with Chinese families. All his MRLA soldiers in the jungle were
Chinese.

'And what other suggestions can you make?' asked Chin Peng.

'Command and control takes too long through the jungle,' said
Ho Peng. 'One comrade at this conference took three months to
walk the two hundred and fifty miles through the jungles from
Johore to join us. In his absence the operations of his unit have been
leaderless.'

Chin Peng nodded, 'You don't have that problem, Ho Peng,
because you're close by, and you have an excellent courier in Liya.'
He observed the slim poorly-dressed girl waiting patiently by a large
tree near the Secretariat hut. 'But the other regiments further away
have severe difficulties receiving my directives.'

'Bring back the wartime system we used against the Japanese.'

'With dead letter boxes only known by two people?'

'Exactly,' said Ho Peng. 'You can give instructions to all the
Politburo members here now, and when they return to their areas,
they will establish a courier chain from Singapore in the south to
wherever you are in the north.'

'Who will be the last link in the chain to me?' asked Chin Peng,
conscious of the danger should the British subvert the person in
direct contact with his Headquarters.

'Comrade Liya,' said Ho Peng without hesitation.

Chin Peng stopped walking and stared across the clearing at Liya
while Ho Peng willed him to agree. With his courier in pole
position, his own position in the Party would be stronger still.

'Are you sure of her?' asked Chin Peng.

'She dare not disobey me,' Ho Peng asserted grim-faced.

Chin Peng believed him. He said, 'Then we'll talk to her, but
there is a better motivation than fear, Comrade Ho Peng.'

'Dedication to the Party,' intoned Ho Peng like a penitent to his
priest in responses.

'Like yours and mine,' said Chin Peng with apparent candour, but
when he left with Liya the following day Ho Peng was still suspicious
of the remark. As they walked towards Tranum in silence, he

150

brooded. The sun was high, the tarmac road hot under foot and their clothes, soaked with sweat in the humidity of the jungle, soon dried out.

After several bends in the road, when he was sure they were out of sight of the 'tappers' guarding the entrance to Chin Peng's jungle camp, Ho Peng suddenly lashed out back-handed and knocked Liya sideways off the road. As she rolled through the buffalo grass into a ditch, he bounded after her and whispered harshly, 'You may be courier to our Comrade General-Secretary Chin Peng, but your first loyalty is to me!'

'Yes! Yes,' Liya replied in a small voice, wriggling through the dusty grass out of his reach, but he moved along the top of the ditch, hovering over her. This was the first time he had been able to impose his discipline on her out of sight of others since the new arrangements had been made with Chin Peng.

'You will bring me everything Chin Peng gives you. Understand!'

She nodded quickly, her eyes big with fright, and he stood up to let her out of the ditch. Bruised and cut, she scrambled back to the road and walked on, keeping a few paces in front of him, her skin tingling with expectation of another blow.

Behind Ho Peng had eliminated her from his mind and was thinking about the details of war. He had gained political power and influence during the last few days but, as a field commander, he found the lack of substance infuriating. He suddenly asked Liya, 'Did you see the Chinese Red Army officers from the People's Revolutionary Army at the conference?'

'Yes,' she said in a voice so low he hardly heard her. The three Chinese had been hanging about in the Secretariat hut near her position at the back. But she said no more because she was afraid Ho Peng would hit her again.

The road twisted uphill, flanked by jungle beyond the ditches on each side, and was quite deserted. 'They were from Mao Tse-tung's Eastern Field Army,' Ho Peng said.

Liya nodded and Ho Peng fell silent again. He could not understand why Chin Peng had not presented those Chinese Red Army officers with a formal request to Mao Tse-tung asking for financial and material support. He supposed it was political pride, because Chin Peng knew the facts. Ho Peng's own spies had informed him from British sources that, whereas the communists had succeeded so far in killing nearly five hundred soldiers, policemen and civilians, they had themselves lost four hundred, and another two hundred and eighty had been captured. Ho Peng, in his new role on the Central Military Committee, had advised the renamed MRLA to follow his own example, quit the big camps, which the British could find, and work in smaller units, but Chin Peng had refused to agree because it was politically weak. He also refused to supply the heavy support weapons like mortars and heavy machine-guns which they needed to seize and hold the Liberated Areas. Finally, Chin Peng had not answered his question about how to finance the new courier network, paying for buses and trains, let alone fund the cost of his political manifesto for the new Communist Republic. Bitterly, Ho Peng remarked, 'Their fight is over'.

'What d'you mean,' Liya asked, glancing round, but Ho Peng's face was dark and closed.

He said simply, 'They've won. Mao Tse-tung's armies captured Peking a week ago, after the battle of Huai Hai. Only Shanghai remains and it will fall in a month or so.'

Liya was overcome. They walked up the narrow road in the hot windless silence, one behind the other, tantalised by the staggering success which Mao Tse-tung had achieved. The whole of China, with all its millions, would soon be communist.

Edward, at breakfast, looked up from reading an article in the *Straits Times* which descrubed the Red Army seizing Peking. He stood up as Diana came out on to the verandah to join him.

'D'you see much of Sean Tallard any more?' she asked blithely. She was wearing a voluminous blue maternity dress which billowed out over her long legs, advertising her pregnancy.

'No,' said Edward shortly and drew up a rattan chair for her to sit down, irritated that thinking of Marsha at the 'Black Circle' made him conscious of the gesture.

Diana shrugged her slim shoulders. She was not really interested in Tallard. She could never forget the awfulness of her miscarriage, but Edward had been so short-tempered since Ferret Force was abandoned, she thought he might feel better if he talked about it. Suppressing her fears for her new baby, she reached for some toast and asked, 'You're always very busy with this awful Emergency, but you never seem to go out there any more, do you?'

'Not for ages,' said Edward emphatically, amazed she even wanted to talk about the 'Black Circle'. He tried to bury himself in the article about Peking, but he had lost the thread. The 'Black Circle', Tallard, Ho Peng, and Marsha kept intruding. He had been too busy to see Marsha since, but he was filled with a hopeless certainty that they would fall on each other as before, like foxes mating, and the twisting surge of excitement at the thought of exactly what they would do to each other was unquenched by sensations of guilt.

He glanced over his paper at Diana. She was eating her toast and checking through her diary. Since knowing she was pregnant again she had refused to make love because she was frightened of losing the baby, and as she tried to be so gentle and understanding it was impossible to be cross. The trouble was, the relentless suggestive warmth of Malaya made everyone want to lie down naked in bed just to cool off and her abstinence was more frustrating than he could have imagined.

'Hassan!' she called out.

The houseboy appeared barefoot as usual, from the direction of the kitchen, wearing a clean white shirt and short sarong over his trousers, Malay style. Diana lifted the teapot and said, 'Some more tea, please, Hassan?'

'Yes, Mem Punjang,' said Hassan, using his nickname for her long blonde hair.

Diana watched him scuff back along the verandah and said, 'It really is a bore about Mr Song.'

'What is, dear?' said Edward from inside his paper again.

'His English,' she said, beginning to peel an orange.

'I didn't think he spoke any English?'

'He doesn't,' said Diana slipping a pig of orange into her mouth. Edward hardly noticed what happened in the house. She only saw him for meals and a short time in the evening before going to bed. 'That's what's annoying. Having to give him instructions through Hassan.'

Hassan reappeared clutching the teapot high in front of him, like an offering to the Gods who commanded him.

Edward said, 'Maybe you ought to learn Chinese.'

Diana laughed, 'Me? I'm far too busy. Take today for example. There's a meeting of the Guild of St Helena with Davina Bleasley, then I'm on a committee for the Easter Ball we're planning, and we've drinks tonight with the padre.' She frowned. 'I suppose if Colonel Bleasley keeps you working late again, we'll miss that?'

Hassan put the teapot on the table very carefully, patting it warningly with his brown fingers, and said, 'It is hot, Memsahib. Very hot.'

153

'Thank you, Hassan.'

'Well, I'm determined to have a stab at learning Chinese,' said Edward putting down his paper.

'What on earth for?'

'I'm in Intelligence and our enemy is Chinese,' replied Edward simply. He had not forgotten how Tallard's foreman, Hou Ming, had treated him. 'Trouble is, finding the time. That old bugger Bleasley won't release me to do a course, so I'll have to find someone to teach me in my spare time. God knows where from.'

'You don't have any spare time, darling,' said Diana. 'You spend the whole day in the office reading awful reports about terrorist attacks and then most evenings you and Angus sit about out here on the verandah drinking Tiger and talking shop. I won't see you at all if you start taking Chinese lessons.'

Edward laughed good-humouredly, shaking his head.

'Will Memsahib need anything else?' asked Hassan hovering beside the table.

'No, thank you, Hassan,' said Diana and waved him away. To Edward, she said. 'Anyway, what's the point? By the time you have learnt Chinese enough to use it, we'll be leaving Malaya on another posting.'

As Edward was already looking into the possibility of an extension, he simply said, 'I've got to make the effort'. The British Army in Palestine had after all, been stumped in the Jewish terrorist campaign for lack of people who could speak, let alone read Hebrew.

Diana gave up. She looked at her watch and said, 'I must go! I'm late already. Doctor Hazlitt has asked me to come early. The poor man says he's inundated during the day with soldiers complaining about jungle sores, centipede rashes, hornet stings, snake bites and so on.' She stood up carefully holding the bulge of her stomach. She gave Edward a quick kiss goodbye and added, 'I'd forget Chinese, if I was you. It's absurdly difficult.'

I learned Arabic, he reminded himself obstinately, and sat down again wishing she had been keener on the idea. He heard the big Plymouth start up and listened to its burbling engine purring away up the road. Silence descended, except for the warm hum of insects in the garden.

He quickly sipped his last cup of tea thinking he must leave too, when Hassan came back along the verandah with Lao Song. Edward looked up enquiringly. Lao Song was wearing his simple black working clothes buttoned all the way up the front to his neck and the wisps of grey hair floating about his head seemed to light up in the morning sunshine.

They stopped in front of him, Lao Song old and inscrutably silent as usual, and Hassan looking youthful and awkward, clutching his hands together. Edward imagined they had some sin to confess.

'Tuan, a moment please?' said Hassan, embarrassed. Edward nodded, prepared to act as jury and judge, and Hassan gestured at Lao Song.

The old cook peered down at Edward in his bamboo chair for a moment and then said, 'Hassan tells me you want to learn Chinese?'

Edward was speechless.

A very faint frown wrinkled Lao Song's face and he asked, 'Am I correctly informed?' He looked from Edward to Hassan who nodded vigorously, desperately hoping he had not misheard the Tuan talking to his beautiful wife.

'Yes, yes,' said Edward at last, amazed at Lao Song's impeccable if slightly old-fashioned English. 'I've wanted to for ages but I haven't had the time.'

'I will teach you, here,' announced Lao Song gravely and made a tiny bow as if the honour was all his. 'If you will allow it?'

Edward shook his head and waved his hands all at once, still amazed, saying, 'Yes, of course! It's incredible! It's exactly what I want.' He flopped back in his chair, still disbelieving, and asked, 'How, I mean where did you learn to speak English so well?'

'I was a teacher at a school in Shanghai,' said Lao Song.

'Song is a Professor,' Hassan chipped in excitedly. He revered Lao Song, and his terror at compromising Lao Song had evaporated into ecstatic delight.

Edward could hardly take it all in. 'What happened?'

'The school was destroyed,' replied Lao Song slowly, troubled by the weight of his memory. 'There has been much killing in China for many years. Chinese fighting Chinese, and the Japanese, the communists and the nationalist Kuomintang. Students are always keen to die in such struggles, though they never know how. Our faculty was bombed. Many did die. I left China.'

His black eyes seemed especially hooded at the recollection and Edward asked instead, 'I don't understand. Why haven't you continued to teach here, in Malaya? Why be just—' he hesitated, all of a sudden unsure of how to speak to a man who only a moment before had been nothing more than a servant.

'A cook?'

Edward nodded, embarrassed.

'A cook is more important than a teacher,' replied Lao Song. 'Hsun Tzu tells us that "of all the methods of controlling the body and nourishing the mind, none is more important than getting a teacher", but even a teacher must eat.'

'If you teach as well as you cook I'm the luckiest man alive,' grinned Edward. He glanced at his watch and stood up. 'Can we start tonight?' With Lao Song at home, he could study every night. The opportunity was fantastic!

'Of course,' said Lao Song, bowing imperceptibly. 'I am at your service.'

'Where do we start?'

'With the four different tones in one syllable,' said Lao Song. 'Mā which means "Mother", Má which means "Hemp", Mǎ which means "Horse", and Mà which means "To swear". Each tone gives a separate meaning in Chinese.'

'I don't think I'll be a very good student,' said Edward, finding it almost impossible to tell the difference. 'But I'll do my best.' He looked directly at Lao Song, wondering what they would learn of each other and added, 'I promise'.

Lao Song bowed again, satisfied, silent.

Edward was late and walked quickly back into the house. In the hall he called back to Lao Song who had not moved from the table on the verandah, 'Incidentally, why didn't you speak to us before?'

'The English expect everyone in the world to speak their language, so there can be no dialogue, which is the essence of human contact, but, now you want to learn my language, I will speak yours.'

Edward nodded, drumming his fingers thoughtfully on the door, then left. He could not help wondering what Diana's reaction would be to his working late in the evenings with her cook, even if he was a professor, and whether Lao Song would relax his strict rule of dialogue enough to speak to her as well in the future.

Chapter 10

THE PRICE OF INFORMATION

Lao Tang sat in the shadows and squinted into the sun across a padi field near the Black Circle squatters' village. Several tappers' women slopped slowly through the glittering water up to their ankles, their wide-brimmed Chinese straw hats rising and dipping as they bent to pull green sedge weed from the padi rice. Lao Tang was sentry on this food collection patrol, with a Bren gun, some thirty yards from the main group and was enjoying a moment of rest. Ho Peng had been beside himself since Comrade Li Chi-Chen had disappeared the day before. He had never recovered after the creeping artillery barrage swept over him while he scrabbled about blinded without his glasses, and Lao Tang suspected he had been planning to desert for months.

He wriggled into a comfortable position with his back to a tree, at peace with the insects buzzing round him, and peered through thick vine leaves at the women in the rice padi. One of the women worked her way towards the strip of jungle along the side of the padi field. She was skinny but her oval face was smooth and rather pretty. She stopped pulling weed and stood up to rub her aching back, casually looking around. Then she stepped briskly out of the water, slipped barefoot across the bund at the edge of the field to the jungle edge, loosened her black trousers and squatted with her back almost touching the dark wall of trees behind, right in front of Ho Peng and the main group hiding in the jungle.

Lao Tang doubted she knew she was being watched. She appeared too relaxed, though all the poor Chinese and Tamil tappers had learned to live a double life. They were more terrified of Ho Peng than they were of the Emergency Regulations, and the

157

Min Yuen continued to smuggle food to the fighters in the jungle in spite of the British soldiers. Lao Tang amused himself by trying to see what she was doing, but she was too skilful. All he saw was a young girl relieving herself.

She squatted over a large glass jar hidden in the ground. In a moment, she had dropped rice into it from a sack concealed under her clothes, replaced the jar top, dusted leaves over it, pulled up her trousers and was back slopping through the water in the padi field again.

Lao Tang could almost taste the fresh rice and felt good. As long as the proletariat supported them, the revolution could not fail. The People's Army in China had proved that. He did not much like being cut off from normal life in the jungle, but lurking unseen, the arbiter of others' lives, the tool of their political destiny, he felt powerful.

The curtain of leaves hanging over the jar rustled and a hand reached down to dust away the covering. Liya continued to pluck weeds from the water, but she watched out of the corner of her eye and guessed the hand belonged to Ho Peng. As soon as she had heard on the grapevine in the village that a MRLA soldier had surrendered to Mr Tallard, she knew Ho Peng would be on the food patrol that day, burning to find out what had happened.

The hand unscrewed the lid and reached inside. Liya glanced at the other women further away but they were all busy weeding and seemed unaware anything was afoot to disturb the watery peace of the rice padi. The hand pulled a small black waterproof canvas bag out of the jar and disappeared into the shadows of the palm leaves. Hands came back, reaching out of the jungle to remove the rice and refit the lid. Straining her ears, Liya could hear secret footsteps as the patrol withdrew deeper into the jungle and she relaxed. The moment of danger, when she was in touch with Ho Peng and the MRLA, was over. The British soldiers were getting more cunning and she never knew when they might be about.

'Edward's not back,' said Diana when she opened the front door to Angus Maclean that evening. He was off duty, wearing a white shirt and pale beige slacks, so she added, 'Do come in and wait. It'll be nice to have some company.'

'Bleasley kept him late again?'

'That man never lets up,' she said and sat down on the sofa among the cut-outs of soft cotton which she was making into a baby's night-dress. She rested her hands on her hard, distended stomach and looked at Angus with big blue eyes. 'Then when he does get home, he spends the rest of the evening working with Mr Song.'

'Edward's good at languages,' said Angus conversationally.

'You know Lao Song is my cook?' said Diana frowning. Edward was spending his time with her cook when she needed his support and encouragement so close to giving birth.

'I'd say he's damn lucky to have his own private tutor, in house, free, gratis and for nothing.'

Diana considered the comment typical of a Scot and insisted, 'Besides, Angus, Chinese is an awful language. All wings and wangs and funny noises which seem to float in the air. Does he really need to bother?'

'Chinese would be a tremendous asset to his job. In my opinion it's impressive that Edward is prepared to commit so much spare time to learn it.'

'Yes,' said Diana thoughtfully. This aspect had occurred to her, but whatever it did for Edward's career, it gave them even less time together.

Angus thought he ought to try and explain, 'We'll only beat these communists with a combination of good policework and army intelligence and the more we understand about the Chinese, the better.'

'According to Davina Bleasley, that's not what Colonel Bleasley thinks,' she answered. Edward always seemed to choose the opposite line to his boss, and it worried her.

'No, well,' said Angus, slightly taken aback. 'Colonel Bleasley is a rather traditional officer. He likes a neat division between police and army, such as there was in the war, fighting the Germans and the Japs, but there's nothing conventional about this affair. No neat divisions at all. The communists could be anywhere. Even your cook, Mr Song, might be a member of the Min Yuen.' He smiled at the look on her face.

'I don't like the idea of that at all,' she said.

'We're all having to adapt our thinking to fight this enemy.'

'No-one likes change,' said Diana quietly continuing to sew her baby's night-dress and wondering how she would cope with the birth. 'It's frightening.'

'I agree,' said Angus with feeling. This was not a place to bring a baby into the world. Diana looked complacent and beautiful but his experience told him she was not calm inside.

The sudden screeching rattle of a cockchafer in the clump of jungle on the edge of the garden made her jump.

'The Emergency is very serious isn't it?' she said, dropping her hands to her lap. She looked out through the open french windows into the darkness. Out there was the manic cacophony of night insects, brief flashes of dusty grey wings as bats swooped round the roof and she imagined sharp-eyed snakes and lizards creeping through the grass to find dry cosy places beneath her feet under the house. There were times when the noises seemed to swell in volume and the jungle to creep luxuriantly closer and closer to the house, to smother her with greenery.

A sweaty sheen stood out on her forehead. She dabbed at it with a handkerchief and became aware of Angus watching her.

'It is serious,' he repeated quickly to cover her embarrassment. 'But you'd think the pin-striped politicians in London couldn't care less. The Colonial Secretary hasn't bothered to visit us at all since the Emergency was declared a year ago.'

'Arthur Creech Jones?' said Diana remembering his name from her stay in Palestine. 'I read somewhere the Labour Party majority is so small they daren't let him come out in case they lose a vote in the Commons while he's gone.'

Angus laughed, 'True, but hell's teeth, at least they could send us some cash! We could lose this war without it.' The Malay Police authority refused to separate Special Branch from the CID on the grounds it would place more strain on the hopelessly inadequate police budget. 'Of course, money is not the answer by itself, but if we aren't funded, the best ideas and motivation won't be enough.'

'I can hear Edward,' said Diana suddenly brightening. She put down her sewing beside her on the sofa as Edward strode in from the hall.

'How's the little lad in there?' said Edward, kissing Diana and gently patting her bulge.

'He's fine,' said Diana in an unconvinced tone of voice. She wanted her baby to be a boy, for Edward who talked of nothing else, but more than anything she wanted his support because she was almost due and terrified.

'You had a good day, darling?' Edward asked. The question had become routine when he came home in the evening but before she could answer, he nipped back into the hall to call Hassan to bring drinks.

'Angus and I have been chatting,' she said when he came back.

160

'But I've got no energy. I'm just exhausted by the end of the day.' She immediately regretted putting it like that, as they had not made love for months.

Edward appeared not to notice. When Hassan had supplied whisky s'tengahs and orange juice for Diana, he asked Angus, 'You here on a social visit? Or business?'

Diana pulled a face and said, 'He says it's social, but I doubt it.' It occurred to her that her chat with Angus was more conversation than she had had with Edward for months.

Angus raised his dark eyebrows and admitted, 'A bit of business, then we can relax, eh?'

'Let's talk in the garden,' said Edward. 'And afterwards stay for dinner?' He smiled quickly at Diana and said, 'Darling, would you fix it with Lao Song?'

'If he condescends to speak to me,' she said without enthusiasm. Sometimes, Edward seemed to forget she was pregnant, though he always asked if she was all right. She could not help it but even so insignificant a request as ordering an extra place for supper was a strain.

She watched them walk down the verandah steps into the warm Malayan night and then waddled towards the kitchen.

'Tallard has reported an SEP,' said Angus quietly when they were in the middle of the lawn, far enough from the house so no-one could overhear them. SEP, or Surrendered Enemy Personnel, had become the jargon to describe a communist who had given himself up.

'From Ho Peng's gang?' asked Edward excitedly.

'I'm sure of it,' agreed Angus and added, 'Will you go and pick him up for me tomorrow?'

Edward's face was masked by shadow but he answered enthusiastically, 'Of course!'

'I'd do it myself but the new Police Commissioner, Nicol Gray, is visiting us in the morning for an inspection and I've got to be there. The point is we have to take the armour plating off the vehicles and it would be madness to go out to Tallard's place without it.'

'Why d'you have to remove the armour?' asked Edward, amazed.

Angus grunted cynically, 'There isn't enough money to armour all the police vehicles, so Gray says if we can't all have armour, then it's unfair for only some to have it. So no-one is allowed to use it.'

Edward shook his head. The British capacity for self-destructive 'good form' was astonishing. The Emergency would never be won with rules like that.

'Of course, some do have armour, but we have to take it off for his inspections.'

'And put it on again afterwards?'

'Aye,' said Angus dourly. 'So you can see why I'm not that keen to risk driving out to Tallard at the Black Circle in un-armoured trucks.'

'Why doesn't Tallard drive the SEP to us in his own armour-plated truck? That Monster of his?'

Angus shrugged, 'He's been bloody difficult since Ferret Force was folded up. He's done the odd task for the Civil Liaison Corps helping to train the infantry, but he keeps taking them into the same area of jungle where you found that big camp.'

'I don't blame him for that,' said Edward, though it was undeniably selfish when there was so much else under threat. 'I guess he wants to keep Ho Peng off his own back and stop the terrorists attacking his house.'

Angus nodded, 'They still shoot it up once a week or so, but the odd thing is that they've never hit anyone.'

Edward laughed, 'A lot of Chinese have notoriously bad eyesight. Maybe they're not very good shots.'

'After nearly a year?'

'What are you saying?'

'I don't trust Tallard,' admitted Angus. 'There's something about him and his involvement with Ho Peng that doesn't ring true.'

'You mean more than just digging up wartime caches?'

Angus grunted in the darkness, 'He's certainly a mercenary bastard. He's put in several more claims since those first Stens!'

'Really? I didn't know,' said Edward. He drank his whisky. So much seemed to be wrong in the way the Emergency was running.

'I suppose it's useful to take weapons off the communists,' Angus continued. 'But don't you think it's odd that Tallard knows so much about Ho Peng but never seems to bring his infantry patrols into direct contact with the enemy so we can kill a few of them.'

'And Ho Peng doesn't seem very good at hitting Tallard either?'

'Exactly,' Angus said. He drained his glass and said, 'You just be careful tomorrow. Ho Peng may not be much good at hitting Tallard, but he's been most efficient at killing plenty of other people.'

Edward looked at Angus's dark silhouette for a moment, then

said, 'Let's go inside. See what my professor-cum-cook has on offer.'

In the morning, Edward was out of the house without waking Diana as the first streaks of light cut across the night sky. He was excited at the prospect of seeing the SEP. This would be his first contact face to face with a member of the MRLA, with a Communist Terrorist. He wondered what the CT would look like and what sort of information he might give about Ho Peng. Anything would be better than the little they had accumulated to date. He walked over to the armoury, drew his Sten SMG and crossed to the Motor Transport park where he found a young platoon commander in charge of the convoy.

He had some bad news, he told Edward, 'We've been allocated a truck, an armoured car and two jeeps, one for you and one for me. I'll take the two policemen who'll arrest the SEP in my jeep. But we're diffy the armoured car. It's knackered.' He gestured into the shadows of a shed in the MT park where Edward could just see men stripped to the waist peering into the engine compartment of the armoured vehicle.

Edward checked his watch and said, 'Any chance they'll fix it?'

'I doubt it,' said the young man. His face looked very white under his dark jungle green floppy hat. 'Trouble is all the others are out with the companies, in places like Camp Rideau, or lying in bits all over the workshop floor.'

Edward glanced at the waiting jeeps and said, 'The jeeps are plated. At least on the sides. What about the truck?'

Two lines of infantrymen sat impassively in the open back of the three-ton truck waiting patiently for others to decide their fate. They wore their green jungle patrol gear, '37 pattern webbing belts and ammunition pouches, and they clutched short Lee Enfield SMLE No-1 .303 rifles between their knees, with the butts resting on the floor. Some were smoking, their faces in darkness behind the glow of the cigarette under their hats in the half-light of dawn.

'The men should be all right. The sides of the truck are plated, and the cab.' The young platoon commander gave a short laugh. 'If we are attacked we'll leap over the sides and find some decent cover. Practised it often enough on our anti-ambush drills.' He glanced at Edward, hoping he had impressed him.

Edward heard the enthusiasm in the young officer's voice and looked up at the sky over the roof-tops of the MT buildings. Grey

163

streaks were fading rapidly to pale translucent blue and he already felt the sweat prickling his skin under his shirt. They were losing time if they wanted to be back in Kuala Lumpur before midday.

The platoon commander read Edward's mind. He said, 'I reckon we've enough armour between us as long as we keep our vehicles well spaced apart. All the vehicles are fitted with radios. I'm call-sign "three-one" and you'll be call-sign "nine-four" for a liaison officer. I'll give the mechanics another five minutes. If they can't fix the armoured car, we'll set off anyway.'

Edward agreed, 'In that case I'll go on ahead, and wait for you where the rubber starts, near the junction at Nine-Mile Village. There are some squalid little huts there, on the left.' The escort convoy was not his responsibility. He was there solely as an Intelligence officer.

'I know the place,' said the platoon commander. 'We'll pick you up there.' Clutching his M-1 carbine, he marched off towards the sound of hammering in the workshops.

The two Tamils saw the army jeep pull in to the side of the road beside their house as they were preparing to leave for work. The officer who was driving stepped out and stood looking at the rubber plantation opposite.

Ranjang Hadar looked at Manilingam and said, 'D'you think he knows?' It was nearly six months since they had seen the two communists leave the rubber and walk into town, but the incident had been repeated several times since.

Manilingam could think of no other reason for anyone to stop by their poor wood house. To be on the safe side, they walked briskly on to the road, making a wide detour away from Edward's jeep.

Edward checked his watch. The convoy was taking a long time to catch up. He felt uncomfortable standing about on his own, so he climbed back in the jeep and drove on slowly, repeatedly glancing at his rearview mirror.

Ahead, above a sharp bend on the red laterite road through the Black Circle estate, Lao Tang lay hidden with forty others lined out in cover on either side of him on the edge of the rubber trees overlooking the road. The sun beat down, sweat dripped from his face and ran down his neck and back, mosquitoes buzzed in the hot air and insects crawled through the dry leaves under his body. He gripped his Bren gun with sweaty palms and peered through the scrub concealing his position, trying not to fall asleep.

They had not stopped since Ho Peng picked up the rice cache the day before. Furious, he had led them without explanation at speed to the ambush site and they had spent most of the night camouflaging their position over the road. The site was well-chosen. There was a clear arc either side of the tight bend over the stream and no cover for the British who would be caught on the road in the killing zone. The narrow unsurfaced road ran uphill into view on his left, curled round a sharp bend over a stream culvert directly below them, about forty yards down a gentle slope of scrub, burned stumps and grass, and disappeared from view round the hill on his right.

Ho Peng was kneeling at the mouth of the culvert joining a wire to the wartime Japanese anti-tank landmine he had buried under the culvert. Glancing constantly up and down the deserted road like a bird, he checked the connection, and then walked uphill, tucking the detonating wire out of sight under ferns and weeds as he came. He sank down in leafy cover beside Lao Tang and connected one of the wires to a car battery, leaving the other wire loose to set off the bomb. Finally, he glanced up and down the line of his main ambush party. Everyone was awake and alert.

He looked uphill behind him into the rubber where he had placed a Rear Defence Group. Satisfied, he hooted twice, signalling the trap was set. Answering calls came from two Covering Fire Squads out of sight in their camouflaged positions further round the valley sides, where Ho Peng had placed them to prevent a British counter-attack on the flanks.

They settled down to wait, plagued by flies and mosquitoes, parched and sweating with the hot sun on their backs.

A mile away, Edward stopped his jeep on the side of the road by the rubber and looked at the Sungei Lui which ran right through the Black Circle valley estate. He reached for his radio handset on the seat beside him and said, 'Hallo three-one, this is nine-four. Send location, over.'

'Three-one, we're right behind you, on the Black Circle estate road.'

'Nine-four. Good. I'll drive on to the house and wait for you there. Acknowledge? Over.'

The platoon commander's voice crackled cheerfully, 'Three-one. Acknowledged! Out.'

Edward dropped the handset back on the seat beside him and let out the clutch. He was so close to the Black Circle now, he

165

reckoned he would be safe to drive straight there.

Lao Tang heard the jeep grinding uphill to his left and gripped his Bren. His thumb played over the safety catch. Beside him Ho Peng was completely absorbed, staring at the empty road waiting to see the approaching vehicle. His pocked face was set hard and streaked with sweat and mud.

The jeep appeared round the curve with one person in it. Lao Tang shifted his Bren slightly and filled the sights of his Bren gun. The driver changed down a gear to slow for the sharp bend across the culvert, the sun's reflections off the windscreen cleared and Lao Tang immediately recognised the young British officer with fair hair who had followed them in the jungle. He tensed ready for the explosion under the culvert which was Ho Peng's signal for the whole ambush position to open fire.

Nothing happened. The landmine had failed. Lao Tang's fingers had gone tight white on the pistol grip ready to fire. Almost sick with anticipation, he waited for Ho Peng to give a long burst with his own carbine, the fall-back signal in case the landmine failed.

The jeep picked up speed. Still Ho Peng waited. Lao Tang was aiming directly at the driver's back and almost pulled the trigger in sheer frustration, to relieve the tension, but Ho Peng squeezed his arm and shook his head viciously. He had recognised Edward too, but he wanted more than one jeep. Lao Tang subsided, wondering what the hell Ho Peng was waiting for this time.

Edward drove straight to the Tallards' bungalow using the back road to the house to keep out of sight of the estate offices. He was just about to run up the steps to the front door when Marsha appeared at the door of a bright new corrugated iron shed built at the opposite end of the bungalow to the garage where Tallard kept his armoured Monster. She called out, 'Edward! I heard the jeep and wondered who it could be.'

Edward went over to meet her, surprised to see her dressed in a starched white overall buttoned up the front and white plimsoles. She looked fit and very attractive.

Seeing the lone jeep, she said, 'Jesus, you didn't come alone again? That's madness!'

'No,' he smiled, pleased by her concern. 'There's a convoy close behind.' It had been months since their first encounter but Edward still found Marsha attractive. He could not help staring at the bare flesh of her neck and the gentle curves of her bosom where she had left several buttons of her white overall undone in the heat. He noticed her blue eyes sparkling with amusement and asked, 'What's with the nurse's uniform, Marsha?'

'I'm the Black Circle medic now,' she said and added in a low husky voice, 'And not a stitch on underneath!'

She was playing the same game as before, without complications, and he laughed, saying, 'Are we going to play doctors and nurses?'

'Wish we could, honey,' she pouted and gestured at the shiny new hut. 'But I've got someone in my clinic and Sean's in the house with that goddam communist.' As she spoke, a young Chinese woman appeared at the door of the shed to see who had arrived.

As they walked over the hard sun-baked yard, Marsha explained, 'She's a young mother with a small son, aged nearly two, I think, who's terribly run down with septicaemia from secondary infections set up after leech and insect bites.' She shook her head and Edward could see she was genuinely upset. 'They will let them run round naked in that filthy squatters' village. We can't get penicillin yet, but fortunately the little boy is responding well to a course of sulphonamides.'

'You enjoy it?' Edward said. 'Having something to do, I mean.'

'Of course.'

As they neared the hut, the young Chinese, suddenly vanished inside but reappeared carrying her little son. She ducked away across the yard in the opposite direction.

'Wait!' called Marsha in surprise. 'I haven't finished with him yet.'

'Maybe another day, Mrs Tallard,' the woman said in sing-song bad English over her shoulder. 'I come back another day.'

Crossly, Marsha watched her go and said, 'That's typical of them, Edward. No offence, but she was probably frightened off by your uniform.'

Edward nodded, 'I'm not surprised. We want to help people like her, but the CTs can step out of the jungle and terrorise them at any moment of the day. There are squatter villages like yours on estates all over Malaya and it's impossible for the army or police to watch over them all the time.'

They watched as the Chinese woman walked briskly down the yellow path beside the rubber trees with her black-haired, half-naked son perched on her hip. Her black hair tossed loosely from side to side and her baggy grey cotton trousers flapped round her legs. There seemed something familiar about her but he could not place it.

'Show me your new medical centre,' he said to Marsha.

'Of course, Diana's miscarriage was really the motivation for doing this,' she explained leading the way in.

The building was only marginally cooler inside, despite the shiny reflective roof and gaps all round at the eaves to catch the slightest breeze, and it was equipped with all the essentials of a medical centre: glass bottles of tablets, cotton wool, alcohol and basins with gleaming stainless steel instruments. A washbasin, medicine cupboard, several chairs and table completed the set-up.

'Brilliant,' said Edward, impressed. 'D'you get many coming in?'

'Slow to start with, but more and more now they can see I don't care who they are or what they've done. I'll help anyone as long as they're sick.'

'No questions asked?'

She looked at him frankly with her blue eyes and said, 'What can I do? They won't come if they think I'll tell tales.'

Edward frowned, unsure what to make of that.

She came up to him and said softly, 'Everyone's equal when they're sick, honey.' She put both her hands lightly on his arms, her fingers just touching his skin. 'I can't be selective, or the bandits wouldn't let them come at all.'

Edward was reluctant to admit she was right, but her closeness and the way she was looking at him made conversation difficult. She stepped inside his arms, looking up at him, and he gave in, just as he had known for months that he would, pulling her to him and kissing her hard, remembering the sensuous feel of her soft lips, the way she opened her mouth in abandon, her salty taste and warm feminine smell.

The noise of vehicles grinding up the slope brought him back to reality. Without breaking their kiss, he opened his eyes. Marsha clung to him, her head tilted back, her eyes closed, ignoring everything.

He heard someone shouting orders. Gently, he pushed her away. She let go reluctantly and grinned at him. 'Isn't there anywhere where we can make love without worrying about the goddam Emergency?'

Edward smiled back. 'Or your husband.'

'Stuff him,' she replied, straightening her white overall. Her husband was a functional lover, too often a beast.

They stepped out into the blinding sunshine again. Edward shielded his eyes. Sean Tallard, holding a carbine easily in one large hand, was talking to the young platoon commander in front of the steps to his house.

'Fairfax! Good to see you,' shouted Sean Tallard. 'Come to get this commie bastard?' He waved the carbine at a man sitting dejectedly behind him on the wooden steps.

Edward shook Tallard's hand and looked carefully at the prisoner. This was his first sight of a communist, a member of the MRLA, and he did not look much. His skin was sallow with lack of sun from living in the jungle, he was thin, his pale khaki uniform was dirty with sweat and torn, like the long puttees wrapped round his ankles and his canvas shoes, his hair was cut short and stood up all over his head like a black brush and dark fish eyes stared suspiciously out from behind thick steel-rimmed spectacles.

'He hardly looks like a killer,' he said.

'Anyone can kill women and children,' said Tallard. He glanced at his wife who walked up behind Edward but she ignored him and went up the steps into the house. Edward noticed that the eyes of every soldier avidly followed her slim swaying figure out of sight into the shadows of the hallway.

'Think he'll be any use?'

'I reckon so. He hasn't said too much to me, but he's certainly one of Ho Peng's mob and that's a breakthrough.'

It was a sad comment on the security forces' record in the area, but true. Ho Peng had succeeded in terrorising several Police Districts in the State for months and given away virtually nothing.

The soldiers clambered down from the truck, partly to ease their stiffened limbs and partly as a concession to tactics. The sergeant with them shouted orders for them to deploy to the sides of the open area in case they were attacked. Tallard watched a moment then said, 'These policemen going to arrest him?' He pointed at the two policemen who had climbed out of the back of the platoon commander's jeep. One was a smooth browned-skinned Malay constable wearing a round black songkok hat, and the other was a barrel-chested bearded Sikh, a sergeant of police, with a large white turban.

'Yes indeed,' said the young officer brightly. 'Bit of a job getting these two along. All their colleagues are on parade, vehicles polished.' He had not heard about the lack of armour.

The Sikh sergeant said, 'That is true, Sir, but we are rather being here than there.' He enjoyed being a policeman. The regulations fitted his sense of order, but he came from a small village in open

169

country near Amritsar and hated being in barracks in town, especially when there was an inspection.

'Well, here's your prisoner,' said Tallard cheerfully. During the night, Li Chi-Chen had willingly revealed that Ho Peng had dug up numerous wartime caches in the last months all of which contained weapons but as far as he knew, nothing else. The questions had puzzled Li Chi-Chen, who could not understand why both Ho Peng and a white planter should share the same interest in digging holes in the jungle. He was wondering if he had done the right thing by surrendering.

Tallard said, 'He's a surly sod, but nothing that a balanced diet and some sun shouldn't fix.'

'That is good,' agreed the Sikh. 'He will certainly get regular meals where he is going.'

The Malay constable smiled and the two pulled Li Chi-Chen off the steps, locked handcuffs over his wrists and marched him over to the jeep. He was bundled in the back behind the armoured plates sticking up at the sides and they sat down to wait, their heads just visible over the armoured sides, all three representing quite different but typical parts of Malaya, the Sikh's thick white turban, the neat black Malay songkok, and in between the dirty crumpled MRLA cap on the crewcut Chinese head.

'We better get going,' said the young officer. 'That spot of bother with the armoured car this morning has put us behind.' He thanked Tallard and signalled his platoon sergeant. There was more shouting and the soldiers ran back to the truck. The officer shook hands rather formally with Tallard, which took him by surprise, and the convoy left, the jeep leading. Edward called out to say he would catch up in two minutes. He wanted a word with Tallard first.

'You keeping busy?' asked Tallard suspiciously.

Edward nodded. He did not want to let the convoy get too far ahead, so he came straight to the point and asked, 'Have you found all the wartime caches yet?'

Tallard whipped round, peered at him for several moments trying to work out what was behind the question, his brown eyes bleak and unfriendly, then he laughed, 'Jesus! I do believe you're jealous for the reward money!'

'Of course not!' said Edward, taken by surprise.

Tallard was delighted with his discovery, 'You're all the same, you fine British officers, with your high morals, but it's the sight of filthy lucre that really grips your imagination. Am I right there?'

'Certainly not!' said Edward furiously.

Tallard's laughter died. He gripped his carbine, hitched up his belt over his stomach, and turned to mount the steps to his house. He stopped at the top and said, 'There's not much breaks the surface of life better than a dollop of hard cash, Edward Fairfax, but the stuff can be a terrible burden on friendship.' He held Edward's furious look for a moment then walked inside the house.

Edward could just see Marsha's pale face deeper in the shadow of the hallway, so he forced a smile and turned away. Frustrated and angry with himself at the way he had handled Tallard, he started the jeep and let out the clutch with a jerk, accelerating fast to catch up the others.

He drove past the estate offices where he caught sight of Hou Ming standing thin and impassive in the doorway at the back of the verandah. Everyone seemed to be out and about.

After the buildings, the road narrowed through the rubber plantations, like a thin winding umbilical to the main road six miles away. Almost at once he saw the young Chinese woman who had been in the clinic, with her half-naked son perched on her hip, walking along the side of the road. He slowed beside her and, mustering the best Chinese that Lao Song had taught him so far, he said, 'Can I give you a lift?'

The girl turned her face away behind her black hair and ignored him, quickening her pace.

Annoyed, Edward leaned across the jeep and repeated the question. Still smarting from Tallard's brush-off, he was damned if he was going to be seen off twice.

Suddenly she turned to face him and cried, 'Go away!'

'Liya!' he said in amazement, and nearly ran the jeep off the road. He swerved in front of her, grappled the wheel straight, and said, 'You were the girl in that hotel, in Chinatown!' He understood immediately why she seemed so familiar when she had cut and run from Marsha's clinic.

'Leave me alone!' she said in a high-pitched voice, quite unlike the voice she used in the brothel. 'You must not see me.' She dodged round the jeep through the lallang grass at the side of the road, furious that her curiosity to find out what was going on at the Tallard's house that morning had meant being seen by the British officer, and carried on walking as fast as she could.

Edward came after her, cruising very slowly beside her. In

English, 'Why are you here?' and when she did not answer, he shouted at her, 'Why?'

'I live here,' she said, giving him a quick frightened glance.

'You live here?' Edward repeated, trying to resolve the total contrast of the two places he had seen her, 'And work in town?'

She gave him another desperate look, knowing what he was thinking, and said in a softer but still desperate tone, 'I have to, don't you see?'

'For the money?'

'Yes! For the money! For my son!' she cried out. The features in her perfectly shaped face were so neat that they reflected every subtle change of her mood precisely and she looked utterly miserable, her slanting dark eyes filling with tears. 'Don't you see?' she pleaded with Edward. 'I am ashamed for my people to find out what I do in Kuala Lumpur.'

Edward nodded, suddenly feeling embarrassed that he was poking into her life just to satisfy his curiosity, yet fascinated to have scraped below the surface of her Chinese inscrutability. He said, 'I'm sorry. It's none of my business.'

'I have to do it, for the money,' she repeated desperately, tucking her son to her other hip. There was no point trying to escape him and for some reason she could not define, she wanted him to know why. 'These people mustn't know I am talking to you.' She glanced round but there was no-one in sight. 'You see, I have no husband, here in the village, and there is no-one else to look after my boy.'

'I understand,' said Edward, trying to. He had never thought of it, but he supposed most of the girls in brothels might have similar stories to tell. She looked distraught, her pretty oval face tortured with pain.

'You don't understand,' she contradicted him fiercely, her humiliation driving away her tears. 'How can you? I have to do what I do. I have to!'

Edward was appalled by the image of her sacrifice, when suddenly a massive explosion echoed round the valley, shaking the hot air.

Liya froze, and for an instant, her black eyes held Edward's astonished gaze. Then she wrapped her arms firmly round her baby and sprinted along the path towards the squatters' village as fast as she could.

Over the hill, the culvert heaved beneath the armoured truck and burst in a mushroom of orange flame, hurling the three-tonner up and sideways like a toy. In the roar of noise, Lao Tang pulled his finger tight on the trigger of his Bren. His shoulder juddered as bullets shattered the windscreen of the leading jeep and the driver's red sunburnt face disappeared in a cloud of red. At once, he shifted his body to fire at the officer beside him, following his target as the jeep careered off the road into the ditch. On the periphery of his vision, he was aware of the truck smashing back to earth in a shower of green and pink bodies, clods of earth and stones.

Edward stared at the pall of smoke rising above the rubber trees on the hill ahead, and guessed at once where the ambush had been sprung. He pressed his foot flat on the accelerator, and as the jeep raced along the road throwing up a cloud of red dust behind, he grabbed the radio and began to shout, 'Three-one, three-one, radio check, do you read me? Radio check? Over!' There was no answer.

Lao Tang had been deafened by the noise of gunfire pouring down on to the road. His own target, the jeep, lay on its side in the ditch below him, the wheels spinning, and punctured with bullet holes. It was half-concealed by green scrub but there was no movement and he guessed the occupants were dead. His magazine ran out of bullets. He reached over the top of the Bren to change magazines, and paused, horrified. There was a huge crater where the culvert had been. The remains of the jungle green truck had come to rest twisted and shattered upside down at the side of the road. All over the slope, among the scrub and burned tree-stumps, bodies lay scattered, bloodied and mutilated. Their screams carried over the rattle of gunfire. He wished Ho Peng would give the order and they could move forward in the Charging Unit to finish them all off with hand grenades.

The camouflage of leaves snapped above his head. Instinctively, he ducked and glanced at Ho Peng whose eyes were glittering with excitement. 'They're firing back!' he shouted hoarsely. 'Keep firing!'

Lao Tang sneaked another look over the lip of his fire position. Ho Peng was frantically pointing at the blackened crater where the stream was finding a new path through the red earth and stones, and through the smoke Lao Tang could just see jungle green uniforms moving in the hole. He levelled the Bren and opened fire but the stinking black smoke hanging over the crater made it impossible to see exactly where the survivors were hiding.

Ho Peng shouted down the line, 'Charging Unit! Prepare to attack!' The British were at his mercy and he dared not waste time.

He wanted to seize their weapons and vanish back into the jungle. Fighting the Japanese had taught him that it was fatal to hang about. He gripped two British Army 36-grenades and prepared to lead the assault.

Edward braked before the bend round the hill and stopped. Beside him, the avenues of rubber trees on each side of the road were ominously silent compared to the racket of small-arms fire he could hear over the high ground above him. The continued firing, more sporadic now, was at least encouraging. Someone must be fighting back, but he assumed the CTs would have flank protection parties out and he was afraid someone might have seen or heard his jeep. Feeling very vulnerable, he grabbed his Sten gun and jungle webbing belt, hopped out and crouched beside the jeep. He pulled the radio handset across the seat and called up, 'Hallo zero! Hallo zero!' He had to raise Headquarters, for immediate assistance. 'This is nine-four. Contact! Contact! Over.'

Please, please let them answer, he whispered to himself, constantly looking around him. Sweat poured off him. He wiped his eyes with the back of his arm.

A weak reply buzzed in the earphone but he could make nothing of it. Rapidly he sent his message anyway, 'Nine-four, Contact! At 12.10 hours, on stream-road crossing on boundary of Black Circle Rubber Estate. Enemy ambush of convoy, call-sign three-one, returning with SEP. Three-one not answering radio. Casualties and full details not known. Fighting support and casevac required asap. Am going to render assistance. Over.' He repeated the message twice, in between buzzing, incomprehensible replies and then ran back into the cover of the trees to work out his next move.

Sporadic firing from the other side of the hill made up his mind. Support from Headquarters would take at least an hour to come, assuming they had received his message at all, and he could imagine the plight of the men caught in the ambush. They needed help at once. After a final quick glance round to assure himself he had not yet been seen, he headed up the hill through the rubber at a crouching run, dodging from tree to tree, his eyes hurting with the strain of trying to spot the Chinese terrorists he knew were ahead, before they saw him.

Panting hard, he reached the brow of the hill and the rattle of gunfire was clearer. A few bullets snapped through the branches above him and he threw himself on the ground. No more came and he sheepishly realised they were stray bullets from the few men fighting back. Encouraged but wary, he forced himself to stand up again and move forward. Keeping low, his knees brushing his chest, he advanced towards the shooting. His stomach was liquid with his fear of not seeing the Chinese CTs before they saw him, and his flesh shrank in anticipation of being hit. He told himself he did not mind dying, it was just the pain he was afraid of.

Suddenly, over a rise in the leafy covered ground between the rubber trees, he looked down between the last lines of silver trunks on to the red laterite road eighty yards below him. Shocked, he took in at a glance, the smoking crater, the wrecked truck and the jeep on its side. From his vantage point, he picked out a few green-clad soldiers, hunched behind the wrecked vehicles, firing back up the hill, and he saw the Chinese lying hidden in a series of cunningly prepared trenches between him and the men on the road. He estimated the MRLA party was at least thirty, maybe more.

At that moment Ho Peng, Lao Tang and three others in the Charging Unit stood up and began to weave downhill through the burned tree stumps and scrub, grenades in hand.

Edward saw their intention at once. The men on the road needed help. He forgot how exposed he was in the open rubber plantation, stood up to get a better view, leaned his Sten against a rubber tree, took good aim at the taller bandit in the lead and fired several shots.

Lao Tang sank to his knees gasping with surprise. He clutched his calf. Beside him, Ho Peng swore, 'Comrade Lao Tang, keep going! You are letting down the attack!' He tried to drag Lao Tang to his feet but Lao Tang could do no more than crawl back to his shallow trench. Ho Peng, oblivious of the bullets, kicked him angrily and ran on down the slope. He crouched behind a tree-stump and threw a grenade at the truck. Encouraged by his example, the others quickly threw theirs too.

Edward kept firing but he watched helplessly as the little black objects arched towards the storm ditch where the soldiers were lying. They landed and he counted the seconds off one by one. At eight he realised with a thrill that they were duds. One exploded, making him drop to his knees behind his tree and he never saw what effect it had.

He looked up again and saw the MRLA soldier preparing to throw again. The man was small but plainly a fanatic, wiry and energetic, leading from the front. Edward fired at him, aiming carefully. He grunted with satisfaction seeing him duck and twist, his throw spoiled, and his grenade exploded harmlessly in the scrub.

175

Cursing, Ho Peng turned and doubled back up the slope, cutting and weaving uphill through the rough ground. He searched the rubber behind his men's position as he ran, and spotted Edward moving behind his tree. He flung himself back beside Lao Tang who had crawled back clutching his bleeding leg, and screamed furiously at the Rear Defence Group, 'Stop watching the road! The British are in the trees behind you. Kill them!'

Terrified, six Chinese behind the main line whipped round and loosed off a hail of bullets into the shadows under the rubber trees behind them. Edward flung himself to the ground. Bullets clipped white latex chunks from the tree trunk three feet above him. In a moment of clarity, he unclipped his magazine. Maybe five or six rounds left. Grimly, he rammed it back into his Sten. He had four spare 30-round magazines in a pouch on his belt. Ammunition was not the problem, but the flat leafy ground between the rubber trees all round gave no cover from fire and the Chinese terrorists would soon outflank him. He thought briefly of Headquarters and prayed they had heard his radio message even though he knew they couldn't help him now. 'Come on, the Seventh Cavalry,' he whispered to himself.

They were working round him. He caught sight of a movement through the trees, twisted round on the ground beside his rubber tree and emptied his magazine at a fleeting target of pale khaki fifty yards away. Then he swiftly changed magazines and slithered away to the side, to change position and keep them guessing. Uphill would be suicide, in full view of the enemy below, so he wriggled through the fallen leaves wishing he was a snake, a very small snake, straining his head to see left and right as he went.

Ho Peng was hurling instructions at his men, convinced a patrol of some size was behind him. He sent an Element of ten men uphill to the right with orders to sweep across through the rubber trees just below the ridge of the hill and flush them out.

After forty yards, Edward was filthy, covered with soft damp leaves, soaked in sweat and exhausted. He lay still gulping in warm air as quietly as possible, sure he could hear surreptitious steps coming towards him from all sides. Suddenly a Chinese CT in the same uniform as the SEP stood up silently only thirty yards away and padded across his line of vision, crossing the lines of rubber. Edward stopped breathing. He was in full view. All the CT had to do was turn his head. A second joined him. Edward had to move. Or die. Very slowly he brought his Sten up, took quick aim and shot the first in the chest as he appeared in the centre of an avenue between the trees. The second hesitated and died too. Detachedly Edward watched the expression of amazement on his sallow face as the burst raked him across the stomach. An answering rattle of fire crashed through the trees, but Edward stayed on his belly and wriggled away as fast as he could around the hillside. Behind him Ho Peng's party of ten reached the flank and began moving rapidly through the trees, Ho Peng still shouting at them from down the slope.

Edward came to a pile of dried branches lying on the ground. The plantation spread uniformly in all directions and the rise which had concealed him so far was turning into a convex bowl in the crook of the valley from which there was no escape. He was cornered. The dead branches offered no protection from the bullets but at least he could take the CTs by surprise when they came on him. He crawled behind the branches and lay still, his heart beating hard against the ground. He peered between the branches. A head appeared over the groundline from behind a tree. The Communist Red Star was quite clear on his cap. Three more appeared to the left and right. They were calling to each other as they came in his direction.

He took a deep breath. CTs, he knew well from Intelligence reports, never took British Army prisoners. He determined to die fighting. Very quietly, he took another full magazine from his pouch, ready to fit it, put it ready on the ground beside him, lifted his Sten and aimed at the MRLA man nearest to him. The sweat poured off his forehead, blinding him as he stared through the dried leaves. When they were about thirty yards away, he squeezed the trigger in a long burst. He dropped from sight, and the others vanished as he swung his fire on them too.

To his surprise, there was no answering fusillade. He fired several more bursts, to warn them off in case they were creeping closer for a charge, and changed magazines, trying desperately not to fumble.

Then he listened. A heavy machine-gun was in action down on the road. Keeping a wary eye around him, he concentrated and heard its steady powerful thump beating on to the slope below him. When there was a .50 on your side, he told himself absurdly, there was still hope.

Inside the Monster, stopped on the road in sight of the wreckage of the ambush, Tallard shouted over the din of the .50 Browning, 'Bastards are running away!' Sweat was running down his face in the heat inside the steel truck, but he was grinning and hunched his bulk over the twin handles of the big machine-gun, his thumbs pressed on the trigger.

Three bearded Punjabis were beside him. Employed as estate maintenance men, he had trained them as a reaction force and they were firing their carbines through portholes at the hillside following the markers of Tallard's livid red tracer bullets. The effect on the Chinese MRLA, already unnerved by Edward's activities in their rear, was electric. Ho Peng could hardly keep them from throwing down their weapons as they broke cover and ran uphill into the rubber.

Edward heard them go, running round the hillside out of view, and he fired several quick bursts at two men he glimpsed running between the trees. Finally, all the firing stopped. Silence beat down, like the sun.

He waited. Just to be sure they had all gone. Minutes passed and sweat blinded him. In the silence, he was almost afraid to move. He heard a big diesel vehicle grinding along the road and recognised the sound of Tallard's armoured truck. Cautiously, he stood up. The rubber trees were still in the heat, grey leaves limp, and not a soul stirred. He walked slowly downhill past the bodies of the two men he had shot. On the edge of the rubber, he saw the Monster on the road near the crater and Tallard clambering out. He shouted. Tallard peered up, then waved back.

Edward walked on down the slope, pleased to be alive, but he felt no joy in his survival.

'You were frigging lucky not to be with this lot,' said Tallard when Edward stepped over the ditch on to the road. His hand swept round at the carnage.

Edward shrugged. He had come close enough. Matter-of-factly, he said, 'Let's do what we can for them till the lads get here from KL.'

'If they come,' said Tallard pessimistically, but he left one Punjabi on guard in the Monster, keeping a look-out, then set to with Edward to help the wounded.

They counted the casualties. Surprisingly, only eleven of the twenty-three had died, including the jeep driver and the Malay constable, but all the remainder were hurt, either in the initial blast or with gunshot wounds during the subsequent fire-fight.

Edward found the young platoon commander lying on his back in the ditch near his jeep, with a broken leg and a sucking bullet wound in the chest. 'Strap him up,' said Tallard bluntly throwing across a handful of shell dressings he had brought from Marsha's medical centre. Further down the ditch, he knelt by a soldier whose arm had been shot off below the elbow and wrapped it in a tourniquet. Shaken, he moved on to the next, muttering, 'This bloody rescue party better turn up soon.'

The platoon commander looked up at Edward and whispered, 'Were you in the trees up there?'

Edward said, 'Yes,' and lifted him carefully to slide the strapping round his chest. The young officer's face drained of colour but he made no sound. After a few minutes, he caught his breath again and went on, 'We owe our lives to you. We'd had it,' he gasped. 'When those bastards ran down the hill at us with grenades, we had nothing left. You stopped them.'

Tallard glanced at Edward but said nothing.

'He did, you know,' insisted the young officer leaning round to see Tallard. 'Up there on his fucking own.'

Edward remembered little of the next hour, going round in the blazing sun from one man to the next, from the muddy slimy crater to the dusty scrub where the leaves were spattered with blood and already covered with flies, till all their filthy mud-streaked tortured faces blurred. All except one man, the platoon sergeant, a stocky man with years of soldiering experience. His face remained crystal clear in his memory. He lay calmly on his back staring up at the harsh Malayan sun, his white skin burned red, and his blue eyes watched Edward bending over him trying to bandage his severed legs. The two stumps were cauterised by the fire of the explosion, but he had lost too much fluid. Edward worked mechanically, knowing it was useless without plasma to stop the shock. He felt the man's hand on his shoulder and, like a father, the old sergeant said quietly, 'You did fine up there, lad. You did fine.' Edward looked up at him, astonished his voice could be so peaceful in such a nightmare of destruction but the sergeant had died.

Edward flung the bloody bandages down and punched the red mud. Sean Tallard had been watching and said, 'The British die well in other people's countries.'

By the time the relief force appeared, a convoy of armoured cars, trucks and a doctor with an ambulance, Edward was exhausted. Drained by the heat, the sights and the desperate good humour of the men, he sat down on the bank of the ditch, near the upturned jeep, and let the relieving soldiers take over. In an atmosphere reminiscent of Dunkirk, the wounded had begun to make tea from rations they carried in their webbing and waited patiently, smoking cigarettes. There was a bizarre sense of having won, typical of the British Army, in spite of the terrible cost.

Captain Denton appeared, striding up the road, dapper and handsome in clean jungle greens, his blond moustache bristling under his floppy cotton hat. He took in the scene at a glance, fished in his pocket for a packet of Du Maurier cigarettes and offered one to Edward. They lit up.

Edward drew deeply on his cigarette and felt dizzy. He said, 'What a bloody waste, Harry.'

'Could have been worse,' said Denton quietly.

'No, I mean the whole frigging effort to bring in that SEP.' He waved his cigarette towards the jeep. The SEP lay stretched up under the back of the vehicle, his arms over his head still handcuffed together, and dark red stains, almost like sweat, coloured the front of his pale khaki uniform.

Tallard joined them. He had come down to find the SEP too. 'Ho Peng succeeded in eliminating this bastard, but it's not a total loss.' He prodded the body with his toe. 'I talked to him last night.'

'Why didn't you say so before?' asked Edward tiredly.

Dismissively, Tallard replied, 'Because you were going to ask him all the questions you wanted back in Headquarters.'

'And what did he say?' asked Captain Denton disapprovingly.

Tallard ignored his tone and said, 'His name was Li Chi-Chen, and as far as I could tell, he deserted because he was terrified of Ho Peng. Been beaten up by him several times. Ho Peng took his weapon off him last week, put him on vegetable-growing duties and when that happened he thought he'd be killed. Probably right too.'

It suddenly occurred to Edward that Ho Peng was the man leading the grenade charge and he said, 'At least I know what that little bastard looks like now.'

Tallard frowned and was about to continue describing his talk with Li Chi-Chen when Edward asked bluntly, 'Was Li with Ho Peng in the war?'

Captain Denton looked up at the question and Tallard scowled, 'No. Why?'

Edward shrugged, 'I don't know. Just thinking of Ho Peng and all those caches. Maybe Li Chi-Chen was thinking of rewards too.' He squinted up at Tallard. At least, they were even for the day.

The big Irishman glared at Edward. Then he wiped the sweat off his face and stamped off to his armoured truck without another word.

Harry Denton said, 'What the hell was all that about?'

'I'm not sure,' said Edward, feeling dizzy from smoking and tired in the sun. Tallard, Ho Peng and caches. The significance was there, somewhere.

Suddenly Captain Denton exclaimed, 'Christ, I nearly forgot, seeing all this. But Diana's had her baby!'

'Tell me!' exclaimed Edward sitting up. 'What was it?'

'She went into labour soon after you left and Doctor Hazlitt rang the office about the same time HQ got your message on the radio for help.'

'Yes?' Edward urged, shading his eyes to look at Denton against the sun and thinking she must have given birth about the time the mine went off under the truck.

'A girl.'

'A girl?' Edward repeated, his energy fading. Exhausted after the fighting and helping the wounded, he tried to resolve the news with his conviction that Diana had been going to give him a son.

'She's going to call her Ellie.'

'How is she? Diana, I mean,' Edward asked, feeling guilty that he ought to have been at the hospital.

'Mother and child—' began Denton cheerfully.

'Doing well,' Edward interposed in a flat voice and dropped his head in his hands, suddenly feeling terribly tired.

Chapter 11

ABANDONED

'How's little Ellie?' said Leonard Goodbury solicitously. A fawn tropical suit, black shirt and white dog-collar hung on his gaunt frame like a windsock in dead air, and he held a plate covered with sandwiches from which he ate steadily. 'She must be nearly, what, eight months old?'

'She can nearly stand up on her own, padre,' said Diana happily. She always enjoyed talking about her baby.

'Motherhood obviously suits you,' the padre replied in a toothsome compliment. Diana, blonde and elegant in a light-blue cotton dress and wide-brimmed straw hat, had recovered her figure remarkably well.

Diana beamed at him and sipped her tea. She took the opportunity to look round and see if there was anyone else she ought to talk to. She and Padre Goodbury were standing on the grass near the steps into the garden with a good view of all the guests.

Davina Bleasley entertained a selected list of guests to tea every month, always on a Wednesday afternoon when the offices in the Headquarters closed for sports, and her large verandah was full of people and the hum of relaxed chat. The men wore a mixture of shirts and ties or uniforms, the women colourful dresses. Malay servants in white tunics, because Colonel Bleasley refused to have any Chinese in the house, moved about offering plates of thinly-sliced sandwiches. Diana considered it quite a coup to have been invited as Mrs Bleasley never normally asked anyone of less rank than major, and she was pleased to see Colonel Bleasley talking to Edward on the verandah.

'I was just talking to your very lovely wife Diana,' said Colonel

Bleasley pompously. 'And she tells me Roger Haike is your brother-in-law.'

'Yes, Sir,' replied Edward dutifully. With a sinking feeling he knew exactly what was coming next.

'Good show, eh? Him getting a Military Cross for that train ambush. You must be very chuffed.'

'Delighted,' said Edward.

Colonel Bleasley squinted sharply at Edward, his little eyes searching for disagreement. He went on emphatically, 'Impressive show, mustering the men after the crash and fighting off those Chinese devils.' He dabbed at the sweat on his neck with a large silk handkerchief, glanced about and added in a confidential tone, 'By the way, Fairfax, I've been meaning to talk about that ambush of yours, up at the Black Circle .'

Edward waited politely. Over Bleasley's shoulder, he noticed Diana talking to the padre. He hated tea parties.

'Didn't want to mention it in the office,' continued Colonel Bleasley. 'Not the right place.'

'For what, Sir?' asked Edward, prepared to be bored whatever it was. Colonel Bleasley was supreme at dressing up old news and other people's ideas to sound like his own.

'Wanted to let you know I couldn't put you up,' said Colonel Bleasley blandly. 'Not really on, you know. That young platoon commander was jolly polite about what you'd done and so on, but he did damn well too and we couldn't really give out two MC's for the same "do", could we?'

Edward was stunned. Colonel Bleasley took his silence for understanding, patted the dampness inside his collar again and said cheerily, 'Good man. Knew you'd take it well.' With that he threw a cautious glance at his wife who was busy talking to a brigadier and stepped briskly through wide-open french windows into the house, heading straight for a drinks table in the corner of the room.

Edward watched him go in a daze, trying to grapple with the pleasure of knowing he had been considered for an award and fury that Colonel Bleasley had refused to support it. Through the french windows he watched Bleasley pour himself a large whisky s'tengah and turn to chat ostentatiously to a group of older officers and their wives.

After hearing news like that, the last thing he wanted to do was go on making polite conversation. He thrust his cup and saucer into the hands of a passing Malay houseboy and nipped down the steps into the garden.

'Excuse me, padre,' he said smiling at Leonard Goodbury. 'Must take Diana from you. Suddenly remembered. A million things to do at home.' He took Diana firmly by the arm and pulled her away.

Diana threw a desperate smile at the padre who gallantly rescued her cup and saucer before she dropped them. Puzzled, he watched Edward usher her off round the corner of the house.

'Edward, for goodness sake! What on earth are you doing?' she demanded once they were out of sight and earshot of the party. She hated causing a scene. 'We never thanked Davina for having us!'

'I couldn't care less!' said Edward rudely. 'Her fat husband has just told me he refused to support an award for me. Why couldn't the spiteful bastard have told me before?'

Shocked by his language, she said, 'Maybe there were reasons?'

Edward snorted, 'Who's side are you on?'

'That's not fair!' said Diana. 'We only went to the Bleasleys because I thought it would help you.' She hurried to keep up with him striding across the lawn towards the road, her high heels catching in the grass.

'Well it hasn't and we're going home.' They reached the Plymouth. He walked round, got in the driver's seat and started the engine.

Obstinately Diana stood by the car considering whether she would go back to the party, but the idea of walking home did not appeal, not for the distance, but having to explain why. Silent and angry, she got in the car.

Neither of them spoke until they were back in the bungalow. Edward went straight into the sitting-room and slopped a generous measure of whisky in a glass. He switched on a bulky 'His Master's Voice' radiogram in the corner of the sitting-room as the calm educated tones of a literary reviewer declared, ' "Crawfie", whose real name was Marion Crawford, was the Governess to heir-to-the-throne Princess Elizabeth and to Princess Margaret and she has revealed intimate Palace secrets for the first time in her memoirs serialised in the American magazine *Ladies Home Journal*. We ask the panel if the trust of our future Queen as a little girl should be broken?'

'Certainly not! Dreadful thing to do,' Diana snapped at the radio and went immediately to check the amah who was looking after Ellie.

When she came back, as Edward knew she would, to listen to the six o'clock World Service news, Edward was staring morosely into the garden on his second whisky s'tengah.

'You all right, darling?' she asked, her temper restored. She hated seeing him depressed and had almost forgiven him.

He shrugged without turning round and asked, 'Want to come out for a drink later?'

She glanced at the big tumbler in his hand and said, 'Not really. I'm going to give Ellie her bath after the news.' She had already tied her long fair hair in a knot to keep it out of the way.

'Yes, of course,' he said dully. They seemed to go out so little lately.

Diana hesitated, then made up her mind and said, 'I know you're upset by Colonel Bleasley and I just wanted to say that I don't like him very much either, but aren't there special rules he has to follow?'

She had not meant to sound condescending but Edward snapped, 'Not at all! It's not up to him to decide. I don't care if I get anything or not, but at least he could have put up the citation. Instead, he deliberately scotched it. Out of sheer spite.'

Diana hesitated again then said, 'I hope you won't say that sort of thing to anyone else.'

'Why not?' asked Edward, idly watching the colour fade from the evening sky and the sharp silhouette of a bird flying over the big banana palms standing out of the clump of jungle beyond the garden.

'Well,' said Diana rather desperately, feeling the conversation sliding out of her control. 'We have to keep in with people like Bleasley.'

'The authorities, you mean?'

'Yes, I suppose so.'

Edward swung round, checking his watch, and declared, 'In that case, let's listen to the news so you can hear just what the bloody establishment is like.'

Puzzled, Diana sank on to the sofa. Edward marched furiously over to the radiogram and whipped his hand over the Bakelite volume knob so that the familiar introductory strains of the World Service news signature tune 'Lilliburlero' boomed deafeningly into the room. Then he poured her a drink, shouting over the noise, 'You'll need this.'

She said, 'No, thank you,' but Edward appeared not to hear and handed her a glass which she put down untouched on a table. Since having Ellie, she found alcohol gave her a headache in the heat. Edward said nothing and re-filled his own glass instead.

The music died away, and the prim, cut tones of the announcer echoed from the big mahogany sound-box, 'In London, the Foreign Office has officially recognised China's new communist regime led by Mr Mao Tse-tung. Britain has withdrawn recognition from Nationalist China under General Chiang Kai-Shek and his Kuomintang forces. In America—'

'That's the bloody establishment for you,' said Edward in bleary triumph. He turned off the radiogram.

'It can't be true?' whispered Diana.

'Well, it is,' said Edward. 'I've known all day. We all read it on a signal this morning in the office. It's outrageous! While we are trying to defeat the communists in Malaya, the British Government is voting for the Chinese communists in China! Even the bloody Russians walked out of the United Nations when Mao Tse-tung's representative took his seat in the United Nations. But not our chap. Oh no. He sat there and voted for him.'

Diana could not believe her ears, but her faith in the status quo was not easily rocked and she said, 'I'm sure there must be a reason, darling.'

Edward peered at her crossly, and said, 'Of course there's a bloody reason! People like Bleasley and the bloody Government are a bunch of selfish sods doing exactly what suits them to stay in power. Meanwhile, the rest of us graft our bollocks off fighting to stop Malaya being taken over by the communists.' Hot and furious, the image of the platoon sergeant dying after the ambush slipped through his mind.

Diana needed time to think about it. She stood up and said, 'I must give Ellie a bath.' She was as shocked as Edward but her matter-of-fact tone of voice implied acceptance of London's attitude and infuriated Edward.

'Is that all you can say?'

Diana was genuinely puzzled why he should be angry with her and replied practically, 'The amah has gone home, Edward. There's no-one else to do it.' Actually, she enjoyed looking after Ellie herself, and normally Edward was so busy working on his Chinese lessons with Lao Song at that time of evening that she never thought he cared.

Edward looked crossly at her, gulped down the rest of his whisky and walked out, oblivious of her hurt.

He found the Plymouth's car keys in his pocket as he crossed the grass to the road and drove through the gathering dusk into town, straight to the Coliseum Bar.

In the foyer he noticed there were very few pistols on the table. For eighteen months since the Emergency started all the planters and tin miners had carried guns and, in the Coliseum Bar, they always left them on the table in the foyer. However, by six in the evening, the wise man was already back on his estate, to avoid driving along remote roads at night when the risk of ambush by the CTs was high.

Sure enough, the dark mahogany-lined bar was deserted except for a few at the tables. Mr Wong, the owner, was nowhere in sight. Only Willie the barman stood behind the bar, in his usual white and black waistcoat, working through a backlog of used glasses.

'A bottle of Tiger please, Willie,' said Edward climbing slowly on to a barstool.

'It's been a bad day for you?' enquired the barman as he poured Edward's beer. The customer's fair hair was untidy, his Parachute Regiment tie was awry and he could smell the whisky.

'It's been a bad day for Malaya,' said Edward gloomily.

'You mean the recognition of Red China?'

'Everyone knows now?'

Willie nodded with a serious expression on his thin face. 'The customers talk of nothing else tonight. Everyone very angry.'

'I'm not surprised,' said Edward and drank deeply. Willie hung about wiping the counter-top, as if he wanted to chat, so Edward added, 'What were they saying?'

'They say it explains why the authorities hide the truth from the newspapers, that the situation is more serious but the British Government wants to play it down. D'you think that's true, Mr Fairfax?'

Edward shook his head. 'Nonsense, Willie. You know what the Press are like for finding things out, and there's no Press censorship here.'

'But how can you tell?'

'I read all the official reports, Willie, at work,' Edward said flatly. He drained his glass and pushed it across the bar for another. He knew he was getting drunk but he did not care. He had worked hard for months, trying to stop the communists, sifting reports to build a picture of the movements of men like Ho Peng. He had passed information to infantry patrols, followed up an endless list of horrible murders, many of them by Ho Peng's gang, interviewed the survivors, and doggedly battled to minimise the damage caused by Colonel Bleasley's objections to the police by secretly liaising with Angus Maclean to hear his Special Branch assessments. His effort had been wasted. Bleasley's spiteful rebuttal of his actions at the ambush and the British Government's espousal of Chinese Communism was too much in one day. He felt badly let down.

He said, 'The bloody Government couldn't have given the Communist Terrorists a bigger morale boost if they tried.'

'That's what they all say tonight,' agreed the barman. 'Like it was 1941 all over again. When the British abandoned Malaya to the Japanese.'

Edward nodded. Disbelieving estate managers, tin miners and ex-patriate businessmen had been calling Headquarters all day to register their disgust. 'We didn't deserve it. Things are bad enough here already, Willie.'

'Like what, Mr Fairfax?' asked the barman pouring a bottle of Tiger. He watched the thin froth of beer rising up the glass.

'Like Sir Henry Gurney's National Registration system, Willie,' said Edward, also watching the froth. When Willie slid the beer towards him, he drank deeply, wiped his lips with the back of his hand and said, 'It's a damn good idea for everyone to have an identity card, to tell who's bona fide and who's not, but of course the bloody CTs hate it and they're causing a lot of trouble.' He shook his head sadly. 'Bastards keep murdering the poor photographers we send out to take pictures of all the villagers.'

'And the villagers themselves,' said Willie who always read the newspapers avidly.

Edward stared into the top of his beer and wondered if Liya had been photographed. He had not been out to the Black Circle for months. Too busy, and no excuse to authorise an escort to get out there. Gloomily he supposed she was still leading her double life between the squatters' village and the 'hotel' in Chinatown.

He drank his beer, dropped the glass back on the counter and ordered another. It suddenly occurred to him that she might be a useful contact in the village. He laughed at himself, out loud, startling the barman. He had been dreaming of developing a source for months, but he had been too ambitious and aimed too high. He thought Tallard might have fixed him up with a real CT. Stupid bastard, he muttered to himself. Expecting a social introduction to a real jungle fighter in the MRLA, like at one of Mrs Bleasley's tea parties? Especially from a man like Tallard. He snorted. And all the time that little Liya had been going backwards and forwards under his nose. Too insignificant to notice. He had dismissed her as just a girl forced to flog her body for cash. But she lived in the squatters' village and she would know the others. Maybe some Min Yuen, or even CTs.

'That's the answer, Willie,' said Edward slushing his words. He banged his fist loudly on the bar. 'I'm a fool for not seeing it.'

Willie the barman nodded politely, quietly polishing a glass with a cloth. He glanced at the few other customers at the tables, but no-one had taken any notice. All the white men were getting drunk in Malaya that night.

'Fetch me a taxi, Willie! I've got an idea.' He struggled in his trouser pocket for his wallet and fumbled for Gandra Singh's card. 'This chap will come. Always does.'

The barman took the dog-eared card and disappeared. Edward drank his beer while he was away, gazing vacantly at the bottles on the glass shelves. The barman returned, gave Edward his card and said, 'Your taxi will be here very soon, Sir.'

'Well done, Willie,' Edward slurred, laughing at himself again.

'Three beers, Sir, will be $4.80.'

Edward dropped $6-Malay on the bar, waved his arm expansively and said, 'Keep the change, Willie. Money makes the world go round, eh? That's what someone said to me once.'

He walked steadily out through the foyer to the road, his mind filled with his decision to recruit Liya. By the time he had negotiated the steps and covered walkway, Gandra Singh was waiting for him with his bulbous old black Austin, door open. Edward clambered in, collapsed on the worn back seat and shouted, 'To Chinatown! To the Wild Orchid Hotel.'

Gandra Singh, shaking his head in a mixture of agreement and sorrow, drove the short distance into Chinatown, turned off Petaling Street and stopped outside the hotel. Edward heaved himself off the back seat, fell back, and finally struggled out to the street where he took several deep breaths of warm air, tangy with the smell of frying ginger. He paid off Gandra Singh and shoved through the bead curtain into the red-lit bar on the ground floor of the hotel.

'A beer,' he said in blurred Chinese to the little Malay girl behind the counter at the end of the room. She smiled dutifully, her pale make-up lurid under the red lanterns over her head and reached for a bottle of Tiger in the fridge.

Carefully hanging on to the counter-top, Edward peered through the red gloom and counted five customers, all Chinese, in two groups. Some of the girls were already sitting at their tables. A large, heavily made-up Chinese woman in a bulging red and green silk cheongsam approached on rocking high heels from the end of the bar. She said, 'I'm Lu-Lu Suzie. This is my bar. You like a girl, mister?'

Edward laughed loudly, thinking how surprised the woman would be to know why he wanted one of her girls, and Lu-Lu smiled professionally to match his humour. 'You like joke?' she said, her slanting black eyes wrinkled with pleasure. Drunks always parted with their money and they were seldom fussy.

'Yes,' he said, blinking to see her mouth was full of gold teeth. Frantic erotic images leaped into his furred mind as he imagined what she must have done to earn the gold, capping one tooth after the other. He switched his gaze to her heavily made-up eyes and plunged on with his plan, 'I'm looking for a girl I met here once, called Liya.' Without waiting to see how Lu-Lu reacted, he grabbed the glass which the Malay girl gave him and gulped the beer.

Lu-Lu gave him a beaming smile and asked, 'You see her in here now?' She waved a fat ringed hand at the tables.

'No,' said Edward, nettled. He might be drunk but he had not forgotten what Liya looked like.

'Okay. You not worry. Let me go see,' Lu-Lu whispered, winking conspiratorially. She was an expert at avoiding trouble and did not want to lose this customer. Officers earned much more than Other Ranks, who only received a paltry nineteen shillings a week which gave them no more than $8 spending money. She patted Edward's arm and left him at the bar to make her way through the arch to the stairs at the back of the hotel. She climbed two flights, pulling herself up on the banisters, and stood to catch her breath on the first-floor landing. She was older than she would admit to anyone else and heavier than she would admit to herself.

In the bar Edward accepted a cigarette from the little Malay girl because she had lovely brown eyes, and chatted to her in a mixture of rusty Arabic from Palestine and Malay he had picked up from Hassan. He inhaled deeply on the cheap cigarette and the nicotine made his head spin. The little Malay girl laughed happily at the expression of drugged surprise on his face. She came round the bar

191

to hold him steady as he swayed on his stool and lifted his beer glass to his lips, to help him drink away the taste of tobacco.

In the corridor upstairs, Lu-Lu Suzie knocked on the door of the room with the Royal Doulton Bath. The door opened and a Chinese girl with short dishevelled black hair put her head round the door. She was clutching a sheet round her shoulders and said to someone inside, 'It's Lu-Lu.'

'Let her in.'

The girl let Lu-Lu through and quickly shut the door. Then she dropped the sheet to the floor and walked naked back to the bed.

'What is it?' said the man sitting cross-legged on the bed. He was wearing just a pair of cheap blue cotton trousers which he had slipped on when he heard the knock and his wiry torso showed not an ounce of fat.

Lu-Lu's eyes swept round the room, at the red flock wallpaper, the writing paper on the table, the empty beer bottles and the girl's clothes scattered about. She said, 'There's a British officer downstairs. He wants Liya.'

Ho Peng narrowed his eyes. 'Why?'

The naked girl wriggled sinuously round behind him and her hand caressed along the top of his thigh.

Lu-Lu shrugged her big shoulders, 'I didn't ask.'

'How does he know her name?'

'How should I know?'

Ho Peng angrily brushed the naked girl's hand off his leg and wiped a sheen of sweat off the rough skin of his face. He decided, 'I'll come and look.'

Lu-Lu said quickly, 'I don't want any trouble here. He's very drunk.'

'Then he won't make a sound.'

He smiled at the expression of distaste on Lu-Lu's powdered face and told her as he dressed, 'You don't care either way, do you? Not for him. Just for yourself, but you have to remember that we act for the Party, and even the British Government in London votes for us now.' He laughed at the puzzlement on her face as he tucked in his shirt. He picked a fat-bladed knife from where he had hidden it under a pillow on the bed and walked over to the door. He glanced into the corridor. 'You go first, talk to him, tell him Liya is up here. When he comes, I'll be waiting.'

Edward saw Lu-Lu coming back through the archway into the bar and waved her over impatiently. The little Malay girl deferentially made room for her and returned behind the counter.

'Well? Where's Liya?' Edward asked.

Lu-Lu put on her smarmiest smile and replied, 'Liya is upstairs.'

'Nonsense,' said Edward loudly. 'She's not here, is she?' The little Malay girl had been so impressed at hearing Edward try to speak Malay, and so informative.

'She's up in room, for you,' Lu-Lu contradicted him, frowning. She was not sure what had happened, but Ho Peng would be furious if his fish got away.

Edward wagged his finger ostentatiously, feeling all the frustration of the day boiling up inside him. His idea to use Liya as a source, even perhaps wean her away from her life as a prostitute, was being thwarted at the last by more lies. He shouted, 'She's not bloody here, is she?'

Two Chinese men at one of the tables looked up in surprise. British soldiers commonly caused fights in town but it did not pay to be caught up in one because the police took every advantage of the laws of arrest under the State of Emergency regulations. They stood up, threw some money on the table and scuttled out through the bead curtain.

Ho Peng heard the shouting. He ran lightly down the stairs and along a passage at the back of the bar. A narrow door concealed in a dark alcove behind the bar itself served as an emergency escape for the barman. Ho Peng eased it open. Edward was standing now, with his back to the door, shouting and pointing his finger at Lu-Lu's broad bosom.

She had plastered a wide insinuating smile on her face and was insisting, 'Liya upstairs. I promise!' She saw the secret door open and Ho Peng's face in the shadows but not a flicker changed her expression. Instead, she tried to hold Edward's arm, as if to calm him. Another few seconds she promised herself, and when Ho Peng struck she would spit on this arrogant, drunk British officer.

'Sahib wanting taxi?' boomed Gandra Singh from the doorway. As the bead curtain clattered back into place behind him, he swelled his barrel chest and peered challengingly at everyone over his thick grey beard and moustache.

'The Punjab Infantry Regiment!' shouted Edward delightedly. 'Bloody right I do!' It seemed entirely logical to see the Sikh taxi-driver again. He was disgusted with the fat woman who kept telling him lies and wanted to leave anyway. He swung his arm from her grasp and nearly fell over.

193

Lu-Lu cried out, 'Wait!' She gestured at the shadows behind the bar, but Gandra Singh was quicker. Moving across the bar with surprising speed for a man of his bulk and age, he caught Edward in a bear-like hug and swung him back towards the entrance. 'We go now, Sahib,' he bellowed.

Waving one hairy arm like a windmill in case anyone tried to stop them, he held Edward's body firm with the other and dragged him stumbling across the boards, through the bead curtain and on to the street.

'Yes, Gandra Singh, time to go,' Edward burbled, feeling dreadfully light-headed, like a butterfly.

'Very timely indeed, Sahib,' agreed Gandra Singh panting hard, but without stopping. He could hear frantic shouting inside the hotel and shuffled fast across the street to his taxi holding Edward like a sack.

'Bloody Chinese,' muttered Edward; frustration and alcohol washing over him.

'Yes indeed, Sahib,' gasped Gandra Singh emphatically. 'Bloody Chinese. Always wanting money.' Edward had not paid for the beers. Several Chinese swarmed out of the hotel into the street.

Gandra Singh flung open the back door, shoved Edward unceremoniously inside, slammed the door and jumped into the driving seat. 'No time for saluting now,' he muttered into his beard and thumped the steering wheel, praying his old Austin would start at once.

'Salute be damned!' shouted Edward from the back seat where he lay on his back, vaguely aware they were being chased. 'Remember the Punjab Regiment, Sergeant Gandra Singh! Charge!'

'Punjab Infantry! Very good, Sahib,' grinned Gandra Singh with delight.

Hands beat on the roof and reached for the back door-handles and suddenly the old Austin taxi jerked forward. Edward gazed stupidly for a moment at various upside down Chinese faces which disappeared and were replaced by a blur of multi-coloured neon signs picking up speed past the window. Then his eyes glazed over and he passed out.

Chapter 12

A NEW VILLAGE

Ah Chi stood at the door of his hut, scratching his stomach and looking around the squatters' village. It was mid-afternoon, the sun still hot on his face, but it was now poised to fall behind the jungle over Bukit Chondong to the west. Several tousled-haired children played with pieces of bamboo in the dust in the open area between the huts, among the few chickens scuffing about for pecks of food or insects so small it seemed the stupid birds were eating dust. The tappers had returned from work with their clothes caked in soft white latex, the foreman Hou Ming had measured their daily quota of 144 trees for their pay, and they sat in front of their huts, smoking cigarettes, talking and relaxing. The smell of cooking filtered through from the back of the huts where their women were preparing the evening meal, and columns of smoke rose above the attap roofs from their fires into the still hot air.

Liya laid wood rice bowls on a table and glanced past Ah Chi's skinny silhouette in the doorway at her three-year-old son playing naked in the dirt with the others. He had recovered well from his sickness of the year before and seemed in good health. A movement beyond the village caught her eye, between the silver water of the padi field and a bright green clump of bamboos. She looked hard, squinting against the bright sunshine reflecting off the rice ponds.

Khaki figures were approaching, maybe fifteen in a long line, snaking at a steady pace round the padi field towards the village.

Ten minutes later, Ho Peng strode casually into the tappers' village as if he owned Malaya and the British Army did not exist. Bad-tempered, he put one hand on his hip, beside a .38 revolver holstered on his belt, and snapped an order for his men to bring

195

everyone out of their huts. Behind him one of his soldiers, whom Liya recognised as Lao Tang, held a pole in one hand from which fluttered a long red banner. The Chinese characters on it in gold read, 'Through Violence we shall Conquer!'

The MRLA soldiers herded everyone into the middle of the village, shouting and jostling. By force of habit Liya counted ten MRLA armed with a mixture of Stens and carbines, and supposed the others were deployed out of sight behind the clumps of bamboos at the back of the village to stop people sneaking away. Liya followed behind Ah Chi and his elderly wife who was grumbling volubly about leaving her cooking. As the men and women gathered round in a half-circle, the young black-haired children, who had been playing in the dirt, ran uncertainly to their parents. Liya's son pushed between the legs of several people in front of her and grabbed her cotton trousers.

'Long live the revolution!' shouted Ho Peng glaring round at the big crowd of villagers. They responded with a lack-lustre echo, impassive, like cattle, and he declared, 'The proletariat must be led towards the true people's revolution.'

Liya wondered what brought Ho Peng out in broad daylight to make speeches in the village, but she recognised the form of words and her heart sank.

'Show your indentity cards!' screamed Ho Peng.

No-one moved. Suddenly, the purpose of the MRLA visit was plain.

'Show them!'

When no-one obeyed, each scared to be the first, Ho Peng became apoplectic. His pock-marked face, dirty and pale from months spent in the jungle, suffused with blood. He flicked open his holster, pulled out his revolver and pistol-whipped the nearest man. The sound of the metal butt plate striking the tapper's head echoed clearly round the village, his legs splayed like rubber and he sprawled senseless on the ground. Ho Peng gestured at one of his men who ran over and tugged at the unconscious man's latex-encrusted clothes. In seconds, his hands found a pocket and he stood up holding a small card high above his head. The passport-sized photograph of the tapper was plainly visible to everyone.

'This card is for the National Registration scheme invented by the British Imperialists to control the free peoples of Malaya,' said Ho Peng as if speaking to a class of school children. He waved his revolver at them. 'You know why the British want to register everyone?'

The motley crowd of Chinese villagers shook their heads.

'To tax you!'

The villagers groaned and nodded their heads. Now they understood.

Ho Peng snapped impatiently, 'They want to control your lives and take away the freedom we in the Malayan People's Communist Party have promised you.' He paused and almost conversationally demanded, 'Who else has an indentity card?'

The crowd of Chinese busily shuffled about, their hands searching in their dirty trousers and shirt pockets, but before anyone could produce one, Ho Peng glanced at the unconscious man at his feet, aimed his revolver at his head and pulled the trigger. The man's head jumped, dust and blood blew up beneath, his body twitched and he lay still. In the silence after the sharp report, everyone froze. A thin Chinese woman screamed, shoved forward through the crowd and flung herself on her husband, trying to pull and beat the life back into him.

Ho Peng ignored her and said in chilling tones, 'Anyone with a card who does not immediately show it will also be shot.'

At once, hands found their new identity cards in their pockets and thrust them forward. One of Ho Peng's MRLA soldiers went round taking them all in and piled them on the ground in front of Ho Peng. Lao Tang stepped forward with a small bottle of petrol, emptied it over the pile and set fire to it.

Clutching her little boy to her knees, Liya watched the flames engulfing her face on the top of the pile and breathed more easily. The moment she had informed Ho Peng that the whole village had been photographed, she knew that blood-letting was inevitable. It was part of the revolutionary struggle, as he had said so often before. She wondered if the whites had heard the shot from Tallard's house, but she suspected Ho Peng had prepared an ambush in case Tallard came to investigate with his armoured car.

Ho Peng tore his eyes from the fascination of the fire and stated, 'No-one will belong to the National Registration scheme. It is an anti-revolutionary crime.'

Liya stared at Ho Peng's face trying to read his mind. She was sure this part was not rehearsed.

'Line up in families!' shouted Ho Peng. 'All men, women and children together.' He snapped orders to his men who shoved the villagers into groups. Liya picked up her little boy and stood beside Ah Chi, his old wife Ah Po, and his family, his sons and their wives and children. Feeling she was being watched, she glanced round and saw, hidden inside the attap hut behind them, an MRLA soldier standing silently with his carbine held across his chest. There was no escape.

The villagers waited silently, docile and afraid. Ho Peng stood at one end of the line and said, 'You will be punished for not fighting the oppression of the British Imperialists and their running dog photographers, and to warn you never to disobey the orders of the Malayan People's Revolution again.' With that, he grabbed a small girl by the hair, dragged her away from her mother, rammed the muzzle of his pistol against her temple and fired.

Blood spewed out of the small head and the body collapsed on to the hard earth.

Liya suddenly felt light-headed and utterly detached. She was in the hands of fate. She gripped her boy to her chest and kissed him. Ah Chi turned his head to look at her but his expression was impossible to read. Another shot made him jump and he looked back in time to see Ho Peng drop a baby boy to the dust, shot through the chest. The villagers stood stunned and speechless, as he stepped over the small corpse and searched among them. 'There will be four!' he hissed. The MRLA soldiers stood impassively round, their carbines and Stens levelled at the crowd.

The mothers of the dead children began screaming and struggling, but their men held them fast, trying hopelessly to comfort their distress. Emasculated by shock, all they could think of was preventing their women running out and being killed too.

Ho Peng marched up the line. Liya was sure he flashed a look at her. Five paces away, he stopped, shoved his scrawny arm into the terrified crowd and grabbed a boy by the arm. His mother screamed and pulled back. Ho Peng swore and his soldiers stepped forward. Encouraged by the screaming of the other distraught women, the mother desperately tried to wriggle free with her child tucked in her arms. Ho Peng switched his grasp, seized a handful of her long black hair, and pulled her out between two men who fell back in terror without lifting a hand to stop him. He flung her on the ground, the child bounced from her arms and he shot it twice.

'No!' screamed the woman, scrabbling on her stomach back to her bloodied baby.

Moving swiftly, Ho Peng stepped over the body and walked

quickly back to the crowd on the balls of his feet. He hated the wailing, screaming women. At the end of the group of villagers, he looked straight at Liya.

'No,' she whispered, holding her son tightly to her front and quietly echoing the frantic screams of the woman she could see clutching her dead baby in the dust. 'No!'

'Give him to me,' said Ho Peng grimly. 'The revolution demands the greatest sacrifice from everyone. Individuals do not matter. Only the Party matters.' He seemed to sneer as he held out his left hand, his right hanging loose by his side with the revolver. One shot left, Liya thought. Just one.

She broke his gaze, knowing what was in his mind. Ignoring him completely, she bent gently over her small son. She kissed him, on his cheeks and eyes, and he smiled at her, and she brushed his straight black hair back from his face.

Ho Peng lost his temper. He lunged forward, grabbed the boy by the leg, and yanked him from her arms. In the second that her arms lost their grasp on her son's warm body she turned to iron, rooted to the ground, detached, like a person dreaming. She never really saw her boy swung like a doll to the ground, or heard his terrified screams and the sudden shot which blew his skull apart. She stood quite still without a word, arms hanging loose, and empty like a shell.

Ho Peng walked past the four little bodies, casually flicking the used cartridges from the chamber of his revolver and replacing another six rounds. Then, he looked up at the stunned villagers, shouted an order and walked out of the village. Lao Tang, with the red banner, fell in behind him, followed by the other MRLA soldiers in their wake.

In a Nissen hut in the police compound in Langat, nine miles away on the road to Kuala Lumpur, an old fan turned slowly on the ceiling of a little room, unable to stir the smell of sweat, linoleum floor polish and paintwork warmed in the sun.

'That finishes my briefing for the Langat District War Executive Committee,' said Edward thankfully after forty minutes talking, sure his words had fallen unheard, like dead leaves. He lifted the collar of his shirt to free the sweaty material sticking to his back and fanned his face with his lecture notes.

None of the four men sitting at the table stirred. A policeman in pale tropical uniform heroically fought to keep his eyelids open, his head nodding erratically; an infantry major beside him in jungle greens, the Company Commander from Camp Rideau, doodled with a pencil on a small khaki notepad; and Sean Tallard, in voluminous safari shirt and slacks, stared out of the window at a palm tree bending in the heat, his mind elsewhere. He was thinking about a wide open space which had been cleared not far from the site of the ambush the year before.

After a long silence, the fourth man at the head of the table, a small Malay neatly dressed in a light-grey silk tunic, said, 'As Chairman, I want to thank you, Lieutenant Fairfax, for a most interesting brief.' His voice was cultured and he spoke very good English.

'Thank you, Datuk Mohammad Razak,' said Edward using the Malay's full title.

The Malay's brown face creased in a pleasant diplomatic smile, showing perfectly white teeth. He raised his voice, 'Perhaps you would summarise the important points?' The change in timbre disturbed the policeman who snapped awake and somehow contrived to look astonishingly alert, leaning forward on the table and shuffling some papers. Sean Tallard looked at him in disgust.

Edward had given six of these briefings to newly formed District War Executive Committees in different areas but he nodded dutifully and repeated, 'General Sir Harold Briggs has just taken up the newly created post of Director of Operations for all Malaya and he is convinced that the only way we can defeat the communists is to win the ideological war. He has instituted these committees, at District level like this one here for Langat, and at State level, to co-ordinate all civil and military action throughout the country. He stresses that the army is in direct support of the civil government which is why he has declared that all these committees are chaired by Malays.'

The major grunted.

Realising the army would now be asking him for information to act on, the policeman asked innocently, 'What are the important elements of the plan?' His eyes had been tight shut when Edward mentioned them first.

Tallard gave a great sigh.

Edward said, 'General Briggs wants us to dominate the populated areas and build up a feeling of security among the people. In other words, to achieve the opposite of the CTs who are terrorising them. Then he wants to break the communist grip on the population, especially among the 600,000 Chinese squatters all over Malaya, and so isolate the CTs from the Min Yuen who provide their food and information supplies.'

Puzzled, the Malay Datuk said, 'I'm really not very sure how this is to be done?'

'Nor me, Datuk Mohammad,' observed Tallard drily.

Edward avoided Sean Tallard's eye and said, 'The fourth point is to destroy the communists by forcing them to attack us on ground of our own choosing.'

'What precisely does that mean?' insisted Tallard. The policeman nodded looking from one to the other round the table.

'Ambushes,' said the major decisively, tapping his pencil on to his doodle. It snapped and he swore, then apologised with embarrassment.

The Malay Datuk nodded vaguely. 'I'm sure you are right, Major. Yes indeed, but how can we woo the Chinese away from the communists?' He frowned. 'We're giving them so much now with agricultural grants and supplies, such as seeds. Even pigs, which I'm told the Chinese people like. But what else?'

Edward said, 'Perhaps the State Executive War Committee will give you some guidance?'

The Malay brightened at this. The strategy of war was as obscure to him as the gore of its tactics was ghastly, but he understood politics. He said, 'Thank you, Lieutenant Fairfax. I shall seek advice from the State Committee, the SWEC as you like to call it, no?'

Edward's brain hummed with the tune, 'Defer! Defer, to the Lord High Executioner!' as he heard brisk military steps in the corridor outside. There was a knock on the thin wood door, it opened and Captain Denton stuck his head into the room wearing a peaked forage cap. He saluted the Datuk, as the senior man in the room, and said, 'Bad news, Mr Tallard. Just heard your tappers have been attacked again. The bastards killed four children this time. A patrol chanced to be in the area and went to the village when they heard the shooting. The sergeant thinks the CTs attacked because all the people had National Registration identity cards. He found a pile of ashes of burned cards by the bodies.'

Sean Tallard swore and demanded, 'They see any CTs?'

'Not a thing, and no-one will talk.'

'They're scared out of their minds,' said Tallard looking back round the men round the table. 'And that's the bloody problem!' He apologised to the Malay, and stormed out of the room.

The policeman followed him, properly alert now. Harry Denton looked at Edward. He said, 'You'd better come too.'

Tallard led the way in his Monster, Edward followed in the armoured car he had taken to drive to Langat that morning, and the policeman brought up the rear in an armoured 15cwt truck.

Twenty minutes later, as the sun was sinking fast, this impressive column arrived, engines roaring, in the open area among the cluster of poor attap huts in the Black Circle squatters' village. Men in a variety of uniforms, all heavily armed, jumped out of the vehicles.

The Chinese watched from their huts, keeping their thoughts to themselves. The dusty compound was strangely empty and silent compared to the terrible killing ground it had been an hour before. Only a few women knelt in the dirt by the bodies of the dead tapper and three of the children, weeping and alternately wringing their hands or stroking the small corpses, but the fourth child, a small boy, was alone and covered with flies.

The infantry platoon sergeant had deployed his thirty men in groups around the village in case the CTs came back. He saw Edward, the only army officer among the newcomers, came up, saluted and said, 'Pity these poor sods didn't 'ave all this fire-power 'ere two hours ago. Might 'ave stopped it 'appening, Sir.'

'We were sitting in Langat talking about it,' said Edward bitterly.

'Separate the CTs from the people,' quoted Tallard, hands on hips, looking at the scene. 'How, I'd like to know. How the fucking hell *can* we stop them?'

Edward felt sick looking at the single little naked body on its own. Marsha Tallard come out of a hut in her white nurse's uniform and Edward could see she had been crying. She said, 'I brought my First Aid box, but there's nothing I can do. There's no one hurt except these.' She gestured at the little corpses. The policeman, grim-faced, was starting to make notes of the scene of the crime. He stooped down to pick up a couple of brass empty cases which caught his eye, and one of his colleagues was taking photographs.

The sergeant watched them and said, 'I told the villagers to leave the scene as it was. Just like I was told on the radio.'

Edward nodded and asked, 'Have the villagers said anything about the CTs?'

'No,' said Marsha her voice cracking. 'But it's got to be Ho Peng.'

Edward's eyes were drawn irresistibly to the small body lying untended on its own. 'Does this one have no family?'

Marsha looked at him and big tears welled in her eyes. She

replied, 'That's the little boy I helped cure last year, just before that awful ambush.'

Edward stared at her. 'Are you sure?'

Marsha nodded.

Liya's child. He looked at the bloody corpse, trying to imagine the Chinese girl with the little boy, alive and laughing, the reason for her sacrifices in Chinatown. Feeling as empty as if the loss was his, he asked, 'Where is she? I mean, the mother?'

'She lives in that hut usually,' said Marsha, puzzled by Edward's sudden concern. She pointed at the hut she had been in. 'I can't understand a word of Chinese, but she's not there. Poor girl probably doesn't even know what's happened.'

Not in town, Edward thought. Please God, don't let her be in town while this was going on. He turned to the sergeant and asked, 'Did you see anyone on the road, leaving this place, when you turned up?'

'No, Sir.'

Edward thought for a moment and strode into the attap hut. An old man and woman were sitting at the table and other younger members of the family were outside at the back of the hut sitting quietly round a fire. Edward recognised the old man as Ah Chi, whom Tallard had spoken to when he first showed him round the estate. He mustered his Chinese, thankful for Lao Song, and said very carefully to the old man, 'Ah Chi, I am sorry for what happened today.'

Ah Chi did not answer for a moment, surprised to hear a British Army officer speaking his language, even badly, but he said, 'You British have an Empire, yet you are always sorry about killing?'

His accent was rougher than Lao Song's, and Edward struggled with his vocabulary. The old man's lack of interest seemed strange after what had happened. He asked, 'But this child was one of your family?'

'Which child? There are four.'

'The one lying out there on it's own,' said Edward crossly. In the fading light, it seemed more like a pile of earth. The other bodies were obscured by women kneeling and softly wailing. Only Liya's child was alone.

Ah Chi shook his head. 'No.' His wife watched implacable, her black eyes hardly visible in her old face.

Edward changed tack and asked, 'Where is the mother?'

Ah Chi shrugged.

Edward lost his temper and shouted, 'Where is she? Where's Liya?'

The old Chinese looked up, his eyes wreathed in wrinkles and wondered how this British officer knew her name. He observed the white officer was genuinely upset, which puzzled him, but he said, 'That way,' and pointed out of the village. 'Near the rice.'

Edward ducked out of the attap hut and walked quickly towards the padi field. The sun was sinking fast behind the jungle beyond, casting long shadows of the trees across the ground. On the edge of the village, hidden behind a clump of bamboo, he passed a half-section of the infantry patrol and told them he was going out of the perimeter for a moment.

'Right-ho, Sir,' said the corporal and to the man beside him, he whispered, 'Officers like to pee in private.' They laughed.

Edward knew what they were thinking but he did not mind. He looked left and right in the shadows, afraid to lose Liya before darkness made it impossible to find her.

'Liya? Are you there?' he called in Chinese.

She heard him coming and she thought of moving, but the day had robbed her of power as surely as it had robbed her small son of life. She sat on the bank on the edge of the padi field and waited for whatever would happen next, staring at the gold and blue reflections of the evening sky on the water.

Edward almost missed the slight figure in the tall lallang grass. She was sitting cross-legged on an earth bund on the edge of the padi field, quite still, her back straight, her hair loose in a black cascade over her shoulders and staring at the last bright colours of the sunset over the jagged silhouette of jungle trees and the reflections on the water in front of her, with the myriad spikes of rice breaking the surface.

He knelt down beside her and wondered what to say. Finally, he said simply, 'I'm terribly sorry,' in halting Chinese. Even after a year with Lao Song he was not prepared for this.

She lifted her shoulders slightly. She was wearing a short-sleeved shirt and her bare arms hung down with her hands lying in her lap on the grey cotton of her working trousers. She fancied she could still feel the warmth of her son on her skin in those last moments she had held him.

'I wish I could have done something to prevent this,' he said earnestly.

She did not move. There was nothing the British could do. They

204

were a spent force, and had been ever since their defeat by the Japanese in 1942.

Desperate to prove his concern, he leaned earnestly forward and unconsciously put his hand on her knee, saying, 'Tell me, surely there is something I can do?'

She solemnly looked at his hand, feeling its weight and warmth on her leg and he snatched it away in embarrassment. All he could think of was the Wild Orchid Hotel and he cursed himself for being so clumsy. In a rush of English, he said, 'I'm sorry. Really, I meant nothing. I just wanted to help.'

She turned to face him and her slanting dark eyes, wide and dry, explored his face. She saw the lines of worry on his forehead and the serious expression in his blue eyes and she said in a small voice in Chinese, 'You have come here to find me, and you try to speak my own language, and I believe you.' She reached up her bare arm and put her own quite small hand on his shoulder as if to reassure him.

Her face was calm and beautiful, quite unlike the distraught mother he had expected to find, and he gently put his hand back on her leg, without a qualm of embarrassment, for her simple gesture reaching out to him had brushed aside the veil of her grief and silently broken down the barriers between them. For the moment, they were two people uncaring of uniforms, of the social gulf between them or the harsh world.

Conscious of the opportunity, Edward asked casually, 'It was Ho Peng, wasn't it?'

In their peaceful cocoon, the question seemed entirely natural to Liya. All the strains of the years meant nothing after what Ho Peng had done to her, so she nodded, knowing perfectly well that the admission was a subtle but definitive step to tell him other and far more important secrets. To her surprise, she felt no regret, just relaxed and even a little satisfaction.

'What will you do?'

'Carry on,' she answered simply, for there was nothing else she could do.

It was the answer Edward wanted to hear, so he could see her again, for he felt sure she could be a real, if low-level, source of information among the villagers. At that, the soft look in her eyes faded, she took her hand away, and the spell was broken, letting the world back in. He said, 'I'm sorry. The future always spoils the present.'

'Sometimes both can be a dream,' she said lightly, though she believed in it, and she wanted him to believe in it too, although she thought it was odd for her to be encouraging him. She realised her feelings about him had changed. Then she was on her feet, looking down at him still kneeling and thinking how slow these big Europeans were.

He stood up and she walked briskly ahead through the red-grey dusk back to the village, her small feet taking short neat steps along the path compared to his loping stride which she could hear behind her.

The corporal saw the slender Chinese girl with long black hair first, was suspicious of a trick, and then relaxed when he saw the officer in shirt and shorts behind. He said, 'I was just coming to find you, Sir. They're all champing at the bit to go back there in the village. Worried about the regulations, Sir. Getting caught out on the roads at night.'

Edward thanked him briefly, feeling like a traveller in time returning to the planet from a place of peace to find everyone at war. He followed Liya straight past the little group of soldiers. The corporal frowned and wondered what the officer had been doing with the pretty Chinese girl by the padi fields.

Two days later, Colonel Bleasley blustered into the Intelligence office in Headquarters and announced, 'The Briggs Plan is on its way! New Villages for all.'

Edward, sitting at his desk, looked up at Harry Denton who sat opposite him at the other end of the outer office, and they both looked at Colonel Bleasley. Smugly he told them, 'We're going to move all those bloody Chinese into New Villages, whether they like it or not.'

'Why, Sir?'

'Don't be stupid, Fairfax,' snapped Bleasley. 'You know the General wants to separate the CTs from the Chinese population in kampongs and towns. To keep the buggers away from the Min Yuen.'

Captain Denton frowned and said, 'Yes?'

Exasperated, Colonel Bleasley explained, as usual personalising the ideas as if they were his own, 'We move all the squatters into new villages, Captain Denton, and we give them land of their own, freehold land, so that instead of being squatters and vagrants they become part of Malaya.'

'And the Malay Sultans have agreed to give land to all these Chinese?'

'Yes,' said Bleasley piqued that Edward had spotted the crucial link in the plan. 'Sir Henry Gurney has been working on the Sultans in every State since he took over as High Commissioner. Now that Briggs is here as the Director of all combined operations, we can get on with it.'

Harry Denton coughed and asked, 'Pardon me, Sir, but I'm not really sure how this helps?'

Colonel Bleasley blew his nose in his handkerchief which was already damp with his sweat, took a deep breath and said, 'We fence the New Villages with barbed wire, and we put guards on the perimeter. That means we can carry out random food searches when the Chinese tappers or miners go out in the morning, which gives them the perfect alibi for being unable to bring food to the CTs. We'll also ambush paths to the fenced villages to stop the CTs getting back at them at night. D'you understand, Captain Denton?' Colonel Bleasley intoned, 'Isolate, separate, and protect! That's the ticket.'

'There are 600,000 Chinese squatters in Malaya,' said Edward in amazement.

'We're going to move the whole lot,' stated Bleasley.

'They won't like all those restrictions very much,' remarked Denton.

'Better than having your children murdered,' said Edward.

'Quite!' said the colonel and waddled towards his office.

Edward could not help adding, half to himself, 'Isn't it bloody typical that the British Government always acts too late?'

Colonel Bleasley whipped round and shouted, 'How dare you criticise the Government!'

The memory of the children's broken bodies flooded back and before Edward could stop himself he burst out, 'It's now two years since this Emergency was declared! Those poor devils at the Black Circle could have done with all this protection and interest a couple of days ago.'

To his surprise, Colonel Bleasley did not totally lose his temper. Instead, he snorted condescendingly, 'What the hell d'you know about the problems faced by senior Staff or the High Commissioner? Besides, those bloody Chinese are probably Min Yuen, helping the CTs. Serve 'em bloody right if a few get knocked off.'

He stamped into his office and slammed the door. Captain

Denton raised his eyebrows at Edward who was seething, thinking of Liya's dead son. He was about to make another bitter remark when the door flew open and Colonel Bleasley's red face re-appeared. He said, 'Thought that name rang a bell. The squatters at the Black Circle are going to be moved tomorrow! To that bit of cleared land nearer the main road.'

Edward swallowed his amazement at the sheer rotten bad timing of the move which might have prevented the five deaths. Quickly, he asked, 'May I go along, Sir?'

'Certainly not, Fairfax. Out of the question.'

Edward went anyway. He left Captain Denton all worried to cover for him as best he could and, that same afternoon, dressed in jungle greens with his belt of patrol equipment and Sten, he linked up with the infantry company commander from Camp Rideau who was to set the cordon around the village. The platoons moved out in darkness at two in the morning in trucks and, an hour later and grateful for the light of a half moon, Edward found himself walking in a single file of silent shadowy soldiers through the scrub and bamboo around the squatters' village. Edward wondered if Liya was sleeping in her hut, with the old man and his wife and the other tappers and their families. Or was she in town?

The line stopped, the soldiers spread out, far enough apart to encircle the village altogether, but not so far that someone could slip between them in the shadows. They settled down to wait for dawn. As an 'extra', Edward sat near the entrance to the village, hidden in bushes, with the same sergeant who had found the murders in the village two days before.

Dawn came softly, a half-light after five o'clock in which the women of the village stirred and prepared small fires for their tea and morning rice. As thin columns of smoke rose vertically in the still air, the tappers, in shorts, walked to the river to wash, and children scuttled about half awake, scratching themselves and peeing as they felt like it.

The sun broke over the chaotic ridge line of mountains rising above the 'Black Circle' and Sean Tallard drove into the village in his armoured vehicle. He stepped down and shouted at everyone to gather round. Behind him came a government official from the Chinese Affairs department and a policeman in a jeep escorted by a Ferret armoured car.

Edward joined them. Tallard showed little surprise at seeing him and while the villagers emerged from their huts to see what was going on, he said, 'Pity this didn't happen before, but moving down near the main road will cause havoc with my tappers. Hell of a way for them to walk up to do their work.'

Edward sympathised, but there was no alternative to the Briggs Plan for New Villages and Sir Henry Gurney was not allowing any.

For the second time in a week the Chinese stood docilely in the middle of their kampong and their futures were decided. Tallard stood on an upturned Tiger beer crate and told them, in Chinese, 'You're going to be moved. Now! Every one of you, with all your pigs, chickens, children, goods and chattels. One family to each army truck, which will be here soon. You'll be helped by the soldiers. And when you get to the New Village, each family will be given a piece of land to grow your vegetables and raise livestock.'

Ah Chi considered himself old enough to risk asking a question. 'What d'you mean "given land"?'

Tallard grinned and replied, 'Ah Chi, given means given. The land you have by the end of today will be yours in a hundred years. If you live that long.'

Some of the younger Chinese laughed but Ah Chi looked grave, for in his experience nothing was given for nothing. His wife who had heard everything, understood none of it and her old leathery face looked quite blank. She did not want to move.

Edward said in Chinese, 'You will have more than land, Ah Chi. You will own part of Malaya. You will be a part of the future of the country.'

Ah Chi bowed, showing wisps of white hair on the top of his head. He had heard many promises recently, from the communists and now from the British. Time, he told himself, would tell.

Outside on the road, they all heard a distant roaring of diesel engines which grew stronger and soon the first of a column of forty trucks turned off the road into the village. The move began.

Edward found Liya among Ah Chi's family but she was aloof and the bustle of activity made it frustratingly impossible to talk. He watched her packing up the pathetic few belongings in their hut, pots, pans, a kettle, patterned cotton sleeping mats, a couple of battered water-buckets, a cardboard box of food, the table, bowls, three bamboo chairs, and the animals, four chickens, a pig and two mangy pye-dogs. Three soldiers helped them load everything in a three-ton truck after a hectic chase round the mud yard to catch the chickens which the children enjoyed enormously, shouting and laughing with delight.

Before they left, they were all photographed. Proper identity cards were a condition of the New Village, so the army could catch CTs without identity cards trying to slip into the new compound unnoticed. Edward watched Liya as the Indian photographer took her picture for another ID-card, and wondered if she was thinking what the cost of her first one had been but her face was impassive.

When at last the time came to drive away Ah Chi's old wife refused to leave. She sat down in the door of her hut and wailed, overcome with confusion. Ah Chi ignored her and clambered on to the truck, for he knew the British soldiers would bring her. Two young privates, both National Servicemen, sweating in the sun with the effort of loading everything and chasing the chickens, came over to cajole her but she refused to budge, howling louder than ever. 'I'm glad she's not my mother-in-law,' said one.

'Well, leave her,' said the sergeant crossly. 'Or we'll never get this lot moved.'

'Come off of it, Sarge, the family wouldn't be complete without her!' said the other private good-naturedly. The two privates glanced at each other, slipped either side of the old lady and scooped her up between them. 'Just like catching them chickens.'

'Just as scrawny.'

'No-one's going to eat this one.'

'Don't be dirty, you lot,' intoned the sergeant in a low voice as he helped them lift her into the truck.

Still wailing, she sat next to Liya and the truck, one of the first to leave, started out of the village. The infantry sergeant stood with Edward and remarked, 'Ain't that the young bird you found, Sir, couple of days ago? Mother of one of them dead kids?'

Edward nodded. Oddly, it seemed too personal to talk about.

'I thought so,' said the sergeant pleased with himself. 'These Chinks are bloody hard to tell apart.'

Edward watched her go. Just before the truck turned along the muddy track round some tall banana palms, Liya glanced back at him, but she was too far away and her expression seemed no different to all the others sitting on the heaped truck. Then the truck jolted over mud ruts and her hair fell across her face like a black curtain.

The move took all day. The New Village had been selected only three miles away, chopped out of a piece of jungle the other side of the stream where the truck had been blown up over the culvert. Tallard did not like his workers having so much further to walk to

210

the rubber plantations, but at least the operation had cleared all the jungle on the north side of the road between the estate track and the Sungei Lui and gave the CTs one less place to ambush him.

When Edward followed Liya's truck there, the army engineers were still working with big green bulldozers to clear the ground of logs, stumps, branches and the vegetation debris of the jungle. Other work parties were putting up the chain-link and barbed-wire fence around the village compound, to ring a flat area for the New Village huts. Beyond the cleared patch the Sungei Lui ran sluggishly through the bottom of the wide valley, providing water for the villagers.

The trucks from the old squatters' village arrived all day in more chaos of unloading, shouting and arguments. Ah Chi, being one of the first, was allocated a good position on a slight rise, so the tropical rains would not affect their new quarters. They put up temporary army tents until their new huts were built. Liya and the others worked hard to make things comfortable for their first night and she had no time for Edward. He left them to it.

It was hard to believe they would make sense of their lives. He had no doubt that the British Army's passion for organising motley groups of people all over the British Empire would see to it that the New Village was a model of neat new timber huts, lined up with military precision, fenced and guarded, but whether such extraordinary civil upheaval would help defeat the brutal men in the jungle remained to be seen. It struck him as ironic that the British Imperialists were supplying 600,000 Chinese with a revolution which the communists had promised but could not supply themselves.

All the infantry vehicles were busy with the move, so Edward had to take a taxi home from Langat Police Station. Gandra Singh picked him up in his old black Austin. As they drove sedately back to Uxbridge Drive, Edward decided it would not be safe to turn up in the office in dirty sweaty jungle greens without checking with Harry Denton whether Bleasley had noticed his absence.

At the house, Edward noticed the Plymouth was not parked at the end of the cul-de-sac, which meant Diana was out. He paid off Gandra Singh and then suddenly said, 'Come in and have a beer, Gandra Singh. It's a long time ago, but I owe you for dragging me out of trouble downtown.'

'Oh no, Sahib!' replied Gandra Singh shaking his head emphatically. 'I couldn't possibly do that. What would the Memsahib say?'

Edward was not sure, or whether this meant Gandra Singh

thought that British women objected to beer, or to Sikhs, or if Gandra Singh was afraid to meet Diana for some reason, but he insisted. He could not shake the memory of the killings in the squatters' village, and the move, especially being unable to talk to Liya, had left him peculiarly depressed. He had somehow expected her to take more notice of him. He wanted a drink and some company and the one time he needed her, Diana was not at home.

Gandra Singh flapped across the lawn barefoot in his old leather shoes and tried to wipe his big hands clean on his loose shirt and baggy trousers. Inside the house, he looked round apprehensively as if he expected to see Diana at any moment, but relaxed somewhat when Edward went into the kitchen and brought back two bottles of beer. They sat down to drink on the rattan chairs on the verandah.

'This house reminds me of the Punjab,' said Gandra Singh and proceeded to tell a long story of his time in the Indian Army, one big hand waving about in the air, conjuring the characters of his story, the other wrapped hugely round his glass or wiping the froth from his beard and bushy moustache each time he drank. His tale of Prajapati Brahma, Manu, and an enormous fish weaved warm images and made Edward forget his problems in Malaya.

Lao Song brought their second beer on a tray and Edward made him sit down too. Hassan hung about at the end of the verandah on the corner of the house grinning at the three of them but refused to join them.

'He says he's too young,' said Lao Song solemnly, priest-like in his long black working clothes.

Gandra Singh chortled. He seemed to have forgotten his worries about coming into the Sahib's house and stuck his legs straight out under the table.

Lao Song carefully lifted his wispy moustache out of the way with his long fingers and put the glass to his lips.

'I'm very grateful to you for teaching me Chinese,' said Edward in Chinese and quoted the first poem Lao Song had made him learn, to perfect his pronunciation, 'Tian Yuan Di Feng, the sky is round, the earth square.' And then told him about talking to Liya.

Lao Song looked very wise, his face parchment dry, and replied, 'If you wish to speak of death and love, we must apply ourselves in new directions. There is much to learn.'

'I didn't say anything about love,' said Edward laughing.

Gandra Singh chortled again, 'Oh Sahib! You cannot separate women from the talk of love.'

212

Lao Song nodded, 'That is the way of the East.' He pressed his wisps of hair aside and drank again.

By the fourth beer, the sun was sinking, Edward had slumped down in his rattan chair, Gandra Singh was humming a love song in his deep bass voice, and Hassan stood beside the table, contentedly listening to the rhythmic cadence of Lao Song's Chinese quoting the Analects of Confucius from memory: 'When a man's wisdom is sufficient to attain something, but his love is not sufficient to hold what he has obtained, whatever he has attained he will lose again.'

'So love is more important than wisdom?' asked Edward slowly in Chinese.

'Of course,' replied Lao Song sagely.

'What on earth is going on here?' demanded Diana in high-pitched amazement from the french windows. No-one had heard the low note of the Plymouth returning and her appearance was as if by magic.

'On cue for an interesting conversation about love, darling,' Edward laughed, misunderstanding her expression of astonishment.

Tall and beautiful, in a smart blue dress, matching high heels, handbag and pearls, her blonde hair tied back, she gazed at the empty bottles stacked on the table and the look on her face struck Edward as rather funny.

Gandra Singh scratched his hairy chest uncertainly through his shirt, peering up at Diana from his chair. The lassitude of beer was upon him and he was quite unable to leap deferentially to his feet as he would have liked and as he thought the Memsahib might have expected him to do.

'Want to join us, darling?' asked Edward genially. He waved at the bottles. 'Hassan will get you a glass.'

'At once, Mem Punjang,' said Hassan, his big brown eyes willing to appease. He shifted from foot to foot, awaiting the outcome of the conflict of wills between the Tuan and his wife of which the Tuan Edward seemed blithely unaware.

'Certainly not!' snapped Diana, and stood her ground without really knowing what she would do next.

'Where've you been?' asked Edward, ignoring her tone and drinking some more beer.

'To tea with Mrs Bleasley and Padre Goodbury. I gather you're in real trouble. Again.' She emphasised the word, and though she did not mean to, sounded like a schoolmistress scolding an errant boy. 'She says her husband's going to give you some extra duties.'

213

'Stuff him,' said Edward pleasantly and told Hassan in Malay to fetch more bottles of beer. He listened to the satisfying sound of Hassan's bare feet scuffing along the verandah boards and added without rancour, 'Bleasley's a fathead, Diana. Sit down and join us. Lao Song was telling us all about love.'

Lao Song bowed from the waist on his chair with a deeply serious expression on his face but he said nothing, for he was drunk.

'Ridiculous!' Diana snapped. She desperately wanted to join them, but she was fed up with Lao Song's absurd refusal to speak to her just because she could not understand his impossible language, making her feel as if she did not belong in her own house, and she blurted out obstinately, 'I haven't time! I'm going to settle Ellie in her cot, have supper and go to bed for an early night. I'm exhausted.' With that she walked back into the house.

Behind her, Lao Song said something in Chinese and Edward replied in Chinese, and she heard the pop of another bottle of beer, which convinced her she was doing the right thing, to show them she did not approve. However, as she busied herself round the house with her baby, then eating her supper which Hassan slipped in to give her sitting alone in the dining-room, and finally much later lying unable to sleep in the darkness in the big double bed, she could not shut out the constant buzz of low male voices from the verandah, the clink of glasses, the occasional deep rumble of laughter from Gandra Singh and a musical confusion of Eastern languages which she simply could not understand.

Chapter 13

THE MARCH OF THE RED ARMY

The noise of the Dakota was deafening even through the head-phones, and the vibrations of the twin turbo-prop engines all-absorbing. Sitting behind the two pilots, Edward had a good view of the rolling sea of green jungle below, broken by the occasional scarlet splash of flowers covering the Flame of the Forest tree, patchwork kampongs, and cut through the edges near civilisation by winding cords of unsurfaced logging roads.

The pilot's voice crackled through the headphones, 'Think these leaflets will do any good?'

Edward flicked a switch on his headphones to 'send' and said, 'That's what the "Emergency Information Service" believes.'

'Euphemism for propaganda, eh?'

Edward nodded. 'Emergency Info is the new name for the old PR department. What with the commies taking all of China, and now the Korean War, they reckon we need a boost.'

'They're bloody right,' interjected the pilot gloomily. 'Those Inchon landings were all jolly fine, but the Reds are giving us a real trouncing now. China, Korea, maybe Malaya next?' Communism seemed in the ascendant everywhere.

'Maybe the message has finally got through to London. They've sent out a chap called Hugh Carleton Greene to galvanise the new Emergency Info set-up. He's been seconded from the BBC.'

'Should know about propaganda then,' said the pilot.

'I hope so. His chaps reckon that even if we can't persuade Ho Peng to surrender, we might turn the heads of some of his men who will give us a lead on him.'

The pilot snorted his disgust and fell silent. He flew out over the

4,000-foot ridge of mountains above the neat rubber plantations of the Black Circle estate and Edward looked into the bowl of jungle the other side, in Negri Sembilan State. Somewhere down there was Ho Peng's deep jungle base. Edward was sure that the communists could never be beaten until the army confidently patrolled even the deepest areas of jungle, such as this area of mountain fastness where the three States met.

'Odd that we can fly so close to the bastards and not get at them,' said Edward to the pilot.

'I did a drop into that awful place during the war,' announced the pilot.

'What?' demanded Edward hardly believing he had heard correctly.

'Right at the end of the war it was, in May '45. I was flying Liberators then, for Special Operations, out of Ceylon.'

'What did you drop?'

'Eight H-type SOE containers in two passes. I was worried sick we'd get picked up by the Jap night patrols, but the bally place is so remote, we never saw a soul. Thank God.' Even though the British controlled the skies over Malaya again, he still hated the idea of having to bale out or crash-land in the jungle. The only way out was on foot, injured or not, and he was horribly conscious that several planes had already crashed in the jungle during the Emergency and their crews never seen again.

'H-types were made up of drums, weren't they?' asked Edward, thinking of the cache Tallard and he had unearthed the previous year.

The pilot nodded, 'Five drums per container, making forty in all, but they never told us what was inside them.'

Edward's disappointment must have communicated itself because the pilot added, 'All I can tell you is that I remember my airloadmaster saying they were bally heavy that night.'

Edward supposed the drums must have been filled with explosives, though there had been none in the drums Tallard picked up in that camp.

'Ironic, us giving them all the kit they need to fight us,' the pilot remarked. 'Makes you wonder what they'd have done without us.'

Morosely, Edward agreed, 'They aren't being supplied by Communist China or Russia. The troops haven't found any weapons from there during the whole Emergency.'

The pilot made a turn back towards Kuala Lumpur and

civilisation and they swooped down low over the Black Circle valley on a line between the edge of the rubber and the jungle, heading for the New Village. Edward twisted round, left his canvas seat and went down the narrow body of the aircraft to watch the dispatch.

The side parachute door was open and the warm slipstream whipped at the shirts and shorts of the men throwing bundles of leaflets into the air. The fluttering white papers swirled downstream, like confetti, slowly falling over the edge of the jungle and the rubber trees where Edward and the Emergency Information officers hoped they would be picked up by Ho Peng's MRLA when they emerged from their hideouts. The silver plane roared over the New Village, and Edward looked down on the neat rows of new timber houses, the security fence and the plots of land being cleared and cultivated outside besides the glistening Sungei Lui. Surprised round faces stared up, wondering what new trick the British were playing. He wondered if Liya was among them.

He had been out to see her at the New Village several times, on the pretext of watching the new houses being built, but either she had been unable to get away from Ah Chi or his wife without arousing suspicion, or she had not been there at all. Edward was still sure she wanted to speak to him confidentially, because she had certainly had the chance to dismiss him on the few times he had seen her, cooking or washing clothes with Ah Po. Instead, she had given him a quick look of appeal from her slanting black eyes, like a prisoner condemned to silence.

After the flight, the duty driver from Headquarters picked Edward up in a jeep at the airfield. He settled himself in the canvas passenger seat and, as they pulled out through the main gate past the RAF policemen on duty, he said casually, 'We'll go back to the office via the Majestic Hotel.'

'Right, Sir,' said the driver.

Edward glanced at him but the driver was concentrating on avoiding a trishaw pedalled by a very old Chinese. Conscription had lifted him from driving buses in South Harrow to jeeps in Malaya for a year, and his life revolved round his billet, beer and the Motor Transport pool. Officers' reasons for doing things were of no more interest to him than the fares on his bus at home. At the hotel, he parked in the shade of a palm tree and watched the young Para officer disappear into the darkness of the entrance foyer. Then he lit a Woodbine.

The Majestic's bar, with its big fans turning lazily under the high ceiling, was empty and Edward stepped out on to the terrace at the back. Tables were set overlooking the gardens under trees whose leafy branches cast cool shadows and protected guests from the worst of the sun. A few monkeys played about on the branches of one, grunting and grooming each other for fleas.

Edward spotted her in a wide straw sun-hat reading a paper at a table in one corner of the terrace and went over.

'Sorry I'm late,' he said cheerfully.

Marsha Tallard looked up, her eyes deep-blue in the shade of her hat, and smiled happily. 'Edward! So you got the message all right?'

Edward nodded, sitting down. 'You and Sean in town for a few days, away from the "Black Circle"? I don't blame you. You deserve a rest.'

'Yes, we both need a change,' said Marsha vaguely, but she was watching him carefully. 'Will you stay for lunch?'

She sounded light-hearted, not at all as if she was thinking about communists. He said, 'I can't, really. Hell of a lot on, but I'll catch up with you both later.'

She shook her head slowly, and said, 'Sean's not here.'

'I suppose he's gone to the Coliseum Bar?'

'He's gone to Singapore.'

Edward could not stop the thrill inside him. She was observing him, her lips slightly parted with suggestive amusement, blatantly enjoying her plan. He said slowly, 'That note delivered to my office, was signed by Sean?'

She shook her head, delighted with herself.

'You've got me here on false pretences!'

'Nothing false about this, Edward honey,' she replied frankly, knowing her bait was taken. She whispered, 'I want you so bad, that I thought up the message idea the minute Sean said he had business in Singapore. And don't worry about him.'

Edward nodded. Tallard had talked about a fun place called Bugi Street.

'And you're not having a real easy time with Diana, now, are you?'

'How d'you know?'

'I can tell,' she said.

Edward supposed she could, reading some subtle feminine code.

Knowing the effect she was having on him, Marsha put her hand lightly on his bare arm and her finger tips gently scratched his wrist.

Edward felt both weak and frantically excited at the same time and, in spite of his better judgement, his mind was already working feverishly through excuses and ways to meet her, rapidly considering the risks and the lies he would need to tell.

Her fingers pressed on him, demanding an answer, a promise to love her without complications which she knew was the dream of every man and, with the memory of their last time together, impossible to refuse.

He shrugged, lost, smiled and said, 'Where?'

The simple answer gave her a delightful physical thrill of anticipation, and her soft American accent purred like a cat with the cream as she said, 'Why, here, honey, in my room. The Majestic is real old-fashioned and it has an enormous bed.'

Committed, Edward grinned and glanced along the terrace, but it was empty. He took her hand and he said, 'What about the staff? I mean being seen?'

'They're very discreet,' she said. She coquettishly ducked the brim of her hat to shade her face and added, 'And besides, I don't think they'll see much of us, d'you?'

In spite of the shade, he felt hot. He let go her hand and stood up. He had decided on his excuse. A source meeting. That was secret, gave him an open-ended time bracket and allowed him to come to town in civilian clothes. 'I must go now,' he said. 'I'll be back at eight.'

'I'll order dinner in my room.'

Edward left her at once and passed a young Chinese waiter coming along the terrace to take orders. Behind he heard Marsha's voice and thought of the evening, at once guilty, apprehensive, and drugged with anticipation.

He walked down the steps of the Majestic into the hot sun. The noise of traffic and people bustling along the pavement washed over him. The driver saw him coming, flicked away his second Woodbine and started the jeep. Edward climbed in and they pulled away. His eyes passed over the Chinese faces on the pavement, bland and seemingly indifferent to the world, without really seeing them, his mind absorbed with the evening, ironing over every detail of his plan like a military operation to smooth out the merest wrinkle of compromise.

The cinema was cheap, stuffy and hot but Ho Peng bought two tickets, plunged into the dark auditorium and sat down. Liya followed him and sat beside him trying to adjust her eyes to the gloom.

'Why are we here?' she asked quietly. She had never seen him with such nervous energy and put it down to the operation he was planning.

'D'you think that officer saw you?' Ho Peng asked in a low throaty voice.

'No,' said Liya, surprised that Ho Peng had recognised Edward Fairfax. The jeep had almost brushed into her as she turned to cross the road by the big hotel, but Edward had been gazing vacantly into the distance and not focused on her at all. Ho Peng, close behind her, must have seen him quite clearly. He stared hard at Liya for a moment and then whispered, 'He doesn't matter for now. We completed our reconnaissance and they suspect nothing.'

'Shall we go now?' Liya asked, trying to understand why Ho Peng had bothered to hide in a cinema to question her about the Parachute officer.

For answer, Ho Peng pointed at the screen where an advertisement for Martini had just ended and the newsreel was beginning, its beacon lighting up the big screen with black and white rays from side to side. Ho Peng said excitedly, 'We've plenty of time to prepare for tonight but you must see this!' He would not have admitted it, but he had already seen the newsreel piece four times.

Liya said nothing. Businesslike, she would continue to function for Ho Peng but all her enthusiasm had died with those children, all of them, in the squatters' village. Ho Peng sensed something of her antagonism and again tried to peer at her face in the darkness, but the news had started and he sat back to watch.

'Chinese Red Army enters the Korean War!' screamed the newspaper headlines being filmed, while the measured but musical English public-school tones of the newsreel announcer was saying, 'On Sunday 26 November, 200,000 Chinese troops of Mao Tse-tung's Red Army swarmed over the Yalu River and inflicted an overwhelming defeat on United Nations forces fighting in Korea. GIS of the American 8th Army fighting for the UN must have thought they had successfully ended the Korean War by pushing the North Koreans up to the Yalu, which forms the border between North Korea and the newly-recognised Communist State of the Republic of China. Some GIS could even see mainland China on the other side of the river! Then, the Chinese Communist attack came as a total surprise. The 8th Army tumbled back in disarray making a desperate fighting withdrawal to avoid being cut off altogether. Elsewhere, there are fears that the US Marine Corps is trapped at the Changjin Reservoir in terrible snow and ice, and trying to fight its way out on frozen roads to the Sea of Japan to avoid total encirclement. UN Casualties are feared to be high.'

Ho Peng could hardly keep still in his seat. This was the march of the Red Army he had long predicted. Liya felt his enthusiasm but she also sensed unusual interest among the mix of Malays, Chinese and Indians in the stuffy little cinema.

'They were warned,' exclaimed Ho Peng. 'The Chinese Foreign Minister Chou En-lai warned the stupid Imperialist Americans not to invade North Korea. Now they are defeated.' He turned to look at Liya, the bad skin of his face terribly streaked by the reflections of the black and white pictures on the screen, his eyes gleaming in the dark, and whispered, 'We must go, you and I. There is work to do for tonight. The fight must intensify here in the towns. With Red China on the march with us, we shall win, I'm sure of it!'

He gripped Liya's arm hard and stood up, pulling her with him. 'Come on! The British must be made to feel unsafe throughout the country and know that we are in control!'

'I've got to go out tonight,' Edward shouted over the sound of the shower cascading over him.

'Where are you going?' Diana called back from their bedroom. She had Ellie on the bed, completely naked after her bath and free of towel nappies which gave her prickly heat, kicking her short fat legs in the air.

'A meeting,' shouted Edward through the tumbling water. He soaped himself all over and felt himself swelling with the thought of Marsha preparing herself for him in that enormous bedroom. 'A secret meeting. You know the sort of thing.'

'Yes, I see,' said Diana frowning at Ellie who was crawling across the bed. She had no idea what he meant. 'When d'you have to go out?'

'A bit before eight.'

'Before supper?'

'I'm afraid so,' he called. He stepped out of the shower and quickly began to rub himself down hoping Diana would not come into the bathroom and see the state he was in. It was easy lying when he was shouting from one room to the next, but face to face naked like that he was not at all sure he could explain himself.

221

Diana was thinking of supper and wished he could have warned her before. Edward was always working late on some staff intelligence paper or going to see Angus. Without enthusiasm, she said, 'I had better tell Mr Song.'

'I'll do it,' said Edward. 'I'm going to have my lesson with him now, before I go out. And by the way, his name is Lao Song, not Mr Song.'

Diana did not reply. She felt left out. She wanted to watch Edward dressing, but he put on his clothes in the bathroom, a shirt and tie and white duck trousers, and she wanted to spend time talking with him, enjoying Ellie together, seeing her crawling and trying to talk, and she wanted to have supper with him, not on her own. But he gave her a quick kiss on the cheek and walked out of their bedroom to find Lao Song in the kitchen.

Edward and Lao Song sat as usual in a spare room which Edward had set out as a study, with chairs and a table, a blackboard he had signed out from the quartermaster's stores and rows of Lao Song's books.

Half-an-hour into the lesson, discussing the news about the Chinese Red Army in Korea in Chinese, Lao Song observed Edward across the table, his long fingers placed carefully together at the finger-tips, his eyes hooded with thought and said, 'You are not concentrating, Mr Fairfax.' Even after eighteen months, Lao Song was politely formal, not deferentially as a cook to his employer, but in control as a teacher to his pupil, and they both enjoyed their daily lessons together. 'This is a subject which greatly interests you, yet your mind is elsewhere, in the heat of the night, and reminds me of so many of my students in the past. He paused, thinking then added, The Master Confucius was right to say, "In youth, when the physical powers are not yet settled, he guards against lust".'

Edward glanced quickly at Lao Song, annoyed the old Chinese could divine his thoughts. Rather sharply, because he was afraid Diana might have noticed too, he said, 'Forget it, Lao Song. Let's get on.'

Lao Song shook his head and replied, 'We cannot learn when the mind is full of obstacles and the fury of expectation. The Master said that "when a person is strong and his physical powers are full of vigour, he guards against quarrelsomeness".'

Edward finally recognised one of Lao Song's favourite quotes from the Analects. He apologised for the flash of bad temper and completed it, 'And when he is old, and the animal powers are decayed, he guards against covetousness.'

To his delight, a faint smile wrinkled Lao Song's parchment skin as he replied, 'I am surely too old even for covetousness, but be careful, Mr Fairfax, with what you do tonight.' He began closing the text books in front of him, emphatically ending the lesson before time.

Shortly before eight, Edward drove the blue Plymouth along the Batu Road towards the Majestic Hotel and kept his eyes open. Lao Song was wise and observant, but Edward was irritated with himself for showing his feelings and had no intention of being caught out twice. He parked the Plymouth two blocks off from the Majestic so no-one could identify the conspicuous blue American saloon outside the hotel, and set out to walk there through the darkness.

Few people were about, as the High Commissioner and General Briggs had clamped down with harsh new food control measures which had seriously dampened night-life in the towns. A long list of food, including rice and dried fish which the CTs especially liked, was forbidden to be sold without a detailed written record of sale, many restaurants and cafés had been closed down, and Briggs had banned the movement of food at night altogether. Activity after dark was much reduced.

Fully alert, Edward forced thoughts of Marsha to the back of his mind, and cautiously scrutinised the Chinese, Indian and Malay faces which passed him on the pavement.

The odd mix of Victorian-Muslim architecture of the Majestic Hotel loomed ahead behind the tall palms, and Edward wondered which of the lighted windows upstairs belonged to Marsha's room. He was about to cross the last road running down one side of the hotel into the square, his precautions almost utterly submerged by his imagination of the next few hours with Marsha, when he saw Liya.

She was leaning against the corner of the block, in shadows, with her back to him looking into the square, in a white short-sleeved shirt and black cotton trousers, but her slender and perfectly-proportioned profile reminded him so much of the time he had found her sitting by the padi fields after the massacre that he had no difficulty recognising her.

In soft suede shoes, he walked up silently behind her and said in Chinese, 'Liya? What are you doing here?'

She spun round and gasped, 'Lieutenant Fairfax!'

'You waiting for someone?' he asked, seeing her flick a nervous

223

look into the square. His assignation with Marsha Tallard suddenly made him think that Liya was meeting a lover herself, though she was dressed very ordinarily in working clothes.

She shook her head, wishing he had not seen her.

'Then can we go somewhere?' he asked. 'Just for a few minutes?'

'No!' she answered rather fiercely, shrinking further back into the shadows of the building where the lights of a café reflected in her slanting black eyes.

'Why not?' asked Edward puzzled, still looking around suspiciously. He quickly made up his mind. Marsha could wait but he had to seize this extraordinary opportunity with Liya, even for a few minutes. He said, 'You've been avoiding me for weeks, Liya, but I always thought you wanted to see me, to talk?'

'I do,' she insisted, abashed by her earlier surprise at seeing him and recovering herself. She had thought very carefully about what she had told him after the massacre of the children and decided that she must see the keen young British officer. She put one of her small hands on his arm and told him in a low sincere voice, 'I've thought about you a lot, and watched you when you came to see me in the New Village.' He seemed to have a genuine interest in her and she was impressed with his Chinese. She said, 'I think you do want to help me, and I want to see you, but this isn't a good time.'

'Where then?' Edward asked, delighted with her reaction. 'And when?'

Round him she could see a large motor car crossing the far corner of the square. Desperately, she looked up at him and said, 'You can always meet me at the Chinese Theatre. I've a friend who is an actor.'

'How does that help?' Edward asked, puzzled.

Behind him, Liya could see a slight wiry figure step from the darkness of a clump of red canna plants on the other side of the square and cross the road close to the car. She even fancied she could see the black object in the air but it was too dark and too far away and her imagination was working overtime.

'Leave a message with him,' she said in a rush. 'He's called Liao Ting-chi.'

The grenade exploded inside the car shattering the warm peace of the square. The Majestic Hotel and the stately palms all round seemed to reel back in shock.

Instinctively Edward grabbed Liya, pulling her close to protect her. She could feel the tense excitement in his body, wrapping her in

224

his arms like a lover, she thought with detached and puzzling clarity.

He twisted round. The car was still moving, the driver dead over the wheel, and it ploughed over the pavement into a palm trunk. Flames flickered inside and, as they stared, the fuel caught and a ball of orange flame billowed with a roar up the palm tree making the hanging branches flail and rattle in the blast. They both felt the rush of heat on their cheeks.

Edward whipped back to face her, his grip on her arms tightened and he shouted, 'You knew!'

Vehemently, she shouted back, 'No! I didn't. I promise!'

Men in tropical suits and women in dresses were pouring out of the Majestic Hotel among waiters and hotel staff, uncertain what to do. They walked slowly into the square, staring in horror at the blazing wreck. Far off, Edward heard sirens. He shook Liya, surprised how small and light she was, and demanded, 'Why were you here?'

She refused to answer for a moment. He was hurting her arms and her mind whirled with possibilities. She watched the little black silhouettes moving helplessly round the burning car, and the dried palm leaves set alight in the tree above. Then she lifted her face and met his furious look. She put her hands on his chest to steady herself as he shook her roughly, insisting she answer, and finally she admitted, 'Because I thought you might be here!'

Edward stopped shaking her and stared at her open, frightened face, lit by the fire behind in the square, and the frank expression in her dark eyes. Amazed but still suspicious, he demanded, 'How could you possibly know?'

She stared earnestly into his eyes, determined to convince him, and said in a small vulnerable voice, 'Because I saw you here this morning, in a jeep.'

Edward frowned, disbelieving. Behind them, the sirens burst into the square. He could feel duty pulling him away. Doors slammed, soldiers began shouting orders and the sound of boots drummed on the tarmac. He wanted to believe her but he said, 'I don't understand.'

'I promise, Edward,' she said softly, hanging limp in his grip, and desperately trying to persuade him with her eyes, knowing she had confused him. Quietly, she repeated, 'I promise. I thought you would be here.'

Soldiers doubled past them. A truck drove up and stopped in the street between them and the Majestic. Coils of barbed wire were flung out and pulled across the road, and the milling curious crowds pushed back around them.

'You're hurting,' she said.

He apologised quickly and released her, letting his arms drop to his sides. The attack on the car and her sudden revelation she had been looking for him had quite disorientated him. He supposed he would have to go into the Majestic to make certain that Marsha was all right, but after what had happened he felt oddly disengaged. He was strangely relieved that the mêlée of troops and police made their original assignation out of the question. Vaguely conscious of Liya rubbing her arms where he had been gripping her he turned, embarrassed, to watch the soldiers setting up their road block. He observed from the cap badges on their berets that they were Artillery. They were putting on a fine display of military efficiency but it all seemed totally pointless. The groups of Malays, Indians and Chinese who had gathered were paying them no attention. They were looking at the wrecked car at the bottom of the palm tree in the middle of the square. Everyone could see that the people in the car were already dead and burned beyond recognition, and their attacker long gone.

When he turned back for Liya, she had disappeared in the crowd behind him.

The following evening Roger Haike came to the house dressed in jungle pea-greens and forage cap to say goodbye. Trying to ignore the bright new purple and white medal ribbon of his Military Cross on his shirt, Edward gave him a whisky s'tengah and they sat outside on the verandah. Edward sipped his drink, listening to the cicadas out in the garden, his mind on Liya, and Roger announced, 'I'm posted to Korea.'

'The Western world can relax,' said Edward half to himself, staring into the darkness. He could smell the sweet scent of the big banana trees in the clump of jungle beyond the ditch.

'Eh?' grunted Roger.

'The war will be in safe hands, Roger.'

Diana smiled sweetly and said, 'Edward's only joking, Roger. What are you going to do there?'

'I'm going to be a Foo,' he drawled, still frowning.

'How very appropriate,' said Edward.

Diana kicked him with her foot under the table, and before Roger

226

could take offence, he added, 'Didn't you do that for us in Six Airborne Div.?'

'Yes, but that was during the war.' Roger smiled cleverly. 'Before you joined. You wouldn't remember.'

'What's a Foo?' Diana interrupted quickly. She was doing her best to avoid an argument. Besides, the recent United Nations setbacks in Korea had been well reported and she was genuinely worried about her brother.

'Forward observation officer,' said Roger importantly. 'I sit up-front with the action and give my chaps in the gun lines their targets over the radio.'

'You looking forward to it?' she asked dubiously.

Roger was not sure about that. The British troops with the American 8th Army had suffered heavy casualties in freezing winter conditions, and they were still retreating south pursued by the victorious Chinese Communist Army. On their eastern flank, the Marines were fighting desperately from town to town, to break out towards the Sea of Japan. He answered obliquely, 'I'll be pleased to leave this mess in Malaya.'

'Some serious fighting going on in Korea,' said Edward happily and was delighted to see a shadow flicker across Roger's smooth face.

Roger leaned back in his chair, making the rattan squeak and retorted, 'I shouldn't wonder that my experience in Korea will be useful here in Malaya soon. China or Russia are bound to throw their full support behind the Malayan cause sooner or later and they'll need people like me who've seen a bit of action.' He drained his glass and said, 'By the way, Edward, a chap could die of thirst here. What say a refill, eh?' Imperiously, he held out the empty glass.

Edward ignored him, called for Hassan, and said, 'What makes you think Malaya will go the same way as Korea?'

After Hassan had refilled his glass, Roger spent the next half an hour telling him, only Edward did not bother to listen. He let Diana interpose various questions while Roger talked endlessly and consumed two more whisky s'tengahs. Edward was immensely relieved when Roger finally said, 'Got to go now, Diana old thing. We take the troop train to Singapore tonight. Lots of packing to do in my room in the Mess.'

Diana stood up, a worried expression on her pretty face, and said, 'Please be careful of yourself Roger.'

227

'No scenes now,' said Roger smiling bravely and brushing his small black moustache in a cavalier manner. 'I'm sure it'll all be over by the time we get there.'

'I'll see you out,' said Edward politely. Diana hugged her brother and gave him a kiss goodbye. Despite being unbearably pompous, he was still her brother. She watched the two men walk through the sitting-room into the hall and gave a sad little wave when Roger turned to see her for the last time.

Edward opened the front door, sickened by the theatrical little departure scene. Roger passed him with haughty disdain, with all the vanity of a volunteer, a sacrifical lamb on his way to the altar, but he stopped outside the front door in the shadows on the verandah and suddenly declared, 'By the way, Edward, bit of advice before I go, as a sort of elder brother, eh? Stay on the straight and narrow, old man. Hate to see old Diana put through the hoop.'

Edward stared at Roger. All his dislike of his brother-in-law mustered into a ringing response of righteous indignation, 'What the hell are you talking about?'

Roger laughed unpleasantly, like a man who has all the answers, and retorted, 'Don't come the old soldier with me, Edward, old man. That Tallard woman. Bloody bad show for Diana, socially and all that. Besides which, she's a bloody Yank.'

Edward boiled. All the guilt of the first time with Marsha, months before, surged together like a wave with the frustration of the previous night and he snapped, 'I don't know who the hell you've been listening to, but—'

'Don't have to listen,' Roger interrupted rudely. 'Saw you with her last night. At the Majestic. Flousy piece with red lipstick and blonde hair.'

Edward remembered the Artillery cap badges. He said, 'You were with the soldiers who set up the road blocks?'

'That's right,' said Roger, nodding smugly. 'We were called out to reinforce the police. Saw you plain as a pikestaff with that American tart.'

The irony that Roger had not seen him with Liya was nothing short of absurd. She, a genuine intelligence source, had been wrapped in his arms to protect her from the blast, whereas he had seen Marsha, his intended lover, merely to tell her their plans were ruined by events. To Roger's surprise, Edward smiled.

Piqued, Roger said, 'Always knew you were a bad egg, Fairfax. Never should have married Diana.'

Edward refused to rise, but he stepped on to the verandah and genially prodded Roger on the chest on his shiny silver and purple ribbon, looked him straight in the eye and told him, 'Maybe in Korea, you'll get a chance to earn that Military Cross.' Then he turned to go inside. People like Roger Haike in the world were better ignored. They could not be trusted with the truth.

Furious, Roger fired one last dart, from the shadows of the verandah steps, shouting, 'You can't tell me you weren't up to no good with that woman. You're a liar, Fairfax! Just like your bloody father.'

Edward stopped in the door, gave a swift look back at Roger and saw the smug self-satisfaction on Roger's face that hurt as much as the pain of hearing his dead father's name attacked, and he lost his temper. Without a word, he took a couple of quick steps back across the wooden boards of the verandah, and hit Roger twice, with a hard right into his ribs, knocking the wind from his lungs and bringing his head down which he smashed with his left, ripping his cheek. Roger grunted, blood spewed out of his nose, and he collapsed backwards over the steps on to the grass. Edward followed him and stood over him for a moment to see if he needed more, but Roger lay still, moaning quietly and hoping no-one would hit him again.

Without a word, Edward went inside and slammed the front door behind him.

'What have you done?' Diana demanded in the hall, her blue eyes wide and fearful.

Edward shrugged and said bluntly, 'He was rude about you, about me and then about my father. So I hit him.'

Shocked, Diana gave him a fearful look and slipped out past him. He heard her gasp. Then she was inside again, furious, and shouting for Hassan to bring towels and water, ignoring Edward.

He stood in the hall and as Hassan passed him with a jug of water and a hand towel, he said, 'He asked for it, so whatever you do, don't bring the little shit back in here.'

Diana gave him another furious look, for speaking to her like that in front of the servants, and snapped, 'Don't worry, Edward. I'll drive him to the Officers Mess myself.' She took the things from Hassan and ran out on to the verandah.

Edward shrugged and wandered out to the garden side. He poured himself a large whisky and slumped down in a rattan chair.

Nothing seemed to be going right. Maybe Roger was the lucky one, leaving Malaya for Korea.

A cock-chafer started up his screeching musical rattle in the jungle. He sipped his drink and watched the fireflies glowing, dipping and vanishing over the trees in the garden.

Tallard, Ho Peng, Liya. All the loose ends had to tie in somehow. He could not just give up, though he wished he could see some way forward. Then he muttered to himself, money makes the world go round, wondering how he was going to pay Liya for her information. If he could find her again.

He heard Diana come back later, but she did not bother to find him. Glumly, he supposed she was still angry with him for hitting her brother, and also for volunteering to stay on in Malaya for another tour of three years. But he couldn't leave now. He had to get Ho Peng.

Hassan filled his glass and then, as usual, refused to leave him. He was puzzled and frightened by the fight between the Tuans which had surprised even Lao Song when he told him in the kitchen. He sat in the shadows on the verandah with his back to the warm wall of the house, watching Edward sink into his bamboo chair. Several drinks later, as Hassan was nodding off to sleep, Edward shook himself, hauled himself out of his bamboo chair and walked unsteadily through the house to his bed.

Hassan, stepped off the verandah and scuffed barefoot across the warm grass round the house. Under an arch of stars, he stood sadly in the dark shadow of the clerodendron bushes and strained his ears for the slightest sound, but the magic was not working and there were no reassuring little noises from the Tuans' window. Just shuttered silence.

Chapter 14

AMBUSH AT FRASER'S HILL

Edward found the Chinese Theatre on the edge of Kuala Lumpur's Chinatown, in a street market filled from end to end with two-storey shophouses and sweet-smelling food stalls. An exotic oriental arch, surmounted with sweeping green and red tiled roofs, led into a courtyard. Roaring dragons in peeling vermilion paint glared out from circles of bas-relief on the walls of the building inside and red paper lanterns covered in Chinese characters were hooked under the overhanging roofs and turned lazily in the warm air.

The sun beat down on the courtyard, silent except for the burr of a cricket in some weeds in one dusty corner. As Edward walked into the building a thin Chinese voice asked out of the darkness, in English, 'What d'you want, mister?'

Edward blinked to see who he was talking to, concentrated on his Chinese and replied, 'I have come to see Liao Ting-chi.'

'Liao!' said the voice in a tone of surprised amusement. Edward's eyes accustomed to the gloom after the bright sunlight outside and he made out a slim Chinese boy with bright black eyes.

'He's an actor here.'

'Oh yes!' said the boy lightly, in Chinese. 'He thinks he's a famous Manchu Warlord! Please, follow.'

He led the way through the empty auditorium to the back of the theatre by the stage and pointed to an outside door. Edward looked through suspiciously and hesitated. All he could see was an alley filled with refuse.

He repeated firmly in Chinese, 'I want to see Liao Ting-chi.'

The boy just grinned, waving Edward into the alley.

Edward put his hand in his pocket, gripped the 9mm Walther

pistol Angus Maclean had given him for such meetings, and stepped into the alley. An old wooden staircase to the roof was tacked to the outside wall of the building and the boy gestured to him to go up. Suspicious, Edward mounted the stairs, testing each rickety tread. At the top, the roof was flat. He could see across the tiled roofs of Chinatown, the theatre's façade of dragons and garishly painted characters at the front of the building over the street, and near-to was a line of ramshackle timber changing rooms which made Edward think of Victorian beach cabins. He picked his way over a tangle of electric cables, rotting paper and rusting tins to the first changing room, banged on the door and called out, 'Liao Ting-chi?'

A voice shouted in Chinese, 'Ta Ma De! Go away!'

Edward kicked the door. There was muttering and the door opened slightly. A bleached face peered out, black hair plastered flat, eyebrows plucked and dark red lipstick thickly layered on to disguise thin lips.

Edward demanded, 'Liao Ting-chi?'

A blunt hand shot into view and pointed at a hut further along the line.

This time, Edward banged on the door and walked straight in. The changing-room was long and narrow and smelled of joss sticks. The walls were hung with coloured silk costumes, glittering with diamante jewels, plumes, and sashes. A bed on one side was draped with rugs and cloaks. Opposite were open wood boxes filled with small Chinese shoes, pots of paint, wigs looking like dead animals, and bottles of Chinese medicines with shrivelled things inside. Facing him at the other end of the little room was a skinny figure naked to the waist, perched on high-platform brocade shoes with curled toes, and wearing baggy silk trousers tied at the ankles and fastened at the waist with a broad cummerbund. Above his chest, which showed every rib, his neck and angular bony face were white with grease-paint, his unusually wide mouth was coated in carmine lipstick, and black eyebrows slanted up to a tall yellow hat encrusted with sparkling glass and sprays of feathers.

Edward was gripped by his expression of wide-eyed surprise through a full-length mirror on the end wall which was lit all round by glowing electric bulbs. He asked, 'Liao Ting-chi?'

The actor turned with theatrical poise and observed Edward without saying a word. Irritated, Edward repeated his question. The thin Chinese opened his mouth and nodded, shaking the feathers on his hat. He had long black hair hanging down to his waist. Coyly, he pulled a handful over his shoulder and began to plait it with surprisingly long and graceful fingers, as if he were embarrassed. Impatient, Edward took a menacing pace forward and shouted, 'Are you Liao Ting-chi or not?'

Terrified, the actor dropped his hair and fell back into a chair in front of the mirror like a puppet with its strings cut. He gurgled inarticulately, his fingers fluttered round his face and neck, repeatedly drawing a line across his throat and touching his ears.

After a moment, Edward sat down on the bed and burst out laughing. Liao Ting-chi was deaf and dumb. For almost a year he had worked on his Chinese with Lao Song and his first real contact with the underground world of intelligence could not even hear what he was saying.

But Liao could lip-read and recovered fast when he saw Edward understood. He had known at once that this was the man Liya had talked about, so when Edward mouthed her name, he nodded happily, waving the tall feathers of his yellow hat back and forth, and mimed writing gestures. Edward produced a notebook and pen from his pocket and Liao slowly wrote a date and time in fine calligraphic letters.

Impressed, Edward mouthed, 'Where?' shrugging his shoulders and looking around as if he were playing charades.

Liao nodded, smiling horribly with his red lips and began writing again, holding the pencil so delicately the script was hardly visible. Methodically, he wrote the name of a small park not far from Kuala Lumpur's main padang. Delighted, Edward thanked him and left.

The following evening, Edward found the park, a small square with a number of cafés around the sides where people went after work with friends at sunset to enjoy the pleasant warmth after the heat of the day. Edward sat on a bench, idly watching a small green pitta bird pecking nervously for ants and smoked a cigarette. Thinking how their roles were reversed from the chance meeting outside the Majestic Hotel, he checked his watch and just after the appointed time, when he was beginning to think Liya would not appear, she walked out of the darkness behind the bench and sat down beside him.

When she pretended not to know him, he offered her a cigarette which she refused. She opened a shoulder bag and took out an orange which she began to peel and eat. In a low voice, she asked in Chinese, 'Did you find Liao all right?'

Edward frowned, 'He's a bit peculiar.'

To his surprise, she laughed softly repeating his phrase, 'Yes, he is peculiar,' and gave him a quick look. 'He wants to be a girl.'

'That's plain enough,' said Edward matter-of-factly.

Liya nodded, smiling. 'I found him that job, and he loves it. He's always dreamed of dressing up, since he was a little boy, and putting on make-up. Now he can mime on stage too.'

'I know he can't give much away being deaf and dumb, but can we trust him?'

'Yes,' she insisted. 'And no-one will ever suspect you going there.'

Edward gave her a wry look and said, 'Because they'll think I'm going up to see him for pleasure?'

Liya giggled and offered Edward a bit of her orange, pleased he had not taken offence. The orange was delicious and sweet. Edward swallowed and asked bluntly, 'What can you tell me?' They both knew they ought not to spend too long together.

She nodded, serious again, and told him that she had seen rice being smuggled out of the New Village and hidden in a jar on the bank of the Sungei Lui.

'How are they doing it?'

'Maybe in the frame of a bicycle. Or the tube of a wheelbarrow.'

'Who does it?' asked Edward.

She was reluctant to implicate individuals who obeyed Ho Peng only through fear and said, 'I don't know but I've heard them talking.'

'For Ho Peng's group?'

She nodded again, then asked, 'What will you do with these things I tell you?'

Angus Maclean had warned him to expect this question and he said, 'I'll pass it to the people in my office. They're collecting information about all the New Villages and how people are settling in.'

She looked relieved, then took his wrist, looked at the time and said, 'I must go!'

He watched her walk swiftly away among the crowds, wishing there had been time for all sorts of other questions, like why she had wanted to see him outside the Majestic, whether she was still working at the Wild Orchid, how often she came into Kuala Lumpur, where else she went and when they could meet again.

As the weeks passed, all their meetings took the same form. First,

234

Edward went to see Liao Ting-chi above the theatre and the actor became increasingly friendly. He took to giving Edward tea out of a small aluminium pot and tiny china cups. The one-sided conversation was always difficult as Edward's Chinese pronunciation was not good enough for Liao to lip read accurately and Liao often curled up gurgling with laughter on the bed at some unintended innuendo or pun. Then Edward left, ignoring the knowing glances of the boy downstairs and the other 'actors' on the roof, with new instructions to meet Liya.

She always chose a different place and a different time, and he began to appreciate how careful she was. Angus gave him advice to pass on to her, to help her set up meetings, but she hardly needed it, never setting a routine.

She admitted once she was scared to death of Ho Peng and that the communists' network was spread so wide it was impossible to tell who was involved. Sometimes, they never spoke. She just passed by him in the street and slipped a paper in his pocket. Another time she left a letter in the left-luggage at the vast Islamic-style main railway station, or gave him a sweet in a crowd round a café, the message in the wrapping. Over the weeks, Edward really looked forward to seeing her slim shape and pretty face appear one way or another from the crowds of Chinese, Malays and Indians on the streets, and when she slipped away, he was always left feeling he wanted to know more about her.

She did still work at the Wild Orchid, but when he pulled a face, she smiled, pleased he seemed to care, and promised him that she only served drinks. She never answered his question about why she had wanted to meet him that night outside the Majestic Hotel and he never pressed her. He kept reminding himself that their relationship was strictly business, and dangerous.

'What makes someone want to talk?' he asked Angus Maclean one weekend as they walked together in the garden. The sun shone, a golden oriole sang melodiously from the top of an Indian laburnum in pendulous yellow flower and the fragrant blue stephanotis filled the warm air. Diana sat in the shade on the verandah reading a book, keeping an eye on Ellie crawling about on the grass.

'Good question,' replied Angus. 'Important that you understand your source's way of thinking.'

'It could be her political beliefs?'

'Yes, or a feeling of intellectual superiority. She obviously sees things going on she doesn't like and she's obviously intelligent.

There are all sorts of reasons. Money is often a factor.'

'But not in this case.'

Angus nodded, 'Which makes her unusual. Most of the Chinese sources we've come across so far are rabid communists one minute and the next they've changed sides, telling us everything they can remember and demanding every last cent of reward money for finding weapons or betraying old colleagues. Your source is an exception.'

Angus had offered Special Branch funds to pay Liya for her information, but she had refused, and it was easy to pretend her material came from the police, so Colonel Bleasley could not accuse Edward of acting without his authority, or, worse, try to control the source himself.

'What about hate?' asked Edward, thinking of what Ho Peng had done to her.

'Always a good clean motive,' agreed Angus. 'Difficult to say without knowing more about the background.' Edward had let slip early on that his source was a girl, and Angus was intrigued to know more, but he knew better than to ask. It was a principle of Special Branch work that the indentity of a source was kept absolutely secret. Each one was given a code name. Liya was called 'Red Dragon'.

'D'you think she's worth going on with?' asked Angus suddenly.

Edward was half expecting this question. Liya's information was hardly going to win the war, but she was building up a picture of life in the New Village. The jar of rice by the river was picked up without incident after an infantry patrol from Camp Rideau had sweltered in ambush for two days. Another had been found near the new padi fields. Two women had been arrested for smuggling rice out of the gate in their clothes, and a cache of rusty Japanese rifles had been uncovered in a clump of jungle near the old squatters' village.

He answered, 'What have we got to lose? I don't mind spending the time.' Actually, he looked forward to every meeting.

'Doesn't leave you much time at home,' Angus observed, casting a glance at the verandah. Diana was watching them over the top of her book and he knew she was jealous of Edward's commitment to his work.

Edward shrugged and said, 'We shan't win the war out here sticking to regular office hours.'

Angus agreed but said, 'Don't overdo it, though. That old sod

Bleasley keeps you at it and your Chinese lessons take up a fair bit of time. I'd hate to see your marriage suffer as a result of running a low-level source.'

'You leave my marriage out of it,' said Edward good-humouredly.

Angus saw the iron behind the smile and backed off with, 'Only mentioned it as an old friend. And as your Special Branch advisor.'

Edward smiled and said, 'Well, then, as my assistant SB officer, doesn't it seem a waste to let Red Dragon go when she costs us nothing except a bit of my spare time?'

'You're appealing to my Jock instinct,' Angus grinned, 'and you may be right. We all put in more than our fair share of hours fighting this Emergency, and I fancy the communists put in the overtime as well, but the bottom line always seems to be hard cash.'

Edward admitted frankly, 'I know it's not as if we're handling a member of the Central Executive Committee of the Malayan Communist Party, but I'm enjoying the game while it lasts.' He loved the intrigue and their short chats so much that he would have hated to stop. Fearful of the answer, faced with unrelenting office work as an alternative, he asked, 'Seriously, Angus, you're the expert. What d'you think?'

'Let's keep going.'

When Edward met Liya next, by one of the river ferry stations on the Sungei Kelang which ran grey with mud and flotsam through the centre of Kuala Lumpur, she said quietly, 'Ho Peng is gone away.'

This was the first time she had given him information about Ho Peng without being asked. Edward paused before replying and checked around. It was midday, and they were sitting side by side on a couple of old chairs outside a wood hut selling coffee as if they were waiting for the ferry. In the heat, there was no-one else about except some men in shorts sitting on the planks of the old jetty mending fishing nets. He asked, 'D'you know where he's gone?'

She shook her head and frowned, 'North, I think.'

Edward tried to jog her memory, 'To Tanjong Malim? Or further north, to Ipoh?'

'I think he's in the jungle, somewhere just north,' she said. She was terrified about giving details in case Ho Peng found out, but in this she felt safe as Ho Peng was so expert at avoiding British patrols in the forests.

Edward frowned, 'D'you mean he's left his usual haunts near the villages round Ulu Langat?'

237

'Yes.'

'Maybe he's in his camp in the deep jungle, in the mountains?'

Liya wondered how much Edward knew, but she said, 'The gossip in the Village is that he's gone away from this area altogether.'

'For ever?'

'No. Just for a meeting, I think.'

'But you've not heard where?'

'No,' she said.

'Ho Peng sounds rather like the High Commissioner,' Edward remarked. He glanced at her and saw her frowning so he added, 'It would seem that neither of them likes to say where they're going.'

'Really?' She found it hard to believe that the movements of the British High Commissioner were not known by all sorts of British officers like Edward, and it was just this sort of insight into the British way of life which she enjoyed about their meetings.

Edward said, 'Sir Henry Gurney's travel arrangements are dealt with by his private secretary and only a very few people know where he is going next.'

'Why?'

He laughed at her naïvety and replied, 'To prevent him from being attacked by people like Ho Peng.'

As soon as the meeting was over and Liya had disappeared into the alleyways between the old riverside houses, Edward returned at once to the Intelligence Office in Headquarters. Captain Denton was reading through some Intelligence summaries on CT activity. He looked up as Edward came in and walked straight over to the family tree on the wall showing the organisation of the MRLA.

After three years the gaps were gradually being filled in, ranging from Chin Peng, the General-Secretary, at the top, down through the branches of State Committees, showing the political and military wings, branching out in each State to the District Committees, with names like 'Happiness District', 'Rural District' and 'Construction District', spreading further in each District to lists of 'Elements' or 'Independent Platoons' responsible for Bodyguards, Food Supply, Propaganda, Couriers and Armed Attack. Finally, at the bottom, lists of individual CTs were named, with cross-references to card index files elsewhere in the office. Special Branch estimated there were still 5,000 MRLA in the jungle, in spite of several hundred losses during each of the three years of the fighting so far. The Min Yuen were continuing to supply new recruits.

Ho Peng's name was at the top of the tree, fixed in the Central

Military Committee and pencilled in with a question mark for membership of three State Committees; Selangor, where Kuala Lumpur was the capital, Negri Sembilan and Pahang.

Then Edward moved to the big operational map of Malaya and looked at the area around Kuala Lumpur. Ho Peng was believed to have overall command of the MRLA Regiment round Langat, Camp Rideau and the Black Circle estate. If he had gone north, as Liya said, he could be with the 6th MRLA Regiment in Pahang, the 1st Regiment or even the 11th Regiment which crossed the Selangor – Perak State border, near Fraser's Hill.

Edward walked back to the MRLA wall-chart to see that Special Branch in Tanjong Malim had produced the information recently that a Chinese called Siu Mah commanded the 11th Regiment and that Chin Peng himself was said to be somewhere in Pahang. Since the communist leaders had meetings from time to time, Edward guessed that Ho Peng had gone to one of these, preserving the greatest secrecy, just as any senior British officer would do for his own security.

'You look very busy,' observed Harry Denton.

'Just refreshing my memory on the CT orbat,' said Edward blandly. He did not want to discuss Liya's information until Angus Maclean had 'produced' it through Special Branch. Denton, like Bleasley, thought Red Dragon was a police source and had no idea Edward was involved. He changed the subject and said, 'Didn't expect you in the office at this time on a Friday afternoon?'

Captain Denton pulled a long face and gestured at the papers on his desk. 'Another bloody summary for Bleasley. He's got to brief General Briggs, to summarise how the Emergency is going, and it doesn't make very encouraging reading. Over 3,000 people killed so far and no sign of a let-up.'

'I thought we had captured or killed nearly 2,000 CTs?'

'We have, but Angus Maclean's Special Branch lot reckons they've armed another 5,000 Min Yuen and they're providing a constant source of new recruits.'

Edward had not realised the situation was that grim.

Denton continued, 'On our side, we're in a better state than three years ago, as Nicol Gray has doubled the number of policemen to 25,000. We've got 40,000 troops and the same number of special constables, which all helps, and the infantry are getting quite good in the jungle.'

'It's pretty small beer compared to Korea,' said Edward gloomily, thinking of Roger Haike, who had been taken prisoner there after the Battle of Imjin River in April. Nothing had been heard of him since as the North Koreans refused to admit to the Red Cross how many prisoners were in their POW camps. 'The United Nations has committed 800,000 troops there.'

'And they're still not winning.'

'Bloody Government in London doesn't want to spend the money,' said Edward. 'They would soon take notice if they lost the Malayan tin and rubber revenues, though God knows they've been hit hard enough as it is with all these murders and attacks. D'you realise, the Emergency is costing half a million dollars a day!'

'They'll have to spend a lot more than that to win,' retorted Captain Denton.

The conversation flagged in pessimistic contemplation of the work they were doing while the distant British Government continued to be unmoved by the very real danger that the communists might win.

After a moment, Harry Denton said, 'By the way, Diana has been trying to get hold of you. I said you were out.'

'Did she say what it was about?'

Captain Denton shook his head, frowning. She had sounded tense on the phone. 'No, but she said it was important.'

Edward nodded, went over to his desk and picked up the phone. He asked the operator to put him through to his house and Diana answered at the second ring, 'Edward? Thank God!'

'What's the matter?' He could hear the panic in her voice.

She replied in a rush, 'It's Ellie. She's got some sort of fever. She's awake and cheerful enough but she's very hot and sweating.'

Her panic reflected on Edward for a moment, then he controlled himself, knowing there was an explanation. 'Sounds like another attack of that flu she had ten days ago.' Babies and small children often had brief illnesses, coughs, colds and unexplained flushes, and the heat in Malaya was always a problem for them. Calmly, he said, 'Have you called the Doc?'

'He came earlier and gave her some medicine,' Diana replied. 'She seemed all right for a while, but I'm not sure now.'

'Call him again.'

'I did and he's coming as soon as he can, but he's out of camp at the moment.' She paused, then added in a small voice, 'Edward, can't you come home?'

Edward thought quickly. Diana seemed to have done everything she could. She had called the doctor and if she was really worried, she would have taken Ellie straight to the hospital. Edward felt he had time to see Angus, to pass on Liya's information before the weekend. He said, 'Darling, I'll be with you as soon as I can, but I've one job I must finish off before the weekend.'

Diana said nothing.

'Really, darling. It's rather important.'

'Isn't your daughter important too?'

Edward took a deep breath and said soothingly, 'You've done all you can. I'm sure Ellie will be fine, and the doctor will be with you soon.'

'That's not the point,' Diana began. She wanted Edward with her, not his opinion over the telephone. She felt terrified and lost, unable to help her daughter.

'I won't be long, really, darling,' Edward insisted.

'Please don't be,' Diana said in a flat tone of voice, and rang off.

Forty miles North of Kuala Lumpur, a narrow metalled road cut back and forth through dense jungle, rising several thousand feet from the flat lands of Selangor State above Kuala Lumpur to the ridge of mountains on the border with Pahang State. On the other side of the pass, beyond Fraser's Hill, the road wound down to Tras, Tranum and Bentong where Comrade General-Secretary Chin Peng was hiding out in some of Malaya's remotest jungles. Above one curving S-bend, Ho Peng lay in the shade of the canopy behind a large boulder cradling his carbine, and picking his teeth. The man crouching beside him whispered, 'How long d'you think we'll have to wait?'

Ho Peng replied, 'As long as it takes, Comrade Siu Mah. My information is that he goes up to Fraser's Hill on weekends.'

Siu Mah nodded, 'That's borne out by our Min Yuen workers in Tras township. They've seen his car. A Rolls-Royce.'

Ho Peng spat expressively on the ground and went on, 'Today is Friday. He's a busy man but he could still come up here as late as Sunday, for the day out, maybe for lunch. The British like to go to places for lunch.'

The Rest House at Fraser's Hill had always been popular with the British. Its mock-Tudor design, with black and white half-timbering like a golf club in suburban Surrey, reminded some guests of England and looked decidedly bizarre in the jungle, but they came for the cool mountain air and to enjoy temporary respite from the

241

sweltering humidity of the lowlands.

'Till Sunday afternoon it is, then,' Siu Mah agreed. He stood up and padded silently along the path they had cut the day before through the thick undergrowth behind their ambush position. He and Ho Peng had placed thirty-eight of their best men in a line overlooking the bend in the road. There were riflemen from Siu Mah's Armed Element and Ho Peng's Bodyguards, with three Bren guns, making up a fire-power equivalent to any British infantry platoon. Each man had carefully parted the foliage in front of them for a perfect view and clear field of fire on to the road below. That short stretch of tarmac and the deep monsoon ditches at the side of the road had become a killing zone.

Siu Mah moved quietly down the line telling the men they would stay another two days if necessary and checked they were properly alert. Ho Peng's savage reputation inspired respect and confidence. All the men in the ambush felt it, and were burning to succeed.

Siu Mah returned to the middle of the ambush position to find Ho Peng peering through the bamboo curtain in front of the boulder, unruffled by the wait. He crouched down beside him. They heard the sound of approaching vehicles grinding uphill and tensed. A convoy of army trucks came slowly into view and passed below them. Ho Peng shook his head with professional disgust, seeing how the protecting armoured cars were out of sight at the front and the back when the vulnerable trucks were in the centre of his killing zone. Silent, hidden in the trees, they let it pass.

Edward took two hours to find Angus Maclean and pass on Liya's information about Ho Peng. When the duty driver dropped him back at his house, he recognised the second car parked beside the blue Plymouth as Doctor Hazlitt's. He walked briskly inside, threw his briefcase on the hall table and went straight to Ellie's room. Diana was standing with her hands clasped tight together on her chest watching Doctor Hazlitt kneeling beside the high-sided cot with his hand on Ellie's forehead. Ellie's face was blotchy and flushed, her blonde curls matted with sweat and she cried in pain as the doctor touched her. Edward noticed she had a thermometer under her arm.

'Doctor Hazlitt arrived a moment ago, just before you,' said Diana. Edward heard the tension in her voice and put his arm round her shoulders. Her shirt was damp with perspiration. She just leaned against him, thankful he was with her at last. Ellie's fever had worsened, in bouts, making her sweat and shake but hardest to bear had been her heart-rending crying.

The doctor nodded and said distantly, his mind on Ellie, 'Yes, I'm sorry I was so long. I had to go to King's House this afternoon to see Sir Henry Gurney. He's off for the weekend to Fraser's Hill or somewhere tomorrow.'

Diana and Edward hardly heard him. They could tell from the expression on his face how worried he was about Ellie and, as if mesmerised, they watched him pull the thermometer from under Ellie's small arm and study it. He turned to them and said, 'She must go into the hospital at once, Mrs Fairfax.'

'What's the matter with her?' asked Edward. 'Could it be malaria?'

'But I give her quinine regularly!' exclaimed Diana. 'And she always sleeps with a mosquito net.'

Doctor Hazlitt agreed, but the little girl was obviously in a lot of pain and he did not like the faint yellow tinge of her skin. He said, 'I think we should get her into hospital as soon as we can, for tests. We've got the best facilities in the country there.' He pulled his stethoscope off his neck, coiled it up and stuffed it in his pocket.

'Can I stay with her?' asked Diana at once, stepping over to the cot to comfort her daughter. 'In the hospital, I mean?'

'Of course,' said Doctor Hazlitt.

Edward stared at Diana bending over Ellie, smoothing her forehead and quietly talking to her, and felt helpless. The doctor had a job, Diana too as Ellie's mother, but he felt useless. He did not realise how much better Diana felt just for having him there with her.

The doctor asked, 'May I use the telephone?'

'Of course. I'll show you where.'

Edward's sense of unreality and disjointed participation continued as he drove the big Plymouth on his own to Kinrara Hospital while Diana sat with Ellie inside the ambulance. At the hospital, Edward parked in the visitors' car park and walked back to the big colonial building while Ellie was whisked into a ward. He found Diana in the passage outside, walking up and down and wondering if the pendulum of life and death was going to claim her second child too, after losing his first.

A nurse brought cups of tea. They sat down on metal chairs in the passage to wait, each with their own thoughts.

Hospital staff in white coats and nurses in crisply-ironed uniforms

243

walked up and down the wide, high-ceilinged passage, their shoes squeaking on the linoleum. From time to time, they could hear Ellie's crying in the ward. After an hour, a doctor in a white coat came out of the ward and joined them.

Diana stood up at once. 'What's the matter, Doctor?'

'May I ask a couple of questions first?' he asked, and carried on straightaway with, 'Has Ellie been anywhere near pools of water or streams?'

Diana shook her head, but Edward said, 'What about that ditch on the edge of the garden? Bordering the jungle on the rough ground beyond the perimeter. She was crawling about there when Angus was round the other day.'

Diana nodded slowly.

The doctor pursed his lips. He said, 'I think that may account for it.'

'For what?' Diana burst out. 'What's the matter with her?'

'I think she has Weil's disease, or leptospirosis,' the doctor replied trying to sound as calm as possible. 'Her attack of flu-like symptoms ten days ago, and what you've just said about the ditch, would seem to confirm it.'

'Leptospirosis?' asked Edward.

'It's a disease associated with rats,' explained the doctor reluctantly. 'A small spiral bacterium called icterohaemorrhagiae which is picked up from rat urine in water courses near human habitation.'

Diana felt sick and sat down heavily on her chair. It was impossible her baby girl could be ill with such a thing.

In a kindly voice, the doctor said, 'We're doing all we can, with nursing and a course of M and B.'

'Sulphonamides?' asked Edward.

'Yes, from May and Baker,' said the doctor, his face a mask of professional kindliness which concealed very real concern. He knew the sulphonamides had little effect, but it was all they had. The battle was up to Ellie. But she was so small, and already her skin was turning dry, febrile and yellow, indicating the kind of serious liver disorder which made leptospirosis a killer. He said, 'We're doing blood tests now, and I'll let you know as soon as we have some news from the lab.'

'Can I be with her?' asked Diana. She brushed her fair hair back from her face and tried to look competent. The doctor hesitated, as it was always worse with children and Ellie's bouts of fever were disturbing even for the nurses. No-one, least of all the parents, liked to see a small two-and-a-half-year-old girl crying and fighting a fever which could not be explained to her because she was too small to understand. However her mother might make all the difference. He said, 'All right, but don't tire yourself out.'

He was rewarded with a flashing smile of gratitude and Diana pushed through into the big ward, with Edward close behind her, just as Ellie was gripped with another feverish attack, filling the room with her cries.

The big ward was lined with white beds, all empty except Ellie's near the other end. Two nurses were busy on each side of her bed, one trying to calm her, the other checking the drip feed which hung from a metal stand over the end of her bed.

'What's that for?' asked Diana. The drip looked awfully serious.

'This will restore fluid loss,' said the nurse with a confidence she did not feel. She saw the expression in Diana's eyes watching her daughter rolling about in the bed and added, 'Perhaps you'd like to help change her bedclothes and nightie after she quietens down?'

Diana nodded and took over, sitting on a chair beside the bed, sensitive to every movement and cry Ellie made, gently padding her hot skin with cool linen and lifting her back and forth to change her night-dress between attacks. Edward fetched tea from time to time, for something to do, as Diana refused to leave Ellie's side. She was not excluding him, because she needed to know he was nearby supporting her, but she was determined to let no chance slip by to do her utmost to help her little girl herself.

The afternoon faded into evening, the shadows lengthened across the lino floor, and disappeared as night fell. A nurse switched on a light by the bed and Edward went over to the window. He could just see the dark shapes of the big trees outside, the night was filled with all the familiar sounds of crickets, shrieking cockchafers, frogs and geckos. The air was heavy, building for a storm, and his clothes were tacky on his skin after a long day running round in the heat. Vaguely, he thought about all the things he had done in Malaya, his enthusiasm for learning Chinese, the frustration of working out how to beat the communists, and meeting Liya, but none of it seemed to matter any longer. He would have given up everything to have Ellie well again. Behind him, by Ellie's bed, Diana hardly moved on her chair, watching her daughter's flushed face. Ellie lay breathing harshly but calm, between bouts of fever, and a nurse busied herself monitoring her temperature. The doctor came in and joined Edward by the window. He looked over at the bed and said, 'The tests have confirmed it's leptospirosis.'

'So what next?'

'We just keep fighting on.'

'You mean Ellie keeps fighting on,' snapped Edward.

The doctor nodded rather hopelessly.

'Can't you do something? We can't just let her fight this on her own!'

'We're doing all we can,' the doctor said firmly. 'I promise you.' But he looked across the ward and wished his patient was bigger and stronger.

Edward felt a tightness in his chest, as if he were short of air, and he wanted to shout at the doctor, but he knew it was fruitless.

The doctor said, 'I expect you'd like to spend the night here? I'll sort it out with Matron but I'm sure you can use these empty beds.'

Diana refused to leave Ellie. As the long dark hours passed, every time she thought she might lie down for a quick nap, Ellie started another bout of fever, filling the ward with her crying and thrashing about. Edward looked after Diana, changed her cups of tea which were often untouched on the table by the bed and persuaded her to eat a little supper one of the nurses brought. By morning they were all exhausted but the fever seemed to have subsided.

Ho Peng sat on the ground where he had slept all night and leaned back against the boulder. He chewed a piece of sun-dried river fish which looked like a length of old sisal rope, unconscious of the smell. He heard diesel engines straining uphill. There had been little traffic apart from a few commercial lorries and some motor cars and the whole ambush line stood-to every time they heard a vehicle approaching. He checked his watch. A few minutes before one o'clock. It would be hot in the sun on the road, in the killing zone. He stood up.

Siu Mah peered with him over the boulder between the bamboos and atap leaves on to the tarmac road winding through the jungle trees. Round the corner came an open jeep carrying six Malay policemen, wearing their traditional round black Malay songkok hats and armed with Stens. Behind, came a large black Rolls-Royce with sweeping mudguards, huge coach headlights in gleaming chrome and a brave Union Jack flying from a pennant on top of the famous square Rolls-Royce radiator grill.

'That's it!' hissed Ho Peng, spitting out bits of dried fish. If the Union Jack was not enough, identification of the person in the car

246

was confirmed beyond all doubt by the number plate, just as he had told every man in the ambush line it would be. Instead of the usual letters and digits was a single large crown. This was the crown of office of the High Commissioner for Malaya, the Queen's personal representative, the most prestigious target in the country.

Coolly thinking how absurd the British were to allow Sir Henry Gurney about with such a feeble escort, he rested his carbine over the boulder, took aim on the driver of the Rolls-Royce and opened fire. At once, the whole ambush line poured fire on to the road in a harsh roar of noise. The jeep slewed to a halt in the ditch, pursued by raking bursts from the Bren guns, with all but one of the Malay policemen dead or seriously injured, and the Rolls cruised silently to stop sideways on the road, the dead centre of the killing zone.

To Ho Peng's amazement, the back passenger door of the Rolls opened and a tall figure in a suit stepped out very leisurely, shut the door behind him as if he had all the time in the world and walked casually away from the car towards the ditch. Grimly, Ho Peng switched his aim and fired again. Sir Henry Gurney collapsed, struck by bullets from the trees all round him and crumpled into the monsoon drain beside the road.

Fire continued to pour into the Rolls and at the jeep behind from which one lone surviving, and extremely brave, Malay police sergeant was firing back at random into the trees because he could not see any of his attackers' positions.

Ho Peng turned to Siu Mah and shouted over the din of the shooting, 'Withdraw!' The object of the ambush was achieved. It was time to escape.

Siu Mah signalled to a man near him who stood up and blew a long blast on a bugle. One by one, the ambush party appeared walking swiftly along the track behind their positions. Opposite the boulder they turned down a track which had been specially cut for their escape into the deep jungle. Within minutes of the ambush, the whole group was over the ridge above the road. The sound of the lone policeman firing sporadically into the trees faded away and was replaced by the noises of insects, birds and the rhythmic scuffing of their soft plimsoles on the jungle floor.

Later that afternoon, Edward saw two nurses talking in hushed voices at the end of the ward and noticed the shocked expression on their faces. He left Diana by Ellie who was lying jaundiced and drained on her bed, and went over to them. In a voice dulled with tiredness, he said, 'I know it's looking bad for her, but I'd like to know the truth.'

The nurses looked at him and one said, 'You haven't heard?'

'Heard what?' said Edward. His eyes ached with lack of sleep and he tried to remember if he had missed something one of the duty doctors had told him.

The other explained, 'Sir Henry Gurney has been assassinated. In an ambush on his way up to Fraser's Hill.' She was whispering as if she might prevent the news spreading like a forest fire across Malaya, and making every single person feel that, if the High Commissioner himself could be gunned down, what hope was there for anyone else?

Edward blinked at her, trying to absorb her words, dislocated by his awful pessimism about Ellie.

'The High Commissioner?' The man who engineered the New Villages and gave the Chinese squatters their own land.

The girls nodded.

'Dead?'

'Yes.'

Without a word, he turned around and walked slowly back to Ellie's bed. Fraser's Hill. North of Kuala Lumpur. Liya had been right. He suddenly recalled their conversation, comparing the High Commissioner's movements to Ho Peng's and felt sick with the thought that he might have given away something she might have repeated and which had been overheard by the enemy. 'Surely I can't have been responsible?' he said to himself, but he was so tired he could no longer remember what he had said to her. He just knew he had to find out what had happened.

Diana was asleep in her chair leaning forward on Ellie's bed, her head cradled on her arms. Ellie was quiet for the moment, taking shallow breaths. The two nurses came over and Edward said, 'I'm going over to Headquarters. Shan't be long. D'you think she'll be all right for an hour? She looks quiet now.'

The nurses looked at each other, for they knew the little girl was more prostrate than ever. One put her hand on Edward's arm and said reassuringly, 'You nip off, dear. Leave everything to us. You need a break.'

Edward looked across at Diana and the nurse added, 'Don't worry about your wife. We'll look after her.'

He knew he was exhausted. He drove the Plymouth slowly and with great deliberation while his mind whirled guiltily with snippets of talk and memory. Liya's information that Ho Peng had gone 'north' had been vague, but he was stupid not to have linked it with seeing Siu Mah's name beside Fraser's Hill and with Doctor Hazlitt's remark that Sir Henry was planning to go there at the weekend.

'Nonsense,' said Angus Maclean on the telephone when Edward called him. Edward dared not go into too much detail on the open line, but self-guilt burst through the veiled expressions he used to explain his failure to see what was going to happen.

Angus was dismissive. 'Not even Sherlock Holmes could have made a linkage like that.'

'I don't know,' repeated Edward. In front of him on the desk was the first official signal about Gurney's death.

Angus sensed Edward's exhaustion in his slurred speech. He changed the subject. 'I gather Ellie's not well?'

Edward nodded as he replied, 'She's in Kinrara. Leptospirosis. I've just come from there.'

Angus was appalled, and said, 'Listen, old mate. The damage has been done. Poor old Gurney's dead. You get back to the hospital pretty damn quick. Diana needs you.'

When Edward dropped the phone back on the cradle, he felt as if he would like to sink on to the desk and fall asleep but Angus's words about Diana rang terrible alarm bells.

He heard heavy footsteps in the corridor, the door was flung open and Colonel Bleasley marched in. He was wearing uniform, and looked pink, bleached and scrubbed after his usual post-prandial shower.

'What the hell's going on?' he demanded, observing Edward's damp civilian shirt, his badly creased cotton trousers, the stubble on his chin and his hair all over the place.

'Sir Henry Gurney has been murdered,' said Edward hoisting himself to his feet and knocking over his chair.

'I know,' snapped Colonel Bleasley. 'But it doesn't give you the right to walk about looking like that. Standards, y'know. Important to keep them up at times like this.'

Edward gazed at him for a moment, then walked unsteadily out without a word, leaving Colonel Bleasley speechless with surprise. Angus was right. He had to get back to the hospital, to Diana and Ellie.

He was almost asleep on his feet by the time he shoved through the door into the Ward again. Ellie's bed at the far end was

249

surrounded by a blurr of nurses and doctors in white and he could not see Diana. They looked up as he came over, but no-one spoke or moved and he knew what had happened. All he could hear was a tortured muffled sobbing which he recognised as Diana.

Angus had been right. Diana needed him, and he had let her down.

Chapter 15

NADIR

The dead are buried quickly in the East. Under a tropical sun, Ellie's funeral at St Mary's Church in Kuala Lumpur was well attended by the friends Diana and Edward had made over three years, and Edward could not help thinking of the contrast with his father's burial in Jerusalem in July 1946. Then, apart from the priest and bearers, only Diana had been there, before they were married, with her father, Angus Maclean and one other good friend and fellow officer in the Parachute Regiment, Aubrey Hall-Drake. When Ellie's small coffin was lowered into the rich Malayan soil, more than fifty people came to give their support. Even Sean and Marsha Tallard came all the way into town from the 'Black Circle'.

A few, like Angus, the padre Leonard Goodbury, and Harry Denton came back to the house after the funeral for tea and eats which Hassan and Lao Song had taken immense trouble to prepare, but Diana seemed detached from reality, and the atmosphere was leaden. Everyone left as soon as they decently could after making Diana and Edward promise they would not hesitate to ask for their help if they needed it.

For Edward, the whole ritualistic procedure seemed extraordinarily unreal, quite unconnected with the bright little girl who had died. When he came back out on to the verandah after saying goodbye to the last guests, he found Diana sitting in one of the bamboo chairs gazing across the garden. She looked very pale but composed and beautiful, wearing a dark black silk dress which hung softly over her figure and her long fair hair bunched with a black ribbon at her neck.

She turned her blue eyes on him as he came through the french windows and said, 'I'm leaving.'

251

'What?'

She nodded very slightly, as if any such reinforcement of her feelings was really quite unnecessary, crossed her legs and said, 'I've decided. I've had enough, and I'm leaving.'

Edward was astonished. She was so calm, after the pain of losing Ellie, and her eyes were unnaturally free of tears. He expostulated, 'You've decided? But I've just been given an extension!' Bleasley, reluctant at first, had realised the kudos of having a Chinois speaker in the Intelligence Office, and had told him his appointment was extended only the day before.

'I know. That was what made up my mind for me.' Her reasons spilled out in bitter confusion, one after the other. 'Malaya's not for me. I thought I'd like the heat, but I don't. I do my best with the other officers and their families, but I feel left out. God knows, I've made an effort, but I don't understand the army and I don't understand the languages here. Mr Song still makes little effort to talk to me in English, though he's quite happy to teach you Chinese every day. And I can't bear the endless violence.'

'It's not so bad here in Kuala Lumpur,' said Edward. 'In the barracks, I mean.'

'The bloody camp is horrid,' Diana contradicted him. 'Corrugated iron everywhere, sandbags, and Nissen huts. It's so claustrophobic! I daren't go for a drive into the country to explore, for fear of being ambushed and killed! Frankly, I'm terrified all the time and only want to get away.'

Edward was silent. It was true, the Emergency had spoiled so much of what they had originally expected from their time in Malaya. Even without ambushes, driving anywhere was a bore, always running into road-blocks of soldiers trying to prevent locals smuggling food to the CTs. General Briggs had ordered that Europeans suffer exactly the same delays and searches as Malays, Chinese and Indians.

'And how I hate the jungle,' she stated flatly, glancing at the banana palms waving gently over the clump of jungle beyond the garden and shivered. She had been over there once, across the awful ditch with the rats, with Ellie toddling along beside her, just to see, but when she parted some big attap leaves to peer into the green gloom, with the sun hot on her back, the chaos of leaves seemed to surge towards her and drove her off in panic with a roar of insects, birds and horrid slithering noises in her ears.

'It's not as bad as you think,' said Edward rather desperately.

'Why don't you let me take you in sometime, and I'll show you.'

'What a horrid thought!' she said and then snapped, 'Besides, that's just the problem. You'll never find the time. I hardly see you. You're always busy. I know Colonel Bleasley's not easy, but if you're not at the office, you're with Angus doing some secret thing you can't talk to me about. Even when you're home you spend all the time learning Chinese with our bloody cook!'

'Lao Song is not just a cook. He's a Professor of languages from Shanghai University.'

Diana shrugged. It was true but it hardly mattered any more.

'And Colonel Bleasley should be posted soon,' continued Edward lamely. 'I thought that would make the extra time here worth doing?'

'To you, Edward, but not to me. You like the Emergency, with all the terrible things that happen, but I don't. I suppose it's something to do with your missing the war, but I've had enough drama, losing the first baby and now poor Ellie.' She paused, her voice breaking for the first time. 'Her coffin was so tiny, and you wouldn't even throw a little soil on top of it.' She looked angrily at him.

Taken aback by the truth of her remark about the war, Edward retorted angrily, 'No, and nor did I on my father's coffin either. I think it's a meaningless, crude ritual which has nothing to do with faith or belief. Perhaps it's supposed to be cathartic, for our grief, which makes it condescending too, but it has little to do with losing Ellie.' There seemed to him no way that any religion could satisfactorily explain the death of a pretty, growing child. 'A handful of soil seems such a barbaric gesture.'

'There was nothing barbaric about Ellie's funeral,' snapped Diana matching his irritation. 'And you upset the padre. I saw his face.'

Amazed, Edward shouted, 'Stuff the bloody chaplain! Ellie is my daughter! Was, I mean,' he corrected himself, and immediately regretted losing his temper.

'And mine! I count too, you know, though I doubt you've noticed in the last three years. You weren't even there when she died. When we needed you most.'

Edward curled inside with guilt and asked quietly, 'Well then, what about us?'

She looked at him pityingly and said, 'I wondered when you'd come to that.'

'What d'you mean?' he asked. She was hiding something.

'You should have thought about "us" before you went off with that Marsha Tallard woman,' said Diana. The hammer blow at their marriage seemed so easy to talk about in the end.

Edward's expression hardly changed. Marsha was a long time before, though the adulterous cut felt suddenly as raw as ever. For safety, he repeated evenly, 'What d'you mean?'

'Roger wrote to me from his prisoner-of-war camp in Korea,' she said calmly, fishing in her handbag on the boards beside her rattan chair. She pulled out a creased and torn airmail flimsy. 'This letter only reached me yesterday, months after he sent it, because the North Koreans are swine and refuse to co-operate with the Red Cross.'

'He's all right?' asked Edward. When he had heard Roger was a POW, he had felt guilty about knocking him down the night he left.

'I'm surprised you care,' remarked Diana.

'I admit I never liked him very much.'

'You'll like him even less when I tell you he wrote that he had seen you with that Tallard woman. In the Majestic Hotel of all places! Goodness knows who else might have seen you!' She closed her eyes a moment wondering if she was the last person to find out, and added, 'God, I wish I'd known earlier.' She might never have had Ellie, or the pain of her illness and death.

Edward sat quite still, recalling the whole occasion exactly. He had seen both Liya and Marsha, and snorted ruefully at the irony of how his expectations for that night had been turned about.

Diana lost her temper and shouted, 'Do you deny it?'

To his relief, instead of demanding an answer to that drastically simple question, she shook the letter at him and added, 'Roger is quite specific!'

Edward shrugged and said, 'He would be. You know perfectly well what he's like. You don't like him any more than I do.'

'He's my brother and at least he supports me.'

'Only on his terms.'

'They're better terms than yours and this' – she gestured frantically around, encompassing everything about Malaya – 'this awful place!' She stood up, smoothed the black silk down her slim hips and stated finally, 'I've had enough. I'm going back to England. The fighting is almost over in Korea and Roger might be released soon. He'll be flown back to England and I want to be there to meet him.' Then she walked inside and went to their bedroom, to pack.

Stunned by the speed of events, Edward watched her walk through the sitting-room, elegantly sure of herself, till she disappeared in the shadows in the hall. Hassan drifted unhappily through his line of vision clearing up the teacups and empty sandwich plates from the funeral tea party.

The next three weeks passed too quickly for Edward. He spent as little time as possible in the office, he avoided another meeting with Liya, though he was desperate to ask her for more information about Ho Peng and the High Commissioner's murder. And he spent as much time at home as he could trying to persuade Diana to change her mind. She refused.

'Are you saying you want a divorce?' he demanded exasperated.

'I don't know,' she shrugged, sliding away from the issue which would so utterly change her way of life. There had been too much reality and death and she was simply not ready to grasp the implications of killing her marriage too. 'All I know is that I have to leave Malaya,' she said.

She booked her train to Singapore and a cabin on a liner from Singapore to Liverpool, and, on the morning of departure she said practically, 'You can keep the car, it's no good to me, but don't bother to see me off. We've nothing more to say to each other. Leonard Goodbury has arranged transport for my baggage and he'll drive me to the station.'

Edward lost his temper at last and shouted, 'What's it got to do with the fucking padre? You're still my wife and I'll drive you to the station!'

'Don't worry,' she snapped back, shocked by his language. 'I haven't told him, or anyone else, why I'm going. Just that I have to go back to England for a month or two to see family and get over Ellie's death.' Then she turned away and left him fuming. She felt battered by Malaya, and the nearness of departure had steeled her mind. Edward, she decided, had changed.

When the Transport Corporal came to fetch Diana's suitcases, there was nothing Edward could do. His anger at Diana's refusal to discuss their future had swamped any latent feelings of guilt over Marsha Tallard, but he was powerless to stop the soldiers carrying her cases to the truck in the road outside. Fighting over whether suitcases should be in one place or another seemed foolish and had no bearing on Diana's decision to leave.

He surprised himself by feeling the same way about the padre. Later that evening, innocent of their marital strife, Leonard Goodbury arrived in his army Humber to drive Diana to the station. She was as usual looking very beautiful in smart travelling clothes and high heels and she kissed Edward goodbye on the cheek. This struck him as perfectly absurd after all the frantic arguments they had had, so, rather as if she was a departing guest rather than his wife walking out on him, he asked casually, 'When shall we see each other again?'

For the first time since Ellie's death, her armour of detachment was shaken and she said uncertainly, 'I don't know, Edward. It's just Malaya—' Her voice trailed off, she turned away and walked down the path to Leonard Goodbury's car. As the padre held the door for her, she stopped and looked back at the house. Edward was standing on the verandah with the front door wide open behind him. She gave him a little wave, got in to the car and was gone.

As Edward watched the black Humber move up the short road and saw its small red tail lights flick out of sight around the bushes on the corner, the image of Diana giving him that silent wave stayed fixed in his mind. Then he went back inside.

He walked on to the verandah at the back of the house, and looked round the garden. He breathed in the scent of the stephanotis by the steps, the night sound of insects, the frogs and geckos buzzed reassuringly and the warmth enveloped him. Malaya had seduced him. He loved it. After all the arguments, shouting and recriminations, he felt strangely relieved, almost light-headed, a single man again with the knowledge of experience and without any of the inhibitions or confusions.

Unasked, Hassan brought him a large whisky s'tengah. He smiled and thanked him. He sipped his drink contemplatively and made up his mind. If Diana had left him because she could not cope with his obsession for Malaya, for his Chinese, for the demands of his job, then he had better feed the obsession.

He slugged down the last of his whisky, changed into cotton ducks and a white shirt and left the house. It took him only a few minutes in the Plymouth to reach the centre of town and he parked the car by the central police station. Dark clouds covered the sky and intense humidity threatened rain as he walked briskly into China-town.

The Chinese theatre was in play, filled with a sea of excited Chinese in white shirts, a cacophony of high-pitched voices and brass cymbals, and actors in gorgeous costumes stalked the stage in a mixture of Eastern charade and mime. Edward squeezed through the crowds in the yard who were pressing forward to see, and slipped into the dirty side-alley, hoping Liao Ting-chi would not already be on stage. He took the rickety old ladder two at a time, picked his way over the rubbish on the roof and knocked on the door of Liao's changing room. The gesture was a formality but Edward often wondered if Liao could feel the vibrations. As usual he shoved open the door and pushed inside.

Liao was standing at his mirror, resplendent in a full-length tunic of red silk and brocade, curving shoulders, and wore a great black head-dress. He smiled happily in greeting, almost cracking the fierce black lines of his grease paint and long Chinese finger-nails fluttered round his costume, describing it for Edward in mime.

'You look superb, Liao,' said Edward truthfully.

Laio Ting-Chi beamed with delight.

The smell of grease paint and joss sticks was heavy but, in the gloom behind Liao himself, away from the lights around the mirror, Edward became aware of someone else who was smoking a pipe. A slender Chinese of indeterminate age and sex, with long black hair and narrow feminine features.

'Liao is playing Duke Hsiang of Lu tonight, the terrible Chinese warlord of the State of Ch'u,' this person explained in a high-pitched voice, 'in the time before Confucius.' He offered the pipe up to Liao who held it delicately, put it to his lips, inhaled the smoke and closed his slanting eyes in bliss. His white face, made up with arching black eyebrows and a fearsome mouth of carmine lipstick, relaxed and Duke Hsiang lost all his legendary terror.

Liao opened his eyes and offered the pipe to Edward.

'What is it?'

The person on the bed observed Edward languidly, impressed with his Chinese.

The room was so small, Edward took the pipe anyway, as Liao looked as if he might drop it, and asked, 'Where is she, Liao?'

Duke Hsiang's theatrical curved shoulders lifted slightly and he gestured for Edward to smoke the pipe. His expression under all the make-up was impossible to read.

Edward looked at the pipe. It seemed well-used, and he was suspicious but, with Diana leaving, nothing much mattered any more and his mood was one of commitment. He put the pipe to his lips, smelled a thick sweet odour and inhaled, as if he was smoking a cigarette.

Instantly light-headed, reeling and soaring among the lights which seemed to have set up a jive around the mirror, his legs turned to rubber and he reached out to hold himself against the side of the

257

room. His hand grasped a shelf which collapsed, cascading bottles over the floor.

Liao gurgled with delight and the other Chinese shrieked with laughter.

'What the hell was that?' asked Edward, steadying himself and trying to concentrate. The Duke Hsiang of Ch'u appeared to have swelled in size.

'Opium,' said the shadowy Chinese on the bed.

'Stupid sods,' said Edward automatically, but without animosity. He struggled to control his whirling mind and demanded again, 'Where is she?'

'She's not here,' said the Chinese, tears of laughter running down his cheeks and without the slightest idea who the Englishman was talking about. He reached across and took the pipe from Edward's limp grasp and passed it to Liao again. Edward watched him inhale blissfully and realised he would get nowhere with either of them.

'Stupid sods,' he repeated and lurched backwards out of the little changing-room. The warm night air was clean and light compared to the thick atmosphere inside Liao's changing-room. He took several deep breaths, and when the lights of Chinatown stopped bobbing about him like bright corks on the sea, he made his way unsteadily down the staircase into the alley, sublimely unconscious of the wobbly handrail and broken steps.

His decision to go and find Liya in the Wild Orchid was taken without a moment's reflection. He walked under the archway into the road, and set off in that direction with ungainly steps.

Lu-Lu Suzie was in the bar, dressed as before in her voluminous silk cheongsam and heavily made-up. She recognised Edward as he pushed through the bead curtain and smiled, showing her gold teeth. The nasty little chase when she had last seen the young English officer was both a long time ago and not of her making. This time she did not expect Ho Peng, who had been away for some weeks, and as the Englishman had come back he would be sure to spend his money.

'Have a Tiger,' she said to Edward beckoning him over and ordering the pretty Malay girl behind the bar to pour a glass.

Edward accepted and was soon sitting on a barstool feeling more relaxed than he could remember. He knew he was floating on a cushion of alcohol and Liao's opium but he felt remarkably lucid.

'What can I do for you tonight?' asked Lu-Lu in English.

'I want to see Liya,' stated Edward in Chinese.

Lu-Lu narrowed her eyes, surprised by his Chinese and the blunt request to see Liya. There were few customers she allowed to ask for individuals and Liya was not one of her girls anyway. However the Englishman was drunk and maybe he would never notice who came to see him.

'Is she here?' asked Edward happily drinking his beer.

Lu-Lu shook her head. 'No. She's not here, but I can give you a room where you can wait for her.'

Edward nodded as if this were the most natural arrangement in the world.

'Only you have to give me a deposit first.'

Without demur, Edward fished in his pocket for his wallet, nearly falling off the barstool in the process, and handed over a twenty-dollar bill. Lu-Lu stuffed it away in her capacious bosom inside her silk dress and told him, 'Follow me'.

He dropped off the barstool, and walked with great care after Lu-Lu who grunted slowly up the stairs and along the worn carpet to her best room on the first floor.

'You wait here,' she said expansively, waving her arm round the room.

Edward took in the heavy red flock wallpaper, the marble-topped table, the big green armchair and the large double bed covered with white sheets. The decoration was bare but the Wild Orchid had been a private house once, so the room had a certain old-fashioned character to it, with curtain rails and a polished wood dado all round the walls.

'What's in there?' asked Edward pointing at another door in the corner of the room.

'A bathroom,' said Lu-Lu.

'Very good,' Edward nodded, as if he were being shown a suite in Kuala Lumpur's finest hotel. He stared at the door for a moment and turned to ask Lu-Lu another question but she had gone. Edward shrugged. His mind had stopped flying and he suddenly felt terribly tired. He drained his glass, let it fall on the marble table and lurched over to the bed. He collapsed on to it, lay full length on his back and stared at the ceiling.

The real world flooded back. Everything had gone wrong. After three miserable years fighting the communists, two High Commissioners had died in the driving-seat, one murdered by the CTs. A police state had been imposed on Malaya with road-blocks and restrictive commercial regulations about food supplies, but no-one could see a way to halt the endless attacks on planters, miners, police, army or anyone else the CTs wanted to kill. The authorities were unable to persuade the British Government to spend the necessary funds to combat the threat to Malayan society and most people still thought the communists might win, as they had done in China and as they seemed to be doing in Korea. After all, they had been able to murder Gurney. No-one believed the official line that the assassination had been sheer chance. Finally, in the nadir of his gloom, Edward thought about the failure of his own life and losing his family, his daughter and his wife. Confusions settled over him, but oddly there was no pain. He supposed it was Liao's opium. He closed his eyes.

Ten minutes later, the pretty Malay girl reported back to Lu-Lu that the Englishman was so fast asleep she could do nothing for him. She had stripped him naked and done her best but he was dead to the world. Lu-Lu Suzie shrugged. She would charge him for the room all the same.

Even the impending storm which broke with lightning and torrential rain over Kuala Lumpur did not wake him.

Around midnight, Liya walked through the pouring rain into the Wild Orchid by the back way, completely soaked. Her samfu working clothes were sodden and filthy, as if she had been in the jungle for a week, but Lu-Lu never asked questions. She merely said, 'I didn't expect you back so soon?'

'My work was finished quicker than I thought,' said Liya.

Lu-Lu nodded, and said bluntly, 'Your room is occupied.'

Liya pulled a face, though she was not surprised. Lu-Lu Suzie never missed a chance of making a few dollars. Cross, she said, 'But I wanted a bath.'

Lu-Lu observed Liya's filthy clothes with distaste. She never went outside Kuala Lumpur herself. She said, 'You can probably use the bath. There's an Englishman in there, but he's on his own and fast asleep.'

Liya guessed intuitively that it was Edward, but she played safe and asked, 'Who is he?'

'That officer who caused trouble here a while ago asking for you.' Lu-Lu shrugged her big fat shoulders and said, 'Men are all the same, but he's learned Chinese quite well. If you want a bath, you don't have to worry about him. He's been drinking and judging by the expression in his eyes he's drugged as well. Even Anim couldn't wake him when she went up to entertain him.'

'I'll have a bath and find another room,' said Liya and made her way up the old stairs, pleased Anim had not succeeded with Edward. She slipped silently inside the bedroom, locked the door behind her and tiptoed over to the bed. Edward was sleeping peacefully and she watched him for a moment, thinking of all their meetings and conversations and how he had tried to speak Chinese and understand her way of life. The Malay girl had left him under a sheet, piling his clothes on the floor in the corner. At that moment, he was completely at her mercy.

In the bathroom, she carefully closed the door, filled the deep old-fashioned bath, stripped off her dirty clothes and wallowed in the hot water. Bathing was possibly the only luxury in her life. She loved being able to come back after her trips and feel clean again. This time, as she washed, she had no doubt what she was going to do.

She stepped out, dried herself and, still naked, walked soft-footed back to Edward. She looked down on him for a moment, loosening her hair from the knot she had tied for the bath, and then slipped under the sheet next to him. For a while she lay still beside him, getting used to his warmth, listening to his steady breathing and enjoying the surprise that his skin was as soft as hers. Then, lying on her side, she began to explore him with her fingers, still surprised and delighted at the fortune which had brought him to her like this, vulnerable and shorn of the barriers which normally kept them apart, almost like a baby. Exciting herself, she caressed the smooth muscles of his chest, his arms and slid down across his flat stomach to his legs.

Her roaming fingers found his penis and scrotum. He stirred, coming awake, which thrilled her, and by the time he was half awake and aware what was happening to him, she was as aroused as he was.

He opened his eyes and saw her leaning over him, her black hair like a soft curtain over her pale shoulders.

'Liya?' he asked, utterly confused.

She nodded and when she was sure he knew her, she bent forward and kissed him. He responded, but she had not stopped the delicate dance round his groin with her finger-nails and he gently slipped his arm round her, exploring her back and feeling her small breasts and rigid dark nipples.

Gently she pulled him towards her. She wanted him at once, without spoiling the moment with pointless questions and talk. He

261

leaned over her, suddenly desperate for her, but hesitated, frightened of hurting her. She pulled harder with her arms and urged him into her, wrapping her slender legs around his waist. As they began moving slowly together, he was surprised how strong she was, and demonstrative, writhing under him and calling out incomprehensible little words in Chinese, and when they reached their climax she bit him in the neck and scratched his back and arched up beneath him before falling still, drenched in sweat.

'Lu-Lu Suzie said you were drugged,' she smiled down at him after they had disentangled themselves and lay side by side on the bed.

Edward smiled, idly stroking her arm across his chest and said, 'I was. With Liao Ting-chi's opium.'

She laughed out loud, imagining the scene as he described it, then she slid over him, lying full-length on his body with her legs wide apart, and kissed him full on the lips.

In the bungalow in Uxbridge Drive, Hassan had not gone to bed. He was wandering round from room to room, recalling things from happier times and seeing nothing but emptiness now. Even Lao Song had disappeared that evening and the house was deserted. So much seemed to have changed, he told himself, and he wondered pathetically if the Tuan would return at all. Finally, he plucked up courage and went into the Tuan's bedroom. He sat cross-legged on the bed under the big white mosquito net and looked round. He often went there by day, but at night the room was forbidden, like a temple, which he had only approached from the garden, to worship at the soft little noises of pleasure he had heard through the window. Now, there was nothing.

BOOK FOUR

November 1951 to June 1955

'All hearts in infancy are good and true,
But time and things those hearts derange.'

Shih Ching, 3,3,1.
(The Book of Poetry, Chou Period, before
Confucius)

Chapter 16

SIX PROMISES

Lao Tang was observing Tallard's house from the jungle fringe. On his right was Ho Peng and, behind them, thirty other soldiers of the MRLA. They owed their lives to Ho Peng. After the assassination of Sir Henry Gurney, the British had angrily swamped the jungle round Fraser's Hill with patrols, but Ho Peng's group had escaped intact.

Ho Peng had kept his men on the move for weeks. He laid confusing trails back and forth through the jungle while the monsoon rains poured down through the canopy, refused to allow them to make any noise, and imposed rigid discipline on their leaving any signs of their presence. He seemed to sense the nearness of the British and had sometimes refused to let them cook or smoke or make a proper camp at all, forcing them to sleep on the wet ground wherever they ended up at last light. They hated it, but one morning Ho Peng silently woke them in the blackness before dawn to sit on the damp leaves gripping their rifles and Stens, water dripping down their necks from the sopping branches above. Lao Tang could still recall his fear as he became aware of the unmistakable sounds of many people secretively moving about close by in the inky dark, the occasional clink of a mess tin, and smelled the tantalising waft of cooking. They had nearly walked right on to a British patrol and had slept all night only yards away, saved by the thickness of the jungle and Ho Peng's strict discipline. As a misty grey dawn light filtered down through the canopy, they saw a long line of British soldiers walking past them, still filled with sleep as they plodded on into the jungle, unaware that the enemy they sought was watching them.

But the Peng's men were tired, hungry and very thin. Being on the move meant they were separated from their usual sources of food supplied by their Min Yuen contacts, and they had lived off the jungle as best they could. Lao Tang was fed up with eating palm hearts and acrid slimy Kladis, and he had been very ill indeed after eating a wild pig he had shot at a salt lick. It was full of worms and had not been cooked enough.

The noise of a vehicle made him look up. Tallard's armoured 'Monster' was coming up the hill from the estate offices to the house. They watched him drive the truck into the garage and Ho Peng whispered hoarsely, 'We'll wait till dark.'

Daylight faded into night rapidly, as always in Malaya, and an hour later Ho Peng stood up and walked calmly into the open towards Tallard's house. Lao Tang was in charge of the ten-man Armed Element behind him, giving him close support in case they met trouble, and the other two Armed Elements took up positions on the road to the house, cutting it off from help.

Ho Peng's technique for entering the house was simple. He walked up the front steps, shot the lock to bits with a burst from his carbine and ran inside followed by Lao Tang and two others. As he had guessed, Sean Tallard and his wife were having a whisky s'tengah in their sitting-room. Ho Peng appeared in the doorway and shouted in English, 'Halt! Do not take a gun!'

Tallard froze, his hands reaching into his gun cabinet, and turned to face his intruders.

'What took you so long?' he said. 'You little bastards have been shooting this house to shit for three and a half years and now you decide to visit, just like that?'

Shocked, Marsha sat in one of the two armchairs clutching her drink. The intrusion was all the more terrifying because she was showered and comfortable in a clean sarong after a long day working in the New Village medical centre, while the Chinese were filthy dirty, their MRLA uniforms torn, their leggings caked with mud, their faces pale and drawn and the expression in their black eyes was pitilessly suspicious, like wild animals entering a house for the first time.

Ho Peng stepped forward. Marsha wrinkled her nose at the smell. He ignored her and said to Tallard, 'I could have killed you any time.' He waved his free hand at the dado concealing the sand-bagged reinforcement of the walls which he had seen at once and added, 'This was not able to stop me.'

Tallard, enormous in front of Ho Peng, shrugged his shoulders and replied, 'It's worked so far'.

Ho Peng's eyes narrowed and he said, 'Times have changed. I need answers now.'

Tallard looked puzzled. 'Answers?'

'You know what answers!' shouted Ho Peng, his pale pitted skin colouring with anger.

'Whatever he's talking about, Sean honey,' said Marsha in a hollow voice, 'you better tell him or we're in trouble.' She did not like the way the three dirty Chinese behind Ho Peng were staring at her.

Ho Peng pointed at her and said, 'This woman is your wife?'

'Yes, but she's nothing to do with this.'

'With what?' snapped Marsha.

Ho Peng's eyes travelled from Marsha's blonde hair, down her slender neck to the shadows of her bosom underneath the soft sarong, over her narrow waist and hips to her long legs and feet. She felt like a piece of meat in a butcher's shop.

He spoke rapidly in Chinese and Tallard shouted, 'No!' but the three Chinese at the door ran forward, grabbed Marsha by the arms, knocking her drink to the floor and dragged her screaming and fighting from the room.

Ho Peng carefully closed the door after them, without taking his eyes off Tallard. He ordered him to sit in the soft armchair Marsha had been in, so he could not do anything unexpected and covered him with his carbine. He said, 'You heard what I said?'

Tallard nodded.

Ho Peng waited and his eyes never left Tallard's face. The silence was oppressive. Sweat stood out on Tallard's forehead and dark patches stained his shirt. The man had to tell him.

Distantly through the closed door they heard a long female scream.

Tallard cringed inside. The sound faded away and he waited in spite of himself for the next scream. He squirmed in the deep soft chair, measuring the distance between them, but Ho Peng lifted his carbine a fraction and he stayed put.

The scream came again.

Tallard's imagination ached with what they might be doing to Marsha but he said with a thick, obstinate voice, 'Why didn't you kill us before?'

Ho Peng did not answer.

Male laughter and another series of pathetic cries echoed through the wood house, lower in tone but Tallard could not help straining his ears and heard every syllable. He wondered why Ho Peng had not left the door open, so the sounds of torture would carry clearer.

Ho Peng leaned forward and whispered, 'I'll stop them if you tell me.'

'No you bloody won't!' Tallard bellowed suddenly, to drown out the noises. 'I know you, remember? From the war. You'll kill us both.'

Thinking of the war helped. Tallard suddenly realised why Ho Peng had not killed them before. They both knew how easy it was to kill someone if you wanted to badly enough, especially with a force of soldiers to help. Plainly, Ho Peng had wanted him alive. Forcing himself to ignore Marsha's cries, Tallard said, 'You've closed the door so the others won't hear us. And you're speaking English as a double measure, so they can't understand us. You never killed me, because you need me.' Not, as Tallard had always blindly prided himself, because of the care with which he changed his routine, used the 'Monster' whenever he could, and the sandbagged walls of his house.

Ho Peng glared at him. The MRLA needed resources badly and Ho Peng still wanted the advantages he could obtain by providing them.

The British did not know it yet, but Chin Peng had admitted the campaign was going badly in his October 1951 Directive, in spite of the killing of Sir Henry Gurney. Not a single Liberated Area had been established anywhere in Malaya and the MRLA were losing as many men as they had killed civilians, army and police. Worse, the British patrols were increasingly effective in the jungle. The Malayan Communist Party desperately needed funds to finance new initiatives. In between attacking the British or being chased by them, Ho Peng had searched for the gold in all the old wartime hides without success. He said, this time in Chinese, 'It's hidden in the jungle, isn't it?'

Tallard nodded. There was no harm in admitting that.

'Where?'

'Want the gold yourself, do you?' asked Tallard unpleasantly. He leaned back in his chair and tried to show a confidence he did not feel. 'To run away to a more comfortable life, like your old General-Secretary Lai Teck?'

Ho Peng swore and aimed his carbine at Tallard's head. Tallard stared back at Ho Peng's face behind the muzzle, at the cold black eyes and broad nose flattened over his filthy pitted cheeks. He felt sick. More faintly now, he could hear Marsha's cries but there was only one option for their survival, if she still had an option. He said in a hoarse but firm voice, 'If you murder me, you'll never find out where the gold is.'

The small round muzzle of the carbine did not waver. Ho Peng was seething to kill Tallard, but he controlled himself and asked, 'What happened after the parachute drop? I had to go and see General-Secretary Chin Peng. When I got back, you had gone and so had all those containers.'

Tallard lifted his shoulders. He was not going to be drawn into detail, though he could still hear whimpering down the corridor and it took all his self-control not to launch himself at Ho Peng.

'You couldn't have carried all those containers by yourself,' continued Ho Peng.

'I didn't,' said Tallard truthfully.

'I found a dozen men missing when I got back. I was told they had been ambushed by the Japanese. I suppose you killed them after they had carried the gold off for you?'

Tallard shrugged again and said, 'Think what you like, Ho Peng. Apply your own standards.'

For a long moment, Ho Peng stared coldly at the big man sitting in the armchair. Slyly he said, 'We can make a deal. You can't get the gold from the jungle without my protection, and you don't want to tell the British, so why don't we find it together and share it?'

Survival gave Tallard no choice in his reply. As dismissively as he could, he said, 'Get the hell out of my house!'

The barrel of Ho Peng's Sten moved a fraction and he pulled the trigger, three times.

Deafened, Tallard flung himself sideways in his chair, and Ho Peng laughed. He said, 'You'll change your mind, Tallard. Remember, I know you too, from the war. I'll smash this house of yours and terrify you from now on till you tell me.'

'It hasn't worked yet,' Tallard retorted desperately.

Lao Tang burst into the room, carbine at the ready, with the other two MRLA soldiers behind him. Ho Peng flicked his head and they all ran outside the house.

Tallard hoisted himself up and raced down the passage, hardly daring to think what he might find.

Marsha was in her bedroom. She was sitting on her bed, naked, rubbing her wrists where she had been tied up, and crying. Her face was bruised and she ached all over. He sat down beside her, pulled her into his arms, stroking her hair and asked, 'Are you all right?'

She shook her head, sobbing like a little girl, feeling safe in his powerful grasp and comforted by his familiar smell. For a long time, she let him hold her, as she grappled with what the three had done to her and how she could never tell anyone, least of all her husband. Eventually, she said, 'Those goddam yellow bastards never touched me, Sean, I promise, but they frightened the goddam life out of me.' She looked up at him with her tear-stained face. 'It was awful! I screamed and screamed because they had knives and I thought they were going to cut me apart.'

But they did not, Tallard thought. He tucked her back into his chest and said nothing. He knew Ho Peng. Nothing was done without a purpose, nor did he ever make idle threats. He had proved he could force his way into the house when he liked and he had deliberately spared Marsha, for the moment. The stakes had suddenly gone up.

Tallard wasted no time alerting the authorities. He needed support. He contacted Angus Maclean and they met in the New Village, in Marsha's medical centre. Edward came too, on the pretext of seeing the District Executive War Committee at Langat and because he hoped to find Liya at the New Village.

'Why are we meeting here?' Angus asked quietly, looking round the shiny corrugated tin hut which was lined with shelves of bottles and dressings. He and Edward were sitting on wooden chairs, the only two in the room, Tallard was leaning against the wall and Marsha was fiddling with her box of prescribed drugs which she never left in the hut for fear they would be stolen for the CTs. She felt dirty thinking about the attack and wished she could be left in peace to forget it. 'Wouldn't it have been better at your house, where it all happened?'

'I'm a busy man,' said Tallard brusquely. 'I have to come here to see my tappers and it saves you the extra mileage to the house. Now, d'you want to hear what happened or not?'

Angus listened carefully while Tallard described the attack, omitting all mention of the gold.

'You mean to say he just came in, beat you up a bit and then left?'

Tallard said aggressively, 'That's what I said.'

Angus looked at Edward and said, 'Well, it's useful to know that Ho Peng is back.' The attack on the Tallards confirmed what Red

Dragon had told Edward. Ho Peng was back in the jungle around Langat and the 'Black Circle'.

'Useful!' exploded Tallard. 'I want something done about it!'

'What?'

Tallard took a deep breath and said, 'Winston Churchill's new Tory Government in London has had the common sense to send the Colonial Secretary out to see what the hell is going wrong in Malaya, as you well know, and we all heard his radio broadcast at the end of November telling us what the new administration is going to do to win the war.'

Edward was watching Marsha. She lacked her usual vivacity and refused to catch his eye. He felt sure she was hiding something.

'He promised more protection for the squatters and New Villages and I want that right now.'

Angus smoothed back his dark hair, instinctively disliking the Northern Irishman, and said, 'Aye, you can have that. I'll get a small squad of Special Constables sent up tomorrow. But there'll be other changes too.' Tallard's hearing of Oliver Lyttelton's radio broadcast was obviously selective.

'Like what?' demanded Tallard.

'Lyttelton made six promises. He also said there would be a compulsory education programme, to win the war of ideas, and a Home Guard in these New Villages, made up of the villagers themselves.'

Tallard was shocked. 'You're not suggesting you're going to arm these bastards?' he said, his voice rising.

'Aye,' said Angus softly. 'Give them a school and make it Malayan, not just Chinese, to show them the British mean to build up Malaya as a country in its own right, and give them the responsibility to protect it themselves.'

'Ah Chi would make a good leader,' said Marsha quietly from the corner.

Tallard snorted, 'He's too old.'

'Maybe, but I've seen him helping other families settle into this New Village and I don't think he likes the CTs. You can always find younger men to help him.'

Tallard glared at her but she refused to meet his look.

'I think Mrs Tallard's right,' said Angus firmly. 'In any event, Mr Tallard, you won't get my support unless I get yours in these new measures for the villagers here. Lyttelton also announced that the police will have supremacy in the fight against the terrorists.'

'They'll need bloody reorganising!'

'He promised that too,' said Angus calmly.

'And who's going to provide this utopia?' demanded Tallard.

'The man who takes the place of Gurney. He'll be a general and have complete authority over all civil and military affairs in Malaya.'

'The bloody country's becoming an all-British police state,' grumbled Tallard, but in the face of Ho Peng's threats he agreed to Angus's terms. Edward left them to work out the details and went for a walk round the village to look for Liya.

The sun was hot on his shoulders as he walked down the line of new timber huts and along the perimeter fence. Beyond, men and women were working on new rice padis beside the Sungei Kabal. The same chickens and children rootled about in the dirt between the houses, but the New Village was cleaner compared to the old squatters' village nearer the 'Black Circle'.

There was no sign of Liya, but Edward greeted Ah Chi outside his hut on the high ground and asked him if he had seen her. Ah Chi shook his head and said she did not come out to the New Village as often as she had done to the squatters' village. He smiled toothlessly, 'We are better organised now. We have more pigs and chickens and rice, from the Government.'

As they drove back to Kuala Lumpur, Angus asked, 'Where did you get to just now?'

'Just having a look round the village,' Edward lied blandly. 'The government agricultural aid programme seems to be working, for Ah Chi at least, and I tried to imagine a school there.'

'Helps being able to speak Chinese,' said Angus jealously. He added casually, 'Seen Red Dragon recently?'

'Not in the last week,' said Edward awkwardly. They had met once a week since that first night together, and twice spent the night together in the Wild Orchid. Liya promised him she wanted to see him, but she was reluctant to break her rule of setting a routine for their meetings. She was frightened of being surprised by Ho Peng. She only let Edward come to the Wild Orchid when she was quite sure he was away.

'Has she said anything more about Ho Peng?' For the moment Red Dragon was the only source of information on him.

Edward shook his head. He wondered if he should tell Angus about Liya. There were anomalies in her way of life which he did not understand. She seemed to travel such a lot, which maybe explained Ah Chi's remark, and he thought about her too much.

Becoming personally involved with a source was unprofessional and dangerous. But he was afraid that, if he said anything, Angus would make him give her up for someone else to control and he would never see her again. He dismissed the idea. Liya was not important to Angus. She was nothing more than a young woman scraping a living in various places as best she could, like thousands of other Chinese, and she picked up the occasional bit of interesting information on the grapevine. Being involved with her would make little impact on such low-grade information or the Emergency as a whole, and, understanding her more, he might be able to help her. He deliberately changed the subject and said, 'D'you think Lyttelton's six promises were genuine?'

'Certainly,' said Angus. 'We are going to see big changes in Malaya soon and I'll tell you something else, in the strictest secrecy. The Police Commissioner, Nicol Gray, is going to get the sack, so this absurd "no armour" policy will go too. We'll be able to armour all our vehicles. Not just the odd one like this without telling him.'

'Maybe Lyttelton's broadcast wasn't just political guff after all.'

'London is at last beginning to take an interest,' Angus insisted. 'The best news is that they're going to separate Special Branch from the CID. We've been given a base outside KL now, hidden in the middle of a rubber plantation, and to underline the promises, we're getting all the funds we need.'

Angus dropped Edward at the gates of the Headquarters. He had to catch a special RAF flight down to Singapore. The new resources for Special Branch had allowed him to mount a number of long-awaited operations. In addition to his interest in catching Ho Peng and breaking up his CT gang around Langat and the 'Black Circle', Angus, now a Chief Inspector, had been charged with tracking down the MRLA courier network.

Special Branch had deduced that Chin Peng must use a chain of couriers running up and down the length of Malaya to keep in touch with his commanders. Each courier operated in his or her local area, collecting the messages and passing them on in clandestine meetings, at most knowing only two people in the chain, either side of their own area. Meetings were always secret, like a 'chance' brush-past in a crowd, on a stairway in a shop, or at a bus queue.

Sometimes the couriers never met at all and used 'dead letter boxes' instead. A courier might leave a message hidden in an old cigarette packet in a pre-arranged spot, and later the next link in the chain would arrive and pick it up. Couriers leaving messages used secret signs at the dead letter boxes to tell the other courier that the box was empty or full or not to come there again, like a small pile of stones or a beer bottle-top left in an agreed position which could be seen by anyone casually walking past.

After months of work, Special Branch had identified the first link in the chain in Singapore and Angus could hardly wait to start. He knew they would have to be very careful, but with the ever-essential element of luck, the surveillance operation would unravel Chin Peng's courier network from south to north, revealing one courier in the chain after the other, till they reached the final link to Chin Peng himself.

Then Special Branch would be able to intercept and read all the MRLA's orders, administration and secret papers. For this, the courier chain would be left in place. Some couriers would be left unwitting players in the game, some would be 'turned' to work as double agents, and some would be arrested, imprisoned or executed. The Emergency Regulations were quite specific. Anyone, whether male or female, found carrying a weapon, grenade, or even a single bullet faced the death penalty.

Chapter 17

TANJONG MALIM

During the morning of Monday 24 March 1952, Ho Peng was sitting at the marble-topped table in the room with the bath in the Wild Orchid, and looking at an old road map of Malaya. A string vest hung loose round his skinny chest and he wore clean black cotton slacks. He rested his arms on the table and pushed his finger along the road north from Kuala Lumpur past Kuala Kubu Baharu, where Sir Henry Gurney had driven to his death on Fraser's Hill, through Tanjong Malim on the State border between Selangor and Perak, through Bidor, and to Ipoh, State capital of Perak. An important MCP member, a girl, one of the Perak State Committee, called Lee Meng lived there.

He reached over the map for a lightweight airmail letter-pad, put it on the map and began to write with a fountain pen. He wrote slowly, with great deliberation. The nib of his pen was very thin and his Chinese script tiny. After an hour he had written much but covered only a strip of paper an inch wide the full length of the pad.

Then, he took a length of electrical cable, cut a piece just over an inch long and eased the wires out of the rubber sleeve. He cut out his strip of Chinese characters with scissors, rolled the thin paper tightly, like a tiny carpet, and slipped it inside the rubber tube. He sealed the tube by softening the rubber over a lighted match and sticking the tiny round lips at the ends together.

He pushed back his chair, went over to a small grip bag on the floor and came back to the table with a new bar of Palmolive soap. He began to drill out a cavity in the body of the bar of soap with a drill bit, rolling it between finger and thumb, collecting the fine flakes of soap as he worked. Every few minutes, he measured the

275

little rubber tube against the drill bit for size. Eventually he was satisfied and slipped the rubber tube snugly in its hole in the centre of the bar. He took the bar and the flakes of soap to the bathroom and, softening the flakes with a little hot water, he packed them back in the hole over the rubber tube, hiding it completely and smoothing the end of the soap so it showed no sign of disturbance. He returned to the table to tidy up all signs of his work, scrutinised the bar for any defects and finally went back to the bathroom and washed his hands with it.

He left the soap in the bath tray, dried his hands and went back to lie down on his bed. The soft sheets and the comfort were an unaccustomed luxury compared to his weeks away in the jungle and he slept.

At midday, a knock on the door woke him. He slipped off the bed, checking the time on his watch and called softly, 'Who is it?'

A female voice answered, as expected, and Ho Peng unlocked the door. Liya walked in.

'I want you to take something to Ipoh,' he told her. They were the same height, but a complete contrast to each other.

Ho Peng stood on short bandy legs, his big hands hanging loose and his hair standing up all over his head in short tufts where someone had cut it badly in the jungle. His pitted skin was clean now after a bath but tell-tale pale after weeks under the canopy, and his eyes always shifted restlessly, always seeking danger signs.

Liya stood calmly deferential in front of him, like a schoolgirl before her headmistress, her neat figure concealed in a shapeless faded blue working samfu. Her long hair was bunched plainly at her neck and her pretty oval face was smoothed of all expression except bland obedience.

'Some toiletries,' he explained. 'For someone in Ipoh. She's a school teacher and hasn't much money.' He gave Liya the small grip bag. 'Give her this grip.'

'Where does she live?' Liya asked. She noticed Ho Peng's ribs showing inside his vest.

Ho Peng gave her the address in Ipoh of a small Chinese house, two blocks from the FMS Bar, a very popular place with planters and tin miners, and to Liya's relief, he told her to leave at once. But, as she reached the door, he suddenly said, 'Wait!' He watched her face suspiciously for the slightest flicker of annoyance, then nipped into the bathroom and returned with the bar of Palmolive. 'Might as well give her this too,' he said. 'It's very important she gets everything.'

Liya understood. She put the used bar of soap in the small grip bag and slipped out of the Wild Orchid into the busy streets of Chinatown in the heat of the midday sun. She hated and distrusted Ho Peng. She knew there was a secret message in the grip but she had to obey him. For the time being.

'The bloody water pipe's been blown again,' said the Assistant District Officer to himself in his house late that evening. Michael Codnor left his hand on the old kitchen sink tap, willing it to produce water but it gurgled coyly and remained dry. He was thirty-two-years-old, a keen administrator and well-liked by the people of Tanjong Malim, a small town of some 5,000 people in a rubber-growing area on the main road north. He knew that the local CTs were responsible. They had cut off the town's water supply from the reservoir in the hills in the jungle five times before, and Codnor, who had escaped from a German POW camp during the Second World War, had no illusions about the danger of a trap. This CT gang had terrorised the area for more than four years. In one highly successful jungle ambush they had killed seven soldiers, and in a total of forty incidents had murdered seven civilians and eight policemen since the start of the year, just under three months ago.

Accordingly, a strong force gathered just before dawn the following morning to escort the repair team out along the pipeline. With Codnor were a jungle police squad of fifteen men and W.H. Fourniss, the Executive Engineer of Public Works, with four of his men to repair the pipe. They left the town at sunrise, following the pipe and looking for the break. The police squad marched strung out each side, weapons at the ready. By the time the pipe plunged into the narrow avenue cut through the jungle, the sun was warm on their backs and they were sweating.

No-one talked much. Fourniss and the repair team concentrated on looking for the leak, while Codnor tried to see into the green shadows to each side of the avenue, feeling the danger and knowing there was nothing they could do to avoid it. The pipe had to be mended.

Two miles later, the soft swish of their boots against the weeds growing thickly in the damp tropical heat was drowned by a furious rattle of gunfire. Fourniss died instantly. Codnor was wounded and then shot dead trying to crawl out of sight into the jungle. Behind him, the police jungle squad and repair team stood no chance and were cut to bits in the centre of the ambush. The CTs kept firing till the leaves concealing them in the jungle edge were shredded, muzzle smoke wafted about and the acrid smell of cordite mixed with the sweet odour of blood in the narrow defile between the trees.

In the silence after the slaughter, the CTs, nearly forty of them, crept out of their hiding places, stripped the dead and dying of their weapons and ammunition, and stole away. They left twelve dead men and eight seriously wounded. One pipe-repair man at the back of the patrol was miraculously unharmed and ran terrified back to Tanjong Malim to give the alarm.

Liya reached the town two days later, on 27 March, on an old bus. She had been delayed by other visits Ho Peng had asked her to make closer to Kuala Lumpur, during which she had learned of the killing at Tanjong Malim, but she thought nothing of it. Ever since the start of the Emergency four years before, the newspapers had been filled with accounts of similar killings all over Malaya, averaging fifty civilians a month, month after month. What puzzled Liya more was that, although the British seemed impotent to stop the CTs attacking at will from their jungle hideouts, the CTs continued to lose over forty MRLA fighters a month, double the rate they had inflicted on British soldiers and the police. She went to see Ho Peng's Min Yuen contacts in a shop-house selling hardware in the Chinese quarter and was not surprised to find the murders were almost forgotten.

If the people were indifferent, General Sir Gerald Templer, the new High Commissioner who had taken over in Malaya only a month earlier, was not. He arrived in Tanjong Malim an hour after Liya, in a column of armoured vehicles and the police gathered some three hundred and fifty of the community's most important figures into the meeting hall of the Sultan Idris Training College. Templer, a tall spare good-looking man fifty-four-years-old, in civilian clothes, gave them a lecture.

'You are all aware of the outrage which took place near here forty-eight hours ago,' he told them in a bleak voice. 'It could only have taken place with the knowledge of certain people in this town, people some of you will know.' He glared at them and said, 'But you and the rest of this town are too cowardly to give that information to the police!'

His words were translated through Malay, Chinese and Tamil interpreters, which slowed matters, but the harangue lost none of its impact. The town's leaders were left in no doubt of Templer's savage anger. After an hour, when some of them began nodding their heads, punch-drunk with the oral assault, Templer shouted, 'Don't nod your bloody heads at me! I haven't started!' To their horror, he declared the whole town subject to a twenty-two-hour curfew, allowing people only two hours when they could leave their homes, between midday and two o'clock. The buses would stop, the rice ration, centrally dispensed, would be halved, and no-one would be allowed to leave the town, indefinitely.

As he spoke, the soldiers who had escorted the General to Tanjong Malim were surrounding the town and the iron terms of the curfew were already in place.

There was nothing secretive about Templer's fury. His Staff in the Headquarters in Kuala Lumpur had spent two hectic days preparing this response to the ambush and numerous Pressmen stood at the back of the hall to hear it. They were astonished at the dynamism of the new High Commissioner and the news of this new driving force in Malaya's administration spread across the world like wild-fire.

The news spread even faster through the town itself. Liya, who was with her Min Yuen contacts above their hardware shop, had planned to spend one night with them and then travel on to Ipoh. Outside a loud voice boomed in the street, 'Return to your homes immediately! No-one is permitted on the streets except between twelve and two o'clock.' She looked out of the window and saw a jeep full of policemen driving slowly up the street. A Chinese, a Malay and an Indian were taking it in turns to shout through a hand-held cone.

'You must go!' said Huang Chi-dao, the shopkeeper.

Liya wasted no time. She grabbed Ho Peng's small grip and slipped out into the alley behind the shophouse. She made her way through narrow streets to the back of the town, planning to walk into the rubber plantations and loop around to regain the main road to the north and carry on to Ipoh.

She left the last tumble-down houses on the edge of town and walked briskly into the rubber. She came to a dusty red laterite track cutting through the plantation. As she stepped out of the shade of the trees into the sun, a soldier rose from behind a clump of dusty bushes and shouted, 'Halt!'

Astonished, she stood quite still, tightly holding the grip. Detachedly, she observed the soldier was a private, which gave her hope. He ambled towards her but held his carbine level at her stomach. Her spirits sank when another soldier, a lance-corporal, appeared out of the bushes to cover him. They were young and pink-faced, probably conscripted men, but she recognised the West Kent cap badge on his blue beret. The battalion had been in Malaya for some time and were experienced troops. There was no chance of escape.

'What's yer name?' said the private genially. 'Where's yer identity card?'

Liya nodded and fished out her card from a pocket in her samfu.

The private studied the photograph on the card and looked at Liya. 'Long way from Langat, ain't yer, love? Wot yer doing up 'ere then?' he asked, but he gave up quickly when she shrugged and looked pathetic, pretending to speak no English. He turned to the other soldier and said, 'Could be a right little cracker this, wiv a bit of lipstick and the like.'

'I'll radio the escort patrol,' said the lance-corporal. 'They can take her back to town.'

The private turned back to Liya and, more to occupy himself because she was nice-looking, he said, 'Wot's in that bag, eh?' Without grabbing, he reached for the bag. Liya let him take it. At that moment she knew that she depended wholly on Ho Peng, on how well he had hidden his message, and that she would suffer jail or even death if this young soldier found it.

'Bloody women's poofta stuff,' said the private peering into the grip. He held up a bar of soap. They laughed, but the private searched beneath the cardboard floor of the grip and felt the handles to see if there was anything concealed in them before he handed the grip back to Liya.

She went back to town in a police jeep, knowing the British High Commissioner meant business over his curfew of Tanjong Malim.

The Malay policeman wanted to know exactly where she lived and reluctantly she let them drive her to the shophouse in the Chinese quarter. The streets were already deserted and the police watched curiously as she hammered on the door for the shopkeeper to let her in.

Inside, she sat with the family in the upstairs room, conscious of their acute embarrassment that she had been brought back by the police. More to bolster his own confidence, Huang Chi-dao said, 'It won't last. They can't close down the whole town!'

No-one answered.

After two days, it was apparent that General Templer was taking no notice of a storm of international protest. In Britain, the

Manchester Guardian described the punishment curfew as 'odious' and the *Observer* warned that the co-operation of the people 'will not be achieved by collective punishments'.

In the little shophouse the long hours passed slowly for Liya. She sat in a corner in the upper room, apart from the family, and waited for the gong to sound from the central police station at noon. Then the whole town disgorged on to the streets, not just to buy food, but to escape the oppressive atmosphere. Stale with sweat from sitting inside the stuffy little room all day long, Liya used her two hours' freedom to enjoy the fresh air and wash, with Ho Peng's bar of soap, at a stand-pipe in the street. The water supply from the reservoir had been mended when the bodies of the ambushed party were retrieved.

After a week, the police came to every house with confidential forms. General Templer wanted everyone in Tanjong Malim to answer questions about anyone they suspected of being a communist, courier or in the Min Yuen, and the forms had to be returned to the police completed or not. Huang Chi-dao was the only person in his family who could write, though Liya knew he had grown-up sons and wondered where they were.

Huang Chi-dao took charge of the form and said to Liya, 'Don't worry, I'll just put down I don't know anything. You're safe with me here!' Then he stuck down the flap without telling her what he had written and slipped the letter into the sealed box which two Malay constables brought to the door later that day.

Another two sweltering days passed before they heard, through gossip on the street during the two hours they were allowed outdoors, that all the letters had been personally opened by General Templer himself, at King's House in Kuala Lumpur, and that six community leaders had been specially driven there to witness him do it. Awestruck by the grand surroundings of the High Commissioner's residence, the six had watched him break the seal on each box, read every letter with the assistance of official translators, make notes from time to time, and then they had watched him supervise the burning of all the forms. The word on the streets was that General Templer was tough but he dealt fairly.

Huang Chi-dao was no longer saying the curfew could not last. Instead, he became very irritable. Liya knew he was trying to remember if he had given offence to anyone living close by or who had come into his shop, who might have named him, and he kept looking at Liya. She doubted he would have dared write about her, because Ho Peng had sent her, but she doubted he would stay silent if he were arrested.

The conditions in the shophouse were unbearable. The shopkeeper, his shrewish wife and their small children argued constantly and they were all hungry. Food was scarce in town as there was only two hours to bring anything in and distribute it, and water was at a premium. Liya stopped washing with the used bar of Palmolive soap, as there was insufficient water in which to rinse, and just splashed her face at the stand-pipe instead.

After ten days, the British made everyone fill out a second issue of confidential forms.

This time, Liya never saw Huang Chi-dao complete the form but she saw his face when he slipped the sealed letter into the box brought by the Malay policemen, and she decided on the spot that she had to escape. She had considered dumping the grip bag, but someone was sure to find it, and in the atmosphere of the curfewed town they might well hand it in to the police, to prove they were law-abiding. In any event, if she did not complete her mission, Ho Peng would find out from whoever the message was intended for in Ipoh.

At midnight, she slipped out of the shophouse with the small bag and made her way towards the outskirts. She made no sound in the muddy alleys, but there were pye dogs everywhere, in yards and alleys, which barked furiously. When she reached the edge of town she crouched in the shadows of a poor wooden building and her heart sank. The West Kents had been busy. The open ground between her and the rubber plantation was now ringed with barbed wire and lit, not particularly well, with bare yellow bulbs on poles strung along as far as she could see from left to right, but enough to make crossing the lighted area impossible without being seen.

She waited for twenty minutes. A patrol of soldiers walked slowly past in the lights. What concerned her more were the soldiers hiding in the darkness of the rubber trees beyond the glow of the makeshift lights, like the two who had stopped her before. On her own, she would have risked it, banking on her femininity to carry her through, but not with Ho Peng's bag.

She spent two more hours circuiting the inside of Tanjong Malim, easily avoiding police jeeps and foot patrols with the aid of the dogs, but unable to find a chink in the British fence. Streaks of pale pink were cracking the dark sky in the east when she crept back into the shophouse and lay down exhausted to sleep on her bamboo and felt mat in the upper room. She was still free, but she felt friendless. The world was closing in around her.

The next day, 8 April, the hall where General Templer had lectured the Tanjong leaders two weeks before was again a hive of activity. Lines of six-foot wooden tables stretched from end to end covered with papers, envelopes, forms, typewriters and card index boxes. Teams of plainclothes Special Branch officers and a special draft of men in uniform from Army Intelligence worked at the tables, sifting, recording and collating the information from the thousands of confidential forms in the second batch of responses.

'I do believe we've broken through, Sergeant Ci Guo,' said Angus Maclean to one of his Chinese Special Branch detectives. 'This second batch has done the trick. After the General's little piece of theatre at King's House, they know their letters won't fall into the hands of the CTs who'll murder them for telling tales, and they're mustering the courage to say what they know. How many have we got on our list of suspects?'

'Over thirty,' said Sergeant Ci Guo. He handed a list of names to Angus who cast his eye down the paper and asked, 'How many forms to go?'

'Maybe five hundred.'

Angus passed the typed list to Edward who was standing behind him. 'Look, Edward! We'll need all the help we can get from your chaps in Intelligence. There'll be forty-odd arrests to be made tomorrow morning. We don't want a single slip-up or the General will be down on us like a ton of bricks.' He had called in Army Chinese speakers to boost numbers on the simultaneous arrests they were planning for the following morning, and to help with the initial interrogations. After Diana left, Edward spent more time than ever talking to Lao Song, and now, after three years, his Chinese had become quite good.

'We'll do our best,' said Edward grinning. Templer's treatment of Tanjong Malim was a supreme example of taking the tough line which everyone in uniform had wanted to take for years, but more than that, the curfew and the confidential forms were producing results.

Angus walked on down the line of tables and Edward read the list of names. Halfway down, he saw Liya's name: 'Liya, female, about twenty-five years, at the "Kok Wan Lo" General Trading Store in the Chinese quarter, suspect Min Yuen.'

He read it several times, disbelieving. He glanced up, but

Sergeant Ci Guo was busy with a fresh form and no-one else was taking any notice of him. Edward noted the address of the shop-house in the Chinese quarter. He was sure there was a mistake, but he took no chances. As one of the few Chinese-speaking army officers, it was easy for him to pick which arrest team he accompanied.

The night passed slowly. He tossed and turned in the heat on his camp-bed in a classroom taken over as a dormitory and worried how Liya would react. His real fear was that she would prove to be one of the enemy, as the anonymous writer of the confidential form claimed, but he kept pushing the idea to the back of his mind, sure that she was nothing more than the victim of jealousy.

Edward was up in darkness at five o'clock the following morning, and after the British Army's usual breakfast of fried egg, sausages and baked beans, Angus Maclean briefed all the arrest-team leaders at six o'clock in a school lecture-room. After that, at dawn, Edward went out to give his own orders to his two jeep-loads of police, and, at 0730 hours, in broad daylight, a dozen similar teams drove fast through the deserted streets to various addresses in Tanjong Malim to make the first of thirty-eight arrests.

The uniformed Malay police with Edward jumped off the first jeep as the driver braked to a stop by the shophouse. He read the name, 'Kok Wan Lo' General Trading Store above the window while two of his team ran round into the alley at the back. After a minute, Edward drew his own pistol and knocked loudly on the front door. Three other Malay police waited silently, their Sten guns ready for trouble. Edward peered through the window at the pots and pans hanging inside. A nervous thin Chinese came through the shop and opened the door. In Chinese, Edward said, 'Are you Huang Chi-dao?'

The shopkeeper nodded, glancing past Edward at the police.

'Have you a woman here called Liya?'

Huang Chi-dao nodded again, 'Oh yes! Upstairs. I'll show you!'

'No,' Edward said bluntly, pointing his pistol at the man's chest. 'You're under arrest.' One of the police snapped handcuffs over the astonished shopkeeper's wrists. Edward and the other two police-men ran up the stairs.

Edward hardly needed to be there to identify Liya. Huang Chi-dao's family were standing apart from her, as if she had typhoid. She looked pale but quite composed and gave no sign of recognising Edward. For a long moment he stared at her, wanting her to say something, to react somehow, to reassure him she felt no animosity towards him, but she waited demurely, looking vulnerable and saying nothing. Finally, feeling foolish, he asked, for the sake of formality, 'Are you Liya?' and she nodded.

Impressed by her composure the two Malay constables did not handcuff her. Liya walked downstairs in front of them as if she were showing them to the door, and climbed into the jeep beside the shopkeeper. She suppressed a smile at the miserable expression on his face. Plainly, his neighbours did not like him. As they drove off, she glanced back to see the Malay police from the second jeep march into the shophouse to search it.

In the Sultan Idris Training College Liya and Huang Chi-dao were taken to guarded classrooms being used as holding rooms and Edward settled down to his preliminary interrogations. He left Liya to last. When Angus had asked him to join the Special Branch team Edward had been thrilled. This was his first real chance to conduct a formal interrogation, though he had had experience of field interrogations with the Special Squads in Palestine which had been rough enough to make even the most hardened Malay constable blench.

'We don't want you sticking freshly boiled eggs up suspects' arses,' Angus Maclean had remarked. 'Even though the hard men at SB headquarters find the trick dramatically successful at loosening tongues. I just want you to run through a routine preliminary interview to sift the real suspects from those who've merely been fingered because of personal vendettas.'

To Edward the offer was a compliment to his ability to speak Chinese. When it came to the point, however, the image of Liya waiting to be questioned would not go away and Edward found no pleasure in the task.

The shopkeeper put up some resistance, simply denying everything, until the search party came back with notes of supplies he had taken to the CT gang in the jungle outside Tanjong Malim. With Sergeant Ci Guo's help, Edward established Huang Chi-dao was the only person who could have written the notes, and stated incredulously, 'This is an invoice of supplies rendered to the MRLA. You've even written the name of the MRLA as the debtor clearly on the top of the paper!'

Squirming, Huang Chi-dao burst out, 'They never pay me! They just demand things and never pay!'

Edward had the man formally charged and taken away. He would be interrogated later in greater detail, tried at the Perak State Court in Ipoh and jailed. During a break he remarked to Angus, 'If the communists paid their bills, they would be a formidable opposition.'

Angus replied, 'Considering they're getting no financial help from the Russians or the Chinese, they're not doing badly.'

Finally Sergeant Ci Guo brought in Liya. Edward waved her to a chair on the other side of a bare wooden six-foot table and asked the question which had been burning his consciousness.

'What were you doing here, in that shophouse?'

'I was on the road selling toiletries. I had some samples.'

'Why Huang Chi-dao?'

'He runs a store which carries these sort of goods. I go all over the place to people like him.'

In English, Edward said to Sergeant Ci Guo, 'Have the searchers found any such samples?'

Sergeant Ci Guo left the interview room. As the door closed, Edward leaned forward over the table and said earnestly, 'I'm sorry, Liya.'

Liya shrugged. She knew very well that the Emergency, or war as it really was, placed them apart, and the pleasure they had together could only be snatched during calm periods. They looked at each other, separated by the official table but there was no time to say more. Sergeant Ci Guo returned with the grip and put it on the table in front of her.

Edward asked her, 'Is this yours?'

Unenthusiastically Liya said, 'Yes.'

Edward emptied the bag on to the table, spreading out her few personal effects, the used bar of Palmolive and the boxes of new soaps, powders and sprays. He felt dirty, as if prying into her private affairs, and was both relieved and surprised when she smiled. He asked, 'What's the matter?'

'Some of the samples have been stolen.'

'By the shopkeeper's family?'

'I suppose so,' she said. 'When I left the bag in the shop, when you arrested me.'

Edward continued with his questions for another half hour. Liya's answers all tallied, as he was sure they would, Sergeant Ci Guo produced further information that the shopkeeper's wife had been found with new toiletries, and when Edward asked him for his opinion in the passage outside the interview room, he replied, 'She seems clear. There's nothing to implicate her and I guess she just got caught up with the curfew when the General turned up.'

Edward did not want to compromise Liya as his source, but that very commitment to her made him insist on one last thorough check. He asked, 'Will you have your technical boys look at her samples and the bag?'

Liya was returned to her holding room and two hours later Sergeant Ci Guo returned with the grip bag. It appeared just the same. The soap, spray and powder samples were still in their wrappings and looked untouched, but he said to Edward, 'They've done a thorough job. I told them to check all the samples. They cut the soap, checked the sprays and opened the powder bottles which is a favourite place to hide things. They even checked the boxes and wrapping paper, and they examined the bag itself. Nothing. She's clean as a whistle.'

Immensely relieved, Edward went back to the hall to arrange for her release papers and found the curfew had been lifted. Angus had decided to fold up the police operation in the Sultan Idris College and take everyone back to Kuala Lumpur where he had the facilities to pursue interrogations and enquiries at Special Branch Headquarters. In the chaos of packing up, Edward was suddenly out of a job and went to find Liya. She was on her own in the holding room.

He waved the release papers and said, 'You're free to go.'

She leaped up, flung her arms round his neck and gave him a big hug. The moment she saw him in the jeep from the shophouse window, she had been worried that all the time they had spent together meant nothing. But now she was convinced he wanted to understand her.

Edward felt terribly self-conscious in uniform in the impersonal surroundings of the classroom, holding her official papers of release in his hand, but her warm body pressed against him melted the formality and he wrapped his arms round her. She looked up at him. He kissed her and she responded urgently, thankful he had been there to help her. He said, 'The curfew's over. We're all going back to KL and I've got a jeep to myself. D'you want a lift?'

She hesitated, but the expression in his eyes was so clear and honest she accepted, half-knowing what would happen.

The fifty-mile drive south took two hours, because they were delayed by three road-blocks where soldiers were making food regulation checks. They talked happily all the way, enjoying the sun and the warm breeze whipping round them in the open jeep, and by the time Edward drove into the outskirts of Kuala Lumpur it was four o'clock in the afternoon and Liya had agreed to come back to the house with him. He wanted to recompense her for the unpleas-antness of being arrested and questioned, and let her relax in comfort he was sure she had never experienced before, away from the maelstrom of life and conditions in Chinatown. And he wanted to make love to her.

She wanted him too. He parked the jeep outside the house and led her inside, carrying her grip bag.

'It's a lovely house,' she said admiring the weeping acacia trees and bougainvillea. 'Does it have a bath?' She had been two weeks in the shophouse.

Edward laughed, and led her through his bedroom to the bathroom. Delighted, she touched the big towels Hassan had put out clean on the hot rail and Edward was about to leave her there when she turned and stopped him with her hand. The smokey look in her dark slanting eyes fired him in a way he could not remember and he let her take the small bag from his grasp and slide into his arms.

They made love in the shower, under the cascading water. She made him laugh taking a bar of soap from her grip, and they washed each other tenderly until they could stand the excitement no longer. With the water beating down on their naked bodies, he lifted her to his chest, light as a feather, her long black hair tumbling over them both and she wrapped her arms and legs round him, wriggling and arching back in her abandon.

Later, Edward left Liya in bed, put on a towelling robe and went to find something to eat from the kitchen. Hassan was out but Lao Song prepared a tray of salads and Edward opened a bottle of French wine he had bought in the Officers' Mess.

'You are not surprised?' he asked Lao Song in Chinese.

'The Master went once without touching flesh for three months.'

Edward grinned, 'And I'm not the Master?'

Lao Song's wrinkled eyes flickered with amusement.

'But aren't you shocked?' Edward persisted, trying to settle the nagging sliver of guilt at the back of his mind.

Lao Song stopped chopping a cucumber and said seriously, 'The Master Confucius told us that "If the Will be set on Love there will be no practice of wickedness".'

'Not everyone thinks like that.'

The old Chinese shook his head sadly and added, 'Confucius had no sympathy with those who cared only for outward form and ceremony. He described people like that as "Thieves of Virtue", and placed his emphasis instead on inward spirit.'

Edward took the tray back to the bedroom and put it on the middle of the bed. Naked, Liya sat up cross-legged, her back straight and shook her hair behind her to dry. She caught Edward watching her and smiled, 'No! I'm hungry!'

She pulled a towel over her knees, like a napkin, and looked at the tray. With the clean linen sheets and great white mosquito net fixed to the high ceiling above them, she felt like a princess feasting in a luxurious tent, and she ate ravenously.

'Didn't that shopkeeper's family look after you?' he asked sitting opposite her and pouring wine.

She shook her head, waving a chicken leg in one hand, and said, 'It wasn't their fault really. There was so little to eat after two weeks.'

Considering Huang Chi-dao had denounced her in his second form, he admired her tolerance. 'D'you see a lot of people like them?'

She smiled quizzically at him and asked, 'Are you still interrogating me?'

Shocked, Edward said, 'No! I'm interested, that's all. It must be difficult finding work.'

She nodded and told him truthfully, 'I have to do a lot of travelling.'

'You don't spend much time in the New Village?'

She looked him straight in the eyes and said, 'Memories keep me away from the village.'

'Of course,' said Edward embarrassed. 'I'm sorry.' After Ellie's death, he had a greater sense of what the loss of her child must have cost her.

He changed the subject, and the hours slipped past. Naked, they talked, they ate and drank, and they made love, sleeping and waking each other again with new and tender embraces, uncaring of the time, until the early hours when they slept deeply sated and at peace with each other.

In the morning Liya slipped from under the white mosquito net in the dark, dressed in her samfu and silently collected up the bar of Palmolive soap and her grip from the bathroom. She paused to look tenderly at Edward. He was breathing regularly, fast asleep, one arm flung out where she had been lying beside him.

In the darkened sitting-room she stopped to admire the fine furniture and artefacts which Diana had bought, gently touching a deep blue porcelain jug on the mantelpiece and letting her fingers feel the smooth polish of an old table. Then she collected herself, left the house and ran lightly across the garden, making for the boundary ditch and the clump of jungle beyond.

When Edward woke, he looked in all the rooms of the house to be sure she had gone. His feeling of loss, which was more regret they could not prolong their uncomplicated pleasure in each other, was balanced by a great sense of confidence. In the bathroom, he found she had drawn Chinese characters on the big mirror over the basin with a corner of a bar of soap. He called Lao Song in to translate.

Lao Song stood quietly in his long black tunic and said nothing for a moment, observing each curl of the script.

'Well?' said Edward impatiently. 'What does it mean?'

'Benevolence and Love,' said Lao Song reverently. 'The greatest of all Confucian virtues.'

Lao Song hesitated, still looking at the characters on the mirror, and Edward asked, 'What else?'

'All Chinese can speak their language, many can read, but few study enough from childhood for the years it takes to write as well as this'.

Chapter 18

JUNGLE DROP

The extra work at Tanjong Malim, had side-tracted Angus Maclean's Special Branch team from their surveillance operation of the courier network in Singapore, but the effort had proved worthwhile. The people in the town accepted they could rely on the police and continued to give information readily, so much so that the Min Yuen dared not smuggle food to the CT gang any more and the CTs, cut off from their rear-area support dispersed. Soon afterwards General Templer authorised and armed a Home Guard contingent in Tanjong Malim which became one of the safest areas in Malaya.

All the rest of that year and into 1953, Angus concentrated again on the south. Gradually the Special Branch was building up a picture of all the important CT commanders in the MRLA, but by July 1953 the operation in Singapore had revealed a link in Chin Peng's courier chain that led to the deserted east coast, north of Mersing.

Angus drove to Mersing and stayed in the Rest House, a comfortable, old-fashioned white-painted hotel on a slight rise overlooking the rambling flat-roofed houses of Mersing harbour and the South China Sea.

The pace of Malay life was slower than ever on the coast, the kampongs fewer and the endless miles of sandy beaches empty of everything except turtles, small crabs and crocodiles basking in the estuary mud where brown rivers spewed into the sea. Inland, hundreds of square miles of untouched jungle and mangrove swamp pressed on one bad road which stretched uncertainly up the coast to Kuantan, Kuala Trengganu and the Thai border. In 1942, this remoteness had attracted the invading Japanese Army as it swept unopposed down to Singapore, and ten years later the same remoteness attracted the MRLA.

Angus, in safari-style shorts and shirt and posing as an Agricultural Advisor, happened to mention to the Rest House manager in the hearing of various Malay and Chinese staff that he was in Mersing to make an agricultural field-study of the monoecious oil palm, comparing mesocarp thickness in Tenera and Dura varieties. The manager nodded intelligently and no-one thought anything of his disappearing off every day in a Department of Agriculture 15cwt Dodge truck to an oil-palm plantation on a hill a mile south of the town. Here he joined Sergeant Ci Guo, his 'field-study assistant', in a small attap hut.

In turns, one man moved about the low fat palm trees chopping off bulky fruit samples of oil-palm nuts in case anyone was watching, while the other remained hidden in the deep shadows of the hut, listening to a radio and peering through powerful binoculars at the beach two hundred yards away. There, under a clump of tall coconut palms at the top of the beach, where the white sand ran up under ziglap grass and scrub, a pile of empty Tiger beer bottles, half filled with wind-blown sand, and a burned-out fire marked the spot where someone had cooked a catch of fish.

It was also the dead letter box where a man the surveillance team had followed from Johore Bahru, twenty-four miles away, had left a message in a battered tin of Gold Flake.

On the third evening, as the shadows of the coconut palms lengthened over the white sand towards the deep blue sea, Sergeant Ci Guo saw a slight figure walk down the beach.

'That's our boy,' said Angus leaning forward. 'See anything?'

Sergeant Ci Guo answered slowly, straining his eyes in the fading evening light, 'No. He's just a silhouette. Can't even say whether it's a man or a woman.'

Angus grunted but he reached into a large briefcase marked, 'Agricultural Department', pulled out a radio handset and alerted the other surveillance units staked out round the area.

'Must have been checking the area,' muttered Sergeant Ci Guo, for the figure on the beach wasted no time. With a quick look round, it bent, retrieved the Gold Flake tin from beneath the empty beer bottles and walked briskly along the beach out of view.

'Not well enough,' smiled Angus when he heard the radio crackle and another SB agent reported he was observing the figure approaching the Mersing road. Angus and Sergeant Ci Guo could hear the distant rumble of an old diesel engine on the road at the bottom of the oil-palm plantation.

A moment later, the radio crackled again, 'Subject waited on side of road for only two minutes when a logging truck stopped. Subject boarded truck. Going in direction of Jemaluang.' The SB agent described the truck and gave the registration number.

'That's a Kuala Lumpur number,' said Sergeant Ci Guo smiling. They were on to the next link in the chain.

The following morning dawned bright and fresh after torrential downpours during the night and Edward took his breakfast on the verandah as usual. The cicadas chirruped, drying out, and a bright green pitta bird was busy on the lawn looking for ants and grubs. Edward drank orange juice and re-read an airmail letter from Diana in England in which she said that Roger had finally been repatriated from North Korea.

Ever since she had left Edward, the POWs had been pawns in the first bitter war between mainland Chinese Communism and the West. Appalling casualties seemed to be the only result as both sides fought to straighten their battle lines along the 38th Parallel. By the time the final Armistice was signed, 690,000 soldiers had been killed in the Korean War, of whom 615,000 were Chinese or North Korean communists, another million soldiers were wounded, of whom 790,000 were communists, and there were a further two million civilian casualties. Malayan losses were not on the same scale, but the measure of Communism's self-sacrifice and determination to win, was dauntingly similar.

Diana now wrote that several RAF Hastings transport planes had been adapted for casualty evacuation, and the British POWs, many of them like Roger captured at the Battle of the Imjin River in April two years before, had been flown back to Lyneham in Wiltshire. Roger was in poor condition and still terribly thin, so she would not be coming back to Malaya for some time. She was at pains to explain that it was not that she wanted a divorce, which Edward suspected did not suit her any more than the fuss would have helped him, but she felt she must help her brother to recover. This was the latest of Diana's excuses for not returning to Malaya. Each letter to Edward had contained yet another reason for her not wanting to join him . . .

Edward looked up from the letter at Hassan's beautifully tended garden and breathed in the warm fragrance of Frangipani blossoms. In the eternal tropical warmth of Malaya, he occasionally hankered for the green fields and cool wet winds of Wiltshire where he had served his first months in the army in the summer of 1945, but at that moment he neither wanted to go back to England, nor did he want Diana back in Malaya.

As a soldier, he liked the Malayan war, or Emergency, all the more so because, since the arrival of General Templer, and his policy of 'Hearts and Minds', the country's confidence had returned, and now, during the last year, his life and work were marching hand in hand.

At work, he routinely saw the strategic overview of Army Intelligence, and occasionally he escaped Colonel Bleasley to join jungle patrols with contacts he had built up at Camp Rideau, to keep himself up-to-date with grass roots infantry work. At the same time his friendship with Angus Maclean gave him access to Special Branch which had become the linchpin of the fight against the CTs in the MRLA.

At home he saw Liya about two or three times a month, which seemed to suit them both. Edward worked long hours and she was often away from Kuala Lumpur with various samples. However, seeing her for sketchy information about Ho Peng became less important than seeing her for herself. Sometimes, they met clandestinely in town through Liao Ting-chi, but mostly she came to Uxbridge Drive. The house was so conveniently at the end of a cul-de-sac and on the perimeter of Headquarters land, that she was able to slip past the clump of jungle into the garden in the evening, spend the night with him and leave in the morning without anyone knowing, except Lao Song and Hassan.

Liya's presence in the house seemed quite natural. Edward had become quite fluent after four years, and with or without Liya, he spoke Chinese all the time with Lao Song. He could also manage reasonable Malay with Hassan, liberally mixed with Arabic and pidgin English. In the evening after work, he wore a sarong and went barefoot. Hassan kept the bungalow clean, but, without Diana's influence, Chinese grammars, dictionaries, notebooks, paper and newspapers lay piled on tables and chairs. Edward usually burned joss sticks or a smoke coil to keep the mosquitoes away and the house relaxed under the influence of the East, almost as though, standing on the edge of the army camp, it might slide out of army control altogether.

Edward finished his breakfast and thought of the night before. Liya, Edward and Lao Song had had dinner together on the verandah, as they often did, served by Hassan who refused to presume on his position and join them, and anyway understood no Chinese.

They chatted about all sorts of things, but of course they could not escape politics. The American Secretary of State, John Foster Dulles, had just warned the world of the Domino Theory and they argued how anyone could really tell 'who knows best for the people' when the methods of each camp seemed at times as brutal as each other. Edward favoured General Templer's pragmatism, which reflected his own personal experience. Lao Song had also seen years of fighting in China before coming to Malaya, and his political views were coloured by his love of Confucian philosophy. Liya's approach seemed altogether more idealistic.

Edward wished she would tell him more about herself. She had admitted she was an immigrant, which put her near the bottom of the social scale in Malaya, but her vitality, understanding and education spoke of a quite different background. In the end he did not care, as long as they continued to see each other, for the evening and night, like so many others, had been a wonderful and therapeutic antidote to the relentless effort of fighting the war, and his life had found a rhythm he wanted to keep.

On his way out, he stuffed Diana's letter in a drawer in the sitting-room, called out to Lao Song that he would be back for supper as usual that evening, and walked briskly across the lawns to the Intelligence Office.

'You're looking cheerful,' smiled Harry Denton as Edward flicked his red beret over a hook on the back of the door.

'And so are you,' remarked Edward, sitting down at his desk opposite him.

'Three bits of good news,' replied Denton. He stretched back in his chair, brushed his bushy blond moustache and grinned broadly.

'First, the good Colonel Bleasley was sacked last night by General Templer, personally.' Seeing Edward's incredulous look, he explained, 'We went to King's House to give Templer an Intelligence summary. Bleasley said the army should have some of the thousand new armoured cars being given to the police just now.'

'And?'

Harry Denton's grin widened. 'It was classic! Very quietly, Templer said, "Really?", and he let Bleasley blunder on with all his hoary old chestnuts about civvies and the cops.'

'Surely he knows Templer places the highest emphasis on the police?' Edward laughed. 'All those bitter wartime personality clashes have been ironed out, they've recruited another 7,000 men, they've totally reorganised themselves, spent £30 million doing it and given Special Branch a free hand. 'Struth! The present Police Commissioner is ex-Special Branch and one in five senior police officers are in the SB now!'

Captain Denton agreed, 'Templer simply said, "Plenty of obstinate buggers like you in the army, Colonel Bleasley, but this isn't the campaign for them. Time you went!" '

'Where is he now?'

Denton said, 'Sulking in his house, I suppose, but I couldn't care less. The second bit of good news is that I'm going too. I've been posted.'

'Where?'

'To command the armoured car squadron operating out of KL. They're going to be equipped with the new Ferrets. Just what I wanted.'

'Congratulations,' said Edward. Life was looking up. Colonel Bleasley's departure meant he could no longer sit on Edward's application for a further two years in Malaya. He said, 'What's the third bit of news?'

'A real scoop! Chap called Lao Tang surrendered early this morning. One of Ho Peng's mob!'

At once Edward reached for the phone on his desk and called Angus Maclean who invited him to join in Lao Tang's debrief. Edward was at Special Branch Headquarters within the hour, a series of low buildings hidden in a rubber plantation on the south side of Kuala Lumpur, Top Secret, fenced and heavily guarded.

'Why did he come in?' Edward asked. This was the first breakthrough into Ho Peng's gang of CTs.

'He walked into Langat Police Station with a Safe Conduct Pass he'd picked up from one of the RAF leaflet para drops. Five of them were going to pick up food from some Min Yuen near Langat but they ran into a Gurkha patrol quite by chance. He was one of the lucky ones to escape. I presume he preferred to surrender to the Malay police in Langat rather than the Gurkhas. He's badly in need of a square meal, but he's a bright lad, about late twenties, and proving most talkative.'

Angus led Edward through rows of wood and corrugated iron

huts where the Special Branch technicians worked on breaking CT codes, concealment of equipment for surveillence operations, interpretation of aerial photography, and police forensic work. The building used for interrogations was made of sinister concrete blocks and set apart from the others in a compound of its own. Angus showed Edward into a room adjacent to the interview room and they observed Lao Tang through a one-way mirror.

The room was plain with a table and four chairs. Lao Tang sat on one in a clean shirt and slacks, his skin was terribly pale, his eyes were sunken, his face thin, and his black hair short and badly cut; but he appeared calm. He was smoking and a packet of Capstan Full Strength lay on the table. Sergeant Ci Guo came into the room, notepad in hand, and Angus said, 'Let's join them and hear what this sod has got to say for himself.'

'Why did you surrender?' asked Angus through Sergeant Ci Guo. For the moment, they would not reveal that Edward spoke Chinese and the Sergeant would pick up nuances of language Edward might miss.

'Everything is different,' said Lao Tang simply.

'What?'

Lao Tang did not hesitate, he had known they would ask a lot of questions. 'After four years, we have achieved none of the objectives we set ourselves. We have no Liberated Areas and the people do not want the revolution. They are terrified of us.'

'That's hardly surprising!'

Lao Tang agreed. Edward listened grimly to Lao Tang's detached description of the first attack, when Ho Peng chopped off the hands of the Indian manager on Bowman's rubber estate, and to Ho Peng's murder of four children at Black Circle village. 'In his October Directive of 1951, General-Secretary Chin Peng ordered us to stop controlling the people with terror, but by then it was too late. If we had encouraged the proletariat, helped them and given them money, they would be on our side now. Instead, you British gave them the things the Malayan Communist Party promised but never gave them, like pigs, corn seed and new villages. You've got the money.'

Angus grunted. The British Government had taken four years to provide the necessary resources and he hated to think what might have happened if the CTs had had external support. He said, 'You could have asked the Russians or Chinese?'

Lao Tang snorted in disgust, 'Fine words! I heard the Chinese talking in Calcutta once.' The conference seemed so long ago. 'They've sent officers to us in the jungle, to advise, but they've given us nothing. No money. Not even weapons.'

From his Intelligence summaries, Edward knew this was true. He could not recall a Chinese or Russian weapon being recovered by any patrol. The Malayan CTs depended on British and Japanese weapons left over from the war, or weapons taken off bodies after ambushes.

'The results are obvious,' said Lao Tang bitterly. 'Four years ago, we ruled the jungle. We had a big camp, for four hundred men. We sang songs, we had shooting practice, and political discussions. Now, we creep round in small groups of thirty, we have to whisper, we sleep on the jungle floor, and we dare not make fires to cook our food, which we have to grow ourselves, because food regulations and New Villages have cut us off from our Min Yuen support.' Lao Tang paused, allowing his exhaustion to show. He looked Edward straight in the eye and said, 'You remember our big camp. You went there after we wrecked your train, with that fat planter called Tallard.'

It was only Edward's surprise that prevented him replying at once in Chinese, but he waited for Sergeant Ci Guo's translation and asked, 'You saw us?' He remembered his uncanny fear that someone was watching them.

Lao Tang enjoyed the surprise on Edward's face. After another translation, he nodded, 'Ho Peng and I watched you pass in the jungle. We could have killed you then, but we tracked you to the camp and we watched that soldier die when he disturbed our booby trap.' He paused thoughtfully and asked, 'What were you looking for?'

'Tallard was searching for weapons,' replied Edward through Ci Guo.

Lao Tang frowned, 'Ho Peng made us dig holes too. All over the jungle.'

'For weapons?' Angus asked, puzzled that Ho Peng should be looking for his own caches.

Lao Tang shook his head, 'We found some, but I always felt he was searching for something else.'

'What?'

'I don't know.'

Angus asked, 'How can we catch Ho Peng?'

Lao Tang became animated 'You must! He pretends to obey the

Party, but he's a hypocrite. We stay in the jungle, we have no women, and we get no pay.' He did not mention that Ho Peng's iron jungle discipline had enabled them to escape the Fraser's Hill follow-up patrols. 'But he comes to Kuala Lumpur, he has women there, he eats what he wants and spends money. He's no better than a capitalist!'

Edward was far from sure whether Lao Tang had given up being a communist or just given up the struggle in the jungle. He reminded himself that it did not matter. General Templer's aim was to destroy the MRLA, whatever it took.

Through Ci Guo, he asked, 'Where is he?'

Lao Tang answered readily, 'He's in a camp in deep jungle, over the ridge of mountains above the Black Circle estate.'

'Where the borders of the three States meet?' asked Edward. Everything seemed to go back to this area, where Ho Peng and Tallard had worked together against the Japanese.

Lao Tang nodded and lit another cigarette. 'He feels safe there because you can't reach him without alerting the aborigines. You British can't protect the Orang Asli because where they live is too remote, so he's terrorised them to keep look-out.'

Sergeant Ci Guo fetched a map. Lao Tang put his finger on a spot in the circle of mountains where the three States met and Angus asked him, 'Will you take us there?'

'No!' said Lao Tang, shocked. He drew nervously and deeply on the strong tobacco. 'It would be suicide for me!' Ho Peng would somehow find out that he had been talking to the police.

'We can't do it unless you show us where to go.'

Lao Tang looked cornered, his thin face more pinched than ever. He willingly answered all their questions but refused to go back into the jungle.

Later, during a break, Angus and Edward watched him through the one-way mirror from the room next door. Edward said, 'Bastard's still a communist, so why's he surrendered?'

'He's an idealist. He's convinced himself his precious Party has lost the purity of its cause.'

'All the same, he's been through a lot with his mates out there in the jungle, and yet he sits and betrays them without a qualm.'

'Money,' said Angus dryly. 'Ho Peng is on the Central Military Committee and three State Committees, so he's worth $200,000 Malay dollars reward. Let alone the other members of the gang. Even a lowly CT private is worth $2,500 dollars.'

'That's a bloody fortune!' said Edward angrily. He watched Lao Tang light another Capstan. The ashtray was full.

'The other reason is he needs to be certain we'll kill or capture his mates who can recognise him. All the reward money in the world won't help him if he leaves men alive who can say he's a traitor. The CTs are particularly hot on vengeance killings.'

'Sending a patrol that deep into the jungle will be very risky indeed,' said Edward. 'Why should we risk our necks so this sod can enjoy a fortune he's made by murdering people?'

Angus agreed. Paying rewards worked, for increasing numbers of CTs were surrendering or being betrayed for the money, but it raised emotive moral arguments. He said, 'Don't worry. I shan't let the bastard off the hook.'

Edward had work to do in his own office in the early afternoon, but he went back to SB HQ that evening. Angus took him straight to a planning room which had been set up specifically for the operation. A large 50,000-scale map of the area was fixed to the wall, descriptions of Ho Peng and some photographs of other CTs were pinned up, and Sergeant Ci Guo was reading through Lao Tang's statement again, looking for any other details which might prove useful.

A tall dark-haired officer in jungle pea-greens was bending over notes strewn across a table. As Angus and Edward walked in he looked up and drawled, 'How are you doing, Fairfax, old thing?'

'Aubrey!' Edward exclaimed. 'What the hell are you doing here? And they've promoted you to captain too!' He also recognised a broad-shouldered sergeant with a barrel chest beside Aubrey Hall-Drake and said delightedly, 'And you're with this Irish maniac, Sean Brogan! By Christ, it's good to see you two again!' They pumped each other's hands and Edward laughed at Brogan, saying, 'So you finally made the Sergeant's Mess?'

'They grew tired of marching me in and out of the colonel's office,' Sean Brogan replied in his soft Southern Irish brogue, 'so when I reached corporal again, they gave me a third stripe, to keep the second in place, so to speak. I can't tell if it'll last.'

Edward laughed and asked Angus, 'What's the reason for this Palestine reunion?' Aubrey Hall-Drake and Edward Fairfax, as platoon commanders in the same Company in Palestine, had shared a tent, while Sean Brogan had been on the ill-fated Police Special Squad which Edward had joined to find Jewish terrorists. Angus Maclean, the briefing officer then, took the same role once more and explained, 'These two reprobates are in the SAS Squadron just posted here, at Dusun Tua. They'll produce the patrol we're sending to find Ho Peng.'

'I didn't think you'd like sitting about in England,' said Edward, grinning at Aubrey.

Hall-Drake smiled. 'It was General Harding's idea to bring the SAS to Malaya, so I thought, with an example like that, I should join in. The selection was pretty arduous but worth every sweaty minute. Since which time, I've been learning a good deal from your old colleague Sean here.'

Angus went on, 'Lao Tang is right about the abos. They're very shy, live off the jungle and CTs like Ho Peng can terrorise them without fear of retribution. The Orang Asli tribes are very remote. In fact, the violence is bringing to light some tribes which even the Malays never knew existed.'

'We could reach them if the British Government gave us helicopters,' growled Brogan. 'Jesus! The Yanks used helicopters in an airborne assault in Korea nearly two years ago, and we still haven't got them!'

'Not even to ferry senior officers about,' remarked Aubrey.

'So we walk in,' said Edward, looking at the map and tracing a route from the Black Circle estate through thick jungle over a mountain range thousands of feet high. The idea did not appeal.

'We drop in,' corrected Aubrey casually. 'By parachute.'

Edward looked at Sean Brogan for confirmation of what sounded utterly mad. The jungle trees looked soft from the air, like green clouds, but before the parachute tangled in the tops, they might smash into huge branches beneath, and the canopy was nowhere lower than a hundred feet above the ground. If the parachute slipped through, the drop would be fatal.

Brogan was nodding, 'We land in the trees, nice and soft like, and then abseil down from the canopy on a length of rope.'

Aubrey was enjoying himself. 'You shouldn't have any trouble, old cock, with your experience. Seem to remember you parachuted on to the only tree in the Sinai desert.'

'A bloody thorny acacia,' admitted Edward.

'And a wog nicked the boots off your feet while you was hanging there,' said Brogan.

'You're all qualified, then,' Angus grinned at Edward. 'And thank God I'm a policeman.' He summarised the operation, 'You fly over the mountain ridge and drop into the jungle two days march from Ho Peng's camp. That should avoid being spotted by the aborigine look-outs but at the same time be far enough away so Ho Peng won't hear the plane. In fact, Lao Tang says the camp is near an abo settlement and some open ground where they cultivate yams, rice and so on.'

'Lao Tang's given me details and I've drawn a sketch map,' said Sergeant Brogan, indicating the table behind them.

Edward shook his head, 'It's not enough. We need to know *precisely* where the camp is. If we just blunder into the area we'll alert Ho Peng and could waste days searching for it. We must persuade Lao Tang to guide us in.'

Aubrey smiled, 'Angus has fixed it. Lao Tang is going back to re-join his friends which gives him three days. He'll verify Ho Peng's there and then meet us at a rendezvous to lead us straight in for a camp attack.'

'Just like that?' said Edward sarcastically. Being in deep jungle hours or even days from any reinforcements was the last place to walk into a CT ambush. 'How on earth can we trust him?'

Angus pulled a photograph from his pocket and pinned it on the wall by the map. The freshly printed picture showed Lao Tang standing in a circle of grinning policemen in uniform. One constable had his arm round Lao Tang's shoulders. Angus said, 'We took that this morning. I just told our chum Lao Tang if he didn't co-operate, I'd have 50,000 of these little snaps dropped over the jungle and kampongs where nice Mr Ho Peng lives and then release him. You should have seen his face!'

They all laughed and Angus summarised by saying, 'Lao Tang is your guide. Edward goes as interpreter, and Aubrey commands the SAS patrol. Good luck!'

The rest of the day passed in a flurry of detailed planning and preparation for Edward and the fifteen-man SAS patrol. Rucksacks were packed with the barest minimum of food to last five days, to keep the weight down, weapons were test-fired on the SB range, spare magazines were filled with ammunition, grenades primed, radios checked, escape and evasion kit stowed in belt pouches, and, after Aubrey gave his patrol orders in the special operations room, they spent two hours practising the immediate action drills in case they were ambushed in the jungle, how they would deploy for the rendezvous with Lao Tang, and the sequence of manoeuvres they would use in the camp attack. Every detail was thought out and rehearsed. Finally Aubrey said, 'We've done all we can.'

'To be sure, but my mate Murphy says it'll all turn out different,' observed Brogan.

Edward had confidence in the team, but he could not shake off his apprehension at jumping into the trees.

Before dawn the following day, in darkness, Lao Tang was issued with his MRLA jungle uniform again, which the SB had specially kept as filthy dirty as when he had surrendered and which he had hoped never to see again. He was dropped off near the Black Circle estate from a plainclothes Special Branch armoured saloon car. The two Chinese SB Sergeants who drove him out promised him that there were no British infantry patrols in the area to bother about.

'All you have to do is walk,' said one, waving encouragingly at the dark hills above them. 'And fast.'

Lao Tang was gloomy. Ahead lay the high ridge of mountains between the peaks of Gunong Nuang, 4,908 feet high north and Bukit Batu Bulan, 3,306 feet high to the south. Beyond that, in the hills which spread towards the Sungei Kenaboi, lay Ho Peng's camp. He was not looking forward to explaining why he had got lost in the jungle, and he dared not think what would happen if Ho Peng did not believe him. He knew. He tried to push all these thoughts to the back of his mind by concentrating on his reward money and freedom from the jungle once it was all over, and he set off into the jungle along a track which was hardly visible but quite familiar to him. He made good speed but kept alert. He did not trust the Special Branch when they said there were no other British patrols in the area.

At the same time as Lao Tang stepped into the jungle, Edward and the SAS patrol strapped on their parachutes in a hangar on the RAF airfield on the south side of Kuala Lumpur by the railway line. Sergeant Brogan helped pull up Edward's straps tight and remarked cheerfully, 'We've averaged one serious injury every time we drop in the ulu, so keep your feet and legs close together, sir.' He showed him how to tie on the length of rope which they would use to abseil down from the tree tops to the jungle floor.

'Remember you're talking to a tree expert,' said Edward flippantly, but never had he felt such pre-jump tension before as when the big, box-like Beverley transport aircraft took off into the brightening eastern sky. They flew south to make a long loop to their Dropping Zone. They did not want the people in kampongs near Langat or the 'Black Circle' to see the aircraft flying towards Ho Peng's camp area.

They sat in two rows on either side of the plane on canvas seats

303

facing each other chatting cheerfully while the RAF dispatchers moved up the two lines, checking everyone's equipment. They examined the chin strap of their steel helmets, their parachute harness straps, the attachment hooks of their rucksacks squashed in at their feet in the centre of the plane, and of course the abseil rope. Finally, everyone hooked their static line on to the two steel wires running down the body of the aircraft to the doors.

After an hour, the doors on each side opened and the dispatcher shouted, 'Action Stations!'

The chat died away. Everyone had their own way of dealing with this. Adrenalin pumped. They all stood up, confident in the drill, checked the parachute of the man in front, shuffled towards the doorway encumbered by the rucksacks banging heavily on their knees, with their carbines and Stens strapped to the side, and stood uncomfortably waiting for the final orders.

Edward was not first out, which he preferred, but he could see out of the door around the helmeted heads of Aubrey who was and two others. Five hundred feet below, the green jungle blurred past as the pilot steadied on his run-in.

The dispatcher stared at his wrist-watch, listening intently to the pilot's voice in his earphones.

His bare arm shot up, finger pointing at the red and green lights by the door and he shouted, 'Red on!'

The little red light glowed. Seconds to go.

'Green on! Go! Go! Go!' he shouted as the men shuffled towards him, turned like automatons to the open door and stepped out into space. Aubrey first, the second man, the third man, then Edward.

The rush of warm slipstream air tossed him upside down. The sea of green below mixed chaotically with the blue sky above until the static line ripped his parachute from its packing and a familiar bone-jarring jerk hung him swinging free beneath the canopy.

To his relief, he had no twists in the rigging lines stretched tight above him and the canopy was safely round over his head. He released his rucksack from its hooks, slid it down his legs so he could stand on it to smash through the trees and took a quick look round. He could see several others floating into the jungle canopy not far away and on the horizon mountain ridges curled round them on two enveloping ridge lines, rising towards the high peak of Gunong Nuang which marked where Selangor, Negri Sembilan and Pahang all met. Somewhere under the green mess of trees coming up fast to meet him was Ho Peng.

304

Suddenly he was no longer floating earthwards, but plunging into the trees, bursting through the leaves, breaking branches, praying his parachute would catch up somewhere, anywhere for Christ's sake, as long as it was really solid. He cannoned on to a big branch, bruising his chest and knocking the breath from his lungs. By the time he could breathe again, he realised he had stopped moving. He was suspended from the branches of a huge tree and his harness was pulled tight by the heavy rucksack swinging just below his legs. He could see the main trunk a sickening empty space more than twenty feet away. To his surprise he could not see far below him. The space between him and the ground far below was filled with layers of leaves, bromeliads and hanging vines.

The parachute slipped, dropping him, and he gripped the harness in terror. Foolishly he realised that was hardly going to save him. He had to get down. Trying to work as smoothly as possible without jerking the rigging lines, he dropped the end of his abseil rope, clipped his rucksack to his harness, fitted the figure of eight descender to the rope and began to let himself down. He dared not go too fast. Every time he moved erratically, the canopy jerked spasmodically lower, settling, he hoped, into the branches. When he emerged through the last layer and saw the ground thirty feet below him, he gauged he had abseiled down over one hundred feet.

He had never felt so pleased to stand on firm ground. To his amazement and joy, he was bruised but had escaped serious injury. He wriggled out of his harness, put on his jungle belt kit, with its ammunition pouches, long parang knife, water bottle pouches and emergency rations. He untied the abseil rope from his back-pack and checked his new Sterling. Using Special Branch influence, Angus had obtained the new issue Sterling 9mm sub-machine-guns and Aubrey had opted to take several fitted with silencers, the L34A1 model. Edward had one. It was slightly longer than standard, but when it came to the shooting, it might keep the element of surprise on their side a fraction longer. So far from any support, reinforcements or medical, they needed every advantage. He pulled out his compass and began walking.

Mustering all sixteen of them in one place in the jungle took all their patience and three hours. The high primary jungle helped, as visibility was as much as fifty feet in places, but for hours all Edward could hear were owl hoots, whistles and shouts as the men slowly gathered on Aubrey, the stick leader who waited at a stream junction. Both he and Edward were relieved to find no-one was missing but two had broken ribs and one of the troopers had a badly broken arm. When they were all together, Sergeant Brogan splinted the man's arm, shared out the equipment of the wounded men and they set off. They had two days to reach the rendezvous with Lao Tang.

The lead scout, a thin trooper with sharp features who moved smoothly through the jungle like a deer, carried another silenced Sterling. Behind him Aubrey carried another, as did Edward, but the man behind Edward carried a Bren light machine-gun, one of two in the patrol, to boost firepower for the camp attack.

Moving very carefully, they covered four miles the first day through good jungle, a mile an hour, stopping at four o'clock.

Aubrey guided the patrol in a loop back on his tracks so they could ambush anyone following them and they made camp. He had spent several months with the SAS Squadron in the jungle and was impressed with the way Edward quietly ate his hard biscuit and tin of stew cold like the others. Aubrey had banned all cooking and smoking to minimise the chance of being picked up by the aborigines. He whispered casually, 'Where did a base rat like you from Headquarters learn about the jungle?'

'I've been in the jungle longer than you.' Edward grinned back and told him about Tallard and Ferret Force at the start of the campaign. 'He worked with Ho Peng during the war in this area and there's nothing much he doesn't know about the jungle.'

'Wouldn't he know where to find Ho Peng?'

'No. He used the excuse of Ferret Force and later the Civil Liaison Corps to check every camp he knew about, but the Chinese kept a lot of camps secret even from the Force 136 officers we sent into the jungle to help them.'

'Buggers must have been planning their bloody revolution even then.'

'Hoarding weapons and equipment in hides in the camps, too,' said Edward and told Aubrey of the booby-trapped cache they had found after the train ambush.

The talk helped, but neither of them expressed the questions uppermost in their minds. Had they avoided being seen by the aborigines? If not, would they be ambushed by the CTs? Was Lao Tang frightened enough by the SB threats to re-join Ho Peng? Would Ho Peng accept him back? Was Ho Peng still there, or had he moved already? What would they do if they met a powerful

CT force and were outnumbered? Were they walking into an ambush anyway?

The questions, Edward told himself, were unanswerable. They had covered as much as was humanly possible with their plans and rehearsals. The rest was up to Fate.

After their meal, they moved once more, just in case anyone had located them while they were eating, or heard the signaller tapping out the evening report on his radio back to base in Kuala Lumpur. Aubrey led them several hundred yards distant, round in another loop and they lay down on the ground in a circle, alert at 'stand-to' for the transition from day to night. Half an hour later, when they were enveloped in total darkness, Aubrey whispered, 'Stand-down!', and each man was alone in the unique privacy of the jungle night.

Edward made a final check for leeches, running his fingers over his legs to feel for the soft bodies sucking his blood. He found one which had slithered in through the eyelets of his canvas boots and removed it with a squirt of mosquito repellent. Then he settled down on the ground, pulled a lightweight blanket over him praying it would not rain during the night and went to sleep.

Lao Tang reached Ho Peng's camp in the middle of the following day, tired and damp with sweat after crossing the high ridge of mountains. He avoided the outer sentries easily, as he knew where they were, and sat for an hour watching and listening to the camp to give himself the confidence to face Ho Peng before he walked in.

Like at their first big camp, the area around had been cleared of all undergrowth between the big trees but had one important additional defence. Ho Peng had made them stack all the vegetation they cleared in a six-foot-high barrier around the living area, with zig-zag passages through, like an African kraal under the green canopy of the jungle. The wall had become a crisp brown tangle, making it impossible to see into the camp and impossible to cross the dead thorny branches without making enough noise to wake the dead.

Lao Tang arrived in the middle of a trial.

Outside the Secretariat attap hut, Ho Peng was squatting on the ground faced by three men in MRLA uniform. Two were armed standing at attention and the third, between them, was on his knees with his hands tied behind his back. Behind them the rest of the platoon sat on the ground. Ho Peng was making a speech and angrily waving a slip of paper. As Lao Tang approached with the inner sentry from the gap through the wall of branches, he stopped and everyone looked round.

'Where have you been, Comrade Lao Tang?' demanded Ho Peng. His voice was menacingly quiet but every man in the camp heard.

'We were ambushed and I twisted my knee,' said Lao Tang. The excuse sounded hopelessly feeble but anything more complicated, especially involving other people or places he might have been seen, would compromise him. 'Near the leg wound from the ambush at the "Black Circle" years ago.'

Ho Peng said nothing. He stared unpleasantly at Lao Tang and waited for him to explain himself.

'Our food patrol was attacked by the British and we were dispersed,' said Lao Tang as diplomatically as he could. In fact, they had run for their lives. In the gloom the Gurkha lead scout had seen the CTs leading man first, shot him and the next at once, then charged with the rest of his four-man patrol, killing another and wounding a fourth. Lao Tang had only escaped because the dreaded Gurkhas followed up the blood spoor of the wounded man. Lao Tang said, 'We fought back as best we could but we were separated by an overwhelming force of the enemy. I don't know what happened to the others.'

There was a long silence in which Ho Peng sat and stared at him, like a toad. He was intensely suspicious and there was no proof of the story. However, Lao Tang had always seemed a stout supporter so far, and at least he had come back. Finally, he said, 'No-one but you has returned, Comrade Lao Tang.'

The shock in Lao Tang's eyes saved his life. The Special Branch had not told him the outcome of the Gurkha ambush. Lao Tang had been so relieved to find he was well-treated on surrendering, contrary to what he had been led to believe by the Party, that he had not asked.

Ho Peng decided to put Lao Tang's loyalty to immediate test. He pointed at the man on his knees, waved the piece of paper again, and said to Lao Tang, 'While you were away, this and other criminal enemy documents were found under this man's bed roll.'

Lao Tang felt sick. The paper was a Safe Conduct Pass leaflet, exactly the same as the one he had used to surrender. On the ground in front of Ho Peng were other papers, a copy of the propaganda magazine *Sin Lu Pao*, or *New Path News*, which ex-CTs produced for the British, and several leaflets warning rank and file CTs that their leadership was corrupt. Lao Tang was amazed to see that someone else in the platoon felt the same way as he did and wondered how many more there might be, men too terrified of Ho Peng and rigid Party discipline to act. He tried to keep the surprise out of his face, conscious Ho Peng was watching him closely.

'We have held a trial and the traitor has admitted trying to escape,' Ho Peng continued, his voice rising with anger. 'And he will be punished. He will be executed!'

The man's head jerked up and he began pleading with Ho Peng who stood up, stepped forward and kicked him in the stomach. The man fell on his side, retching painfully.

Lao Tang's common guilt with the condemned man made him want to speak out and overturn Ho Peng's power in a sudden coup. He was sure others would stand up to denounce him too, but events moved too quickly for him, binding him implacably into the iron Party system as if he had never wavered. 'You will show your dedication to the Party,' Ho Peng announced coldly. 'You will assist with the execution.'

Ho Peng sent one of the two guards back to the platoon and they all sat motionless, more as if they were watching a film than reality. Lao Tang stood in his place. Ho Peng produced a rope, he gave one end to the remaining guard and the other to Lao Tang, he looped the middle of the rope around the man's neck under his chin and shouted, 'Lift him off the ground and strangle him!'

The other guard reacted obediently at once. The jerk on the rope forced Lao Tang to pull too, appalled but driven by fear and self-preservation. At once the condemned man struggled to his feet to stop the rope throttling him on the ground, futilely trying to prolong his life by keeping the rope loose. With Ho Peng watching, Lao Tang and the guard took in the slack at once.

As the rope tightened round his neck, ripping his skin, the condemned CT fought and kicked out. Ho Peng ignored his flailing legs and stepped close to watch Lao Tang's face. He observed the other guard take a final bight in the rope round his hand and whispered, 'Comrade Lao Tang, you're not pulling very hard?'

Suddenly Lao Tang wanted to finish it. Somehow, the dying man had twisted to face him, with the other guard pulling at his back. His eyes were staring, conscious and pleading, his mouth was open, dribbling, and he was desperately trying to drag air down his throat into his lungs. Lao Tang gripped the rope in one hand, jabbed his other elbow on the man's chest and pulled the rope hard over the crook of the elbow. Ho Peng circled round the three, like a boxing referee. The sweat poured off them. Even the dying man suspended between them sweated, desperate to live.

It seemed to take ages. Lao Tang had never realised how difficult it was to strangle someone. When the man stopped moving, Ho Peng made them both hold him up, sagging between them, till Lao Tang's arms ached with cramp. The stench of the dead man's sweat and the sight of his tongue protruding from purple lips, round and swollen like a parrot's tongue, stayed fixed in his mind long after the body was dragged away and the parade broke up.

No-one dared speak to Lao Tang. Later that afternoon, when Aubrey's patrol were only a mile away, moving slowly and with extreme caution towards the rendezvous point, Ho Peng came over and said, 'You need to give your knee a rest, Comrade Lao Tang. Take a few days off working with the food growing element.'

'Thank you, Comrade Ho Peng,' replied Lao Tang evenly, trying to hide his panic. Although the food plot, with rice, tapioca and vegetables, was vital for the platoon, being disarmed and put on the "gardeners" detail was a disgrace from which most did not recover. He told himself that at least he could still shoot the two guards who usually went with the garden detail and escape, when Ho Peng suddenly leaned forward and picked up Lao Tang's carbine. 'You won't need this for a while. We're a bit short, so I'll give it to one of the others.'

Edward and the SAS patrol passed another night on the ground and it rained all night. The patrol medic jabbed the trooper with the broken arm with plenty of morphine but he had lost fluid and was in a lot of pain. At dawn Aubrey left him with one of the other injured men and all their rucksacks and they moved in light order to the rendezvous with Lao Tang, well spaced out and with extreme care. The lead scout stopped every few minutes to peer into the green shadows ahead, strained his ears for noises which did not belong and sniffed the air for human scent.

Aubrey, Edward and the lead scout had made a reconnaissance the night before, leaving the patrol to eat their evening 'meal' of cold tinned food, so they reached the rendezvous without error through thick jungle shortly after dawn. They spread out and sat down in a screen of good cover on the edge of a small open area in a narrow flat valley where the Sungei Kenaboi emerged from the jungle. Edward guessed the area had once been well cultivated but the upland rice padis were unused, covered with sedge weeds and the bunds had crumbled away. There was nothing to attract the RAF spotter planes looking for the CTs' jungle 'gardens'. However, along the edge of the jungle, hidden under the overhanging branches of the big trees at the jungle edge, were strips of neat cultivation. This was the place. Ho Peng's food supply. Edward squashed his already sopping jungle hat to his forehead to wipe the sweat out of his eyes and tried to control his excitement. After four years and all the things Ho Peng had done, they had found his deep jungle hide-out at last.

'D'you think Lao Tang will come?' whispered Aubrey, finally expressing the crucial question which justified the whole operation.

Edward shrugged, never taking his eyes off the CT 'garden'. 'I don't know, but seeing those little lines of veg. confirms what he's told us so far.' There was nothing more they could do but wait.

They waited all day, the day of the rendezvous, and no-one came. The sky darkened with black rainclouds and the rain poured down all afternoon. Edward became almost mesmerised by the big drops splashing and bouncing in the padi water and streaming off his hat.

Soaking, they returned to the two injured men for another damp night on the ground. Aubrey and Edward talked for a while in the dark, unable to see each other's faces, but there was no comfort in speculating about Lao Tang and the rain drove them back under their ponchos. It did not let up till dawn and sheer misery drove them early back to their ambush position overlooking the CT 'garden'. Thick mist hung over the open valley, filling the banks of the narrow river and clinging eerily to the branches of the jungle trees.

After only half an hour, Edward saw the mist stirring about a hundred yards away along the jungle edge. The heads and shoulders of four men appeared through the mist. They were in uniform. He whispered, 'There they are!' and pointed, careful not to disturb the leaves hiding them.

'Why the hell has he brought three friends?' Aubrey hissed, kneeling to see better. This was not part of the plan at all. 'And which one is Lao Tang? They all look the bloody same!'

Behind him, Sergeant Sean Brogan knelt and gripped his Sterling. He had already decided to shoot them all if necessary, rather than let them get away.

The four CTs walked closer and they were only forty yards distant in the mist when their features emerged distinguishable in the translucent early morning light, Lao Tang's narrow pale face at the back. Edward whispered very softly, 'Lao Tang is number four!' He wondered if the CT had deliberately chosen to be the last man, guessing what was going to happen.

Aubrey knew what he had to do. In total silence, he coolly indicated who should open fire at whom, and they all took aim, easing the Sterlings up between the leaves. When the four CTs were hardly thirty yards away, almost in line in front of the SAS hidden in the bushes, Aubrey, Edward and the lead scout fired a long burst each.

The suppressed Sterlings spluttered, like rain drops, and the three leading CTs dropped on the spot, like rag-dolls. Lao Tang stood frozen with astonishment, seeing the sprays of blood but hearing none of the familiar racket of gunfire. Before he could move, Sergeant Brogan and another trooper burst out of cover and flattened him in a pool of padi water. Aubrey and Edward checked the other three. They were all dead.

Several members of the patrol dragged the dead CTs into cover in the jungle. Aubrey left Brogan to supervise removing traces of the ambush and sat down beside a large buttress tree with Edward to talk to Lao Tang.

In Chinese, Edward said, 'Is Ho Peng in the camp?'

'Yes,' said Lao Tang, still in shock and now amazed to find that this British officer he recognised spoke Chinese. 'But we must move quickly! He's very suspicious. He took away my carbine and I don't know how long he will stay there.'

Calmly, through Edward, Aubrey made Lao Tang confirm the layout of the camp and the numbers. He was not pleased to hear there were over thirty men there and that the camp was surrounded by a wall of dried undergrowth. 'Bloody thing will force us through the zig-zag entrances,' he said to Edward and Sergeant Brogan who had squatted down to listen.

Lao Tang watched the three British soldiers coolly discussing the options and grabbed Edward's arm, saying, 'Tell this officer we must go!'

Edward translated and Brogan said, 'This little Chink seems awful keen. Could be a trap?'

'Not a very good one,' said Edward. 'We've shot three already.'

'Ah, but we cheated, remember, with them silencers. Now, if we hadn't had silencers, they would have heard the shooting, if there had been any shooting,' said Brogan, pursuing his own brand of logic. 'Which there has been, but they didn't hear it, so they might still be out there waiting for us. D'you see?'

'No,' drawled Aubrey. 'But we can't sit here jawing or Ho Peng will escape us. We'll just hope the sentries think we're the garden boys returning to camp early.'

Lao Tang's relief at the brisk decision to move soon faded when Aubrey put him in front and Edward informed him he would be shot if he tried to escape. Lao Tang took one look at Aubrey's smooth, black-barreled silenced Sterling and the determined expression on his stubbled face and set off without a word, unsure whether to fear Ho Peng more or the British. Aubrey's lead scout fell in behind Edward who stayed close by ready to translate if necessary.

He was surprised how swiftly and silently Lao Tang moved through the trees and undergrowth. They were all sweating with effort by the time he paused where he had waited two days before, to observe the camp thirty yards up a slight slope cleared of all cover. They crouched behind bushes. Edward wondered what Ho Peng was doing at that precise moment inside the camp.

Aubrey said, 'I don't like that wall of brown leaves.' The protective wall was simple but effective, circling the camp and there were six entrances, in-built for escape, and hard to stop up.

Lao Tang turned to Edward, his eyes huge in his starved face, and whispered in Chinese, 'There's a sentry in each entrance.'

As Aubrey whispered, 'What's he say?' a rustling noise made them all look up. A CT stumbled out of the entrance above them, rattling the dead branches, and ran down the slope towards them. Two more CTs appeared in the entrance, shouting.

At once Lao Tang threw himself on the ground, the two CTs opened fire down the hill and Aubrey fired back. The running man was caught in the cross-fire. He stopped dead in his tracks, hit several times in the face and chest, and spun like a top to the ground.

Plans to the winds, Aubrey shouted, 'Charge!' and set off up the hill firing his Sterling in short bursts. Edward tossed reason to one side, convinced they would all be cut to bits on the open slope by the CTs who were twice their number, and followed.

'Keep to the right,' shouted Sergeant Brogan, beginning to pant up the slope with the lead scout. And to the men behind him, he bellowed, 'Gun group! On the left, rapid fire!'

The familiar British Army fire orders galvanised the rest. Behind him, the two SAS Bren-gun teams stepped sideways over Lao Tang's prone form to give themselves an angle and put down

313

supporting fire at the wall of branches, their bullets making a noise through the dead leaves like a raging forest fire.

Aubrey reached the zig-zag entrance first, shot one of the two CTs who was wounded and crawling away by the wall of leaves, and ducked into the camp closely followed by Edward and the lead scout. They took cover behind the first attap hut to catch their breath, frantically looking round for the enemy.

Nothing moved in the camp.

In moments Sergeant Brogan and the other six men had charged into the camp and they all began to move from hut to hut, covering each other as they went, expecting a fusillade of counter-fire at each step. They found slit trenches and bunkers defending each hut, but every one was empty. The CTs had vanished.

'Well fuck that,' announced Brogan angrily when they had cleared every part of the camp and stood at the wall of dead leaves on the far side. Ho Peng had vanished, probably thinking that the camp was under attack by a large force. Aubrey, Edward, Brogan and all the others knew that if he had been aware only nine men were charging up the hill, he could have stayed, defended the trenches and bunkers, and murdered every one of them.

Seizing the camp was a hollow victory. There was a deep sense of disappointment and Edward could not help mentioning, 'Aubrey, that first CT charging down the hill, the one you shot, was trying to surrender.'

'Nonsense,' Aubrey snapped. The implication was that if they had captured him, they might have used him to find out if the camp was alert and defended.

'That's what the others were shouting about,' Edward explained. 'He was making a bolt for it.'

Brogan shrugged. It was too late anyway. He said, 'I don't think we'd have got through this wall of dead stuff easy one way or the other. Maybe we were lucky after all, to catch them wrong-footed.'

They had been so close to catching Ho Peng in his lair. Even the five dead CTs, a good number in a war in which each 'kill' represented a statistical 1,800 man-hours of slogging through the jungle, could not allay the feeling that they had failed. Three men in the patrol had been injured on the parachute drop, and when they went back down the slope outside the camp, they found another SAS soldier had been wounded, shot in the shoulder during the cross-fire which initiated the charge uphill, and he had lost a lot of blood. Lao Tang had also been hit in the chest as he dived for cover.

314

He was conscious but badly wounded. The SAS patrol medic thought he had a collapsed lung and told Aubrey, 'We must get these two out as soon as possible. Or they will die.'

Aubrey was blunt. 'I couldn't care less about the Chinaman,' he said. 'Just my gunner.'

'I want Lao Tang alive,' Edward butted in. 'For the moment, at least. The camp has almost certainly got hides in it, probably still full since Ho Peng's lot scarpered in such a hurry. Is he conscious?'

The medic nodded and led Edward to the trees on the side of the clearing. Lao Tang was lying down beside the wounded soldier, bandaged across his chest with a shell dressing and crepe. His face looked even paler than before.

'Can you speak?' asked Edward.

Lao Tang nodded weakly.

In five minutes, Edward had coaxed him to explain the location of two hides in the camp above. He said, 'Are they booby-trapped?'

'No!' whispered Lao Tang and began to cough painfully.

'Should leave him now,' said the medic.

'We'll move them both into the sun,' Aubrey decided. 'Cut some of these thin trees, make stretchers and carry them to the fresh air. It's bloody miserable in here.' He had studied the map and wanted to signal base for an infantry unit to meet them at the nearest track-head. 'I've seen a village called Kampong Esok, about ten miles south of here along the Sungei Kenaboi. They should be able to get a jeep there for the wounded. Ask Lao Tang if there's a track down the river bank.'

When Edward knelt by Lao Tang and translated, he confirmed there was a track beside the river and croaked, 'A day to Kampong Esok. Two days to walk over the hills.' Lao Tang, convinced he was dying, hardly thought he would manage to survive the day, let alone being dragged up steep slopes in the mountains for two.

'Maybe more carrying these two stretchers,' stated Brogan grimly.

Aubrey left Edward and Brogan to search the camp with two others while he supervised moving the wounded men to the open cultivations. He also sent four men to bring in the two injured men and the pile of rucksacks they had been guarding in their night camp.

'We can't spend long looking for these hides,' said Brogan as they panted up the slope for the second time. 'We'll have to get off along

315

that river as soon as possible. I don't like the look of either of them wounded.'

Edward agreed, but he was determined not to lose the chance of finding information which might be vital to Angus's Special Branch teams.

They found the first hide inside Ho Peng's attap hut in the centre of the camp. Ho Peng had been there not half an hour before, relaxed and drinking tea. A small fire was still hot, his bedroll was still there, the indent of Ho Peng's body on it, a colourful china teacup lay on the earth floor, incongruously bright in the jungle, matches lay on a low table made of small poles and he had left behind a glass jar of sugar.

'Must have been making a brew when we dropped in,' observed Brogan drily. Sugar was a vital food supplement in the jungle.

Edward pulled the bedroll to one side, knelt down and poked gingerly in the earth beneath with his parang knife. They heard a hollow noise. Using the knife, he carefully brushed the dry earth aside and six inches down he found a round metal lid about fifteen inches across.

Brogan leaned over to look and said, 'That's an old drum from an SOE parachute container. Type "H", if I remember correctly.' He had fought with the SAS behind German lines at the end of the Second World War.

Edward wondered if this container was one dropped by the Dakota pilot he had talked to, and if Tallard had been there when Ho Peng took the drop. But time was short and he said, 'Got some cord?' Whatever Lao Tang said, he was taking no chances on booby-traps.

Brogan fished in a back-pouch on his belt kit and handed over a length of abseil rope he had kept from the parachute jump. Edward tied one end to the metal lid and they both retired out of the hut and dropped into Ho Peng's defensive slit trench outside.

They crouched down below the lip of the trench and Edward pulled on the rope. Nothing happened. He pulled again, harder, and suddenly fell on his back in the trench. Inside the hut, they heard the drum clattering over the mud floor.

Brogan laughed as Edward picked himself up saying 'Better safe than sorry', and they went back into the hut.

The old drum lay on the floor, the lid bent and pulled half off. A quick inspection showed it was not booby-trapped inside and Edward opened it completely. Inside was a sheaf of papers and three notebooks. With mounting excitement, he leafed through a notebook and said, 'Chief Inspector Angus Maclean of Special Branch will be bloody delighted with this!'

'Can you read that stuff?' asked Brogan amazed.

'Just a few title characters,' Edward replied. 'But there's no doubt this is a real find. Communists are obsessed with keeping records of all their actions and details on their members. Sort of like confidential reports.'

'Doesn't sound any different to the British Army,' remarked Brogan.

Edward grunted thinking of Colonel Bleasley writing his annual confidential report. 'Wouldn't like anyone to read mine. Nor yours, Sean, the amount you've been up and down the ranks.'

'All done from the best possible motives,' retorted Sergeant Brogan in a hurt voice.

Edward stuffed the documents back in the drum and they went across the camp to a huge teak tree rising up to the canopy beside the CT cookhouse. The embers of a fire still glowed in a pit outside another attap hut, an oil drum half full of water stood on one side and the area was strewn with rusty tins of condensed milk, tins of tuna fish and 'Milo' chocolate jars.

'Looks like they raided the bloody NAAFI,' said Brogan.

'Maybe they did,' said Edward. The Min Yuen had sympathisers in jobs everywhere. Even Sir Henry Gurney's butler had been revealed as a communist, after the assassination on Fraser's Hill, so it would be no surprise to find other communists among the civilian labour in army camps.

They found the hide in minutes, between two huge sweeping buttresses of the big tree. A long plank was concealed beneath soft rotting leaves. Very carefully, Edward tied the abseil rope round one end and they went through the same routine as before. Neither of them expected an explosion as they assumed the CTs had not had the time to set the trap.

They retired the other side of the thick tree and pulled the rope. The plank lifted clear, without a sound.

Underneath, they found a row of five gallon glass carboys with wide screw tops. They opened each one and found they were all nearly full of fresh rice. Brogan whistled, 'A supply like that should last them months!'

'Bound to come back for it, don't you think?'

'Jesus, wouldn't you?'

'Then I've got just the thing,' said Edward brightly, reaching into an extra pouch on the back of his belt. He produced a bulky waterproof canvas bag, untied the mouth and began to sprinkle a white powder in the top of each carboy.

'What's that stuff?' Brogan demanded.

'Ground glass. Helps the digestion!'

Brogan laughed out loud. 'You've learned a few tricks since we worked together in Palestine.'

'Special Branch idea,' Edward admitted, smiling. After all the brutal things the CTs had done, he had no qualms. He cleaned his parang blade and mixed the ground glass in with the rice, saying, 'It'll tear their stomachs to bits. Either kill them or they'll lose enthusiasm for killing the rest of us and hand themselves in.'

'Or both.'

They took great care to leave the 'booby-trapped' rice carboys and the plank exactly as they had found them, smoothing the leaves back over the top. Then they walked back along the now well-defined track through the jungle to the open valley.

After the rainfall of the previous night, the weather was being kind to them. The sky was blue, the last traces of mist were burning off the weed-infested padi fields and the men were sitting on the edge of the open area drying out their sweat- and rain-soaked clothes in the sunshine.

Aubrey Hall-Drake was too experienced a soldier, with a wartime Military Cross, to be caught napping. He had deployed the Bren gunners in defensive positions just inside the jungle, in case Ho Peng came back. He spread the rest out but he could not avoid some bunching together at the centre of the group where the medic was busy with the five wounded men.

Edward and Brogan found him sitting on a rice padi bund, his Sterling across his knees, and told him of their finds. But he said morosely, 'Things're not looking good for Lao Tang and I don't think our chap knows the time of day. The others will survive, though I wouldn't like to face a day's rough marching to Kampong Esok with a broken arm or broken ribs myself.'

Sergeant Brogan said, 'Any news on the infantry?'

'That's why we're waiting,' said Aubrey in a tired voice. He gestured over to the trees where an SAS trooper was sitting with headphones on beside a small radio. Line aerials stretched from the radio into the trees in a 'V', one on either side of him. 'Buggers in HQ are taking a hell of a time to reply.'

'So what's new?' grunted Sergeant Brogan. He tucked his Sterling under his arm and went off round all the men in the patrol, stopping to chat with each, a confident burly figure in dark sweat-stained jungle shirt and trousers.

Aubrey said to Edward, 'Want a cheroot? No point worrying about the No Smoking rule now.'

Edward shook his head. Aubrey shrugged, pulled a thin waterproof tin from his pack and lit up. The smoke rose slowly in the hot still air. Brogan had reached the line of five dead CTs who had been dragged into a rice bund and Edward was about to join him when a low call alerted everyone.

'Abos!'

One of the Bren-gun teams on guard cheerfully waved them on and three Orang Asli men walked over glancing nervously at the wounded men lying in the shade under the trees. They were small, very brown, naked except for a cloth codpiece tied round their waists and up between their buttocks at the back, and they carried long bamboo blow pipes. They grinned shyly and Edward greeted them in Chinese.

The youngest smiled and replied in Chinese, 'We are very pleased you have come.' The oldest, whose brown skin was very wrinkled, nodded seriously.

The sound of chopping interrupted them. Brogan was swinging his parang in big sweeping arcs over by the jungle edge, hacking at something out of sight behind a rice bund beyond the wounded men.

Edward said to the abos, 'We have killed some communists terrorists.'

The young aborigine translated and all three nodded vigorously.

'They have taken our men,' said the young one.

'And our women,' he added after a short discussion among the three. 'But you are here now. To protect us from them.'

Edward said to Aubrey in English, 'They'll be shattered if we tell them we're leaving them again.'

'It's all right,' Aubrey replied. 'Tell him we'll get more soldiers to protect him. I know HQ want to build forts in remote places like this to wean the aborigines away from the CTs. I'm sure we'll get one put here, to put the pressure on Ho Peng.'

By the time Edward had finished explaining all that to the three aborigines in Chinese, Brogan had finished chopping. Suddenly the youngest aborigine burst out laughing and pointed. Edward and

Aubrey turned round. Sergeant Brogan was marching over with the severed head of a Chinese terrorist in each hand, gripped with a fistful of black hair.

Aubrey took his cheroot from his lips and drawled, 'Is that really necessary?'

'Jesus, Sir! We couldn't bloody carry them bodies all the way to Kampong Esok!' replied Brogan briskly. 'Not in one piece that is. And those Special Branch friends of Mr Fairfax here will want to identify their little faces. Am I right?'

Edward nodded, fascinated.

Brogan dropped the two heads on the ground with the words, 'We'll wrap them up in poly bags and share them out to carry in our rucksacks. Plenty of room now we've eaten all our rations.'

Aubrey stared at the heads by his feet, their eyes half-open and filthy with earth and caked blood, and enquired, 'Why didn't you get Edward here to ask Lao Tang to identify them? Colleagues of his, weren't they?'

'Bugger's unconscious now,' responded Brogan. 'Not looking at all rosy. I doubt he'll last the journey.'

'I suppose you'll want to chop his head off too.'

'No Sir!' said Brogan turning back for the next two heads. 'We already know his name, Sir! And there's a nice picture of him back in Special Branch HQ, to be sure.'

The aborigines were mightily impressed, chatting among themselves excitedly and pointing at the growing pile of severed heads. Edward listened to another hesitant translation through Chinese and told Aubrey, 'Couple of these chaps were responsible for murdering several of their tribe.'

'I'm glad they're happy,' said Aubrey, catching sight of his signaller busy tapping his Morse code key, 'but we need to go. I'm going to ginger up a bloody reply from HQ.' He strode over to the signaller leaving Edward to chat with the aborigines.

Ten minutes later, Aubrey came back smiling broadly. 'Sorry if I'm interrupting anything,' he said seeing the old aborigine gesticulating wildly in the air with his hands. 'But HQ have said they're sending a helicopter. A real bloody helicopter!'

The news passed quickly round the patrol, as if by telepathy, and spirits soared. Their relief at not having to walk for hours through the jungle, on a path or not, carrying two stretchers in turn and all the injured men's equipment, not to mention Brogan's heads, was indescribable. Sergeant Brogan came over again. Suspicious of all good news from HQ, he insisted his Troop Commander show him what the signaller had written down. He said finally, 'For all of us?'

'Yes!' exclaimed Aubrey. 'For the whole lot. The helicopters are Navy Sycamores. Off the carrier in the Straits of Malacca. They take four men each, but probably only two as they've got to get over the mountain ridge to find us, so they'll need six or seven lifts.'

'Incredible!' muttered Brogan. 'It's going to take hours.'

'The five injured men will go first,' Aubrey decided, 'and as the rest get flown out we'll leave all our spare ammunition, except one magazine each, with the men who stay behind till last.' He paused and said, 'If I may say so, you don't look very pleased, Sergeant Brogan?'

'I was just thinking, Sir, I needn't have chopped off those heads if I'd known they was coming in with helicopters.'

'I didn't think you cared?'

Brogan grunted, 'The Chinks believe a man must be buried in one piece, for the good of his soul.'

'They're not Catholics, Sean,' said Edward laughing out loud.

'No, well, maybe not,' said Sergeant Brogan and wandered off again to make a brew.

In the event, the Navy sent two Sycarnores and Edward had never seen a more welcome sight. Like dragonflies, with bulbous cockpits, rubber wheels like feet on the end of short legs, and a long tail, they buzzed across the open valley and came in to land on the overgrown padi fields. The three aborigines terrified, fled into the jungle where they watched with astonishment. Navy pilots stepped out, like angels, incongruously dressed in gleaming white shirts and shorts and a complete contrast to the filthy jungle patrol who came to meet them.

The pilots had stripped their machines to carry the maximum weight and the injured men were loaded swiftly on the first lift.

'I don't fancy his chances,' said Aubrey of Lao Tang as he sat down again on his rice padi bund and lit up another cheroot.

Edward agreed, but he was their only link with Ho Peng. Apart from the documents. It would be a pity to lose him.

The Sycamores were back in an hour and Brogan took the container drum of Ho Peng's documents to give to Angus Maclean. Two lifts later, when Edward was beginning to think he would have to spend another night in the jungle, far too close to Ho Peng's platoon of thirty men, the two helicopters reappeared.

The last five wasted no time climbing aboard, the rotors whined, taking the full weight, and they juddered off the ground. Edward had never been in a helicopter before, and where he might normally have been apprehensive at the shaking and rattling din, he was so thankful for the free lift home, he did not care. Aubrey sat beside him looking through the open door at the jungle beneath them, enjoying the breeze. Neither spoke. Their return journey on foot, with the injured, would have been a nightmare.

Aubrey looked at Edward. He admired his ability with languages, and was thinking the patrol had not been such a failure after all, much due to that ability, when the helicopter turned into the afternoon sun and the light glinted on something in Edward's hands. He nudged him, pointed and shouted over the din of the rotor blades, 'What's that?'

Edward opened his hand to show a small gold coin. He shouted back, 'It's a King George V gold sovereign, 1929. One of those abos gave it to me. For saving them.'

'Where did he get it?'

'He said he found it there, on the rice padi, during the war.' The old man had waved his brown arms wildly at the sky to describe the event, and been interrupted by Aubrey announcing that the helicopters were coming. 'He thought it was a gift from the gods.'

Chapter 19

AN OPEN AND SHUT CASE

Months later in May 1954, after the French had been disastrously defeated by the Vietminh at Dien Bien Phu in Indo-China and the expansion of Communism in south-east Asia seemed unstoppable, Angus Maclean again invited Edward to Special Branch HQ. 'Those documents you found in Ho Peng's camp were invaluable,' he told him.

The news added to a list of good fortune since his jungle patrol with Aubrey. First, the officer who had replaced Colonel Bleasley had immediately seen the value of Edward's experience in Malaya and his language ability and extended his posting. Better still, he supported Edward's promotion to captain and made him the army's Special Branch Liaison Officer with an office of his own. Often now Edward drove across to the south side of Kuala Lumpur to visit Angus in the secret SB complex. Apart from a large map of Malaya, and a photograph of Angus in uniform in Palestine, the office was bare except for a desk, two chairs and a cold water dispenser with a big bottle upside down over a tap. Special Branch material was so highly classified that all the files were kept in the secure registry.

Edward asked, 'What took you so long?'

'Most of the papers were in code,' said Angus. He leaned back in his chair. 'But it's given us a much clearer picture of the MRLA and Chin Peng's problems. We now know for certain that Ho Peng is on the Central Military Committee. He probably runs it, for he has been sending endless messages to Chin Peng complaining about the lack of finance to support his military effort. Chin Peng is not producing the cabbage. The MRLA have had no new weapons at all. For the last six years they've kept us on the hop with a

323

hotch-potch of British and Japanese equipment they managed to hide after the Second World War plus weapons they've stolen on raids and ambushes.'

'No sign of support from the Chinese?'

Angus shook his head. 'They've had visits from Chinese Red Army commissars, but they've provided nothing more substantial than a lot of hot air about Mao Tse-tung's theories on Protracted Guerrilla Warfare.'

'Sounds like politicians are the same on both sides.'

'Nor have the Russians helped,' Angus went on. 'Ho Peng says that even a few extra million dollars would do the trick, but they've had nothing.'

'So poor old Ho Peng is not happy.'

Angus brushed a hand over his dark hair and grinned. 'Plus, we believe his brave General-Secretary Chin Peng is now hiding in Thailand. We've had no reports of him in Malaya for months.'

'Anything on where Ho Peng might be now?' asked Edward. 'Like the location of camps?'

Angus shook his head. He stood up to stand under the fan and poured a glass of water from the dispenser. He handed a glass to Edward, poured another for himself and said, 'No. But what we learned in those documents corroborates a surveillance operation I've been running for over a year to penetrate the CT commanders' courier network.'

'So we can tap into what goes back and forth to Chin Peng?'

'Yes.' said Angus and sat down on the front of his desk facing Edward right under the fan. 'We've been following the chain all the way from Singapore. Look at these.' He reached back to his desk, picked up a sheaf of 8 in. by 10 in. black and white prints. 'Pics of a CT courier picking up a message on the beach near Mersing. Last year.'

Edward stared at the blurred shape in the photograph and said, 'It's not a very clear picture.'

'Aye,' Angus agreed. 'It was evening when the photograph was taken and the light wasn't good, but the photo lab boys have blown the prints up as far as they can and we're sure it shows a girl.' Angus watched Edward studying the pictures. 'We think she's Chin Peng's personal courier and a very high-ranking member of the Malayan Communist Party indeed.'

'Excellent,' said Edward, impressed. 'Who is she?'

'She's got various aliases,' said Angus, easing himself off the desk. He wandered over to the dispenser to pour another glass of water. 'But her real name is Liya.'

The blow was physical. Edward stared in utter disbelief. If Angus had not had his back to him at the water dispenser, he would have seen the stupefaction on Edward's face. By the time he sat down again, perched on the front of his desk, Edward had gripped himself but could not help bursting out angrily, 'You can't even make out whether this is a man or a woman!'

'I agree,' said Angus. 'But she's mentioned in the documents and we've got plenty more on her.' He sipped his water. 'I called you in because the final operation is in KL and I thought you'd like to join in.'

'What operation?'

'I'll show you.' said Angus, standing up.

Edward followed Angus out into the sun. They walked through the Special Branch complex to a secluded compound behind high corrugated iron security fences painted an unobtrusive green. An old Dodge diesel truck with a battered red cab stood in the middle of a yard between two Nissen huts, its chassis bending hopelessly under the weight of its load. Boxes of vegetables were stacked high on the back and two Chinese coolies in shorts were pulling a tarpaulin over another stack of boxes on the ground.

Angus climbed up behind the red cab on to the stack of boxes and, when Edward joined him, wondering what the point of it all was, he found himself looking into a timber-lined cavity in the middle of the stack. The truck's 'load' of vegetable boxes was hollow, with just a lining of boxes to make it look loaded. Angus pointed at the stack on the ground and said, 'We've taken out all those boxes to make this cavity. Of course, we roof this hole and put a few back on top to complete the image. We've even added a chunk of lead, to make up for the weight of the missing boxes, and bring the old crate really down on its springs like every other Chinky commercial vehicle.'

'What's the point?' Edward asked dully. All he could think about was that Angus had said Liya was a CT, a communist, a top CT courier. It seemed impossible. Suddenly, his private life was threatened. Her visits when she appeared once or twice a week from the clump of jungle beyond the garden and which he looked forward to so much, her company and her love were suspect. All they had done together would be sifted over, scrutinised and exposed as a sham. Even his work was fatally compromised. No-one would believe she

325

had not fooled him into giving away secrets during all the time they spent together. The whole structure of his life had begun to evaporate like early morning ground mist in the hot Malayan sun.

Angus was explaining, 'It's a mobile observation position. Two people can just squeeze in here with a camera and radio. No-one can see them and the veg boxes seem to deaden any noise they make.'

'What about the food regulations?' demanded Edward, deliberately trying to pick holes. The Chinese Min Yuen look-outs would be sure to check the driver's papers if they were at all suspicious.

Angus looked smug. 'This old Dodge belongs to a genuine grocery company registered in Johore Bahru, in the name of two Special Branch officers.' He gestured at the two Chinese in shorts who grinned. 'The people of Ipoh are desperate for Chinese cabbages, though I hope they don't rot before we can make delivery.'

'We guarantee the freshest Kai Lan kale and Teochew Choy Sam mustard,' declared one of the Chinese in shorts.

Angus laughed. 'And after our operation, they'll re-load all the boxes they've taken out to make this hole in the back. Then they deliver the full load to Ipoh as ordered. All above board and no slip-ups.'

'What bloody operation?' said Edward testily.

'You and I will go in the back of this truck to Chinatown, and with a bit of luck, we'll pin down the final link in the courier network.'

Reluctantly Edward climbed into the cavity at the back of the truck with Angus and they sat down on wooden chairs which had been fixed to the floor. The two Chinese fitted the roof above them, stacked more cabbages on top and tied a tarpaulin over the whole pile. The old diesel started up and rumbled out through a gate in the green corrugated iron fence, through the rubber plantation and into Kuala Lumpur by a roundabout route.

In their dark hide in the back, Edward felt trapped, out of control and the sweet smell of cabbages was unpleasantly strong in the heat. A surprising amount of light filtered through the gaps in the boxes and he found the Chinese SB had deliberately made several extra narrow gaps at eye height to make observation and camera work easier. Angus put on a radio headphone over one ear, leaving the other free to listen out for trouble, hung the radio mike on a hook beside his chair and said to Edward, 'You speak the lingo, so your job is to listen out and try to hear what's going on around us, in case they spot us. If they shoot us up in here, we'll end up like meat and veg soup.'

Angus's heavy attempt at humour was lost on Edward. He asked, 'What is the target area?'

'Chinatown.'

That seemed inevitable too.

For nearly an hour, they were jolted about in the back of the old Dodge until it finally stopped and the noisy diesel engine died.

'The driver has immobilised the engine,' Angus whispered in the dark. 'Something to do with the electrical system. It can't be repaired till we're ready to go, whatever a mechanic does.'

Edward could hear Chinese voices shouting and swearing outside. Someone was banging the truck in fury. He peered between the boxes of cabbages and saw the bead curtain of the Wild Orchid Hotel. He slumped another notch deeper into black depression.

Angus was peering across the dusty little street through another gap between the vegetables. He whispered, 'See the Min Yuen look-outs?' He pointed out two young Chinese sitting at the corner of the street, near a Chinese apothecary's shop. 'They'd pick us up in no time if we tried to watch this place any other way. They check all round from time to time.'

'Including the houses?'

'Yes. Most people round here pay protection money to the CTs.' Angus paused. 'I suppose I would too if the alternative was having my throat cut.'

'How did you find out about this place?' Edward forced himself to ask.

'From those documents and our surveillance of the courier chain from the south. We've had our eye on it for months.'

Edward slumped again. He wondered if he had been seen coming here by the Special Branch, and whether he should come clean about Liya. He was about to start his confession when Angus whispered from the shadows in his gentle Scottish burr, 'I bet this is where Ho Peng comes for a fuck.'

The remark killed his intention to confess. He remembered Lao Tang saying how Ho Peng banned his men from having women in the jungle but then came into town himself. Edward wondered how close he had been to Ho Peng in the past without knowing it, how close Liya had been. His depression settled deeper still, beyond the point where he could talk about it any longer. He decided to close out the world and say nothing. He convinced himself Angus could not know about his affair with Liya, or, as an old friend, he would not have made him come along and witness such complete humiliation. He told himself that the Special Branch could not have seen him at the Wild Orchid as Liya had been coming to the house in Uxbridge Drive for more than a year. Whatever happened, they would never know he was involved. Unless they found Liya and she told them.

To Edward's relief, the whispered conversation died as the two Chinese look-outs sauntered across the street. Edward tried to concentrate to hear what they were saying. There was some swearing, the engine cover was opened and someone began knocking about with a spanner or hammer.

The look-outs went back to their post, apparently satisfied. The atmosphere in the middle of the vegetable boxes became intensely oppressive. Edward sweated terribly, hating the inactivity. He wanted freedom and movement, to clear his mind, but dared not move, not knowing who might be quietly standing close by.

Ho Peng stepped off an old green and white Bedford bus near the Coliseum Bar and disappeared into the crowds. Dressed in a blue check short-sleeved shirt, old blue shorts and sandals, he looked like any other coolie, but, as always, he checked around, stopping every few minutes at a food barrow or paper stall to look around. The final approach to the Wild Orchid, or any other permanent base, was always the most dangerous part of any journey, and sometimes he took more than two hours circuiting the narrow and busy streets before he was certain no-one was either following him or waiting for him near the hotel.

He was just another black head on the street as he approached the old Chinese apothecary's shop. With only forty yards to go to the Wild Orchid, the bead curtain in the entrance parted and Liya slipped on to the street. She was wearing her old samfu working clothes, a long blue tunic shirt, baggy cotton trousers and white plimsoles, and she carried a small grip bag. She paused a moment by the door, with the bag on one knee, looking inside, much as any young woman might do if she had forgotten something. Ho Peng turned into the apothecary's shop.

He stood in the darkness just inside the door where he could see Liya and a broad arc of the street. Apparently satisfied, she straightened, lifted her hand to push a strand of hair back into the thick plait at the back of her neck and began walking. As she passed the apothecary's shop Ho Peng moved into deeper shadow and then back again towards the door to watch her through the crowds.

At that, he nearly walked back into the sunlight and across to the Wild Orchid. He had had a long journey from the jungle and spent more time than usual clearing his tracks through Kuala Lumpur, and he was so close. But he suddenly caught sight of someone else watching Liya, most intently. A young Chinese was standing idly by the driver of an old Dodge truck stacked with vegetables working on the engine. For a moment, Ho Peng almost excused him. Liya was attractive, slim and athletic, even beautiful, easy for a young man to watch. Then, as she passed, the young Chinese began to walk after her and glanced behind him. Thoroughly alarmed, Ho Peng followed the glance and saw another Chinese further up the street casually nod his head in acknowledgement. The alert expression in his eyes was far from casual and he began to walk too.

Ho Peng's grim pleasure at identifying the first and second followers in a typical Special Branch surveillance team was swamped by other, more immediate concerns. He tried to spot the trigger observation position he knew the police would have to start the surveillance team off, to tell the followers their target was on the way. His eyes swept the people in the street, but they were all moving back and forth. He hesitated over the old truck, noting the name painted on the side to check it later, though even from inside the apothecary's the cabbages smelled genuine. He briefly looked up at the first floor windows of the houses, but Min Yuen regularly visited these. They were supposed to watch for police too, but a quick look through the apothecary's door showed him the two on the corner were busy watching the truck driver under his engine and they had noticed nothing.

All this took a second. In the same time, he assessed the damage. The Wild Orchid was no longer a safe house. Worse, Liya was totally compromised. Furious, Ho Peng shoved past the old apothecary into the back of his shop, knocking some vials from a shelf, and pushed through a wood door into the alley behind. For the first time in six years of war with the British he felt hunted.

The Special Branch surveillance team followed Liya out of China-town. The driver of the old Dodge miraculously started the engine again and, as it rumbled off in the same direction, Angus radioed the uniformed police he had kept standing by to arrest her. Two dozen men descended on Liya in three jeeps as she was walking briskly towards the railway station on the east side of the river, to catch a train out of town on to the road to Langat, and bundled her into a police van. The SB surveillance officers melted away in the crowd of curious spectators, their job done, and by the time Edward clambered thankfully out of the stinking hot hide in the middle of the stack of cabbages back in SB HQ, Liya was already in a police cell in Kuala Lumpur's central police station.

Re-loaded, the truck set off again on its legitimate journey to sell Chinese cabbages in Ipoh and Angus and Edward walked across the SB compound between rows of Nissen huts. Angus was delighted with his catch and said, 'Coming to see how she measures up for questioning?'

Edward shook his head, disgusted with himself. After being cooped up in the truck, his clothes were soaking with sweat and he felt dirty, like a voyeur. Angrily trying to be impersonal about her, he said, 'How can a girl like that be a top communist? You heard what they said on the radio.' Liya had offered no resistance to her arrest and said nothing but protest her innocence.

'I'm telling you we've been watching her for months,' said Angus, nettled that Edward was spoiling his moment of triumph. 'Besides, how's she going to explain the grenade they found on her?'

Edward stared at Angus in complete astonishment. Under the Emergency regulations, anyone found carrying arms could be executed. He whispered, 'I don't believe it!'

Angus shrugged and said, 'We'll see. With the death penalty hanging over her, I'm sure she'll spill the beans and help us wrap up the rest of the courier network. Surprising how talkative they become when they're faced with a choice like that. And of course there's reward money for turning in old colleagues. Mercenary lot really.'

Edward knew about police questioning. The idea of Liya being brow-beaten by policemen shouting and cajoling, thinking they were being frightfully clever and knowing nothing, sickened him. 'Just leave out the beatings and the boiled eggs,' he snapped at Angus. 'Or there'll be trouble.' Not at all sure what trouble he could cause, but desperately hoping the threat was enough, he stamped off to his jeep to drive home. He felt drained and filthy, and he needed time on his own to think.

Seven days later Angus called Edward into his office and admitted that Liya had consistently denied everything. She had been moved to Pudu Prison on the corner of Jalan Pudu and Shaw Road, and Edward decided to go and see her. He had thought of nothing else since she was arrested, he had been bad-tempered at work, and terrified Hassan in the house. He told Lao Song the bare facts of what had happened but could say no more. He was simply not able to talk about Liya without being swamped by a mixture of emotions he could not control. He had not realised how much she meant to him until she had been taken away from him.

He used his authority as SBLO to enter the prison, and was escorted by Malay policemen through several barred gates, each one clanging shut behind him with hollow finality.

Liya was in a cell on her own at the end of an empty wing. She was sitting on the teak bench-bed when she heard ringing male steps approaching on the concrete floor. Though she recognised the sound of Edward's step, she kept her face empty of emotion for the warder.

Looking at her through the bars, Edward felt like a stranger. Without taking his eyes off her, trying to see if she was hurt or unwell, he said to the portly Malay warder in charge of the wing, 'Lock me up inside with her, and I'll call you when I've finished.'

The Malay agreed, 'I'll be at the end of the passage if you need me.'

'Need you? D'you think she's dangerous?'

The Malay warder smiled in a smooth well-fed brown face and shook his head, 'I've seen some real villains here, but this one? Not at all, Tuan!'

They listened to him chortling all the way back along the passage, watching each other, Edward standing and Liya sitting quietly on the bench bed, and the formality between visitor and prisoner melted away with the dying prison echoes.

Finally, in the silence, Edward said tentatively in Chinese, 'Liya, darling, how are you? Have they hurt you?'

For answer she flung herself into his arms, sobbing on his chest, saying over and over, 'No, they threatened and tried but they haven't, and I promise you I'm innocent. I promise!'

Edward wrapped her up in his arms, loving her, so small and light, holding her warm body close to his, and experienced a feeling of immense relief. He hated Angus for making him spy on her and the hard uncompromising reality of a Special Branch interrogation. He had tortured himself for days thinking she blamed him.

'You do believe me, don't you?' she asked, her face against his pea-green uniform shirt, making dark stains with her tears.

331

Mark Bles

'Of course, Liya. Of course,' replied Edward soothing her. He gently stroked her hair down her back, feeling the familiar sweep which he loved so much, so feminine and incongruous in the little concrete cell.

Calm again in his arms, she said in a small voice, 'They say I am a courier for the communists.'

'I know,' he replied.

Something flat in his tone made her look up at his face where she saw a shadow of doubt. Not fiercely, she pulled away from him and sat down on the wood bench-bed, saying, 'You don't believe me!'

Hating himself, Edward asked, 'I do! But I have to know the truth!'

She composed herself – as she had done for days when the police asked her endless questions over and over, stupidly asking her to betray other communists for reward money – and waited, knowing what he was going to say.

'Was that you on the beach at Mersing?'

'No.'

'What were you doing in Tanjong Malim?'

'Selling those samples,' she said, her slanting dark eyes wide and full of sadness as she watched him summon the courage for each unnecessary question.

'Have you worked in the jungle for the communists?'

'No.'

'Have you carried messages for Ho Peng?'

She shrugged and said, 'Edward! They are mixing me up with someone else. I'm not what they think! I'm not a beast!'

Edward slumped down on the bench beside her, sure of that, but wishing he knew the truth of all the rest. Knowing his confusion, she said softly, 'You don't really need to ask me all those questions, do you? Haven't the police told you what they've asked me, and my answers.'

Miserably, Edward said, 'What about the grenade they say was found in your grip bag when they arrested you?'

He was not really surprised when she laughed, 'I have no idea how it came to be there! What would I do with a grenade? The police must have put it there.'

Edward nodded hopelessly. The transcripts of her interrogation had proved absurd, a week-long litany of police repetitions and her simple answer to everything was that they had mistaken her for someone else.

332

She wriggled up close to him. He put his arm round her and they sat like lovers on a park bench. For several minutes they said nothing, each content in the other's company, grateful for a moment without the frustration and confusion of speech, as they had so often lain together in bed after making love.

Edward broke the silence and asked in a hollow voice, 'Have they said anything about me?'

She had been expecting the question and guessed how much he hated himself for asking it. 'No,' she said, twisting to look him in the face to convince him, and before he could ask another question, she put her fingers very gently on his mouth and added, 'And I haven't told them.'

She loved him for the relief in his eyes, knowing he could hide nothing from her, and she felt the threat of solitude fade from her life as it always did with him. In total sincerity, she said, 'Do you think I could betray you? Our love has nothing to do with them. It's none of their business. Nothing!'

Almost fiercely, she leaned forward and kissed him. For the first time since the nightmare had torn them apart the week before, they relaxed. A short half-hour passed in which they talked again as they had in the house and forgot the awful pressure of real life. Then their little world was interrupted by the heavy footfalls of the Malay warder coming up the passage, keys jingling at his belt. 'Time's up, Captain Fairfax, sir. These prisoners have got the tea meal now and all visitors must be out for that.'

Edward stood up with his back to the warder and held Liya's hand. Still in Chinese so the Malay could not understand, he said, 'I'll come and see you again if I can, but use Liao Ting-chi if you want to get a message to me.'

'Don't abandon me,' she asked suddenly, her dark eyes big with worry in her pale face. 'They'll execute me for the grenade if they can.'

The words fell on Edward like a sword. Death for possession of a weapon. He caught himself thinking, if only she was guilty, the information she could give would save her.

She seemed to read his mind and said, 'But I'm innocent!' And squeezed his fingers with her own small hand.

The gesture gave him a burst of energy for hope, and, illogically, except by their own intimate rules which excluded the rest of the world, he said, 'I'll do my best!'

On his way out of Pudu Prison, as the gates banged shut behind him, he wondered gloomily what he could possibly do. The threat to execute her was real if the court were to find her guilty, and her sex was no defence. Numerous female CTs had been executed in Pudu Prison during the six-year-old war.

Four weeks later, the trial opened in the Courts of Justice on Mountbatten Road, five minutes down the Jalan Pudu from the prison. The building was a light stone mixture of Victorian colonial and Muslim architecture, with curving Arab windows, chevrons, and domed pendentives reminiscent of a mosque. Inside the courtroom, fans turned slowly under the ceiling and the high walls were painted cool white above gleaming mahogany wood benches, panelling and seats. Liya sat composed but pale in the dock, ignoring a room full of curious spectactors and Press. Everyone knew this attractive young girl was on trial for her life and the public benches were filled with those who had come out of a prurient curiosity to see if she would be executed. Edward sat at one end of a bench where she could see him easily, trying at once to reassure her and pretend to Angus Maclean beside him that he was nothing more than a disinterested observer. Angus sat arms crossed, sure of the outcome, satisfied that Special Branch had done its job and the rest was up to the Courts.

There was no jury. The Sultan and British authorities in Selangor had agreed that a jury of ordinary men, but not women for this was a Muslim country, could be too easily terrorised by the communists. Instead a Judge sat with two specially appointed Assessors and verdicts were reached on a majority vote between the three, each casting his vote of guilty or not guilty. Liya's spirits sank when the three appointed for her trial came into the court and everyone stood up. Not one was Chinese. The Judge was English and the Assessors were a dark-skinned Tamil and a Malay, civilised men, fully aware of the gravity of their task.

The prosecution, a thin Malay lawyer with an immaculate Oxford accent, wasted no time. Briefed by the police report on Liya's interrogations, his aim was to leave no doubt in the minds of the Judge and Assessors that Liya was a Communist Terrorist. He brought seven different Chinese on to the stand, all of whom said they had been CTs in the MRLA, though not in Ho Peng's group, and they all testified that they recognised the defendant as a member of the MRLA.

'But what proof is there?' demanded Liya's defence council, a short Scot called Andrew McBride with red hair and a gentle

Edinburgh burr in his voice. 'The defendant has strenuously denied all these accusations, throughout police questioning. These men are mistaking her for someone else. Is it not the case that each of these men's testimony is equal against hers? One word against another.'

Four of the surrendered CTs said she had carried messages to them and three stated they had seen her in uniform carrying a carbine in the jungles round Langat.

'Can we believe the word of a surrendered terrorist?' asked the Scot with quiet insistence. 'Mustn't we ask why they might give evidence like this? Won't they say anything to prove they have really changed sides?'

'Remember they are all under oath,' interrupted the Judge wagging his finger at McBride.

The prosecuting Malay produced his next witness, Huang Chi-dao, the owner of the Kok Wan Lo General Trading and Hardware Store in Tanjong Malim, who readily said Liya had been going to his store for three years carrying messages for the communists.

'Did you ever see any of the messages?' asked McBride caustically through the translator when it came to his turn to ask questions.

Huang Chi-dao hesitated and admitted, 'No.'

'No!' McBride repeated in a loud, outraged voice.

'Did you ever see any other proof she was a courier?'

Huang Chi-dao had not.

'Then how on earth can you accuse her of being a courier? No further questions of this witness!'

While her young Scottish defence lawyer attacked the Chinese prosecution witnesses one after the other, Liya sat demurely and shook her head in rejection each time she was accused. On the second day, the Malay prosecutor finally called Lao Tang to the witness stand.

'You never told me he had survived!' Edward whispered to Angus.

Angus shrugged, 'You never asked. He took months to recover and after his rehabilitation course he's been working with C. C. Too in Emergency Information Services on Bluff Road. He's done well and they've suspended his Detention Order. Should make a strong witness.'

The Malay prosecutor was unable to say exactly what work Lao Tang now did, as propaganda was classified work, but made much of his transformation from CT to trusted government employee.

335

Like the others Lao Tang testified he had seen Liya in the jungle, armed, in uniform, with Ho Peng. The name created a stir of subdued whispers among the listening public and the Press made notes. Lao Tang repeated the accusations that Liya had been seen in the jungle, armed, and then added, 'She's known Ho Peng for years. I saw her with him during the Japanese occupation.'

Like a short red-haired terrier, McBride was on to him at once; demanding, 'So she fought against the Japanese?'

'Yes,' affirmed Lao Tang, missing the point entirely through the translator. 'That was when she first met Ho Peng, at the end of 1944.'

The Scot faced the two Assessors as he said, 'She was brave enough to risk her life fighting the Japanese. Could you not be mistaken for thinking that you saw her armed in the jungle then, not later as you claim?'

Lao Tang denied it, but the damage had been done. Men like the Tamil and Malay Assessors had lived through the Japanese occupation, because the British had been defeated, and they knew the tortures those prepared to fight the Japanese had risked. When the Judge ordered a recess for lunch, Angus and Edward went to the Coliseum Bar. Willie the barman served them with beer, they sat down at a table in one corner and Angus was furious. 'Bloody fool Lao Tang nearly blew it!'

'I don't think she's guilty,' said Edward doggedly.

Angus snorted. 'You're just taken in by her little girl look. I'm telling you she's as guilty as sin.'

'You regard the whole trial as a formality, don't you?' asked Edward suddenly.

'I do when people like her have been terrorising and killing thousands of people for six years,' said Angus heatedly. 'God! There have been over 4,000 casualties so far, let alone the CTs we've killed, and they're not finished by a long chalk!'

Edward agreed with him, but knowing Liya made him say, 'All right, but look at it the other way around. What if she's innocent?'

Angus snorted again, 'That grenade will settle the issue. Whatever she says, she can't get round that.'

The way Angus made the remark stuck in Edward's mind. When they got back to the Courts, he left Angus talking with some other policemen and went to find the Scottish defence lawyer. They stood in a quiet corner of the hall outside the courtroom and Edward said, 'The police are banking on the grenade.'

336

'Aye,' said the Scot evenly. 'All the other evidence is circumstantial. Only Ho Peng himself can tell us if she's really a courier, and I don't see him turning up.' He laughed. 'But the grenade is fact. Hard to get round.'

'I'm sure it was planted,' said Edward bluntly. Angus's comments over lunch had reminded him of something his black depression had blocked in his mind at the time of her arrest. Angus had said a grenade was found in her grip bag just after they had climbed out of the truck load of cabbages, yet neither had had a chance to speak to anyone else at that moment, nor had anything been said on the radio about it.

The Scot looked interested but said gloomily, 'A fix? I'm sorry to hear it, but it wouldn't be the first time this has happened.'

Edward's hopes sank. 'What d'you mean?' he said.

'The police are all-powerful here and this is the East. None of your wishy-washy British attitudes to Justice here, particularly fighting these bloody commies. With arrest goes the assumption of guilt and it's too easy for them to plant a grenade or even a single bullet on a prisoner to ensure the death penalty under the Emergency Regulations. Only last week, a Judge in this court peered over his specs and noted that, whereas all the grenades flung into cafés frequented by soldiers exploded with devastating results, an unusual number of Chinese brought before the courts had been found with only a single grenade on them and that in each case these grenades had been unprimed.'

'Without the detonator?' said Edward.

McBride nodded. 'Which would make them harmless for the police putting them there. Makes one wonder how many of the Chinese we've executed really were communists at all.'

As he turned to go into the courtroom, Edward stopped him and, knowing the question was hopeless, asked, 'D'you think Liya's innocent?'

The young lawyer looked serious and replied, 'I'm her defence, supplied and paid by the State and I'll do my best. The evidence against her is telling but all superficial, and if the police planted that grenade they have destroyed their own case trying to ensure it. We all know terrorism undermines the very fabric of our society, but fixing Justice is criminal in anyone's code and places us on the same par as the terrorists. What I really believe is that a Judge and two Assessors is no Justice, not even under Emergency Regulations. No-one should be found guilty and executed except through trial before a jury of twelve men and true. Not infallible, but the best the world has produced yet. Not this,' he gestured through the open door at the courtroom. 'Not the bias of three ordinary lawyers.'

'You haven't answered my question,' said Edward quietly.

'As to whether I think she's innocent?' The young Scot looked pensive and replied, 'She's a beautiful girl, calm and intelligent, perhaps too much so. I've spent hours with her, going over the case, but I really don't know what to believe.' He looked Edward right in the eye and said, 'I don't know what your interest is, Captain Fairfax, but I promise you I'll do my best to get her freed.'

The court filled with people, the Judge and Assessors returned and the public settled down. A policeman took the stand and the Malay prosecution lawyer introduced the grenade which the policeman confirmed had been found in the defendant's possession.

The young Scot took over questioning the witness and asked, 'But were her fingerprints found on it?'

The policeman looked uncomfortable and said, 'No'.

'Were anyone else's fingerprints found on this grenade?'

'No,' said the policeman. He mopped his face with a handkerchief and explained himself, 'What I mean is that no fingerprints were taken off the grenade at all.'

Liya's defence looked astonished and said, disbelief ringing in his voice, 'Do you mean to tell the court that this piece of vital evidence found in the defendant's possession was not minutely examined by scene-of-crime officers to prove she had at least held the grenade in her hands?'

'Yes,' said the policeman miserably.

McBride continued in a loud voice, 'So, there is no proof the defendant touched the grenade, as she must have done to have put it in the grip. Is it possible someone else put the grenade in her grip bag?'

The Malay prosecution objected to leading the witness but the implication of police connivance was clear and there was a flurry of activity among the Press.

McBride had no witnesses for the defence until Edward made a suggestion. He went out to the Black Circle New Village himself, without an escort, in his jeep, and drove Ah Chi back to give evidence about the time Ho Peng murdered the four children in the old squatters' village. Ah Chi made an impressive witness. He was an elderly man and an ordinary Chinese, he had been a squatter before land was granted, but he had become headman of the New Village and was leader of the newly-armed Chinese Home Guard. He was the epitome of the changes being made in Malaya and lived at the dangerous crossroads between villagers and the communists. The court listened in total silence as he described how Ho Peng had moved up the line of families until he tore the child from Liya's arms and shot it dead in front of her with the last bullet in his revolver. All doubt faded from everyone's mind when the young defence lawyer asked the rhetorical question, 'Can anyone imagine a young mother willingly working for the communists or a man who murdered her child?'

The Judge and Assessors took until the afternoon of the third day to make up their minds. Edward hardly slept, refused Lao Song's efforts to make him eat and came back to court early. He watched Liya's face, hoping to catch her eye, to give her his support, but she scrupulously avoided looking at him. She continued to sit pale and composed and awaited her fate.

The Judge asked the Assessors for their verdicts.

With great dignity, the Tamil stood up, swept the crowded court room with his dark eyes and announced, 'Not guilty.'

Everyone switched their look to the Malay who said gravely, 'Not guilty.'

Two out of three! Liya flicked a quick glance at Edward and their eyes met. She had won!

'I don't believe it!' Angus hissed angrily beside Edward. He stared furiously at the Assessors.

'I told you I thought she was innocent,' Edward whispered back, hardly able to contain himself.

Angus glared at him.

The Judge banged his gavel for silence and when the noise in the court subsided, he leaned forward and stated, 'I have listened carefully to the evidence of this trial, and while I concede that much of it is superficial, the defence has done nothing more than claim the whole case is one of mistaken identity. Therefore, how the two Assessors as reasonable men came to their opinion I have no means of knowing. I disagree with their decisions and order a re-trial.'

There was a gasp of astonishment from the public benches and several journalists dashed out to file reports. The Judge banged his gavel for silence and declared the trial over. Stunned, Edward stared as Liya was led away, a small sad figure in her white shirt and blue slacks between two large Malay policemen in khaki uniform and shorts. As she turned through the door to the cells beneath the court, she glanced across the room at Edward, her eyes large and sad.

Crushed, Edward burst out, 'He can't do that!'

'Yes, he bloody can,' said Angus emphatically as he stood up. 'That's the law.'

The re-trial was set for two weeks later. Edward was unable to see Liya in Pudu Prison for only McBride was allowed to visit her. He passed her a message of Edward's support. There was nothing more that could be done except go through the whole process all over again.

At the second trial, which lasted three days, the new Judge and one Assessor were British. The other Assessor was Malay. They listened to the same evidence but the prosecution made none of the same mistakes. McBride did his best, even complaining that the whole trial was prejudiced by the publicity there had been in the newspapers. The Judge over-ruled him, but neither Ah Chi's evidence nor the police failure to fingerprint the grenade made the same impact.

When the Assessors stood up to give their verdicts, the Malay, a small man with a round, kindly face, said, 'Not guilty!'

The British Assessor, his face a mask of disinterest, stated 'Guilty!'

Edward felt sick as the Judge summed up, dragging out long minutes of tension. Finally, he announced, 'Guilty!'

Then, without further ado, he put the small black cap on his head and sentenced her to death by hanging.

At once, there was uproar among the packed public benches, everyone talking and shouting together, standing up and gesticulating. They all saw a beautiful young Chinese woman who had been tried in one case after another until found guilty. All of a sudden, British Justice seemed terribly flawed.

Edward sat quite still, in shock, until a journalist and several others tried to shove past, when he stood up and shoved them roughly aside so that he could see Liya across the court. She was already desperately searching for him as the two Malay constables led her away and stared directly at him as soon as he emerged through the mêlée of people in the public galleries. They no longer had to pretend they did not know each other. It was over.

For a short moment they looked at each other straight across the seething courtroom, oblivious of the noise, wanting to say so much which now could never be said. Then the two policemen, worried by the uproar, took her by the arms and hurried her through the little door behind the dock, down to the cells.

Chapter 20

WHITE AREAS

McBride appealed at once against the Judge's decision on the wave of feeling that Liya had not so much been tried but merely suffered as many court sessions as was necessary to find her guilty. His first appeal to the Malayan Supreme Court was dismissed but, while the ikon of British Justice was bitterly attacked in the newspapers in Malaya, Singapore and 9,000 miles distant in England, McBride had the bit between his teeth and lodged another appeal to the Judicial Committee of the Privy Council in London.

In the meantime Liya stayed in Pudu Prison and was allowed no visitors except her lawyer. McBride took her messages of support from Edward, extra food and fresh clothes. Edward excused his unusual interest by swearing the young Scot to secrecy and admitting that she was a source of Army Intelligence. McBride was not entirely convinced, for he had seen the look between them at the end of the second trial, none the less he found it useful to have someone else to talk to about the case. His appeals had made him quite unpopular among members of the law and the ex-patriate British community in Kuala Lumpur.

'So you believe she's innocent, now?' Edward asked him one day when McBride came to the bungalow in Uxbridge Drive after a visit to Liya.

The young Scot stopped flicking through one of the Chinese grammar books lying on a table among a hotch-potch of other books and study papers and said firmly, 'In my experience, evidence often conceals the facts as much as it illuminates them, especially in the East. Whether she's guilty or innocent is not as important for me as the fact that Justice has not been done.'

'So you're more interested in a point of law than in her guilt or innocence?'

Unabashed, McBride replied, 'Without actual proof, like her fingerprints on that grenade or, even better, on the primer which ought to have been inside but wasn't, we are left with conflicting testimonies all given by people with an axe to grind. Police, CTs, and defendant all have quite different perspectives to pursue which stain or even completely prejudice their statements. The lack of a jury makes it worse, placing awful prejudicial pressures on those assessors and the judges. Here in Malaya it's been too easy for the police to arrest anyone at all, plant a single bullet in their pocket, find a few ex-CTs to back them up, and then trust to the Emergency regulations to see the victim hanged for possession of weapons. That's no basis of Justice!'

Good-naturedly, they argued into the night, drinking whisky s'tengahs on the verandah, but Edward persuaded McBride to admit nothing more than, 'From Liya's own perspective, she's innocent, whatever she's done, but if we can't produce a fairer system of Justice to try her properly according to *our* perspectives, then we have no right to condemn her innocence as guilt.'

Liya sent Edward a single written note, written in Chinese, thanking him for everything he had done for her, and telling him she thought of him all the time in her cell. She wrote she had no confidence in the appeal to London and she was sorry she would never see him again. Thoroughly depressed, Edward showed Lao Song the letter that evening. The old Chinese confirmed Edward's translation and observed quietly, 'She really does write well for someone living as she does.'

'She was educated in China, before she came to Malaya,' said Edward. Lao Song had said that to write Chinese well meant starting to learn as soon as a child could speak, at two years old.

'She is plainly an intelligent girl,' Lao Song agreed.

They talked the case over and over that evening, as they seemed to do every day now, and Lao Song tried to comfort Edward by saying, 'In your own way, together, you were as one, you and Liya, but the divide between the good men of your separate villages, who demand so much of each of you and pull you both in such different directions, is no greater now that she is in Pudu Prison than it was when you lay side by side in this house in bed.'

The old man's hooded eyes were not shuttered with unfriendly criticism, but relaxed and honest. Edward knew he was right.

'It doesn't make it any easier to bear, Lao Song.'

Lao Song nodded wisely and said, 'The thieves of virtue have much to answer for in this world.'

Liya had also written to Liao Ting-chi, the actor, thanking him for his help as go-between, and asking him to do a few final jobs for her in Chinatown. Feeling like a priest going to tell relatives of a death in the family, Edward took the letter to the actor's little changing-room on top of the Chinese theatre. Liao Ting-chi was skinny and pale in just a loin cloth to keep cool in the heat before dressing up in a heavy costume as the Duke Choa of Lu for the next performance. He read the note and burst into tears. He gave Edward tea, but he had been smoking opium again, the atmosphere was thick with joss sticks, and his tears kept dripping unchecked on to Liya's note. so Edward was pleased to get away.

A week later Edward was walking home across the grass after work, passing the Tamil 'Swing sisters' scything the lawns as usual, and found a blue airmail letter from Diana waiting for him. Hassan had recognised her writing and left it prominently on its own on the hall-table where Edward normally threw his beret.

He grunted, seeing by the franking date that the letter had taken six weeks to arrive, tore it open and was surprised to read, 'My darling Edward.' She had stopped calling him 'darling' when she left for England. The demotion in favours had never bothered him but after three years he felt as abandoned by Diana as she may ever have felt betrayed by him. The reinstatement was far more worrying. He read on, 'I have been following that dreadful case in Malaya, of the young Chinese girl who has been treated so badly. Of course I'm sure you know all about her appeal to the Privy Council here in London and we all feel that Sir Winston Churchill will treat her fairly, but why are you involved? Your name has been in the newspapers! In *The Times*. Father was rather shocked. "Not good form for a serving officer," he said rather pompously but I must say I rather agree. Especially as I read something about your helping the defence find a character witness for the girl? I immediately thought of your career, and, whatever may have happened between us in the past, I have always done my absolute best for your army career. So I thought about it a long time, talked it over with Father, and I've decided the best thing I could do was come out and join you at once, to show everyone there is nothing in any of these rumours about you and any native girls.'

Edward looked up from the flimsy blue airmail page in his hands, through the sitting-room with its comfortable spread of books about the place, to the verandah and the green garden beyond. He sighed and rubbed the tiredness from his face. 'Hassan!' he shouted down the kitchen passage in Malay, 'Fetch me a Gin Sling!'

He walked into the sitting-room, feeling his life was now as threatened on the inside as it was spoiled on the outside by Liya's imprisonment. He stood by the drawer in the small desk where he had stuffed all Diana's other letters, and read the last lines with a sense of impending doom. 'For the sake of speed, I'll come out by aeroplane,' she wrote. 'There's a lot of fuss about Comets after those crashes near Naples and in the sea off Elba, but Father thinks it's all an American plot to promote Boeing so I'm going to support Britain and fly out by BOAC Comet. I'll be in Malaya in the first week of December and send you advance warning of my arrival time by telegram.'

He became aware of Hassan standing by him with a tray and a long glass of gin. He took it and drank deeply, threw the letter in the drawer and slammed it shut. Hassan turned to go but Edward stopped him and, just to be sure, asked, 'What's the date, Hassan?'

'It is Juma, 3 December,' Hassan replied.

Diana's telegram arrived three days later on Monday from Calcutta. On Tuesday afternoon, Edward drove along Airport Road in the blue Plymouth to meet her at the airfield on the south side of Kuala Lumpur. The plane was two hours late, so Edward passed the time in a Chinese coffee-house just outside the gates, slowly drinking a couple of bottles of Singa beer and chatting to the locals. He went back into the airport when he finally saw the plane coming in to land over the coils of Danette wire on the perimeter fence and disappear with a roar behind the low airport buildings.

Although she had spent days on the journey Diana came through customs in good spirits wearing a broad-brimmed white sun-hat, a blue and white spotted cotton dress and white gloves. She always liked to look her best when travelling. Edward had forgotten how tall and blonde and white-skinned she looked.

She hugged him, feeling his uniform shirt warm and sticky with the sweat on his back.

He kissed her self-consciously and asked, 'Did you have a good flight?'

'Ghastly,' she said, and went into a long explanation of various places through the Middle East and India where they had been obliged to stop to refuel. Edward only half-listened. When her suitcases had been cleared from customs, he drove her back to town.

'D'you remember the car?'

'Of course!' she smiled at him. 'But it's looking a little old now.'

'You've been away a long time.'

'Well, only because you extended your posting.' She had hoped Edward would come back to her in England soon after she had left Malaya.

Edward fell silent, hoping she would not press for an argument. She said, 'You don't seem very pleased to see me?'

'I'm sorry,' he said, avoiding the question. 'We've been very busy and I'm a bit tired.'

'I'm the one supposed to be suffering from jet-lag,' she said.

The pungent aroma of satay roasting on an open brazier on the side of the road filled the car as they drove through town. It reminded Diana of the first time they had driven from the railway station to their new quarter in Uxbridge Drive, six years before. 'D'you see that old taxi driver still?'

'Gandra Singh?' Edward asked, pleased she had remembered. 'Yes, from time to time. He's still around and talkative as always.'

'All the same stories of the Punjab?'

'Of course,' said Edward cheerfully.

'And what about Hassan and Mr Song?'

'Hassan is ever faithful,' he said, but no-one had called Lao Song 'Mr Song' for three years, so he added firmly, emphasising the 'Lao', 'And Lao Song has been helpful beyond the call of duty.' Or friendship, he nearly added, but there was so much Diana had missed that he could not expect her to take it all in at once.

Diana said nothing. She had promised herself to do her best to cope with the situation in Malaya and had set her mind for the worst.

Instead, when she walked into the house, her spirits soared. A huge bunch of flowers Hassan had picked on Edward's suggestion stood in a big vase on the hall table. Delighted, she was admiring the mixture of gladiolus, Lantana and sniffing the fragrant Ginger Lilies when she became aware how much everything had changed. She walked into the sitting-room and stared round in amazement. Knowing Edward might be sensitive to her criticism, she said lightly, 'I can see you've been spreading about.'

'What d'you mean?' said Edward standing in the door.

347

'Well,' she began, waving her hand about. A single armchair was the only place to sit not piled with books, newspapers or maps of Malaya. Edward and Lao Song always sat on the verandah when they talked. Inside, they used a table at the back of the sitting-room where he was teaching Edward how to write Chinese characters. It was covered with ink pots, brushes and bits of paper where he had been practising. Lamely, she asked, 'What's happened to your study?'

'This is where I live,' said Edward simply. 'Did you really think I was going to hide away in a room in the corner of an empty house?'

The remark convinced her she had done the right thing by coming back. Suddenly contrite, she said, 'You must have been very lonely but, don't worry, I'm sure you'll feel better when you get used to having a woman's touch about the house again.'

Edward doubted it, but Hassan appeared behind him and Diana greeted him warmly, pleased to see his smiling welcome. 'And Lao Song?' she asked, glancing at Edward to check he had noticed her determination to fit in.

Hassan certainly noticed and said happily, 'Yes indeed, Memsahib Punjang. Song is still here too.'

In Malay, Edward said, 'Hassan, go and see if Lao Song can spare a moment to come and see the Mem now she's back.'

Diana frowned, thinking she would be excluded again in her own house by language. Lao Song appeared suddenly, soft-footed up the kitchen passage in his cloth shoes where he and Hassan had been listening when they heard the Plymouth arrive in the drive outside. He bowed very slowly and with great dignity and said in clear English, 'We are very honoured to have you back in our country, Mrs Fairfax.'

'I'm pleased that I came back,' said Diana with pleasure, matching Lao Song's old-fashioned text-book English where she felt safe.

'A great commitment from so far away,' said Lao Song gravely.

The old Chinese's grammar was so accurate Edward could restrain himself no longer. In spite of having set up the little scene in English with Lao Song, just to set Diana at ease, he interrupted with a burst of Chinese, 'Lao Song! What's this about "our" country?'

'I have applied for Malayan citizenship!' replied Lao Song also in Chinese. 'Only today while you were at the airport! So many of my fellow Chinese from the mainland have taken advantage of the offer of Malayan citizenship, so now I have decided to make a new life here too.'

348

'That's wonderful,' said Edward delighted. 'D'you realise over a million Chinese have done this already?'

'More than sixty per cent of all those from the mainland,' agreed Lao Song. He had examined the advantages and disadvantages with academic thoroughness before making up his mind. 'Citizenship will matter. We will have an effective vote. The country's first elections, which General Templer announced in May, will take place next year and the elected politicians will have the majority over the nominated members in the Federal Legislative Council. That is the start of real democracy.'

'What on earth are you two talking about?' Diana interrupted icily, sure the stream of Chinese in front of her was deliberate.

To her surprise Lao Song smiled and explained very carefully in English. He finished by saying, 'My soul lives in China, my esteemed Mrs Fairfax, with the spirits of my family whose graves I can never visit again, but from now on I will be a Malayan.'

'Congratulations, Lao Song,' said Diana smiling vaguely. She had no idea what he was talking about but if her cook was going to speak English, even to call her 'esteemed', she would agree to call him 'Lao'.

Lao Song bowed slightly, serious again and padded back to the kitchen with Hassan following, grinning with pleasure that Lao Song wanted to be the same as him. A Malayan.

Edward and Diana had dinner together but she went to bed early, exhausted after her long flight. Edward sat alone on the verandah, listening to the cacophony of geckos and night insects, the delicious smell of Hassan's Moon flowers thick in his nostrils, and thought of Liya locked in her cell. Lao Song came along the verandah from his quarters by the kitchen and asked in English, 'Shall I join you?'

'I've been waiting for you, Lao Song,' said Edward in Chinese, deliberately standing up as a mark of deference to his teacher. 'We always spend the evenings together.'

'Hasn't life moved on another step?' asked Lao Song quietly, a slight smile in the line of his hooded eyes.

Edward glanced at the wisps of white hair on the old man's head and smiled back. They understood each other well, as professor and student and as friends. He said, 'I suppose it has, but I value our conversations in Chinese too highly to conform altogether.'

Lao Song's smile wrinkled his entire face and he said, 'But women are like farmers and men are their farm. They like to cultivate every little piece themselves.'

349

'Only perhaps in China,' retorted Edward, grinning. 'In England the British are an amateur lot, in spite of what they like to think, and we leave a lot to nature. I suppose Diana will move things about again, but there'll always be a rough patch of ground in my house where you and I can talk unmolested.'

Lao Song bowed his head slightly, acknowledging the new situation and said more seriously, 'I'm pleased but beyond our retreat I feel that time is running out.'

Early the following morning, the telephone rang as Edward was shaving. He walked through the bedroom wiping his face with a towel. Safely inside the tent of mosquito netting, Diana was still asleep in bed, long and voluptuous on her side, her fair hair spread over the white sheets, such a contrast to Liya. He picked up the phone in the hall and said, 'Hallo?'

'Edward? Sorry to bother you so early. Some important news.'

Edward recognised the voice and said, 'What's the matter, Angus?'

'That girl Liya. She's escaped from Pudu Prison.'

Edward was stunned. He asked, 'Are you sure?'

'Of course I'm bloody sure!' snapped Angus.

'I'm sorry,' said Edward. He needed a moment to control his excitement. He asked, 'What happened?'

'She persuaded a fat-bottomed Malay warder to show her a way out of the prison, through the kitchens.'

The cheerful overweight Malay would have been easily flattered by Liya, but Edward said, 'What d'you mean by persuaded?'

'Bribed,' stated Angus. 'He was found drunk in a dirty little hotel this morning in bed with two whores and $10,000 in his trouser pockets. God knows where she got the money. That girl must have some really special friends to pay that much to get her out.'

Edward agreed, puzzled. 'If that's right, I'm not surprised. I don't suppose they believed her appeal to the Privy Council in London would cut much ice. Justice has been looking pretty sick hereabouts recently.'

'You mean the grenade?' said Angus.

'That and other things,' said Edward coldly. The police were under pressure for results in the Emergency but his feelings about Angus had changed.

'Maybe,' Angus conceded, but Edward's understanding of Special Branch work, not to say his language ability, was invaluable and he said, 'But that's why I'm calling. I wanted to tell you myself that

350

she's escaped.' He swore, deliberately, 'God, I don't blame her, given the chance, but she doesn't look quite so innocent now, does she?'

Not to you, perhaps, Edward thought when the conversation ended and he slowly put the phone back on its cradle. He finished dressing absorbed with wondering where Liya had gone. Was she in Kuala Lumpur? Or in the jungle? Had she gone north, or south? He somehow doubted the police would find her and decided to make his own enquiries.

However, he had a busy morning at the Headquarters, briefing the Selangor State War Executive Committee on the security situation. An important item on their agenda was whether or not Langat could be declared the next 'White Area'. General Templer had decided that parts of Malaya could be designated 'White' as soon as they were free of all communist activity, overt or covert, rather than wait till the whole country was freed. The telling incentive for this accolade was that inside these areas all the tiresome Emergency restrictions, especially those about food, were lifted and normal life could be resumed. In September the year before, the first White Area had been successfully pioneered in Malacca on the coast. A few months later, in January 1954, Trengganu was declared White, as the communists were easier to exclude from coastal areas, but parts of Perlis, Kedah and, in March, Negri Sembilan followed suit and soon several hundred thousand Malayans, Chinese, Malays and Tamils, were all enjoying freedom again, and road signs declaring 'You are now entering a White Area' were commonplace.

The Chairman of the Selangor SWEC in Kuala Lumpur was Datuk Mohammad Razak, who knew Edward well and had graduated from the Langat District War Executive Committee. He had a particular interest in Langat where he had property but he thanked Edward for his summary and spoke for everyone when he said, 'We would all like to see a town so close to our Federal Capital of Kuala Lumpur declared "White", but as long as the guerrilla leader Ho Peng is in the Ulu Langat I don't see how we can risk it.'

All civil and military affairs were decided by these War Executive Committees and General Templer had galvanised them, sacking several members to prove the point. Mohammad Razak's committee voted in unanimous agreement with his view on Langat and went straight on to other business so that Edward was able to get away by midday.

He went back to the house and disappointed Diana, who thought he had come back to see her, by saying he had to go out again for lunch. He changed from his uniform into a white shirt and trousers and drove into the centre of town in the blue Plymouth. He parked outside the Coliseum Bar and walked in to find Marsha Tallard was waiting for him. He had not dared tell Diana, but the arrangement had been made before he had even received her airmail letter. Marsha was on one of her trips to town again for ten days while Sean Tallard was away and she had phoned to say she was desperate to see him, purely about security, she said.

Edward picked up a beer and a Gin Sling from Willie the barman and they found a secluded table in a corner of the room against the dark mahogany panelling.

They drank each other's health, pleased to see each other and, smiling, he teased her, 'You going to try and seduce me again?' She was as pretty, slim and tanned though her fair hair was cut shorter than he remembered it.

'I'd love to, honey,' she drawled in her husky voice. Edward was looking lean and fit and there was a frightening hardness behind his smile. Then her eyes clouded over, a wry little smile edged the corners of her mouth and she said, 'But that's not why I wanted to see you.'

'Pity,' he said frivolously. He noticed a strained look in her eyes and said, 'Okay, how can I help?'

'The house is still being shot up, sometimes twice a week, and Sean won't move.'

'Ho Peng?'

'You got it, in one,' she said pursing her lips.

'I thought you had some Police Auxiliaries out there to guard you?'

'They can't stop Ho Peng!' she said desperately. 'They're just not in the same league. We've had infantry patrols laying ambushes too, but somehow he just sneaks through and shoots the house to shit.' She drank deeply from her Gin Sling. 'You should see the place now! Sean has given up trying to hide the sandbags or repair the bullet holes in the walls. It's like the goddam Alamo!'

Edward broke the conversation to order steaks which Mr Wong cooked and brought over. As they ate, he asked, 'Why is Ho Peng taking the risk of attacking the same place over and over?'

Marsha shook her head, 'I don't know. Sean has been nearly killed several times. He never says where he's going to be next, so I

352

never know myself when I'll see him next or even if I will. That armoured car has saved his bacon several times out in the rubber.'

'What about you?' Edward asked, watching her face carefully.

'Meaning?' she replied cautiously, thinking he wanted to know what had happened when Ho Peng had burst into the house. To her relief, he merely said, 'Are they after you or Sean?'

'I've never thought of it,' she admitted. 'I take it pretty personally when they blast my house to bits every week, but now you mention it, I guess they're really after Sean.' She paused. 'Is there a special reason behind the question?'

Edward shook his head. 'A suspicion only. Since I found out years ago that Sean and Ho Peng worked together during the war, I've been sure there's a connection. Why d'you think Ho Peng didn't just kill you both when he stormed into your house?'

Marsha said nothing.

'Because he wanted to talk to Sean.'

'Talk!' Marsha exclaimed, thinking of what the other three CTs had done to her.

Edward nodded, 'The three CTs took you out, leaving Ho Peng and Sean together. Question is, what were they talking about?'

Marsha shook her head. 'I don't know. He never discusses the war, or Ho Peng. That's my trouble. I don't know what's going on and I'm scared to death. We should leave, but Sean refuses. He's so goddam obstinate!' All her worry and fear surfaced abruptly through her tough American façade of self-control and she began to cry. 'Goddamit! Now look at me,' she said angrily, and began fussing in her handbag for a handkerchief.

It suddenly occurred to Edward that her frustration was not for herself, but because she wanted to save her husband, to make him leave the 'Black Circle'. In some surprise he said, 'You're really very fond of Sean, aren't you?'

'I love the fat oaf,' she snapped back, dabbing her face. 'He's a rude bastard, he's rough with me, he plays away, but I don't want to lose him.' She looked up at Edward and grabbed his hand, 'That's the trouble. I've always been able to persuade myself the communists in the jungle never really meant any harm by their attacks. God knows, they're such bad shots! But now, I'm convinced they've changed their tack. These latest attacks have been real mean. Now Ho Peng is trying to kill him!'

Edward noticed Willie the barman hanging about with a piece of paper in his hand, and he called him over, to give Marsha time to compose herself. In Chinese, he said, 'Something for me, Willie? Or Mrs Tallard?'

'For you, Tuan,' said Willie, bowing obsequiously as he interrupted. He passed Edward a sheet of cheap writing paper, folded twice. 'A small boy off the street came in and said to give it to you.'

'Thanks, Willie,' said Edward. While Marsha tidied her face with powder and lipstick, he unfolded and read it.

Marsha snapped shut her compact, her moment of self-pity over, and said admiringly, 'Your Chinese sounds real fluent.' She glanced at the note and caught a shadow of surprise on Edward's face. 'Everything all right?'

'Fine, fine,' said Edward distantly and slipped the note in his trouser pocket.

The rest of lunch passed quickly. Edward promised her that he would arrange for the local infantry unit to increase their patrolling. 'I'll press for a real concentration of effort on the jungle round Langat,' he said. 'It's time we nailed that bastard Ho Peng.'

After coffee, Edward said, 'You here in Kuala Lumpur long?'

'Another couple of days,' she answered, her voice mellow after a couple of Gin Slings. 'You want to meet up?' There was no doubting her meaning, but Edward shook his head. His life was already too complicated. 'Diana's back now.' Marsha pulled a face so he said, 'Why not take the car? Beats taxis and gives you a bit of freedom.' He felt sorry for Marsha, stuck out by the jungle's edge with Tallard, terrified to leave her house for fear of being killed. 'I've got something to do this afternoon and I'd rather take a taxi from here, but I'd love you to use the Plymouth.'

She smiled happily, saying, 'Sure! Why not? I'd like that. Remind me of the States back home. You get on if you're busy. I'll take my time here.' She smiled wickedly and whispered, 'Maybe we can get together when you take the car back?'

He left her and Willie the barman let him call Gandra Singh from the telephone behind the bar. As always, the battered old Austin taxi appeared in minutes, as if Gandra Singh waited exclusively for Edward's custom.

'I am very pleased to see you, Sahib,' announced Gandra Singh, his beard now whiter than ever against his dark skin. 'Where are we off to now?'

'You remember you dropped me once near the Chinese Theatre?'

Gandra Singh nodded his head and let in the clutch rather suddenly, flinging Edward back on to the creased leather seat. 'I remember very well, Sahib,' he said, hooting his horn as he negotiated a path between a trishaw and a towering logging truck.

'Wait for me,' said Edward when Gandra Singh dropped him. 'I may have somewhere else to go.'

'Of course, Sahib,' replied Gandra Singh. He leaned back and slipped his bare feet out of his old shoes to give his toes some fresh air.

Edward walked briskly through Chinatown keeping his eyes open. The note said Liao Ting-chi wanted to see him, and he was convinced the actor had a message for him from Liya, but he was careful to make a couple of stops and false turns to see if anyone was following him. He had been too long in Malaya to be caught out by an ambush. Instead of turning into the alley beside the theatre at once, he ducked into a small coffee-shop opposite and watched the place while he drank a bottle of warm Coca-Cola.

The street was busy, filled with Chinese in vests and shorts, in sandals and barefoot, pushing barrows or bent under sacks of merchandise, on bicycles or trishaws. He could see a patrol of police along the street and several soldiers in jungle green uniforms with their rifles, but no-one appeared to be watching him. Soon impatience to see Liao Ting-chi and hear what had happened to Liya overcame his caution. He paid, crossed the street and walked under the archway into the theatre yard.

Working on the idea that speed would save him if he were walking into an ambush, he took his Walther out of his pocket and ran into the alley. Turning the corner, he cannoned into a Chinese coming the other way, knocking him off his feet. Edward nearly shot him, instantly suspicious of a set-up, but the man, wearing just a pair of black shorts, sprawled headlong, half stunned on the alley wall, his face badly bloodied. Edward recognised him as the Chinese he had seen smoking heroin with Liao but he seemed to be recovering so Edward ran on. He took the rickety staircase three at a time and reached Liao Ting-chi's changing-room in seconds.

As usual, he banged on the door and went in. He was nearly sick. Liao's throat had been cut. His thin body, half-naked in his underpants, lay as if it had been draped like a rag doll over his canvas chair in front of his mirror, where he had been painting his face, with his head hanging grotesquely back and his scrawny neck virtually severed. Edward guessed that he had struggled desperately as he died, for the little changing-room was covered with blood, glistening red on his skinny torso, streaking the mirror, spattering

355

the pots of make-up on the shelves and darkly staining the gold satin costume he had been going to wear.

Edward shoved outside on to the tarmac roof, choking on the thick stench of blood and joss sticks, and breathed deeply. The hot Malayan air in Chinatown, reeking of frying, ginger and drains, had never smelled so sweet.

As he caught his breath he noticed a blood-soaked T-shirt flung down the side of Liao's cabin. He frowned and remembered the Chinese he had knocked down in the alley. The blood on his face must have been Liao's.

Edward ran back down the wood stairs and sprinted through the theatre. The man had gone. Edward stopped under the theatre entrance arch and looked up and down the street, knowing it was pointless. The Chinese was lost in the crowd. Not that it mattered. Liao Ting-chi was dead and Liya gone.

He thought of the Wild Orchid, but she would never go back after being arrested leaving there, and if she tried to enter the Black Circle New Village, she would be picked up by the Home Guard at the gates. She was on the run, the police had already put her on the wanted list and now that Liao Ting-chi had been murdered, Edward had no means of contacting her. He wondered if he would ever see her again.

He walked slowly back to Gandra Singh and called the police. The CID arrived and treated the murder as a civil case. They knew Liao Ting-chi was a homosexual actor and, back on the theatre roof, the CID police lieutenant shrugged dismissively when Edward mentioned heroin. 'Probably paid for one kick with the other,' he said. 'Maybe one of his boyfriends got jealous.' He gave Edward a funny look and added, 'Why d'you come up here, eh?'

Expecting this, Edward ignored the implication and explained his job in Intelligence, which seemed to satisfy the police officer. He turned to watch his team busy inside Liao's changing room.

Edward volunteered nothing else, but it was late afternoon when he left them busily sliding Liao's body into a plastic bag, and Gandra Singh drove him home.

He paid off the Sikh who laboriously turned his old taxi in the cul-de-sac and drove off in the dusk. Inside, he found Diana sitting on the sofa as he remembered her from years before. He was not surprised to see she had cleared away most of his books, not completely, but stacked them into neat piles on the tables. He was too drained to make a fuss. It could wait. Besides, she was listening to the radio, with a whisky s'tengah in her hand, and seemed on edge.

He looked at his watch and said with strained flippancy, 'Drinking early? Sun's hardly over the horizon.'

'I needed it,' she said, aloof.

'You all right?' Edward asked, looking at her more closely.

'No!' she suddenly burst out. 'If you really want to know, I'm in a state! I've been back here five minutes and already you're cavorting with that bloody Tallard woman!'

To her surprise, Edward looked astonished. When she expected lies, he answered with complete frankness, 'How on earth did you find out about Marsha?'

'I thought I could help you by coming out again, but God knows, I don't know why I bloody bothered!'

'I had lunch with her,' said Edward. A vision of Liao Ting-chi's bloody corpse flicked through his mind and left him feeling rather detached. He slumped exhausted into an armchair. 'At her suggestion. That's all. The CTs keep shooting at them out there on the "Black Circle" and she wanted help. She's terrified actually.' He thought Diana would understand that.

'Well, how come she was driving our car?' asked Diana, a little mollified. She could see he was under strain.

In a tired voice Edward answered, 'Tallard's away and she's on her own in town. I had something else to do and I thought she'd like to use the car. Give her some freedom and cheer her up a bit.' He checked himself and asked, 'What the hell's all this about?'

Diana took a deep drink of her whisky and finally admitted, 'It didn't cheer her up at all. She was driving the Plymouth along the Batu Road when a Chinese came up behind the car on a motorbike and shot her through the window.'

Shocked, Edward whispered, 'What?'

'She's in the General Hospital on Jalan Pahang, seriously ill after emergency surgery, but she'll live,' said Diana. She did not like Marsha Tallard but she felt sorry for her and was beginning to realise Edward had been telling the truth.

'When did this happen?'

'This afternoon.'

'Yes, but what time?' Edward snapped. He wanted to know exactly.

'At two-thirty, just after lunch. Angus Maclean came here looking for you and told me.'

'I better ring him,' said Edward automatically but he sat rooted in his chair trying to work out how the ambush had been planned.

After a moment Diana told him, articulating what he feared, as if she were reading his mind, 'Presumably they thought she was you.'

Edward focused on her at that, stood up and went to call Angus on the phone in the hall. Thankfully, Angus was still in his office and immediately gave Edward a complete description, filling out the detail. He said, 'You were set up.'

'I know,' said Edward shortly. It was not a nice feeling.

Angus continued, 'The bastard was told to shoot the person driving your blue Plymouth, since no-one else but you drives it. However, Marsha's hair is so short and the windows of the Plymouth at the back aren't very deep, so he didn't even notice he'd shot a woman till he had passed the car. By that time he had already emptied his revolver through the window.'

'How d'you find out all that so fast?' asked Edward.

'I'd like to pretend the Special Branch is omnipotent,' said Angus 'but unfortunately for him, the little bastard was knocked off his motorbike by another car and a Sikh traffic policeman jumped on him.'

'And you interrogated him?'

'Aye,' said Angus cheerfully. 'He was quite co-operative.'

'Not another boiled egg?'

'Not necessary,' retorted Angus in a hurt tone of voice. 'He knows very well his only chance of avoiding the hangman's rope is to give us everything.'

'Who briefed him?'

Angus paused, wishing he could see Edward's face and said, 'He says he was given a written instruction, so he doesn't know.'

It made sense. That way the police could not find the next person in the chain.

'Any ideas?' Angus asked after a moment's silence. His voice was up-beat, inviting answers, suggesting they should forget the arguments between them about Liya's case. They both knew the war went on and Edward needed his help. He told Angus about Willie the barman giving him a note and said, 'They probably watch the Coliseum all the time. That boy was sent in with the note to make me drive towards the junction where the murderer was waiting. They obviously never thought I would leave by taxi and let Marsha take the Plymouth.'

'What was in the note?'

Edward had been expecting this question. Angus wanted to know why he should react to a note at all, and Edward had to tell him, not least because Angus would eventually see the CID police report about the murder. 'Liao Ting-chi was the link to my source,' said Edward and explained how he had last seen him.

'Not very nice,' said Angus thoughtfully. 'Why d'you think they killed him?'

Edward had racked his brains for a reason and decided the facts spoke for themselves. He said, 'Someone rumbled us, Angus. Probably watched how we set up meetings and decided to rub us all out.'

'Sounds as though your source was more of a risk to the enemy than we thought.'

'It's too late now,' said Edward in a flat voice.

'So Red Dragon is over?'

'Gone.' said Edward. With Liao Ting-chi dead and Liya hunted by the police, he had given up any idea of seeing her again. He had to begin to forget her.

Outside the house, the sun had gone down, the frogs and crickets were building up a volume of ululating inducements to find a mate and bats swooped over the garden. In the clump of jungle beyond the ditch, palms drooped in the warm night air and stirred as Liya stepped out of the deep shadow under the tree into the moonlight.

She had hidden in the clump since early that morning, after escaping from the prison, and was waiting patiently to see Edward. After what he had done for her during her trials, she was sure he felt the same way about her as she felt about him, and she wanted his help. She had no idea what he could do for her, but she had decided at last that her life must change.

Stepping softly through the long grass and scrub, she set off towards the lighted windows of the bungalow which she could see beyond the shrubs in the garden. She walked slowly, stopping frequently, like an animal afraid of being seen. She waited at the ditch on the edge of the garden, then, when she was sure no-one was about, she jumped over and moved across the lawn towards the verandah.

When Edward put the phone down after talking to Angus, he went back to Diana in the sitting-room where she had a whisky s'tengah waiting for him. He accepted the truce, thanked her and drank deeply.

She watched him, seeing the tension in his face, and said, 'I was listening to you, trying to understand the life you've been living here.'

He smiled and said, 'It's not always like this.'

'It's been awful this afternoon waiting for you to come back, not knowing where you were, knowing there was violence out there.' She walked over to the french windows and stared into the black night. Whatever she did she would always feel a stranger in Malaya. 'It's what I always dreaded about this place.'

Outside, in the shadows, Liya froze, one small foot poised to take her weight on the bottom verandah step. The fragrance of the white stephanotis climbing up the pillar mocked her as she watched Diana's shadow cast across the verandah boards and rattan chairs where she and Edward had sat happily together on so many evenings. Stunned, she listened to Diana talking, not really understanding the English but recognising the sympathetic tone. When she heard Edward's familiar deep voice inside the house her heart died inside her. All the hope she had built up during her time in prison suddenly and painfully shrivelled away. She took her foot off the bottom step and walked back across the lawn.

Later, after dinner, Hassan finished the washing-up in the kitchen and said to Lao Song, 'Song, when you become a citizen of Malaya, will you stay here as a cook?'

The old man liked Hassan and his face wrinkled in a slight smile. He said, 'Yes, but only as long as Captain Fairfax.'

'Because he is your student?'

'Because he is my friend,' corrected Lao Song with professorial majesty. He added, 'And you, Hassan?'

Hassan's brown eyes looked sad but he replied, 'I will stay!' He did not want the Tuan to leave, but he felt safe in the army quarters, away from the bustle of town. Lao Song nodded slowly and Hassan slipped out into the night.

He had been torturing himself with questions all evening, after hearing the Tuans talking quietly at supper, seeming to understand each other again. He padded briskly barefoot over the lawn, round the house to the window of their bedroom. He circled the Clerodendron bushes and stopped dead. A figure was already there, sitting bolt upright in the moonlight cross-legged on the warm grass. He nearly ran, terrified, then his eyes accustomed themselves to the dark. He made out Liya's slim shape and recognised her long black hair which he so admired hanging down her back.

Instinctively, he understood. She was like him, thwarted and tortured with apprehension for what might happen inside the bedroom. He felt a warm rush of sympathy for her and sat down in the shadow of the Clerodendrons out of her way, knowing how she must feel.

But there was no magic in the Pagoda flowers of the Clerodendron that night. There were no secret sounds from the bedroom which Hassan had come to hear.

He was nodding half asleep when she stood up and glided silently towards him. She dropped something in his hand, putting a finger to her lips, close enough for him to see the tears glistening on her cheeks in the moonlight, then she passed on, like a wraith into the darkness.

Each light step she took felt heavy as Fate.

Chapter 21

HEART OF GOLD

Sean Tallard's murder at the 'Black Circle' was scarcely mentioned in the newspapers. Malaya was absorbed with the build-up to the first ever democratic elections billed for the end of July 1955. There was a new sense of optimism that eventually the CTs would be defeated, that the British would leave, and Malaya be governed by the Malayans. Besides, there had been so many deaths. Tallard was just one of 2,000 civilians who had died in seven years of war.

For six months, the special army operations which Edward had promised Marsha had kept Ho Peng away from the jungle round the 'Black Circle'. The infantry company based at Camp Rideau had patrolled the jungle endlessly, they had laid countless ambushes and painstakingly reduced Ho Peng's group by fifteen for the loss to themselves of only a few wounded. The British Army had learned much about fighting in the jungle, but Ho Peng himself always escaped with a hard core of his bodyguards.

During the election preparations, extra security demands were made on the troops and less time could be spent 'jungle-bashing' around Langat. The CTs took full advantage. They came back to the 'Black Circle' one night, dug three Japanese anti-tank mines under the road between Tallard's house and the offices, and in the morning, just after dawn, they blew his armoured car off the road into the lallang grass as he accelerated down the hill to work. To make certain, they threw four hand-grenades inside the wrecked cab of the steel 'Monster' before the Special Constables in their quarters in the offices could react, and vanished back into the jungle. Later, a new Sikorsky S-55 Whirlwind helicopter arrived with a tracking team and a doctor who could do nothing more than pack Sean

Tallard's tattered remains into a plastic body bag and fly them back to Kuala Lumpur.

Marsha Tallard was on holiday in America, still recuperating from her wounds, and she missed her husband's funeral which took place the next day. Edward and Diana, Angus Maclean and a number of other planters sweated in the mid-morning sun in the churchyard of the Roman Catholic St John's Cathedral, off Jalan Weld, and watched Sean Tallard's coffin lowered into ground.

Late that afternoon the sky darkened and rain poured down continuously. Diana had repossessed the sitting-room and Edward's books and papers now occupied a large room he called his study in the corner of the house near the kitchen, which he had accepted as Lao Song was close by for advice when he took time to practise his Chinese script.

Edward passed by Diana reading a book in the sitting-room, stepped through the french windows and sat down in his rattan chair on the verandah. He stared mesmerised by the dark curtains of water cascading on to the lawns outside the overhanging roof. The rain glistened in the yellow light of the weak electric bulbs over the verandah and beat incessantly on the roof above.

Silent under the noise of the rain, Lao Song padded along the verandah from his quarters near the kitchen and sat down in his usual chair, facing the garden. 'You are thinking of the past?' he asked, breaking into Edward's reverie.

'I suppose funerals do that to you,' said Edward in Chinese, turning round to face him. 'Don't you think they're really vehicles for self-pity, regrets and lost memories?'

'Of friends, especially.'

Edward shrugged, 'I don't know that Tallard was a friend, but he taught me about the jungle and started my interest in Malaya.'

'I didn't mean Mr Tallard,' said Lao Song, his wrinkled face inscrutable.

Edward looked at his old teacher and smiled. Lao Song knew him so well. 'You mean Liya?'

Lao Song put his long fingers together and nodded. Edward had refused to let Diana change the verandah. The bamboo chairs had become symbols of times past when Liya had sat with them chatting on the verandah and stayed the night. Lao Song and Edward often talked about her, wondering where she was or what she was doing. Occasionally, Diana listened to the soft rhythm of their speech through the french windows but she understood no Chinese and

Edward talked freely, treating their evening chats as confessional, or therapy, Lao Song as priest.

A movement outside in the rain caught Lao Song's eyes and he said, 'We have a visitor.'

He pointed and Edward whipped round, his heart thumping, expecting to see Liya. Instead, a short stocky Chinese emerged out of the rain and stood on the bottom step just inside the overhang of the roof, water dripping off him. His clothes, a shirt and long slacks, were plastered wet to his wiry body and his short black hair stuck up in damp spikes. Watching Edward like a snake, he wiped his face with a large roughened hand and asked in Chinese, 'You are Captain Fairfax?'

He took another step up to the verandah, his plimsoles squelching. Edward sat quite still, half knowing who he was, but Lao Song spoke first and said quietly, 'This is Comrade Ho Peng.'

Ho Peng nodded in Lao Song's direction but without taking his eyes off Edward and announced, 'I've come to give myself up. To you Captain Fairfax, because I think you are a just person.'

Edward stared at Ho Peng, at his sharp black eyes and his pocked skin, at his overlarge hands hanging loose by his sides and the way he stood poised to run, like an animal, and he thought of all the murders Ho Peng had committed, of the children at the squatters' village, of Liya's child, of soldiers, police, Sean Tallard only the day before, and countless others. Yet he looked so ordinary.

Conversationally, Edward said, 'You'd better sit down. Tell me about it.'

To Edward's surprise, Ho Peng smiled, showing a mouthful of rotten teeth. Like anyone in a cafe, he pulled out the third bamboo chair, which Liya had always used, sat down and said briskly, 'You ask the questions, Captain Fairfax, and I'll answer.'

Edward asked, 'Why have you decided to surrender?'

Ho Peng shrugged his thin shoulders and replied, 'I've given up working for those communist people. They're no good. And you're winning anyway.'

Edward was stunned. The sheer scale of the volte-face was breathtaking. The last person he had expected to surrender was Ho Peng, who had successfully avoided every effort to trap him and continued to counter-attack at every opportunity, like a true soldier. He asked, 'What about your Communism?'

Ho Peng replied without hesitation. 'What is dead or no longer appropriate should be ruthlessly excised and cast away.'

365

'New life and new quotations!' observed Lao Song drily. 'That quote is from the teachings of Confucius, not Mao Tse-tung.' He had been watching Ho Peng carefully and added, 'Are you hungry, Ho Peng?'

The look in Ho Peng's eyes was answer enough. The endless patrols and ambushes round the villages, and now in the deep jungle as well, had kept him on the move and made food supply by the Min Yuen very dangerous indeed. He had been living largely off what his group could find in the jungle and he was starved.

Lao Song excused himself and walked slowly off to his kitchen to prepare food.

Still grappling with the scale of Ho Peng's turn-round, Edward asked simply, 'Why come in now?'

'The Communist General-Secretary Chin Peng, leader of the MCP and MRLA, left Malaya for good two years ago in 1953,' answered Ho Peng his voice thick with disgust. 'He fled over the border to Thailand on a pretext of directing the war from there. That was bad enough, but just recently, he wrote a letter to the Planters Association suggesting a peace conference. That was nothing less than an admission of failure and defeat. The communists will never win.'

'What happened to the bright new future he promised us all in 1948?'

Ho Peng smiled easily and went on, 'The communists have lost for lack of resources. Right from the start I told Chin Peng we needed money and supplies.'

'Because you were on the Central Military Committee?' asked Edward, showing off to suggest Intelligence already knew a good deal.

Unconcerned, Ho Peng agreed, 'You knew that from those papers you found in the jungle camp. You will also have read I was involved in raising finance for the Party. Chin Peng told me we could raise dollars from the tappers, the miners and the peasants, but we didn't. He said we'd get support from China and Russia, but we didn't, and he promised us Liberated Areas where we would capture British Army equipment, but we didn't have those either.'

Hassan brought a tray of Tiger beer bottles. Instinctively frightened of Ho Peng, although Lao Song had deliberately not told him the name of the Tuan's guest, Hassan quickly opened two bottles and retreated back to the kitchen. Ho Peng grabbed one and drank in great gulps.

Edward grabbed the other and drank from the bottle too. With the rain pouring down over the roof, he felt warm and damp and just watching Ho Peng made him thirsty. He asked, 'You might still have won, in the early years?'

Ho Peng wiped his mouth with the back of his hand, shaking his head, and said, 'Not when the British began to pour money into Malaya, when General Templer came.'

'You stayed in the jungle another three years after Templer arrived,' Edward pointed out.

'It's not easy to change sides,' said Ho Peng. It took time.

'It is if you've got £200,000 reward money coming to you.'

Hassan came back with a tray on which was a large dish of Nasi Goreng. Ho Peng's eyes lit up at the sight and he wasted no time, scooping food into a small bowl, putting it to his lips and shovelling the food into his mouth with chopsticks.

Edward quietly drank his beer for a moment, knowing he should soon call Angus to arrange for Special Branch support. Angus would ask him to be involved in the debrief, but he wanted to clear up some questions of his own first. As he watched Ho Peng bent over the table opposite, stuffing himself with food, the sad scene in the hot sun in the graveyard that morning sprang to Edward's mind and he demanded, 'Did you kill Tallard?'

Between mouthfuls, Ho Peng shook his head and said, 'No.'

'Who did?'

'Liya.'

'I don't believe it!' Edward burst out, 'I don't believe she's even a communist!'

'She is. And a better one than I ever was,' Ho Peng nodded, looking over his bowl of rice at Edward across the table. He knew the young British Captain was obsessed with Liya but he had not known how much. As he reached over to re-fill his bowl, he added, 'She's been in the jungle as long as me, since we fought the Japanese together. Maybe she's better than me in the jungle.' He smiled faintly.

'Liar!' shouted Edward. 'Tallard would have recognised her!'

Ho Peng paused to drink more beer to wash down the rice and then said, 'She cut her hair short in the war so the Japanese soldiers couldn't tell she was a girl. As far as Tallard was concerned, she was just another soldier in my unit. All Chinese look the same to a European.' Again the faint smile quickly buried in another mouthful of Nasi Goreng.

367

Edward nearly lost his temper but he caught sight of Diana's blonde head peering uncertainly through the sitting-room window, alarmed by the raised voices. Quickly, he stood up and strode through the french windows.

'Is everything all right?' she asked, trying to see who else was on the verandah.

'Never mind,' snapped Edward boiling inside from Ho Peng's accusations about Liya. 'Just leave us alone, will you!'

'Really, Edward!' Diana retorted crossly. 'I don't care for your tone of voice! Who's that dirty little person out there, eating?'

Edward nearly shouted that he was the man responsible for causing her miscarriage six years before, but he knew Ho Peng's surrender must be kept secret till Special Branch had used every last bit of information he could give them to capture other CTs. Instead he took a deep breath and said icily, 'Go to bed, Diana, and don't wait up. I'll be late.'

When Edward returned to the table and sat down, Ho Peng wasted no time in explaining, 'Liya was my courier. She took messages between me and the Central Executive Committee. In fact, Chin Peng regarded her as his best courier.'

'Prove it!'

'I don't have to prove it,' said Ho Peng firmly. 'I'm telling you.'

'So I'm suddenly to accept your word?' Edward laughed rudely.

Ho Peng shrugged. The communists meant nothing to him any more and he explained candidly, 'She went around selling samples to shops and stores which gave her the excuse to travel with things we could hide our messages in. Early on she took tins of food to the squatters' village, to reach me in the jungle, and we hid messages inside the tins. Later we used goods you find in hardware shops, like small radios, pots such as kettles where we hid the message in the rolled metal handles, and toiletries.'

Edward felt suddenly cold and asked, 'Like what?'

'Soap,' replied Ho Peng, helping himself to more Nasi Goreng.

'No,' said Edward triumphantly. 'She was caught up in Tanjong Malim and all her samples were minutely searched. We even cut into the soap and we found nothing. She was clean.'

'She's very good,' agreed Ho Peng, and the faint smile drifted over his pocked skin again. 'It was her idea. People are bound to search the new bars, but you didn't open the soap she was using.'

Edward stared at him, but snapped back, 'What brand was it?'

'Palmolive,' said Ho Peng without hesitation. 'I hid a small tube

368

of rubber inside and put the bar in her grip bag myself. It got to its destination, so you must have missed it.'

'A bit bloody risky, wasn't it?' said Edward sarcastically.

'We never expected Tanjong Malim to be locked up under curfew.'

'You're making it up,' said Edward obstinately. It was unthinkable. He remembered that first shower with Liya very well, and the soap, and all the other times, and flatly refused to believe she had not been wholly committed to him. She could not possibly have deliberately fooled him.

Ho Peng reached across the table to scrape the bowl for the last of the Nasi Goreng when his eye caught a gleam in the ashtray in the middle of the table. Wiping his hands on his damp shirt, he picked up the small gold coin which Edward had left there since the night Diana came back, and demanded, 'Where did you find this?'

'Sort of lucky charm,' said Edward vaguely, thinking how typical of the man to pick up the gold sovereign, but he explained the story about the aborigine in the jungle near Ho Peng's old camp.

Ho Peng was interested. He admitted that he had escaped through the back of the camp when he heard the soldiers storming up the hill on the other side, and showed no regret that he had been driven out by a smaller force than his own, but he said nothing about the sovereign. He supposed the coin had fallen into the rice padi when he and Tallard had checked the para-containers after the drop and the aborigines had found it later. However, he had wasted enough time and energy trying to find the rest of the gold and he had made up his mind. The matter of the gold was over. He let the little yellow coin fall back in the ashtray and leaned back in his rattan chair.

As he finished speaking, Hassan arrived with a tray and more Tiger beer. He took away the empty bowls of Nasi Goreng, cleared away the empty bottles and scuttled back to the kitchen as fast as he could.

They both reached for bottles of Tiger and drank in silence, watching each other, each trying to understand the mentality of the other and finally Ho Peng said, 'How d'you think I knew where to find you, in this house?'

'You've got Min Yuen all over the place.'

Ho Peng nodded, but he said, 'Liya told me.'

'Then where is she now?'

369

'In the jungle, where she's been with me since she escaped from Pudu Prison.'

Edward snorted but before he could reply, Lao Song joined them along the verandah. There was something urgent about his manner and he said, 'You might like to see this.' He uncurled his long thin fingers and showed a gold sovereign on his dry palm. 'Hassan saw you talking about that one on the table but he was too frightened to say anything and came to me.'

'Say what?' Ho Peng butted in sharply, staring at the coin in Lao Song's hand.

Lao Song ignored him and looked instead at Edward, saying, 'Hassan says Liya gave it to him, the night she escaped. She came here to see you. Hassan says when Liya saw Mrs Fairfax in the house she went away. He saw Liya in the garden and she gave him this to keep quiet.'

'Why didn't he tell me?' demanded Edward staring helplessly at the little coin. It physically hurt to think how close Liya had been without speaking to him. 'God knows I've been good enough to Hassan, haven't I? And what the hell was he doing in the bloody garden?'

Lao Song raised his eyebrows slightly and adopted an opaque uncritical expression to say, 'Hassan is a gentle soul. He sometimes sits on the grass outside your bedroom window at night. He means no harm, but he saw Liya there that night and he was afraid you'd be angry if he told you what he'd been doing.'

Slowly, Ho Peng leaned forward and picked the little coin out of Lao Song's hand. This second sovereign changed everything. The search was on again. He said quietly, 'This is the proof you need, Captain Fairfax. This second coin of your houseboy comes from the same source as the first.' Carefully, he placed the two coins side by side on the table, each with the bright golden head of King George V face up and each with the same date, 1929, and he asked rhetorically, 'I know how you found your coin, Captain Fairfax, but how did Liya find hers?'

Lao Song sat down and they all stared at the two coins. Edward felt drained. His defence of Liya was hopeless, magicked away by the touch of two gold sovereigns. He felt bruised and hurt but he looked at Ho Peng and asked suspiciously, 'What d'you know about these?'

'There were 120,000 like this,' said Ho Peng coolly, gulping more beer. He enjoyed the expressions of surprise on the faces of Edward

370

and Lao Song. Then he described the parachute drop, years before
during the war.

'So that was the connection between you and Tallard?' said
Edward, recalling how the Liberator pilot had told him the containers were especially heavy that night. 'That's why you both kept
searching for hides in the jungle?'

Ho Peng nodded grimly. 'Each of us thought the other knew
where the sovereigns were hidden, and all along Liya must have
known.'

'Why?' asked Edward in a tired voice.

'She was my deputy with Lao Tang during that period of the war,'
said Ho Peng bitterly. 'But Lao Tang wasn't at the parachute drop. I
was called away shortly after the drop, to see Chin Peng, leaving
Tallard and Liya. When I came back, the gold was gone, Tallard
was gone, and the war was over. He more or less admitted he had
killed the porters he used to ferry the gold away when I saw him in
his house.'

'Doesn't prove Liya has the gold,' grunted Edward.

'She was at the drop, in the shadows near Tallard and me, and she
saw what was in the containers. Weapons in sixteen drums marked
Bravo-seven, which have all been picked up now from various hides
all over the jungle, and gold sovereigns in thirty drums stencilled
Alpha four-nine.' He had thought about that night so often since, he
knew every detail. 'She moves like a shadow in the jungle, so she
could easily have followed Tallard when he hid the gold and taken it
from him when he left the jungle.'

'All that weight!'

Ho Peng shrugged cynically, 'After murdering the porters, Tallard probably felt safe. British colonialism was comfortably back in
Malaya and there was no rush to go back for the gold. That gave her
time.' Ho Peng's yellowing teeth showed in a hard smile. 'I'd like to
have seen his face when he found it all gone.'

'All very plausible,' said Edward dismissively. 'Maybe she just
picked up this coin from the rice padi, like the aborigine?'

'Maybe,' said Ho Peng. 'But why was she out there on that padi
field in the jungle in the first place?'

Edward stared balefully at the squat ugly Chinese. There was just
too much evidence against her.

Lao Song spoke up. In a contemplative tone of voice he asked Ho
Peng, 'If Liya took the gold back from Tallard, why didn't she give it
to you?'

Edward perked up and added aggressively, 'Yes! After all you were the senior Communist Party officer in the area?'

Ho Peng did not answer immediately, though he had known the answer the moment he saw the second gold sovereign in Lao Song's hand. Liya had not trusted him. She had been the political commissar for his group and, while she could have had no complaints about his military ability, the unpalatable truth must be that she had seen through his self-interest. The thought that she had kept such a secret from him for years was incredibly galling, but years of fighting in the jungle had taught him fierce self-control and all he would say was, 'I was the military commander. Liya was our political commissar and she may have had separate orders from the leadership.'

Edward looked at Lao Song who shrugged. It made sense, as far as any of it could be true. Edward shook his head. He needed to clear his mind and think. He told Ho Peng he was going to call the Special Branch and went through to the hall where he rang Angus Maclean at home.

Bluntly, he said, 'You better come round here, Angus. And bring Sergeant Ci Guo with you.'

'On a night like this!' Even inside, they could hear the rain drumming relentlessly on the roof above.

'I've got an SEP here.'

'I'll send Sergeant Ci Guo,' said Angus, but Edward had no intention of letting Angus off the hook. He said, 'You come. I'm drinking beer with Ho Peng.'

Angus was round in a civilian car with Sergeant Ci Guo in less than twenty minutes. Edward introduced them and Ho Peng, who had not moved from his chair on the verandah, looked them up and down and demanded of Edward in Chinese, 'Can I trust them?'

'What's he say?' Angus asked in his quiet Scots voice.

Blandly Sergeant Ci Guo translated and Angus burst out, 'Bloody cheek! Who does he think he is?'

In spite of himself, Edward laughed. He promised Ho Peng he would be there when the debrief started in the morning and saw them off. Watching the three of them dash back through the rain to their car, Edward found it hard to believe that one was Ho Peng at all.

Then he went back to the verandah and slumped into his rattan chair. Lao Song had gone back to his quarters. Edward listened to the rain hammering on the roof. A gecko hung upside down on the ceiling near the electric light, waiting for insects, and cricked its neck sideways to stare at him. Outside, beyond the verandah rail, the dark curtain of water sheeted down on the grass. He slapped a mosquito on his leg. He could smell the damp, sweaty warmth of his shirt and the beer. He flicked the top off another bottle of Tiger. He had a lot of thinking to do.

The following morning, he drove to Special Branch Headquarters in the blue Plymouth. Diana refused to use it any more. The bullet holes had been repaired on the bodywork and plugged on the wood panelling inside but dark spots of Marsha Tallard's blood were still visible on the carpet.

Angus Maclean was waiting for him and they walked between the Nissen huts to the low breeze-block buildings on one side of the compound where Ho Peng's debrief was taking place in the utmost secrecy. Angus paused at the entrance and said, 'You may not like to hear some of all this.'

Edward looked him straight in the eye and said, 'I spent a good hour with Ho Peng before I rang you, and I stayed up late thinking about what he said.' He was exhausted but he had made up his mind. 'You were right about Liya. She's a political commissar, a courier for Chin Peng, and I was conned.'

Angus could see how tired Edward was and said, 'I'm sorry it ended like this.'

'No you're not!' snapped Edward angrily. 'You knew bloody well that Liya was my source. You were following her ever since you picked up the courier lead in Mersing on the beach. Why else did you get me to join you in that stinking cabbage truck when you picked her up? You weren't surprised at my support of her during her trial and you never asked me why I visited her in prison, which you knew about because SB receive reports of all visitors.'

Angus shrugged, tacitly admitting everything. Early on, when Edward asked him for advice on running a source, he had followed Edward to a meet with Liya in the park and photographed her from a distance. 'At least, I kept your name out of all the official reports.'

'Thanks,' said Edward grudgingly. 'But the Press plastered my name all over the newspapers anyway.' He felt drained in the hot sun.

'Everyone will forget all about that soon enough,' said Angus. He made to open the door into the building but Edward stood in the way.

'I won't,' he said.

Edward had sat on the verandah for hours after Ho Peng left and finally decided what he had to do. 'You just let me carry on making a fool of myself with Liya so you had another lead on her in case your own surveillance failed. Am I right?'

Angus rubbed a hand over his dark hair and nodded. 'I'm sorry, old mate,' he said but the words sounded hollow. The fight in Malaya was uncompromising and he supposed he would do the same again if necessary.

'Then you owe me, you bastard!' Edward said emphatically. 'You bloody owe me!'

Clearing the air between them, he felt less of a fool. The embarrassment of his affair with Liya still hurt but the blame was not all his and he was on the attack again. He flung open the door and walked in to start the debrief.

Edward and Sergeant Ci Guo took it in turns to talk to Ho Peng who proved totally amenable. Bathed and in a clean shirt, trousers and sandals, Edward noticed that, washed, the pitted skin of his face was more striking than hidden beneath a layer of jungle dirt and rain. They sat around the table in the same small room where Lao Tang had been interviewed and drank endless cups of pale China tea while Ho Peng happily revealed all aspects of his activities with the communists as if they had never been his colleagues at all. The questions were going so well that Edward's confidence returned and just before lunch he returned to Liya. He asked, 'Ho Peng, do you really think Liya knows where the cache of gold sovereigns is?'

'Yes,' said Ho Peng. He narrowed his eyes, on his guard for the first time in the interview.

Edward leaned back in his chair, looked at him across the table and said, 'You were fooled by Liya about that gold for years.'

The faintest shadow passed over Ho Peng's face and he bent quickly to sip his tea.

'And I was fooled by her too,' added Edward frankly.

'So?' asked Ho Peng quietly. He glanced at Sergeant Ci Guo who was frowning. Was the British captain departing from the usual line of questioning?

Edward noticed the look and said firmly, 'Sergeant Ci Guo, go and find Inspector Maclean.'

Sergeant Ci Guo looked from one to the other but did as he was told. The interview was being taped and there were armed SB officers watching the other side of the one-way mirror. When the door closed behind him, Edward said to Ho Peng, 'How would you like to get your own back?'

Ho Peng nodded imperceptibly.

Edward tried to keep calm, gearing himself to put forward the plan he had eventually decided to try before he finally crawled into bed early that morning. Speaking very clearly, he said, 'Let's fool her. Let's make her think our combined knowledge means we know where the gold is.'

'What knowledge?' asked Ho Peng pragmatically.

'She might not know that you've come in to us, but she knows we might have found papers in Tallard's house after his death.'

'It's not enough!'

'It is if we let her think we know more, if we let her think we're coming into the jungle to find the cache of sovereigns.'

'How?' said Ho Peng dismissively.

Edward leaned forward and said, 'I was given a note in the Coliseum Bar telling me to go to Liao Ting-chi, by Willie the barman. He said the note had been handed in by a small boy off the street. He was lying. I kept the note and we found Willie had written it himself. I noticed the handwriting was the same as the bill he gave me for lunch and expert analysis here in SB Headquarters confirmed it.'

Ho Peng listened expressionlessly. After years on the run, he was fascinated to hear how the Special Branch worked. He wanted the British captain's plan to work. He too had spent a bitter, sleepless night thinking how Liya had fooled him for so long over the gold, and he wanted revenge. He stated, 'You're right. That barman is a member of the Min Yuen.'

'Thanks,' Edward smiled. It was so easy! 'But he doesn't know we know about him yet. If he overhears two of us talking about going into the jungle to find a secret cache belonging to Liya, the news is bound to get back to her and she just might react.' Quickly he told Ho Peng his plan before anyone could interrupt and at the end the stocky Chinese smiled.

Angus burst in with Sergeant Ci Guo, glanced at Ho Peng and said, 'Sergeant Ci Guo tells me you're doing some work on your own account?'

'Like I said, Angus, you owe me,' said Edward harshly.

'Back off, Edward. This is Special Branch territory,' Angus retorted.

'You used me, and now I want your support,' said Edward. Unruffled, he leaned back in his chair and stared at Angus. He had to have this operation.

'Personal problems aren't part of this war, Edward,' Angus replied flatly. Ho Peng was too big to lose after so long trying to find him.

'Captain Fairfax has a good plan,' announced Ho Peng in a loud voice, in English.

Startled, Angus said, 'You speak English?'

'Yes, a bit,' replied Ho Peng but he switched back to Chinese and rapidly told Sergeant Ci Guo, 'I like this plan, so tell your black-haired Inspector I'll refuse to co-operate with anyone except Captain Fairfax unless he helps us out.'

Sergeant Ci Guo looked uncomfortable but translated, knowing Edward understood everything.

Angus was furious. 'You've been breaking the bloody rules, Edward! First, talking to Ho Peng at home instead of handing him in immediately, and now this.'

'Rules never stopped you in the past,' retorted Edward carelessly. 'And besides, I don't give a monkey's shit. I told you, Angus. You owe me.'

Angus took a deep breath. He had no option. Ho Peng co-operative could break the CTs around Kuala Lumpur and persuade countless others to surrender from three States, but if he refused to talk, they might get nothing till it was too late.

'All right,' he said. 'What's the plan?'

Edward smiled. 'Simple. A classic, co-ordinated counter-terrorist operation, and' he began to explain. 'Special Branch, which is you and me, Angus, start with a little deception plan. We go into the Coliseum Bar and let Willie the barman overhear us saying that we know Liya has a secret, and a very valuable cache in the jungle which we're going to find. Next, Willie tells his Min Yuen contacts and the word gets back to Liya. In the mean time, we get the Gurkha infantry battalion to hide small two or three-men observation groups on the likely CT routes into the jungle. Ho Peng here will give us the details on all of those. We move close to the jungle ourselves with a hunter-tracker patrol and wait. The operation is triggered off when one of the Gurkha groups alerts us by radio that Liya has passed them. Then we track her into the jungle to the cache.'

'Just like that, eh?' Angus said drily.

'Yes, Angus, just like that,' replied Edward in a hard voice staring up from his chair at the slight dark Scot.

Angus mellowed his tone slightly and asked, 'What if she's in the jungle already? What if she doesn't get Willie's message? Or the Gurkhas don't spot her?'

Edward was tired and lost his temper. He shouted, 'There are lots of "what ifs" in every bloody operation! Life's like that, Angus! We're not fucking clairvoyants! If you stopped mounting ops for every pissing little objection we'd never win this fucking war at all, because we'd always find an excuse not to go out on operations at all!'

'All right, all right,' Angus held up his hands in mock defence. 'You get your way. Who d'you want in your hunter group?'

Edward did not hesitate, 'We need a good tracker, and I've not come across any better than Untam, though I haven't seen him for a while. Ho Peng says Liya is good in the jungle and travels alone, so our group must be small and carry minimal kit or we'll get left behind. I think three men from Aubrey Hall-Drake's SAS Troop would do, preferably Sean Brogan and two others. With Ho Peng and me, that makes six, which is almost too many.'

Angus thought for a moment. There was so much he did not like about the operation and the risks were enormous, but he said, 'Let's get on with it. Before the situation changes out there in the real world.'

Angus and Edward walked into the Coliseum Bar the following evening after twenty-four hours of hectic planning and preparation, tying in all the elements of the operation. Edward had briefed the lieutenant-colonel commanding the Gurkha battalion who was delighted to deploy his men on an operation sourced by Special Branch with some chance of success. He was mightily impressed when Edward gave him no less than twenty-six possible routes his 'source', Ho Peng, had said the 'target', Liya, might take into the jungle. Only five of these had been known about before.

Edward then handed him six-dozen good photographs of Liya sitting on a park bench in Kuala Lumpur smiling at someone beside her out of the picture. Angus had cut the negative in half, given Edward his half to destroy and passed the half with Liya to the SB laboratory assistants to print up lots of copies. The colonel merely remarked, 'Good-looking girl! Lucky the chap sitting next to her on that bench, eh?'

'Thanks, Willie,' said Edward cheerfully as the barman slid two Singa beers across the counter. He drank the cool beer and Angus

377

remarked, 'You won't be getting any more of those for a while where you're going.'

Willie studiously polished clean glasses and served other customers, but by the time Edward and Angus had drunk three bottles of Singa, they felt sure he had heard enough to know that Edward was being flown by helicopter into the jungle on the far side of the mountain ridge above the 'Black Circle' to find that 'bloody terrorist girl who escaped from Pudu Prison'.

The operation was on. The Gurkha patrols were in position. Some had gone straight into their hiding positions to watch one of the jungle paths under cover of darkness, the rest had dropped off the back end of larger patrols throughout that day taking care not to return over the same route past kampongs in case anyone curious saw the numbers had shrunk by three. By the time Angus and Edward left the Coliseum Bar, all twenty-six patrols were in position between Camp Rideau in the north and the furthest corner of the Black Circle estate in the south. The net was cast and the bait out.

Edward drove the blue Plymouth back to SB Headquarters in the rubber plantation at speed. They did not expect Willie to pass his information to Liya too quickly, but there was no knowing. Ho Peng thought Liya had several other safe houses in Kuala Lumpur. She might hear within the hour. Edward's hunter-tracker group had to be ready in place as soon as possible.

On the way, Angus looked across at Edward and asked, 'At your orders this afternoon, you didn't say what you were going to do when you find her?'

Edward pretended to concentrate on a timber lorry blocking the way on a crossroads and said nothing. He had to see Liya, for his own peace of mind.

Angus was relentless, knowing indecision could put the whole patrol at risk. He asked, 'Is the aim to capture or to kill?'

'I don't know.'

Irritated, Angus demanded, 'Is this whole operation just to find out what really happened between you and Liya?'

'Yes,' admitted Edward flatly. The operation was under way and it no longer mattered. He accelerated through the rubber plantation. They were nearly there and then Angus would have to stop asking questions because there would be no time.

'Male pride is a terrible thing,' said Angus heavily.

'No-one likes being hurt, especially not by friends,' Edward snapped back. 'But knowing why helps.' Angus fell silent but when Edward pulled up in the yard outside the old plantation bungalow and he opened the door to get out, Edward grabbed his arm in a hard grip and swore hoarsely, 'I'll kill her if I have to. Satisfied? Either me or Ho Peng. We both have a score to settle with Liya. D'you understand?'

The intense expression in Edward's eyes convinced Angus. He nodded and Edward let him go.

The five men of the hunter-tracker team were waiting in the fenced compound in one discreet corner of the SB Headquarters where the truck full of cabbages had been parked. Edward went into a Nissen hut to change into his jungle gear.

'Willie get the message?' asked Aubrey Hall-Drake as he joined him. He had insisted on being one of the three SAS in the patrol and cradled a carbine over the few pouches left on his specially lightened belt equipment.

'Certainly should have,' said Edward as he pulled on his jungle greens and laced up his canvas boots to join the team outside.

Everyone was in jungle greens and canvas boots except Untam, who was barefoot, and Ho Peng who was delighted with his new clothes but preferred to keep his plimsoles. He said they were comfortably worn in. Apart from Ho Peng, they carried a mixture of weapons and grenades. Untam had always carried a carbine, Aubrey too, but Brogan and Edward carried Sterling sub-machine-guns with curved thirty-round magazines. The third SAS trooper carried a Winchester pump action shotgun with nine 8mm-ball-bearings in each cartridge, giving a lethal spread over the short distances typical of contacts in the jungle.

Edward led the way over to a RAF Whirlwind helicopter which was standing silently in the middle of the yard with its rotor blades drooping, as if exhausted in the heat. As the engine whined and the blades began to whirl around shaking the helicopter to life, Edward felt a thrill of apprehension and a savage determination to find Liya. Deceiving him in their affair seemed to him to represent all the frustration of the last seven years of fighting the elusive communists in the jungle. Now at last he felt on top. The operation was complicated but well-planned and had all the ingredients of success which had been lacking in Malaya for so long; helicopter support, without which the whole plan would have been impossible, the Special Branch, a deception plan using Willie the barman, Ho Peng's vital information about the enemy, the experienced Gurkhas lying silently watching narrow paths into the jungle, and lastly his own hand-picked patrol ready to track her down. He was determined to find her, to ask her why she had done it. He needed to understand.

The helicopter landed inside the SAS camp by the hot springs near Dusun Tua village and Aubrey installed them in an attap hut close to the ops room where they could rest for the night, or as long as it took. Edward hoped they would not have to wait too long. As they tucked into a supper of steaming hot curry organised from the SAS cookhouse by Brogan, Edward thought of the Gurkha patrols lying in the jungle rationed with cold food for fear cooking smells would give them away. The Gurkhas were disciplined and experienced jungle soldiers but three men would find it very tiring to keep constant watch for four days, let alone the nights too, as Ho Peng had stressed that Liya knew these paths intimately and was likely to move under cover of darkness.

After supper, Edward and Aubrey checked that the SAS signallers in the operations hut were tuned into the Gurkha radio net, waiting for the trigger signal from one of the patrols. They had orders to wake Edward as soon as word came through. Then they went back to their attap hut to catch a few hours rest. No-one undressed. They lay on their canvas camp-beds, ready to go.

'It's an odd thing lying down to kip next to a cove with a reputation like his,' remarked Brogan to Edward, jigging his thumb at Ho Peng through the darkness. Ho Peng had rolled up in a blanket on his camp-bed and was already fast asleep. 'D'you trust him?'

'What d'you think?' Edward grunted, thinking of Liya. He lay on his back and stared at the attap roof which rattled softly in a slight wind. He never thought he would be able to sleep, thinking how his life had swung between extremes with Liya, from complete belief in their affair to hunting her down like an animal in the jungle. At the back of his mind nagged Ho Peng's warning that she would not be easy to trap. To his surprise, he was in deep sleep when a signaller ran over to the hut at five o'clock in the morning and shook him awake by the shoulder.

'Gurkha patrol just sent the code, Sir,' he said. 'The target went past them fifteen minutes ago. They waited to make certain she didn't hear them use the radio, just like you briefed them.'

She had taken the bait! Edward sat up, rubbing the sleep from his face. The operation was on! He woke the rest of the team and they were outside the hut in less than a minute standing in the warm Malayan night. Edward was pleased to see the sky was clear, filled with stars and a high waxing moon. Liya had just enough light to make reasonable progress even in deep shadow under the canopy.

The signaller reappeared out of the darkness with four cups of hot sweet tea clutched in his fists which they shared. Edward found himself drinking with Ho Peng who grinned, his slanting eyes and pitted skin making him look like a devil in the darkness, and he remarked in Chinese, 'Tea with milk! Is this how the British Army kills its enemies?' Edward did not reply. He needed Ho Peng on the patrol, because Ho Peng knew the side of Liya which Edward did not know, and Ho Peng knew the jungle where she was hiding. What worried him were Ho Peng's real reasons for being so willing to come.

A Chinese Special Branch officer drove them out to the jungle hidden under the canvas back of an old lumber truck, to keep up the deception to the last moment rather than use an army vehicle which might alarm tappers going out to work early from their kampongs. After twenty minutes the truck stopped behind trees on a bend a mile up the narrow unsurfaced road to the 'Black Circle'. They dropped over the tailboard and silently moved out of sight into the rubber trees. Walking briskly, they stretched their legs uphill through the avenues of silver barked trees to the jungle edge. On a corner of the rubber, a dark shape stood up and challenged them in a low voice. They had found the Gurkha patrol.

'She was like a ghost!' said the Gurkha corporal in admiration as he explained what had happened. 'We nearly missed seeing her in the darkness. She was so small and so silent.'

'On her own?' asked Edward grimly.

'With two others,' said the Gurkha. 'But we couldn't see what weapons they were carrying.' He took Edward's patrol into the jungle and pointed out the way they had gone. The shadows between the big trees were impenetrable, just a few leaves spotted with faint light from the moon above the canopy and Untam shook his head. Automatically whispering as they always did in the jungle, he said they must wait for first light before he could begin tracking her.

A frustrating hour passed sitting just inside the jungle trying to ignore the insects, during which Edward tried not to think of Liya getting away. At the first glimmer of grey in the eastern sky, he made Untam take the lead and start tracking.

Edward followed with Ho Peng behind so they could speak Chinese, with Aubrey, Brogan and the trooper at the rear.

Untam moved very slowly until the darkness lightened through greys to green and soon the early morning sun fired ribbons of light through the canopy splashing the leaves and trees on the jungle floor with brilliant yellow. There had been no rain for several days, so Untam moved fast, easily picking out the squashed leaf mould, soft ferns brushed by a passing foot to show their silver undersides and the dry broken twigs which revealed Liya's path. Ho Peng walked like a ghost close behind Edward and helped with the tracking from time to time. Edward's spirits rose as they moved steadily uphill and he began to worry they would catch her up too soon and risk a fight before she reached the cache.

'How far ahead is she?' Edward whispered at Untam.

Untam paused, crouching over a crushed leaf, cocked his head thoughtfully and replied, 'Maybe an hour.'

Maybe less, Edward thought.

Then they lost some height, the track levelled out on to flat damp ground veering towards the Sungei Langat ahead on their left, and they reached a swamp. Finally Untam stopped. Ahead the jungle was flooded, the water's surface thick with ferns, lianas and aerial roots falling from big fig trees like tangled spaghetti. The track seemed to go straight in. Untam cast left and right through boggy ground past thorny palms to check Liya had not cut away to a flank. Ho Peng crouched and peered into the swamp. He pointed at a fleshy root sticking out of the water which showed pale where someone had scuffed the black bark. Edward waded in up to his ankles, tripped on something underwater and fell heavily against the tree roots. When he looked round, Aubrey and Brogan behind him were grinning widely but Ho Peng was in the filthy water right beside him busily feeling about under the surface.

'What the hell are you doing?' hissed Edward in Chinese.

'This is a hidden path!' said Ho Peng, his black eyes glittering with triumph. 'Duck boards below the surface. We often conceal a route through difficult terrain like this.' He looked at the jungle around, frowning and said, 'I know this area but always avoided it. There are several river junctions with the Sungei Langat and too much swamp. Unless you have a path of hidden boards like this, the going is very hard. As you see,' he added matter-of-factly, watching Edward get to his feet.

Gritting his teeth, Edward felt about under water and found Ho

Peng was right. It proved they were still on Liya's track. Untam led again on the hidden boards, feeling his way with his bare feet, finding the edges of the wood slats and stepping forward pace by pace. Edward glanced back. The five behind him seemed to be walking on water up to their ankles, although Edward guessed the water was much deeper as the hidden track was taking them towards the river, crossing a flat bowl of swampland in the foothills of the high ridge above. Ho Peng caught his eye. Edward thought he looked worried.

After half an hour, the path took Untam through the tangled branches of a huge fallen tree. He paused, feeling for the hidden boards with his hands. Then he stepped through a window of thick branches under the massive tree-trunk. As he straightened on the other side the board he was standing on dropped suddenly, the water seem to rear up in front of him, and a wooden spear on the end of a spring bow plunged into his chest like a huge striking snake.

Screaming, Untam collapsed face first into the water and sank writhing and thrashing the water. Instinctively, Edward bent double through the branches, slipped on the loose board which had triggered the booby trap and nearly fell in as he grabbed Untam's shirt to pull him back to the surface. Untam rolled face up, his eyes staring, gurgling for breath to scream but blood and swamp water flooded his throat.

Edward stared horrified at the thick spear buried in his solar plexus. It was tied to a long flexible spring-bow which had been concealed underwater and released by the duckboard which he had stood on. Wet with blood and water, Edward found a grip on Untam's trousers and dragged his twitching body back on to the boards. When he paused to catch his breath, Ho Peng's hoarse voice behind him whispered in Chinese, 'Waste of time.'

Edward looked at Untam. Ho Peng was right. The tracker's body was lying quite still, half beached on the underwater boards, his head lolling back in the water. Edward guessed the spear had ruptured his heart and his blood was spreading in a bright oily patch over the water around. Shocked and angry, Edward turned to Ho Peng and Aubrey who were peering at him through the branches and hissed, 'Don't just stand there! I need help!'

Ho Peng looked cautious and Aubrey whispered, 'What about other traps?'

Edward felt sick. Maybe there was another trap still. He looked round desperately. After Untam's screams and the splashing water, the jungle was suddenly very empty and silent. Except it was not empty. Liya was ahead somewhere, with two others and they had probably heard. Maybe they had been watching. He wondered if Liya knew he was after her, if she was wondering whether his own body was lying pierced by the wood stake, if she cared.

Untam's body began to slide off the boards and he grabbed it. The action helped though his fear remained. He looked back again at the rest on the other side of the mangrove roots and snapped, 'Give me a hand. We'll have to leave him here. Come back for him later.'

Gingerly they joined him and Brogan helped lift Untam out of the water while Edward tied him by the arms and legs into the branches of the fallen tree, out of the way of fishes. The trooper tied an orange air marker panel to his leg to make him easy to see when they came back for him.

Edward said, 'I'll lead.' He knew perfectly well what had been going through their minds. No-one wanted to be the first to walk along the underwater duckboards.

'We could try following the path to one side,' Aubrey suggested.

Ho Peng understood and said to Edward in Chinese, 'No good being off the boards. The water is too deep and we may hit more traps anyway trying to stay close enough to touch the path to see where it's going.'

Edward translated, whereupon Brogan leaned forward round Aubrey and peered at Ho Peng, his face dark with sweat, and said, 'You tell this little shit Ho Peng to take the frigging lead himself. Why should you take the risk after all the people he's murdered?' He added as an after-thought, 'And with all due respect, sir, he's a better tracker than you are.'

In spite of himself, Edward grinned but Ho Peng stared malevolently at Brogan. He understood few of the words but all the gestures.

'I'll shoot him myself now, if he doesn't.' Brogan levelled his Sterling at Ho Peng's stomach and said, 'No-one will notice with all the noise that poor bastard Untam has been making.'

Edward was tempted. The decision was his alone. The operation was his, but he was conscious his one motive had been personal, to find Liya, and he felt guilty about asking anyone else to take the risk. Even Ho Peng. There was no time for debate. Feeling like a man who is about to step into space off a high cliff, he made his choice and declared, 'No. I lead. Ho Peng stays right behind me to track.'

The blood had floated out wide around them and reminded Edward just what he risked with every step he took. Feeling his bowels turn liquid and the sweat cold on his skin, he began walking slowly along the underwater boards. Sliding his rubber jungle boots along the uneven surface, he placed each foot with terrible care before putting his weight on it, like a man walking in total darkness, and all the time he swept the green shadows among the trees and leaves for the least indication of something out of place.

To his relief, the swamp petered out after another four hundred yards. He checked his map again and saw that Ho Peng was right. Liya's path had taken them across the Sungei Langat in a flat area between hills, probably deliberately, to place that booby trap in the water. If she was so obviously determined to protect her cache in the hills, that spear would not be the only trap.

Not a step passed without him thinking of walking into another trap and the sweat poured off him as the trail took them steeply uphill towards the high ridge line on the state border, 4,000 feet up. The forest became more open, with a glimpse of light between the canopy of branches high above, moss covered the trunks, lichens hung like hair from the lianas and lush bromeliads clustered on the branches.

Ho Peng closed up behind Edward like a shadow, constantly pointing out the signs of Liya's path through the ferns and low undergrowth on the steep forest floor. He could never remember moving so carefully, treading lightly from step to step, like a bird. Untam's death had been a shocking reminder how Liya had fooled him for so long. He was determined to find her and he needed the Englishman when he did.

'Much further to the top of the ridge?' whispered Edward in Chinese, pausing to catch his breath and control the adrenalin burning through his body like acid.

Ho Peng shook his head. 'Maybe only a few minutes,' he said shortly. They looked uphill. Ahead was a sharp rocky scramble among ferns and moss, damp and slippery underfoot. Neither said anything but they both knew how easy it was to conceal an ambush in such undergrowth. Liya's trail, where she had dislodged gobs of moss and earth on the rocks, was almost too easy to see.

As Edward scrambled up the rocky wall, Ho Peng's eye caught a fleeting glimpse of a short line beneath some ferns lit by a thin shaft of sunlight from the canopy high overhead. In an instant, he registered the line was straight, too straight for anything natural, that Edward's foot had dislodged a loose stone, and that the line abruptly twitched. He lunged forward, grabbed Edward by the waist and rolled sideways, pulling him to the ground as an explosion ripped past them both.

The shotgun blast hit Aubrey in the shoulder, missed Brogan who was kneeling to look round while Aubrey negotiated a large rock, and struck the trooper in the head as he stood looking back down the track. Ho Peng never stopped moving and rolled out of sight down the line of the trail they had been on. One glance at the British soldiers collapsing behind him told him Liya had placed the shotgun perfectly, pointing the muzzle downhill over the rocks where a patrol would naturally bunch up while they scrambled up the obstacle.

The ambush was covered. Bursts of automatic fire hit them from the flank, catching Brogan in the side as he bent over Aubrey. Edward saw him go down and lost sight of everyone in the low undergrowth. Cursing, thinking Ho Peng had changed sides again, he wriggled into cover behind a tree stump.

The enemy were still firing. The Gurkha had said Liya was with two others but he could only hear two weapons, not three. He peeked round the stump and, forty yards away, he saw a man in the typical pale khaki uniform of the MRLA, not looking in Edward's direction, but kneeling up to fire his carbine at something further down the slope. Edward eased out his Sterling, took aim and fired a long burst. The man cartwheeled backwards and a moment later Edward saw a small black object sail uphill into the position where the CT had been. There was the loud explosion of a British 36-grenade, followed by screams which echoed through the jungle. Another one followed and the screams stopped. Edward wriggled to get a better view and was about to fire at something moving in the ferns when Ho Peng stood up waving his arms. He showed two fingers and drew them across his throat. His message was clear. Two dead. Liya, thought Edward, was now on her own.

He turned immediately to help the others. Aubrey, bleeding heavily from his shoulder, looked terribly grey; Brogan was out of action too, hit in the thigh in the second burst of firing; and the trooper at the back of the line had been struck by a single piece of shot in the head and died instantly. His body lay on its back where it had dropped among the ferns and rocks.

'Bastards covered the trap this time with fire,' Brogan muttered as he tightened his shell-dressing over the wound in his leg. Edward nodded grimly, packing the hole in Aubrey's shoulder with three shell dressings, one after the other.

'Not much use to you now,' Aubrey gasped.

'I'll give you some morphine,' said Edward. 'Safe enough. The damage is all flesh and bone up here. Nothing in the chest cavity as far as I can see.' Aubrey was in shock, but Edward had no plasma drip to give him and could do no more than bind the wound to stop the bleeding. He jabbed penicillin in his leg and hoped the morphine would cut the pain.

'Two dead over there,' said Ho Peng in Chinese when he rejoined them. 'Your firing was just in time. Allowed me to close up to throw the grenades.'

Edward turned on Ho Peng, his Sterling levelled and snapped, 'Where the hell did you get those grenades?'

'From him,' said Ho Peng pointing at the dead trooper. 'I took the sack off him as I worked my way round to attack them.'

Edward stared balefully at Ho Peng. The idea of arming him did not appeal, but he said, 'I owe you for pulling me out of the way of that shotgun'. He gestured at Aubrey's shoulder.

Ho Peng shrugged. The Englishman had risked taking the lead after the tracker was killed. He said, 'We all need help sometimes.'

When Edward translated, Brogan said pragmatically, 'You might as well give the bastard that pump shotgun too. You're going to need help up there against that bitch and, after what she's done to the rest of us, you're in no position to be choosy about your friends.'

Edward realised Brogan was right. He walked down to the dead trooper, picked up his pump-action Winchester and handed it to Ho Peng. 'Used one before?' he asked.

Ho Peng nodded, obviously pleased. In English, he said to Edward, 'It's the only way. She has a sixth sense in the jungle.'

'Like you?' retorted Edward.

'Better,' Ho Peng admitted. His face was streaked with dirt and his jungle greens were soaking with sweat. Edward realised they all looked like that. Under pressure.

'Well, she's on her own now,' whispered Aubrey. 'Go and get her, for me.'

'I'll stay here with these two,' said Brogan interpreting a look from Edward.

Edward stood up. The job was still to be done, and now there was

387

no question Liya knew they were coming. He checked the body of the trooper and the two dead CTs and then set off up the hill with Ho Peng.

They did not follow Liya's trail. Ho Peng whispered at Edward to take a line parallel, aiming directly up the slope, to avoid any more traps. The ground became more broken than ever, with outcrops of rock and narrow gaps between, which seemed to Edward built for ambushes.

Finally, in total silence, they reached the top of the ridge. Just mosses and ferns covered the ground and outcrops of rocks from which curled the black roots of the great trees holding up the canopy above.

Edward whispered, 'We'll never find her in this broken ground.'

Ho Peng nodded. She could have been hiding behind any one of a number of moss-covered limestone formations. He said, 'We'll move forward across the edge of the ridge and try to pick up her trail as we cross it.'

Edward agreed and went first, telling Ho Peng to hang back and cover him.

Ho Peng did not object. Liya knew her ambush had not stopped them all. She would be waiting. If the captain wanted to sacrifice himself, then he would take the chance to kill Liya when she revealed her position.

Absorbed with thinking about Liya's likely reaction, Edward never noticed the expression on Ho Peng's face and set off. After several hours following her footsteps, he soon spotted her trail across his path and turned right to follow her in. He crouched low, moving forward one or two steps at a time, his mind in a turmoil. He prayed he would see her first. He told himself she would not kill him if she spotted him.

The trail of crushed ferns ended beside an outcrop of broken rock overgrown with bromeliads, hanging ferns and lichens. Puzzled, Edward cast about but there was no trace of her footsteps. He looked round. Ho Peng was ten paces behind, grim-faced with his shotgun forward and ready.

Edward stepped silently through a gap in the rocks. Twenty yards away in the centre of a shallow hollow was a small open-sided attap rain shelter, hidden by the boulders and ferns all round, and invisible to anyone from the natural path along the ridge unless they were actually looking into the depression in the outcrop of rocks.

Sitting crossed-legged under the dried palm roof was Liya. She was dressed in the pale khaki uniform of the MRLA, with a red star on her peaked hat and looking directly at him. A M-1 carbine lay loosely across her slim thighs.

For a moment he did not register that he was looking at her and stared stupidly.

'Have you come to kill me?' she asked. Her voice was as he remembered it, but smoothly implacable, and low so it did not carry in the jungle.

'No!' said Edward in a hoarse whisper, though he wondered if he really knew the true answer.

'Come over here,' she said.

Her voice was so natural but the tensions of the last hours had heightened his senses to a degree that he sank suspiciously to one knee beside a rock, his Sterling crooked in his arm, ready to lift and fire. Without looking round, he was conscious of Ho Peng crouching just behind him, out of sight and wondered nervously what the ex-CT leader was going to do now they had found their quarry.

'Don't you trust me?'

Edward snorted, 'You've just killed two of my patrol and seriously wounded the others.' Something told him to include Ho Peng among them. In that uniform, Liya was enemy, and Ho Peng, with all his brutality was an ally. 'Those traps nearly killed me too.'

'I'm sorry,' she said.

'No you're not!' snapped Edward. 'You spent years deceiving me with lies. What was the bloody point of it all?'

'We were people on different sides,' she answered simply. Her hands rested lightly on her carbine. 'You hoped I was going to tell you about the Min Yuen.' She paused and admitted frankly, 'To begin with, I thought you might let slip things about the army.'

Edward said nothing. In retrospect, he had used her, and her admission somehow levelled the score, but then he asked, 'Was anything I said to you the reason for killing the High Commissioner, Sir Henry Gurney?' The thought had tortured him ever since.

She shook her head and said, 'No. There was a Min Yuen spy in Gurney's household and Fraser's Hill is a popular weekend retreat with the British. Ho Peng arranged the whole thing with Siu Mah.'

'Liar!' hissed Ho Peng advancing suddenly past Edward, his shotgun thrust forward threateningly. 'You've always been a dirty little liar!'

Quite poised, Liya stared at him and the shotgun, assessing him and the distances. After a moment, she asked scathingly, 'Are you worried the British will execute you if they find you're the one who killed their High Commissioner? Will that spoil your easy little arrangement to take the reward money and amnesty for your crimes and set up a new life? What will they give you for being a member of the Central Military Committee? $200,000! Or is it more? Traitor!' Her voice was clear and rang with her disgust.

Furious, Ho Peng went on the attack, shouting, 'You are the traitor to the Party, Liya. You stole the gold sovereigns!'

'No!' Liya answered fiercely, emotion appearing in her face for the first time. 'After you went to see Chin Peng, I followed Tallard when he took the porters off the drop zone. I saw where he hid the gold and when he left the jungle after the war, I took it away from him.'

'By yourself?' asked Edward incredulous.

'Over months, yes,' asserted Liya. 'At the end of 1945. Half a drum at a time. I learned later Tallard killed all the porters. He thought no-one else knew. He was so confident he gave me enough time to move it all before he came back for it.'

Edward recalled Lao Song's question and with a sideways glance at Ho Peng beside him, asked, 'Why didn't you give it back to Ho Peng?'

To his surprise, she laughed softly.

Ho Peng lost his temper. In a rage, he took a couple of paces forward, raising the pump action shotgun to his shoulder. Liya flung herself to the ground and Edward lunged at Ho Peng with his Sterling.

The shotgun roared as Edward hit Ho Peng in the back. Liya kept rolling away through the ferns across the bottom of the hollow. Ho Peng stumbled with Edward crashing into him from behind, but he kept his finger on the trigger, pumping the action with his other hand, cursing and firing as he fell.

Wriggling away from Edward on the ground like a snake, Ho Peng worked the pump action. As the third and fourth shots blasted in quick succession across the hollow, Edward realised Ho Peng was desperate to kill Liya, and he went beserk. All the tension of the past hours and his revulsion of Ho Peng, of his cruelty and cynical surrender, exploded in a vicious assault. He dropped his Sterling and fell on Ho Peng, seized him by the throat with one hand and began to beat his head and back with his bunched fist, crushing his face on to the ferns and rocks on the ground.

Ho Peng twisted round like a snake, swung the shotgun back

towards Edward and fired again. The blast was deafening but harmless and Edward hardly noticed. The frustrations and revenge of years fused in a terrible violence. He smashed the shotgun aside with his left hand and punched Ho Peng's head and neck with repeated savage blows. Kneeling in the small of his back, he pummelled the wiry, wriggling Chinese till Ho Peng's grasp on the shotgun loosened. Edward grabbed it and holding it like a club, began to smash it down on his back and arms.

'Stop! Enough!' shouted Liya, breaking through the haze of Edward's fury.

Edward paused, breathing heavily, and looked up, his eyes glazed. Liya was standing by him with her carbine, unharmed. Quietly she said, 'You've probably killed him'.

He looked down. Ho Peng was quite still. His head was terribly cut and bleeding, his jungle green shirt, the shotgun and Edward's hands were covered in blood, but he was still breathing erratic shallow breaths. Edward said harshly, 'You should have let me finish the job.'

'Maybe,' she shrugged. 'He beat me often enough.'

Edward clambered off Ho Peng and sat down on the ground, saying, 'Why the hell did you go on working for him then?'

'I never worked for him,' she said emphatically. 'I worked for the Party and the People.'

'But he killed your son,' said Edward roughly, still hard with the rage of his attack. 'And you still worked for him!'

She frowned and said very quietly, 'I nearly gave up. When you found me in the padi field. I sat and thought about it all so much but I told myself that the revolution demands sacrifices from everyone sometimes.'

'Not that!'

She pulled a face of resignation, and said, 'I should have killed him. I wanted to. But Ho Peng was a brilliant field commander. He was never caught and we needed him. The Party needed him.'

Edward stared up at her, remembering all the times they had spent together and thinking how unreal it all seemed. Something of his thoughts must have reflected in his face for she said, 'I nearly gave up again, later.' She paused. 'Because of you this time.'

Edward waited for her to go on.

'That night I came back to you, after the prison. I wanted to give myself up. After everything you did for me during the trial, I was convinced you wanted me.'

'And didn't you want me too?'

'Yes,' she said in a small voice. 'I trusted you.'

'Then why for God's sake didn't you give yourself up?' asked Edward rather desperately, but he was sure he knew the answer.

'Your wife was back, but she meant nothing. I knew how you felt, because I believed in you by then. What upset me was the inescapable realisation that we were from different worlds and could never go on.' She remembered her tears of frustration. 'There were no normal circumstances. We could only have met as we did, in the calm of those evenings and nights at your house, when the chaos of the conflict which brought us together in the first place continued around us. No-one knew about us there, no-one cared, except you and me.'

Edward said. 'So, we were equal?'

'I wanted to be with you as much as I think you wanted to be with me,' she said and fell silent. The jungle sounds of cicadas and birds absorbed them both for a moment.

Edward heard a distant beating. Liya heard it too and hurried on, 'I gave Hassan a gold sovereign.'

'I know,' said Edward. He fished in his pocket and brought out the two sovereigns. They lay clean and polished in his filthy, blood-stained palm.

'Two!' she exclaimed. 'Where did you find the other one?'

Edward told her and asked, 'Where are the rest?'

She stepped over to him and picked the two coins from his palm. The gesture seemed so intimate compared to all the horrors of the day that Edward hardly focused on her next words. 'These are all that's left.'

He frowned, 'There were thousands of them! What happened?'

She looked pained, 'After I took them all from Tallard, I made a special journey to see our General-Secretary. We could travel more easily in 1946 than now and as a political commissar, I was allowed to see the General-Secretary personally. I told him about the gold and he arranged to have it all brought to him, for the Party he said.' She shrugged. 'That was the last I saw of it.'

'General-Secretary Lai Tek?' asked Edward in amazement. 'The man who did a runner with all your money in 1947?' He recalled reading an Intelligence summary which detailed that, when Lai Tek failed to turn up at a Central Executive meeting in March 1947 Chin Peng had taken over as his successor only to discover that the Party was bankrupt.

She nodded.

Edward snorted a low tired laugh. He looked at Ho Peng's still form and remarked, 'All that for nothing'.

'It's the commitment that matters,' she said in a determined voice. 'Not this.' She dropped a sovereign back in Edward's hand.

The beating noise sounded louder, approaching fast over the ridge.

'Helicopters,' said Edward, looking pointlessly at the thick canopy above them. Brogan must have radioed for support while he lay helpless down the slope. He looked back at Liya and articulated something that had been nagging him for so long, 'Whose child did Ho Peng kill?'

'The father?'

He nodded, looking up at her expression carefully.

She turned away saying, 'It doesn't matter any more.'

'Not Ho Peng's?'

She shook her head and fell silent. She seemed to be looking round the hollow as if for the last time. Edward watched her back, remembering all the curves under her pale khaki uniform.

In a very quiet voice she said, 'There's another.'

Suddenly the beating sounded directly above them. A helicopter down-draft thrashed the upper branches of the canopy in a hover.

Edward scrambled to his feet and shouted desperately against the noise, 'What?'

She turned back, her face desperate too, and said, 'He's yours, I promise, a little boy.' But her words were drowned in the noise of crashing branches overhead.

Edward looked up and saw the feet and body of a man coming through the layers of leaves high in the trees and a rope fell snaking through the air to the ground. When he turned round again, Liya had gone.

He ran across the hollow to the opposite edge and looked down the rocky slope over the ridge. For a moment he caught a glimpse of Liya's pale figure darting downhill between the palms and leaves. He shouted, 'Liya! Come back! You can give up now, with me. This is your last chance!'

Distantly through the warm air, he heard her call, 'It's the commitment that matters, remember?'

Feeling empty, he walked back across the hollow. When he stooped to pick up his Sterling he realised he had one of the gold coins in his hand and realised Liya had taken the other. Hers. It was all that was left.

EPILOGUE

Ho Peng, still alive, was winched out through the canopy with Aubrey and Brogan on the first lift. Edward, the dead trooper and the rescue patrol were winched out by the second Whirlwind and another party went into the jungle from the rubber for Untam's body. While they waited for the second lift, the rescue patrol photographed the dead CTs and took their fingerprints. Edward reflected on the march of technology, recalling Brogan's cruder technique of lopping off their heads, and wished he had killed Ho Peng.

The idea returned to him with a vengeance much later when Angus wrote to say that, after Ho Peng had recovered in hospital and been fully debriefed by Special Branch, he gave information leading to the arrest of twenty-three other CTs for which he was finally given his reward. A free man, richer by $200,000-Malay, Ho Peng started a simple, new, uncomplicated life as groundsman of the Selangor Cricket Club.

The reward system was always bitterly criticised, for it allowed amnesty to men like Ho Peng and paid them for it, but its success in folding up large parts of the communist organisation for little effort or risk of further loss of soldiers' lives could not be ignored.

On his return from the patrol, Edward told Angus he had never seen Liya at all at the top of the ridge, and that he had beaten up Ho Peng when he tried to escape. Ho Peng had never contradicted him, fearful he might be put in prison instead of receiving his reward money.

In the last days of his time in Kuala Lumpur, Edward often sat on the verandah with Lao Song, with the evening scent of the Moon flowers thick in the air, but Liya never came. She had vanished.

On 31 July 1955 his tour of duty came to an end on the same day as the first Malayan elections. Lao Song, Hassan and Gandra Singh voted, with eighty-five per cent of the population, and the Tunku

395

Abdul Rahman was returned with a huge majority of fifty-one out of fifty-two seats on a ticket of compromise between all three racial communities. Malaya began the long road to democracy and freedom.

Hassan was heartbroken to see Edward go and wept. Lao Song was more inscrutable but quite as moved. When he said he was going to start teaching again, Edward offered him the Plymouth to drive about. Lao Song smiled and shrugged his thin shoulders, 'I cannot drive. Give it to someone who understands cars as much as I love language. Give the American motorcar to Gandra Singh.' The old Sikh was overcome, and drove Edward and Diana in the Plymouth all the way to their troopship at Port Swettenham when they left Kuala Lumpur for the last time. He stayed on the dockside, alternately polishing the car and waving at them on the rail, until the ship departed.

The Emergency dragged on. When Edward left Malaya, after seven years, all the foundations for victory were in place but the communists fought on doggedly for another five years. They were prised out in ones and twos from the towns, the kampongs and jungles, and the soldiers, acting on increasingly good intelligence from Special Branch, became very efficient. Over twelve years, thousands did their stint in the jungle. In addition to sixty-four British units were the Malay Regiment, Australians, New Zealanders, Rhodesians, Africans and Fijians. In the end they killed 6,500 communists, mostly Chinese, while another 4,000 were captured or surrendered, for the loss of 1,500 in the army and the police. These awful statistics were mild compared to the horror of Korea, but 2,500 civilians also lost their lives.

Finally, in 1960, when Special Branch estimated that there were only some two hundred communists left all over the country, the Tunku Abdul Rahman declared the war was over.

On 31 July 1960 'Merdeka', or Victory, celebrations were held in Kuala Lumpur and hundreds of thousands of Malays, Indians, and Chinese streamed into the Federal capital in buoyant, optimistic mood. The British had gone, the communist takeover was defeated, and the country was theirs.

On the way home, after dinner one evening, Edward stood alone on the rail of the troopship and stared out over the Indian Ocean. He imagined that Liberator flying over the same stretch of sea ten years before to drop its cargo of gold sovereigns into the jungle. And he thought of Liya: He fished the little gold coin from his pocket and wondered where she was, and he wondered whether he really understood anything about her.

'What's that?' asked Diana suddenly joining him at the rail and catching sight of the dull gleam in Edward's hand.

'A sovereign,' Edward replied evenly. 'An old abo gave it to me in the jungle.'

'May I?' asked Diana and before Edward could stop her, she had picked it out of his palm. Edward watched her nervously, praying she would not let it slip through her fingers into the sea. Frowning, Diana asked, 'How did an aborigine get hold of something like this?'

'It was the cause of all the trouble between Tallard and Ho Peng,' said Edward accurately and briefly. Sure of himself after so much, he added quietly, 'That coin symbolises the real cause of the struggle during the whole Malayan campaign.'

Diana nodded, not really caring. At last, Malaya was behind her, she had Edward back to herself again and they were going home. She gave the coin back and smiled, 'Darling, I'm going down to the cabin. You won't be long will you?'

Edward kissed her lightly on the lips and watched her walk away along the deck. Then he turned back to the rail and looked down on the sea churning past the boat way below, the gold sovereign tight in his hand and his mind on Liya again.

'The Master said to us, "From of old, death has been the lot of all men, but if the people have no faith, they cannot live"'.

Hearing his own language, the waiter's bland oriental expression split in a wide grin of delight and Edward walked away along the deck with a light step.

List of Characters

Ah Chi	Chinese squatter
* Ah Kuk	Communist leader
Ah Po	Wife of Ah Chi
* Attlee, Clement	British Prime Minister, 1945–51
Bickerstaffe, Alan	Sergeant in Intelligence
Bleasley, Davina	Wife of Colonel Bleasley
Bleasley, Vincent	Colonel in Intelligence
* Boucher	Major-General, GOC Malaya District, 1948
Bowman, Mark	Rubber planter
† Brogan, Sean	Sergeant in the SAS
* Chin Peng	General-Secretary of the MCP, from 1947 to date
* Churchill, Sir Winston	Prime Minister, 1951
Ci Guo	Special Branch Sergeant
* Codnor, Michael	Assistant District Officer, Tanjong Malim
* Creech Jones, Arthur	Colonial Secretary, 1948
* Dalley	Colonel and Police officer
Denton, Harry	Cavalry captain attached to Intelligence
† Fairfax, Diana	Wife of Edward Fairfax
† Fairfax, Edward	
Fairfax, Ellie	Daughter of Diana and Edward
* Farran, Roy	Major in the SAS during the Second World War
* Fourniss, W.H.	Executive Engineer of Public Works, Tanjong Malim
Gandra Singh	Sikh taxi driver
* Gent, Sir Edward	Malayan High Commissioner, 1948
Goodbury, Leonard	Chaplain
* Greene, Hugh Carleton	Seconded from BBC to be Head of Emergency Information Services, Federation of Malaya, 1950–51

* Gurney, Sir Henry	Malayan High Commissioner, 1948–51
† Haike, Septimus	Colonel. Diana Fairfax's father
† Haike, Roger	Captain. Diana Fairfax's brother
† Hall-Drake, Aubrey	Captain and Troop Commander
* Harding, Sir John	Commander in Chief Far East
Hassan	Malay houseboy
Hazlitt	Doctor
Ho Peng	Communist leader
* Hor Lung	Communist leader
Hou Ming	Tallard's rubber estate foreman
Huang Chi-dao	Owner of Kok Wan Lo general trading shop in Tanjong Malim
* Lai-Tek	General Secretary of MCP till 1947
* Langworthy, H.B.	Police Commissioner in Malaya
Lao Song	Chinese cook in Edward Fairfax's villa
Lao Tang	Chinese communist
* Lao Yu	Communist military commander
Li Chi-Chen	Chinese communist
Liao Ting-chi	Chinese actor
Liya	Chinese girl
Lu-Lu Suzie	Manageress of 'hotel' in Kuala Lumpur
* Lyttelton, Oliver	Colonial Secretary, 1951
† Maclean, Angus	Special Branch policeman
McBride, Andrew	Lawyer, Kuala Lumpur
* Meng, Lee	Female Chinese communist
Meynell, Erskine	Major in SAS
Mohammad Razak	Malay Datuk
* Mr Wong	Owner of Coliseum Bar
* Osman China	Communist leader
Ranjang Hadar	Tamil roadworker
† Romm, Carole	Nurse
* Siu Mah	Communist leader, of 11th Regiment
* Stafford, Bill	Policeman
Sundralingam	Foreman of Bowman's rubber estate
Sundralingam, Rani	Wife of Sundralingam
Tallard, Marsha	Wife of Tallard
Tallard, Sean	Manager of Black Circle rubber estate
* Templer, Sir Gerald	Malayan High Commissioner, 1952–54
Untam	Sarawak tracker
* Walker, Arthur	Rubber planter on Elphil estate
† Warren, Liz	Girlfriend of Angus Maclean in Palestine

Willie   Barman at Coliseum Bar

Characters marked with * are historical figures; those marked with a
† also appear in *The Joshua Inheritance*.

Glossary

Attap	Palms used for roofing, or a building of palms
Bukit	A hill
Canopy	The 'roof' of greenery of the tops of the trees in the jungle
Cheongsam	Chinese silk dress
CT	Communist Terrorist, a description deliberately chosen to denigrate the enemy
DZ	Parachute 'dropping zone'
Ferret Force	Ad-hoc unit begun at start of campaign
Force 136	SOE (qv) unit in Malaya in Second World War
DWEC	District War Executive Committee
GOC	General Officer Commanding
Gunong	A mountain
Jalan	A street
Kampong	A village
Kladis	Tubers, often called yams
Krani	Foreman, of an estate
Mā (Chinese)	1st tone, means 'mother'
Má (Chinese)	2nd tone, means 'hemp'
Mǎ (Chinese)	3rd tone, means 'horse'
Mà (Chinese)	4th tone, means 'to scold or swear'
MCP	Malayan Communist Party
Memsahib	Woman, or 'Madam'
Min Yuen	Shortened form of 'Min Chung Yuen Thong' which means 'the masses movement'
MPABA	Malayan People's Anti-British Army
MRLA	Malayan Races Liberation Army
Orang Asli	Aborigines
Padang	Field in middle of towns and villages

Padi	Rice field
Pak choy	Chinese cabbage
Punjang	Long blonde hair
S'tengah, or satengah	Whisky drink – half whisky, half water
Sahib	'Sir' or Mister
Samfu	Chinese working clothes
Satay	Roast meat on open brazier
Sawi	Chinese cabbage
SB/SBLO	Special Branch/Special Branch Liaison Officer
SEP	Surrendered Enemy Personnel
SOE	Special Operations Executive
Sungei	River
SWEC	State War Executive Committee
Tuan	'Sir' or Mister
Ubi Kayu	Tapioca, starchy root crop
Ulu	Jungle